"Good morning, an instant he saw rec~~~~~~~~~~~~~~~~~~~~ if she'd never seen him before. "Time for your penicillin shot," she said. Her melodious speaking voice almost matched her singing voice.

"Sure," Milt replied, making an effort to smile despite his pounding head. If she didn't want to acknowledge their brief encounter the previous day, why should he care? It didn't mean he couldn't enjoy having a beautiful singer as his nurse.

"Which side?" she asked.

"Huh?" Had that sound come from him?

"Which side do you want the shot in? Right or left?"

He watched her lips form the words. Soft, expressive lips. He blinked, knowing he had to reply. "Uh, left is okay." The cast on his left arm stuck out so much it made it near impossible to roll onto his left side to expose his right cheek. Which made the left as his only choice. In the last few weeks, he'd gotten so many shots in his left butt cheek it probably looked like a purple pin cushion.

"All right. Just roll over and push down your pajama bottoms." She turned to retrieve a hypo from one of the trays.

Praise for Barbara Whitaker

"Barbara Whitaker's A War Apart is a riveting novel set during WWII that has been researched to perfection. Whitaker brings history to life with her incredible descriptions and presents us with an entirely plausible way for two people to find love during such tumultuous times where war has pushed them apart...This is a fantastic book that will draw you in by the heart..."

~ *Madeline Martin, NYT Bestseller.*

"...achingly beautiful. True to the time...many ups and downs for these characters both personally and together. A great attention to detail from the author in which she uses wonderful imagery to transport you to the time..."

~ *Novel News Network Blog.*

Scarred Dreams

by

Barbara Whitaker

Barbara Whitaker

Scarred Dreams

Cover Art by *Jennifer Greeff*

The Wild Rose Press, Inc.
PO Box 708
Adams Basin, NY 14410-0708
Visit us at www.thewildrosepress.com

Publishing History
First Edition, 2022
Trade Paperback ISBN 978-1-5092-4605-2
Digital ISBN 978-1-5092-4606-9

Published in the United States of America

Dedication

Scarred Dreams is dedicated to all veterans who were wounded, both physically and mentally, while serving our country. These veterans continue to suffer long after their service is over.

Scarred Dreams is also dedicated to all victims of violence who continue to suffer long after the violent event and in ways similar to our veterans.

Finally, Scarred Dreams is dedicated to my husband, Pat, who has had his own struggles.

Chapter 1

July 23, 1944
Palm Beach, Florida

"No!" Annie McEwen flung the letter onto her dresser. He couldn't tell her what to do. Not anymore.

Her father's all too familiar words burned in her memory. "You will do as I say. I know what is best for you." That's how he'd run her whole life. And he might think he could keep on doing it. But no more.

She wouldn't write Brice and she wouldn't go to Washington to meet him, as her father had ordered in his letter. And she certainly would not ask for a transfer to be closer to her father's choice for a husband.

She had defied him by joining the Army Nurse Corps and she had intentionally stayed away when she could have gone home to visit. The Army would decide where she went until the war ended. By then, she'd be on her way to a singing career and a life of her own.

Right now, she had to get dressed for her big night.

With shaking hands, she pulled open the drawer to retrieve her last decent pair of stockings. Amid her soft under things, her fingers collided with something hard and rectangular. She drew it out of its hiding place, knowing what she would see before she laid eyes on the handsome face.

Joe. Her dear cousin gazed up at her, bars

glistening on his Army uniform and eagerness shining from those smiling eyes.

"I still haven't done what you asked. I…just couldn't." She plunked the photo down on the dresser, on top of the discarded letter. "I'm still mad at you, you know." Tears welled and threatened to spill over and ruin her makeup. "You left me to deal with him…all alone." She dabbed her handkerchief at her traitorous eyes. "I know you didn't mean to. I know you …"

She drew a ragged breath. She couldn't think about all that now. She had to get ready for the biggest show of her life.

"Aren't you ready yet?"

Annie jerked around, startled. Stella stood in the doorway.

"Just finishing up my makeup."

Stella crossed the room, trailing her fingers across the silken dress spread out on the bed. "You better get a move on. I thought sure you'd be ready to slip into this gorgeous gown by now."

Annie leaned forward so she could see to apply enough makeup to hide the puffiness brought on by her unexpected tears. Luckily her mascara hadn't run.

Stella appeared in the mirror behind her. "Who's that? He's cute."

Annie kept her gaze on her image in the mirror. "That's Joe. My cousin." She tried to sound casual, but her voice betrayed her emotions.

"Oh." Stella's reaction held a wealth of understanding. She had a brother missing at sea. "He's the one you told me about. Sicily, wasn't it?"

Annie nodded. She didn't want to talk about Joe. She needed to prepare for the show. She needed to be positive and confident and excited. Today was her big day, and she wasn't going to let anything spoil her first time on a real stage singing with a fabulous band.

After she carefully pulled on her stockings, Stella helped slide the borrowed evening gown over her head. Annie could have never gotten this concoction on without help, what with the plunging neckline and the backless illusion of the sheer silk invisibly fastened together with delicate, embroidered flowers. She'd had her doubts about wearing the daring dress, but as it settled around her body and she turned to face the mirror, it worked magic on her spirit.

"Oh, Annie. It's just beautiful." Stella moved around her, smoothing and tugging. "You're… you're just so gorgeous in it."

Annie admired her image in the mirror. She did look good. Like a real star.

Her gaze went to Joe's picture. How she wished he was here to see her, to hear her sing.

A warmth filled her, like Joe's loving embrace. "You are here, aren't you," she whispered. His love and encouragement surrounded her. In that moment she knew he'd be at her side on that stage as she took a big step toward her dream.

****

"I don't want to go to any damn show," Sergeant Milton Greenlee spat out. "I just want to be left alone."

"It'll do you good," the stout, sour-faced nurse insisted.

He gritted his teeth, wishing his head would go ahead and explode and get it over with. "I only got here last night. Talk to the doctor. He'll tell you to take me back to my bed."

"I have my orders," she said with the firmness of an umpire calling him out. "Everyone who can be moved is to see this show."

When the elevator stopped, the operator reached across and slid the door open.

The nurse leaned down and spoke to Milt in a firm yet more conciliatory tone. "A little entertainment will help you relax, forget your troubles."

"The hell it will," he muttered, knowing his objections fell on deaf ears. The unrelenting woman would have made a good Nazi—follow orders no matter what.

She pushed his wheelchair down the wide hallway oblivious to his wishes. A damn show wouldn't fix what couldn't be fixed. And it wouldn't make him forget either.

His chair jerked to a halt in the middle of the hallway. "Annie, you're gorgeous," his nurse exclaimed.

Milt glanced up. A dazzling woman approached. He instinctively straightened in his chair. Even with only one eye, he could appreciate the way the deep blue evening gown set off her curves. How her dark red hair framed her creamy, heart-shaped face.

His battered heart stuttered at the sight.

Luscious red lips curved up ever so slightly. A gentle flush spread upward turning her pale skin a delicate shade of pink as she nodded modestly.

"Can you believe that Margo Van Buren loaned her this fabulous dress?"

He hadn't even noticed the other nurse until she spoke.

"You know. Margo Van Buren. The heiress. And

she had her maid alter it so it fits Annie perfectly."

He caught the name. Annie. Not what he'd have guessed for this classy lady.

Two other nurses appeared, adding their "ooo's" and "ahhh's" in chorus.

"Give us a turn so we can really see it," one of them said.

The glamour girl could have been a model the way she turned on the ball of her fancy, high-heeled sandals, took two steps, and then turned back to face her friends…and him.

He couldn't look away. The vision held him there as his heart pounded in his ears. He should smile but his whole being froze in place.

One of the other women broke the spell when she touched Annie's shoulder. "These flowers embroidered on the sheer silk look like they're scattered across your bare skin."

"The guys will love it. That plunging neckline. How it hugs your body," another nurse said.

"Is it too daring?" Slender fingers smoothed the form-fitting garment.

Milt allowed his gaze to caress her every curve.

She glanced around for an answer from her friends. Heads shook in response.

Then her gaze settled on him, as if she had heard his thoughts. He hadn't intended to get involved but he couldn't help smiling, just a little, to show his approval.

"Oh, no," the first nurse said. "It's perfect."

Annie visibly relaxed.

She hadn't asked him, but he would have agreed that it was perfect. And so was she.

"I'd better get backstage." she said.

She disappeared as suddenly as she had appeared. He knew nothing about her except her name, Annie. That and the fact that she was the loveliest creature he'd ever seen.

Chapter 2

After the blue-clad goddess disappeared, his nurse resumed her place behind him. She pushed him through a wide doorway and paused when someone down front held up a hand to tell them to wait. The room must have once been a night club or ballroom in this fancy hotel the Army had transformed into a hospital.

Milt's anger had cooled at the sight of the beauty in the hallway. Despite the fatigue that weighed on his shoulders, he would force himself to watch the show. Looking at a pretty girl might not be so bad. The pounding in his head had backed off a little, but he knew it would be back. It always came back.

While waiting, he surveyed the room. Compared to what he remembered of the stark hospital in England and the crowded ship rolling with the waves, this place could have been the set one of those Hollywood movies where a bunch of stars put on a show for soldiers.

Band members made their way onto the stage and took their places. One of them played a run on a saxophone, then a trumpet tooted, and a slide trombone joined in.

The musical chaos from the band warming up amplified the pounding in his head. Heavy drapes that should have dampened the sound seemed to deflect it outward to torture the men trapped in the rows of chairs, almost like hiding from unrelenting machine gun fire in rows of fox holes. He pressed his right hand over his ear and wondered how he would stand it when their aim improved, and they started playing for real.

His driver maneuvered him to a row of wheelchair-bound patients up front. Two similarly confined men, also dressed in pajamas and robes, gave him the once-over as he rolled past them. One had a cast on his forearm, a bandaged head and foot. The next one's casted leg stuck straight out in front of him.

The nurse placed Milt at the end of the row, probably thinking it would prevent his protruding, plaster-encased left arm from hitting someone in the face if he tried to turn in his chair.

"I'll be back to check on you later," the traitorous caregiver said as she retreated toward the back.

"Yeah. Well, maybe I'll be here and maybe I won't," he muttered to himself. He definitely wanted to see that gorgeous red head again. But after that he might just make his exit.

Reaching down with his right hand, he tried to roll the wheel forward. It didn't budge.

"Shit!" She'd locked the wheels.

"You need some help?" someone nearby asked.

"No!" he barked.

He didn't like feeling helpless. He didn't want to have to depend on someone else. He was a grown man, not a baby in a stroller.

For the millionth time he asked himself why? Why him? It wasn't supposed to be this way. He should have been killed. He'd resigned himself to that, after all he'd seen. He'd never imagined being like this, an invalid, maybe forever.

He'd made it through North Africa and Sicily

without a scratch, while others around him were shot dead or blown to bits. He wasn't invincible, just damn lucky. Then he made it across that beach, that bloody, watery hell where he'd clung to the wet sand and prayed for the strength to keep going. So naturally, as they moved inland, he'd thought his luck would hold out and he'd be safe. He'd been wrong.

The guy next to him, the one with the broken leg, spoke, but Milt merely grunted in reply. Ducking his head, he avoided eye-contact with the other patients. He had protested coming and refused to be the least bit social. He didn't want to be here, and his splitting head made it that much worse.

Something rammed into his damaged arm. Searing pain shot through his left shoulder.

"Auuugh!" Milt roared. "What the hell!"

Rage coursed through his veins.

He twisted around in the damn chair, toward his blind left side, searching for his assailant, ready to blast him with a string of angry curses.

"Gee, I'm sorry." A young kid with freckles strewn across round cheeks and an up-turned nose met his anger with wide-eyed innocence. "I can't seem to get the hang of driving one of these contraptions."

Milton's pulse pounded inside his skull, matched by the throbbing ache in his shoulder.

Red colored his vision. His good hand clenched into a fist ready to pound the careless kid.

Then he saw the stumps. Legs that stopped just before where his knees should have been.

Milton's gut cramped as if he'd been punched. His anger deflated like a punctured balloon.

Another kid flashed before him—covered in blood,

one leg gone, the other mangled so bad it looked like chopped meat, from the explosion that had blown him up into the air and slammed him hard onto the ground fifteen feet away. The kid had been just one step ahead of Milt when he'd stepped on the mine.

Withering machine gun fire kept Milt and the others from reaching what was left of the youngster. They'd flattened themselves to Mother Earth and watched him bleed to death, heard his cries for help, unable to do anything.

"I hope I didn't hurt your arm," the kid continued. "With it stuck out like that, well, I guess I didn't see how far it stuck out."

"It's okay, kid," Milt said softly. "It's okay."

He straightened in his chair, fighting the cloud of melancholy settling around him. He grabbed his casted arm's prop that attached to the cast around his middle and tried to adjust the arm so that it didn't protrude so far. It was useless. The hard plaster didn't give an inch.

They'd put him in a partial body cast to keep his shattered arm stable during the long voyage from England. Miserably awkward, the slightest movement caused stabbing pain in his shoulder.

The kid maneuvered around in front of Milt. "Are you sure you're okay?"

"Yeah, kid, I'm sure." Drained by the pain, Milton struggled to get a grip on himself. "Just leave me alone, okay?" he said with more anger than he intended.

The boy passed Milt and continued toward an orderly to be added to the line of wheelchair-bound patients. The double-amputee glared at Milt as he went by.

Milt glanced down at his own whole, fully

functioning legs. A pang of guilt had him repeating his earlier question: Why? Why me? Why him? Why any of us?

Wham. Rat-a-tat-a-tat. Crash. Milt jerked violently. His breath caught. His right hand gripped the arm rest. His head swiveled as his mind searched for the machine gun he quickly realized wasn't there.

On the stage the drummer continued to run through his warmup.

Breathe, he told himself. You're in a hospital, in the States, safe.

He glanced around to see if anyone had noticed his unnatural reaction to the loud noise. The guy with the broken leg met his gaze and held it.

He knew. He understood.

Milt forced his body to relax. He nodded ever so slightly to his fellow combat veteran, who nodded back and then turned away.

The noise from the band tapered off while the buzz from hundreds of voices rose as men streamed into the room filling the rows of seats and talking among themselves. Ambulatory patients hobbled on crutches or leaned on canes as they searched for any remaining empty chairs. Late arrivals milled around the doors. Most waited stoically, like they did for everything in the Army. Almost all sported some type of cast, bandage, crutch or limp, evidence of how the war had damaged them.

After sitting side-by-side in silence for what seemed like forever, the man on Milt's right, the one with the broken leg, extended a hand. "Warren Calhoun."

Milt reluctantly shook the offered hand. "Milt

Greenlee."

"Hope it's a good show," Calhoun commented, his voice light, upbeat.

Milt glanced toward the stage and shrugged his good shoulder, trying to send a message that he didn't want to talk.

"You haven't been here long, have you?"

"Nope."

After being shuffled from place to place, moving ever closer to home, exhaustion weighed him down. Milt doubted he'd make it through the afternoon of entertainment his tyrannical nurse insisted he attend.

Two weeks, they told him, since he left England. From hospital to dock to ship, from ship to dock to train, from train to truck to hospital. So many bumps and jostles and apologetic faces telling him that he would be okay, that he was going home. Only he wasn't home, and he wasn't okay.

So why was he sitting here waiting? Oh, yeah. Because the damn nurse said he had to come to this damn show. Well, he didn't care anymore. He didn't care if he missed seeing that dreamboat again. He just wanted them to leave him alone. Give him something to dull the pain and let him sleep. He'd just as soon sleep from now on.

"Gotta be grateful, I guess." Calhoun's comment jostled Milt's thoughts. "At least we're alive, and we've got both our legs." Calhoun nodded toward the freckle-faced kid over to their right. "Not like him. Mine may be busted, but I've still got it."

"Yeah, I guess." Milt tried to feel gratitude, but he didn't. Guilt maybe, for having two good legs, for just being alive.

12

He wouldn't let himself think of what the future held. Even if he hadn't completely lost his eye, he would never have good vision in it. And with a shattered arm and no feeling in his hand, his baseball career was over before he'd gotten to first base.

An officer approached the microphone on stage and raised his arms to get the audience's attention. "Would everyone please settle down? The show will be starting in just a few minutes." He lowered his arms and stood watching the crowd for a moment before speaking again. "Find a seat before we turn the lights down. We don't want anyone stumbling around in the dark."

That brought a response, not a laugh exactly, more a round of groans and "okay's."

Someone shouted, "Let's get this show on the road."

Followed by, "Yeah. Start up the band."

The comments were good-natured and soon the men settled down.

Milt managed to turn in his chair enough to see several nurses huddled in a group as if plotting their next move. They then disbursed around the room.

His nemesis moved into position only a few feet away. She shot him a glance that said stay put and don't make trouble.

Okay. So he was stuck sitting through this thing. No chance to slip out.

It wasn't like he couldn't walk. He could make it as long as he had something to grab hold of when he got too dizzy. But he couldn't escape with her standing guard.

The band struck up a popular tune and the lights

dimmed to near darkness. Spotlights bathed the stage in light. The conductor's arms moved rhythmically as the saxophones and trombones blasted out the swing number. Around him smiles spread across faces and toes tapped along with the rhythm.

Milt tried to relax. He might as well enjoy the music since he was here for the duration.

When the song ended and the applause waned, the emcee stepped up to the microphone and started his spiel. The welcome, the acknowledgement of the band members who were apparently hospital staff augmented by personnel from other bases.

They struck up an instrumental number and Milt's mind drifted back, to England, to dances with English girls and music provided by a record player.

The next song took him back even further. To a girl he'd dated while in training. She'd loved the jumpin' beat and had played it over and over. He'd perfected his jitterbug dating that girl, Jill, a cute blonde from somewhere in Georgia.

Milt's toes were tapping, and despite the pain, he felt the urge to get up and dance. Self-consciously, he looked to his right where others grinned and swayed to the music. When the number finished, the crowd exploded in applause.

Milton pounded on his leg with his good, right hand. Loud whistles sounded behind him. Many jumped to their feet and cheered.

The emcee thanked the audience and called for the band to take a bow which brought on another round of applause.

Maybe this wasn't such a bad idea after all. Milt glanced around to find the nurse, still standing at her post. They exchanged nods. Okay, he guessed she was right after all.

He settled in to listen to the band, allowing the music to flow through him, letting memories of happier times creep into his thoughts.

Chapter 3

Annie wrung her hands to keep from pacing while waiting for her cue to go on stage. She tried to clear her mind and focus on the music, but her father's words crept into her thoughts. *"You're not good enough."*

Today she would prove him wrong. The band leader promised her an introduction to one of the big band leaders he'd worked for before the war.

The applause died down and the band started up the number before hers. She had to relax and get herself ready. She'd never sung for a big audience like this before or with such a great band. She hoped her nerves wouldn't get the best of her, make her lose her place or forget the words. Years ago, someone had told her to pick out one person in the audience and sing to that person rather than thinking about all the people watching her. Could she?

That soldier in the wheelchair with the one blue eye peering out from under the bandages came to mind. His eye had been the same blue as Joe's, deep blue and intense with emotion. The moment she saw him she thought of finding Joe's picture and of the Joe's presence watching over her.

Just thinking about Joe made her feel better. Maybe if she found that soldier in the audience or just pretended to be singing to him, it would be easier.

The band's number ended, and the applause roared.

Her number came next. She walked calmly to the edge of the stage and peeped around the curtain. So many men waited.

The familiar notes played, and she walked out onto the stage, her shoulders back, her head high. At the microphone she stopped and looked over to where the spotlight shone on the trombones playing the lead in.

When her cue sounded, she opened her mouth and pictured that wounded soldier. The words flowed out and blended with the other instruments.

Darkness concealed most of the audience, but she could make out the wheelchair patients across the front. As she sang, she let her gaze roam over these men, imagining that somewhere out there Joe watched and listened. She poured her heart into the song, into its dream of finding someone to love.

****

Milt closed his eye when the strains of a slower tune began. The notes flowed over him. A sweet, soprano crooned familiar words. Her melodious voice wrapped him in a warm blanket of sound.

Memories, of home, of his sister at the piano, he and his mother standing beside her, singing, his father nearby smiling. He felt their presence, here with him as the beautiful voice continued. He blinked back tears, glad to be alive.

The band played an instrumental interlude and he glanced around, self-consciously, hoping no one saw his tears. But everyone else focused their attention on the stage. Milt's gaze followed theirs.

A vision stood before him—the same angelic face, the same curvaceous body swaying with the melody. Her red-tipped fingers caressed the microphone she held near matching red lips. Then she began to sing, and her rich soprano reached out and embraced him with its sweetness.

The beauty from the hallway had the most soothing, melodious voice he'd heard in a long, long time.

She sang of finding a dream and his heart raced.

She was the dream, every man's dream.

The ahhh's from the mostly male crowd told him he wasn't the only one admiring the lovely songstress. They all leaned forward, in unison, to get closer to the beauty on stage.

She sensed their reaction, acknowledging it with an upward curve of her luscious red lips while her rich voice continued its melody. Her free hand added graceful emphasis to every phrase. Her sparkling eyes moved from face to face, touching each of them with her magic.

The spellbound audience somehow fueled the emotion in her voice, as if she were responding to a lover's touch.

Like every other man in the audience, the lovely image and the warm feelings evoked by her voice mesmerized Milt. The dream in her song drew him in until he floated by her side.

As she belted out the final notes, she closed her eyes and raised one hand high. Milt's heart soared with her glorious voice.

When the sound stopped, a split second of silence preceded a roar of deafening applause. Milt pushed himself to his feet joined by every man who could stand. Cheers, whistles, and continued applause rang out.

The singer bowed and mumbled her "thank you's." Her delicate, pale skin flushed pink with pleasure at the audience's reaction. She scanned the crowd, clearly enjoying the approval.

The emcee approached her, and the crowd settled a bit.

Milt returned to his chair, but his ears perked up trying to hear the emcee's introduction.

"Lieutenant Annie McEwen," the emcee announced, setting off another round of applause. "Our very own Nurse McEwen."

She bowed again as she moved backward on the stage and looked to the wings.

"And now, Nurse McEwen will be joined by Nurse Lucy Compton and Tech Sergeant Tom Altman."

Another woman in a flowing pink evening gown and a man in dress uniform joined the gorgeous songstress. They gathered around the microphone and the band leader raised his baton to start the next number. In a couple of beats, the trio sang out the fun, up-beat lyrics in perfect three-part harmony.

Milt focused his attention on the red head as her face, as well as her voice, conveyed the positive message of the song.

Finally, he'd really come home. The music, the roaring crowd, the beautiful songstress, all seemed to welcome him. He'd have to thank that nurse for not letting him skip out on this. Nurse McEwen's performance alone was worth all the hassle.

He settled back into his wheelchair as the announcer introduced another song by the lovely nurse. This time she sang an old favorite of his. As the sound of her voice filled the space, Milt floated into sweet oblivion.

He forgot about the pain in his head and shoulder. About his uncertain future. For now, he focused on her. For now, he let himself drift away into the magic of her voice.

Chapter 4

Annie ran from the stage, adrenalin pumping. She twirled around, bouncing in her high heels, the roar of applause still filling her head. She'd never get enough of the crowd's pure adoration. Never, ever, ever.

At the end of the show the band leader, Charlie Cushman, called the performers out to take a final bow. Annie rushed from backstage to even more applause.

Offstage again, Charlie touched her shoulder. "You were fabulous," he said.

"Thank you so much," she gushed. "So were you. So was everyone."

"Great show," someone nearby called.

She looked around to see who spoke and felt Charlie's hand slip away.

An officer she didn't know grabbed Lt. Cushman's hand and shook it, congratulating him. She took the opportunity to step back.

The other officer complimented her singing, and Lt. Cushman agreed. "Best singer in the show."

"Good enough to sing professionally?" she asked, very much wanting him to keep his promise of an introduction to his former employer.

"Sure. You're a natural. You had the audience in the palm of your hand. Not every singer can do that, you know."

"Then do I get that introduction you promised? I

delivered the goods, didn't I?"

"You sure did. I'll write you a letter. I promise." He moved closer, slipped his arm around her shoulder and gave her a hug. "You were fabulous," he whispered in her ear.

Her body stiffened at his unexpected familiarity, yet her mind immediately told her to relax.

Be happy. Be grateful. This man can help your career.

"Thank you," she forced out with as much sweetness as she could muster. She did appreciate the praise she craved, especially from a professional like him. And he could help make her dream a reality. She couldn't mess all that up by being silly.

Despite knowing that this man might just be her ticket to fame, part of her wanted to pull out of his grasp and run. She'd practically begged him to let her sing with his band. Now she desperately wanted to get away from him.

"Annie! You were great!" Stella ran toward her with a giant grin and her arms wide forcing Lt. Cushman out of the way as she swept Annie into an enormous bear hug.

Tears pricked at Annie's eyes. She welcomed both her friend's joy and her compliments.

Over Stella's shoulder Cassie, another nurse, hung back smiling broadly. Annie gave her a little wave.

"You were swell," Cassie gushed. "The men, they all loved you."

By now Stella had stepped back and Cassie came forward to give Annie a little hug of her own. Out of the corner of her eye Annie saw someone speak to Lt. Cushman and draw him away. She sighed in relief.

"See, you had no reason to be so nervous," Stella said. "You were so good."

"Like one of those famous singers on the radio," Cassie added.

Annie's friends refueled her excitement. Unable to contain it, she kicked up her high heels and danced a little jig. "I did it," she murmured, almost to herself. "I really did it."

Stella and Cassie laughed in chorus, then joined her dance. The three circled around until they noticed all the band members gawking at their antics.

"Let's get out of here," Stella suggested.

"Those boys will never look at you the same again. You realize that, don't you?" Cassie laughed as Stella led the way toward the exit.

"I hadn't really thought about it."

"You just wait. When you walk into the wards tomorrow, they'll perk up. Maybe even whistle at you," Cassie continued.

"Gee, I hope not. Captain Burrows won't like that."

"Too late now. You should've thought about that before you decided to be in the show."

"I guess." Annie leaned closer so her friends could hear her over the din from the crowd in the hallway. "I've been singing at the canteen for months. That hasn't caused a reaction."

In the hallway, still crowded with patients, they stood to the side to give the wheelchairs room to get to the elevators. She scanned them looking for the soldier with the blue eyes but didn't see him.

"Oh, this was different," Stella said. "Up there, in front of a band, in that dress. This is the big time."

"Until the emcee said your name, I don't think any

of your patients recognized you," Cassie added.

Stella laughed. "Cassie's right. You better look out tomorrow."

"Oh, they'll behave. They are all nice boys," Annie assured them.

"Well, those nice boys just got a major crush on you. Isn't that right, Cassie?"

"I'm afraid she's right, Annie."

At that moment Sgt. Lloyd Baker rushed toward her. Before she could even speak, he grabbed her, pulled her into his arms and kissed her, right on the lips.

Ohhhhh.

Her emotions temporarily overruled her thought process.

When he released her, she stared at him in shock, gasping for air from the extended kiss.

"Beautiful!" he exclaimed. "You're beautiful, your singing is beautiful, everything is beautiful!"

Stella and Cassie giggled.

"Th…thank you," she managed. Aware that he still held her by the shoulders, she tried to wriggle free.

"Wasn't she swell?" Cassie added.

"I'll say," Lloyd grinned, releasing her and taking a step back.

Grateful for the space between them, Annie nodded to acknowledge the compliment. She knew she should say something, anything.

"I guess I'd better get out of this dress. Don't want to get it wrinkled."

"Margo Van Buren loaned her that dress. Isn't it gorgeous?" Stella inserted.

"She sure is." He beamed at her. "Lt. McEwen, I mean. The dress is great, too."

Annie had to get away. "Thanks so much." She turned and headed for the nearest exit.

Stella and Cassie followed close behind.

"See ya, tomorrow," Sgt. Baker called.

Annie waved as she pushed the door open and escaped into the night air.

"I thought you said there was nothing going on between you two?" Stella queried.

"There's not," Annie stammered. "We're just friends."

"That looked like a lot more than just friends," Stella retorted.

Annie sighed. Men. Nothing but problems. All of them.

Chapter 5

Milt stirred from half-sleep when he heard a commotion near the door. A starched-white nurse murmured instructions to an orderly who juggled a metal tray loaded with supplies. A second orderly, also holding a tray, managed the door. Once inside, both men obediently followed the nurse to the first bed in the ward, just to Milt's right.

When the nurse flashed the patient a smile, Milt's breath caught. With those red lips curving up, her cheek dimpled and, even across the few feet between them, he saw the twinkle in her eye.

When she turned to take something from one of the trays, he studied her face: pale skin, perfectly shaped, delicate nose, and auburn hair pulled back and tucked underneath her white nurse's cap.

The singer! Could it be her? In his ward?

She hadn't been here yesterday. She must have been off duty for the show.

She plunged a needle into the soldier's exposed buttock. Her face winced as if she was on the receiving end of the stabbing pain. When she withdrew the needle, she vigorously rubbed the site of the injection and gave the patient an apologetic smile. He grinned back at her like a guilty schoolboy who'd taken his just punishment.

"We missed you, Nurse McEwen," the patient said.

"Thank you," she replied.

Returning the hypodermic to one of the trays, the beauty dressed in white moved away from the first bed and approached Milt.

"Good morning, soldier." She met his gaze and for an instant he saw recognition before she shut it down as if she'd never seen him before. "Time for your penicillin shot," she said. Her melodious speaking voice almost matched her singing voice.

"Sure," Milt replied, making an effort to smile despite his pounding head. If she didn't want to acknowledge their brief encounter the previous day, why should he care? It didn't mean he couldn't enjoy having a beautiful singer as his nurse.

"Which side?" she asked.

"Huh?" Had that sound come from him?

"Which side do you want the shot in? Right or left?"

He watched her lips form the words. Soft, expressive lips. He blinked, knowing he had to reply. "Uh, left is okay." The cast on his left arm stuck out so much it made it near impossible to roll onto his left side to expose his right cheek. Which made the left as his only choice. In the last few weeks, he'd gotten so many shots in his left butt cheek it probably looked like a purple pin cushion.

"All right. Just roll over and push down your pajama bottoms." She turned to retrieve a hypo from one of the trays.

Embarrassment bloomed at the thought of this beautiful woman perusing his exposed bottom. Shots in the butt were routine, he told himself. But they weren't usually administered by a lovely red head who sang like an angel. And who had a shapely figure hidden underneath that white uniform. He had to distract her and himself.

"Are those your backup singers?" he asked, finally grasping a coherent thought.

"What?" She turned back to face him. "What did you say?"

Determined to make an impression on her, he turned on the charm. "Your backup singers. Aren't you gonna sing for us?"

Her eyes crinkled up into a shy smile and pink spread across her face. "Not today, I'm afraid."

"That's a shame. I really enjoyed your singing."

She inserted the hypodermic needle into a vial of medicine. "Thanks." Her reply sounded a little distant as she concentrated on getting the exact amount of medicine into the syringe.

Milton lay there watching the vision in white and remembering the sexy blue dress she had worn on stage.

Her gaze returned to his but this time a frown marred her features. "I said to roll over, soldier."

"Oh, yeah." Milton pulled the cover aside with his right hand and rolled his body while keeping his gaze fixed on her face.

"And push down your pajamas," she instructed.

Milton glanced at his casted arm jutting out toward the ceiling and bent at the elbow. His fingers protruded from beneath the hard stuff but remained useless.

Her face flushed crimson as she realized the futility of her request.

"I'm so sorry. Here, let me help you." Her gentle voice conveyed understanding.

He felt the heat rising and looked away before she saw the tell-tale color.

Her cool fingers brushed his skin as she pulled the waistband of his pajamas down to expose his rear end for all to see, including her.

He closed his eye tight and waited for the pierce of the needle. Instead, he felt her gentle touch.

"Just relax." She spoke so softly it felt like her words were just for him. Then he heard her humming the same tune she had sung on stage. His mind drifted back to that vision of loveliness, only this time she sang just for him. He barely felt the needle prick.

"There. All done." She gave the site a gentle massage then pulled his pajamas back into place.

When he rolled back over to face her, a smile lit up her face, not to make fun of him, but to convey her understanding of his awkwardness.

He managed a nod when she patted his leg. Then she and her accomplices moved on to the next bed.

"Come back any time." Milt flashed his most winning smile. She rewarded his effort with a deeper blush. Their gazes locked for a fraction of a second. He wished he could extend that connection indefinitely. Already her attention had shifted to her next patient.

If his bandage hadn't blocked his vision, he would have watched her. Instead, he lay back and listened. She had that magical ability to make each of them feel special, despite their injuries. He'd heard of nurses being called angels of mercy. Now he understood why.

"Was that really you singing yesterday?" The guy in the next bed asked.

"Yes, that was me." He heard the uneasiness in her voice as she tried to maintain a business-like demeanor.

"You sure were swell. Like some big movie star," the soldier gushed.

"Do you really think so?" Her genuine pleasure came through despite her efforts to contain it.

"Sure. All decked out in that fancy dress. Up there in front of that band. Like seeing a show in New York or L.A."

"We didn't know you could sing so good," another patient chimed in.

"She's great," one of the orderlies added. "I've been sneaking down to listen to the rehearsals." He looked directly at the nurse. "Like listening to an angel."

"Well...Thank you. All of you." She stepped out into the aisle between the beds and looked around the room to include them all in her gratitude. And then she moved toward the patient across from Milt. "Right now, we need to finish with these shots."

Milt watched her work with the poor boy strung up in traction. Her sweet voice floated through the ward as she hummed to get him to relax. He took the needle like he enjoyed it.

The last two fellows looked like panting hounds anticipating their turn at the trough. Yet their adoration remained respectful.

At least I have a pretty nurse taking care of me.

That thought seemed to ease the pain in his head. He relaxed against the pillow, closed his eyes, and focused on her melodious voice.

****

Annie hummed softly as she rubbed the skin where she had just injected a dose of penicillin. She offered her most professional smile as the patient rolled over and grinned up at her. She often hummed to relax her patients when she administered the injections. But today they reacted differently, thanks to yesterday's performance.

Her thoughts returned to that one, intensely blue eye that had watched her so closely. The similarity to Joe's blue eyes had initially shocked her. But today he seemed less like Joe. Today he came across as his own person, not a shadow of someone she'd lost.

His awkward embarrassment had been endearing, and his joking had completely disarmed her. But it was that grin that made her heart race. It lit up his whole face so completely that the bandages and scars faded into the background, unsettling her.

She didn't need another man to deal with, what with Charlie Cushman and Sergeant Baker, not to mention Brice Attwater, cluttering up her life. Now this new patient had touched her heart. She'd have to nip it in the bud.

After she finished with his ward, the orderlies, along with their trays of spent hypodermic needles, followed her into the hallway. She mentally patted herself on the back for not glancing back at "him," even though she was sure he was watching her every move.

While the orderlies reloaded their trays in preparation for the next ward, Annie went to the nurses' station and shuffled through the new patient files until she found him. Sergeant Milton Greenlee. Newly arrived from England, wounded in June in France.

Milton Greenlee. She repeated his name in her mind, as she rejoined her orderlies to continue the morning round of shots. Despite that grin, Milton Greenlee was just another wounded patient flirting with his nurse.

She had no intention of getting involved with anyone. Men just caused trouble and heartache.

While on her rounds, many of the patients recognized her as the singer from the day before. A couple of whistles and lots of compliments left her glowing from the praise.

If she played her cards right, Charlie Cushman would give her that letter of introduction and when the war was over, she would be singing with a big band. She'd travel the country, the world even, performing, and never, ever have to go back home.

Chapter 6

When Annie returned to the nurses' station, Lt. Bothley, the nurse in charge of the floor, looked up from her paperwork. "Finished?"

"Yes. That's it for the penicillin round."

"Good. You can change the dressings on one of the patients in Ward 5D. Let's see," she scanned the patient's charts. "Yes, here it is." She handed Annie a chart and returned her attention to her task.

"Charles Worthington," Annie read the patient's name. "His leg stump?"

"It's not healing properly." Lt. Bothley didn't look up. "Take good notes about its condition. The doctor is concerned about it."

"Yes, ma'am."

Annie gathered what she would need from the supply cabinet. Too many men returned without limbs. Whether they'd been blown off or damaged beyond repair, most healed well. And most learned to adapt to an artificial one, thanks to the Army's vigorous rehabilitation program. But sometimes the stump didn't want to heal.

Unexpectedly, her thoughts went to Sgt. Milton Greenlee and his embarrassment at not being able to use his arm. At least he had both his legs and both his arms even if his left arm was incapacitated.

Sadly, that handsome face, a face that would have

been a heart-stopper when he let loose that killer smile, now bore angry, red scars. Time would heal some of the damage but not all.

She wondered how badly his eye was damaged. The loss of an eye was a different kind of injury than the loss of a limb.

"Lieutenant McEwen."

Annie stopped as the familiar soldier approached. "Sergeant, how are you today?" She carefully controlled her reaction.

"You're not still mad at me about yesterday, are you?" Sgt. Lloyd Baker smiled in his mischievous, little-boy way.

"I'm not mad at you," Annie assured him. "But you'd better watch your step. Understood?"

He grinned as he raised his hands in surrender. "Understood." Dropping his hands he added, "You were just so gorgeous. And your voice. You sounded like you belonged up there with that band, just singing your heart out."

"Thanks," Annie muttered, a little perturbed as she continued down the hallway. All this praise was going to take some getting used to.

"Are you coming to the game this week?" he asked, trailing her down the hall. "We're playing Camp Murphy again."

She glanced over her shoulder. "And I suppose you'll be playing?"

"Yep. Best short stop Ream General's got." He beamed with pride. "You gotta come."

She smiled. His boyish charm managed to work its way through her defenses. She liked him a lot. But not enough to break her own hard and fast rule-no dating

34

soldiers, not now, not ever.

And with Sgt. Baker she could hide behind the Army's rule of no fraternization between officers and enlisted personnel, even though nurses weren't real officers. They were given rank just to insure respect. But rules were rules. She and Sgt. Baker could remain friends, as long as he behaved himself and didn't pull anymore stunts like yesterday.

Besides, she had a career to think about. A career away from the Army that was finally getting some traction.

"You will come, won't you?" he pleaded.

"I'll try. If I can get one of the other girls to come with me."

"Great! And you won't have to worry about me. I'll be on the field. Plenty far away."

His kiss flashed through her mind. She'd been shocked, but pleasantly so. And that's what worried her the most. She'd liked it.

She decided to change the subject to something safer. "What are you doing here? You didn't stop by just to invite me to the game, did you?"

"Nah." He sheepishly glanced away as if he'd been caught out of school. "I'm scoping out some of the newer patients." He met her gaze. "You know, kind of like scouting out the prospects."

"You're looking for baseball players?" She couldn't believe it.

"Sure. It's a way to lift their spirits. Just like your singing. Only we can use baseball to get them working on their physical therapy. Get it?"

"Sure. I get it." She shook her head but smiled at him. His heart was in the right place. And he was right.

The patients needed something to motivate them to think about life after being wounded.

"I've got to go," she said, turning toward Ward 5D.

"See you at the game. Okay?"

She nodded and continued toward her task.

Lloyd was a sweet guy. Maybe it wasn't so bad having a Sergeant stuck on her. Even if she had no intention of dating him.

She put on her professional smile and entered the small ward that had been a hotel room before the Army transformed the hotel into a hospital. Instead of a few large wards on the floor, there were lots of small ones, which created challenges for the nursing staff the Army hadn't anticipated.

****

Milt tried to remain still as the orderly scraped a razor across his face. He still couldn't get used to being shaved while propped up in a hospital bed.

Another thing to complain to the doctor about. Milt wanted to get up and shave himself. It would be a challenge at first, doing it one-handed. But he'd learn. He had to. Shaving was only one of the things he'd have to learn to do, so he might as well get started.

"Hi, fellows."

The orderly stopped abruptly, giving Milt the chance to look around and see the visitor.

"Hey, Sarge," the guy in the opposite bed answered.

The Sergeant approached the man but looked over to the orderly and nodded. "Carry on, Smith. I'm just here to visit."

The orderly resumed his job shaving Milt's jaw while Milt listened to the conversation, grateful for the distraction.

"So, Lonnie, how are you doing?"

"Oh, you know me. I ain't gonna start complaining now. I may be a little banged up, but I'm home free."

"That's the spirit."

"How'd the game go? I ain't seen the paper and nobody said how you did."

"You mean when we played Morrison Field the other day? We got beat. One lousy run."

"Too bad. How'd you do?"

"Two hits. An RBI. And, of course, great fielding." He used hand gestures for emphasis.

Milt's ears picked up at the baseball references, a game he loved and had played all his life.

The orderly finished. He removed the towel draped around Milt's neck and wiped his face with it. Milt reached up to feel. "Get this soap off, would you?"

"Sure, Sergeant." The orderly dipped a towel in the basin and wiped it across Milt's cheek.

"I'll do it." Milt took the towel and scrubbed the damp cloth over his face and neck. "Get some clean water, will ya'? That's soapy."

The orderly took the wet towel and gathered the remainder of his things. He disappeared through the door leading to the bathroom.

As soon as the orderly moved out of the way, the visiting Sergeant took his place, grinning.

"You're the new guy, aren't you?"

Milt nodded. His headache had returned, and pain put a damper on his desire to socialize.

"I'm Sergeant Lloyd Baker," He offered his hand. "I'm with the rehabilitation group."

Milt hesitated a moment, trying to figure out what

the guy wanted, before extending his own hand. "Greenlee. Sergeant Milt Greenlee."

The orderly returned and handed Milt a warm, wet cloth which Milt wiped over his face. The warmth felt good. The tension in his shoulders relaxed.

"You like baseball?" Sgt. Baker asked.

"Sure." Milt wished the guy would just move on.

The orderly exchanged the wet cloth for a clean towel. "The Sarge here plays on the hospital's baseball team."

"Plays?" Sgt. Baker retorted. "Why, I'm the star player."

That was all he needed. A small-time ball player who thought he was somebody.

"Bet you played. Am I right?"

Milt looked up. "Me?"

"Sure, you. Just asking if you played baseball. Did you?"

"That's all in the past." He wasn't ready to dredge up his feelings about baseball. To contemplate the fact that he would never play again.

He looked around wishing someone would say something and draw this guy's attention. Maybe change the subject.

"What position?" Baker continued ignoring Milt's obvious lack of interest. "No. Let me guess." Baker looked around. "What do you think, Lonnie? Center field. Or maybe third base?"

"Naw, he looks like a first baseman to me," Lonnie chimed in from across the room.

Great. Now Baker had help humiliating him.

Baker leaned closer. "No. I think Milt here was a pitcher. And captain of the team."

His serious stare dared Milt to reply.

"What of it. None of that matters anymore." The last thing Milt wanted to talk about was his past…especially related to baseball.

"You're wrong. It matters a lot. It says something about who you are. Even all shot up you're still that guy, underneath. We just have to help you find him again."

Fury erupted from his depths. Milt gripped the towel, his fingers digging into the rough cloth. If he wasn't so damn weak, so damn incapacitated, he would hit the sorry so-and-so. How dare this state-side jerk preach to him. What did he know?

Baker must have recognized the signs because he shifted his attention to the other patients. "We've got a game coming up. Ream General versus Camp Murphy. You're all invited to come watch. Just tell the nurse and she'll arrange for you to get there."

"I'd sure like to see it," the patient in the bed beside Lonnie spoke up.

Baker stepped toward the man. "Miller, right?"

The boy nodded.

"And let's see," Baker rubbed his chin. "You played first base on your high school team, and you scored the winning run in a big game."

"That's right. You remembered." The young man beamed.

"I know my baseball players."

"And what position do you play?" Milt surprised himself when he asked the question.

"Shortstop." Baker whirled around to face Milt. "And my batting average is 282. At least that's what it is in the Army league." Sergeant Baker returned to

Milt's bed. "It'll do you good to come watch a game. I'll tell Nurse McEwen to put your name on the list."

Milt opened his mouth to object but stopped when he heard Nurse McEwen's name. Would she be the one to take him? He wouldn't mind her company. Maybe going to a baseball game would be okay. Even sitting in one of those damned wheelchairs.

Sgt. Baker took his leave and Milt settled back against the pillow. He'd avoided even thinking about baseball. Tried to put it out of his mind. He'd never play again. There was no doubt about that.

No spring training. No chance to play with the big boys. Not now. Not ever. All he'd ever wanted...gone.

He'd agreed to go to a game. To watch.

It would be pure torture.

He couldn't wait.

Chapter 7

The nurse turned off the light and Milt's good eye adjusted to the semi-darkness. A dim light from somewhere behind the doctor provided enough illumination for him to see the two figures hovering nearby.

Milt stilled as the nurse carefully removed the bandages from his face. He knew what to expect. They had done this in England, in another dimly lit room. He'd learned then that the sight in his left eye wasn't completely gone. It had been dim and blurry, but he'd been able to see shapes. Pleased with Milt's progress the doctor had re-bandaged his eye for the trip across the Atlantic. To protect it, he'd said.

The nurse peeled away the final bandage and Milt blinked several times. The doctor stepped forward and looked into his left eye with one of those lighted instruments. The brightness blinded him momentarily.

"Good," the doctor murmured.

Next came the drops. Milt blinked again to clear his vision.

"Cover your right eye and tell me what you see," the doctor said.

Milt followed instructions and cupped his right hand over his right eye.

Even in the dim light everything went blurry. He blinked, trying to clear it, but it was no use.

41

"Not much," he said. "Everything's blurry."

"Okay." The doctor turned away. Suddenly light flooded the room.

Milt blinked furiously and finally shut his eyes. A tear slid down beside his nose.

He sensed the doctor's presence and opened his eyes again.

"Cover your right eye again," the doctor instructed. "All right. What do you see now?"

"You," Milt replied. The man's face was only inches away.

"Describe me."

"You're a big blob. Wearing glasses. Bushy eyebrows. Moustache, maybe."

"What color are my eyes?"

"Brown…I think." It was a guess. "Dark."

"Good." The doctor pulled back and stood a few feet away. "Now, can you still see my face?"

"Yes. But it's a smaller, blurrier blob."

He stepped back further. "How many fingers am I holding up?"

Milton blinked but the blurry shape wouldn't come into focus. "Uh…two…no…I don't know."

"How about now?"

He held up his other hand, off to the side. Milt tried to focus on it but couldn't. He hated to strike out and that's exactly how it felt.

"I don't know. It's too blurry."

The doctor came closer and held up one finger directly in front of Milt.

"I want you to keep your eye on my finger. Follow it with your eye without moving your head."

"Okay," Milt said, blinking to focus.

The finger moved from side to side, up and down, at angles and back to center.

After instructing Milt to uncover his good eye, the doctor proceeded to examine his injured eye more closely with his fancy equipment. Finally, he stood in front of Milt, arms crossed, and an unreadable expression on his face.

"They did a pretty good repair job. Your eye movement is good. There's some vision." He nodded to the nurse as if giving her a silent command. "We'll let you adjust to having the bandage off for a few days, then look at it again."

"Will glasses correct my vision?"

"That's the hope. But I don't want to fit you just now. Let the eye settle down a bit."

"No more surgery then?"

"No. Not on the eye at least. The plastic surgeon will want to do some work." He turned to leave.

Milt had made up his mind. This time they were going to show him. No more excuses or putting him off. He wanted to see. No. He needed to see.

"Wait a minute," he said. Belatedly he remembered he was still in the Army. "Sir," he added.

Captain Balentine stopped by the door and stared at him.

The sweat rolled down Milt's back. His teeth were locked tight.

"I want to see what I look like," he blurted out.

Surprise flitted across the doctor's face before he got it under control.

"Now. I want to see it now."

"We're not going to re-bandage your eye. You'll be able…"

"I want to see it now," Milt interrupted. "Before I leave this room. Before everybody but me can see what I look like."

The doctor looked resigned and a little worried. He glanced over at the nurse.

"I'll get a mirror," she said and hurried out of the room.

"What you will see today looks much worse than it will later."

Dr. Balentine was hedging. That meant it was bad, so bad he had to warn Milt.

The nurse appeared with a hand mirror like the one his sister kept on her dresser. She handed it to the doctor.

"Just remember, we've only started. There's much more for the plastic surgeon to do. I promise, you will look much better in time."

Milt reached out his hand and the doctor placed the handle in it. Gripping tightly, Milt brought the mirror up in front of his face.

For a few seconds he just stared. A monster stared back. Like Frankenstein. Only this was his face, and the stitches weren't stage makeup or a Halloween costume. No, it was his face.

His throat tightened and his gut clinched. His hand began to shake so the doctor reached out and steadied it.

His damaged eye stared out from red, ugly, scarred flesh. The horrid mess of scar tissue covered his left temple and the left side of his forehead, lines of stitching clearly visible. The inflamed scars ran into his hair, or rather where his hairline had been, from a couple of inches above his ear to his forehead and back onto his head where short hairs emerged from his scalp. Half of his head must have been shaved so they could sew it up. Another jagged scar split his left cheek down to his jaw line. Even his left ear appeared to be misshapen.

His stomach churned even more. Bile rose in his throat. He feared he might up-chuck all over the exam room.

The doctor's cool, but firm, hand remained wrapped around Milt's. He didn't take the mirror away. Instead, he let Milt look his fill.

"The damage to the eye socket has been repaired. The eye lid as well as the eyeball itself were stitched up." The doctor pointed to where his eyebrow had been. "The fractures appear to be healing well. So does the eye. There are numerous skin grafts to do yet, but so far it is progressing nicely."

"Nicely." Milt mocked the doctor's words.

"You insisted on seeing it."

Milt could tell that Dr. Balentine's patience was running out, but he didn't care. It was his face. His horrible mass of a face. A face that would test even his mother's smothering love.

"The redness will fade in time. As will the smaller scars. It will be up to the plastic surgeon to determine what can be done to improve your appearance." He paused and studied Milt for a moment. "Have you seen enough?"

Milt nodded ever so slightly. He'd never forget what he'd seen.

Dr. Balentine nodded to the nurse who reached toward Milt for the mirror. He gave it to her. When their gazes met, he saw pity, the last thing he wanted.

The doctor stepped back. "You're scheduled to see Dr. Fairchild. See what he has to say. And we'll talk again after a few days and look at that eye." He turned to leave and then stopped. "Oh, yes. We'll give you some sunglasses. I suggest you keep them with you and wear them at all times when you are outside. The bright sun isn't good for your eye."

Milt nodded. He wanted to thank him, but he couldn't speak. Not now. Not with the terrible images still so fresh.

At least now he knew what he had to face. Ha! Face. What a joke...on him.

Chapter 8

The orderly left Milt sitting in the day room in his wheelchair. A newspaper lay on the table nearby, but Milt didn't want to struggle to read the words or think about what was going on in Europe or in the Pacific. The orderly had pointed out a desk in the corner with writing supplies, in case he wanted to write a letter. Something else Milt didn't want to think about. He should write his folks, but not now.

Sunshine streamed through the open French doors that lead to a small balcony only a few feet away. He looked down at his perfectly good legs. He needed to try them out, see if they still worked.

Using his right arm to steady himself, he pushed up until he was standing on his own two feet. Slowly and deliberately, one step at a time, he made his way into the bright sunlight.

Grasping the door frame, he drew a deep breath of fresh, sea air. He'd made it. And his head wasn't spinning. His legs, though shaking, hadn't given way.

Another soldier, he didn't recognize, stood on the balcony with his back to Milt. Not that it mattered, there was plenty of room for both of them. To put the other patient on his good side, Milt maneuvered to the man's left.

Unprepared for the sparkle of sunlight on the water, Milt's breath caught. He'd known they were near the ocean. He'd heard it and smelled it, but until this moment he hadn't seen it.

What a view!

As far as he could see, sparkling, dancing blue water stretched to the empty horizon. Not a single ship in sight.

Waves crashed onto the pristine sand. No ugly obstacles, no landing craft, no bodies, no blood. Just the gentle waves and the endless motion of the water.

"It's nothing like the beaches over there," the man next to him said.

"Yeah." Milt looked at his fellow patient and saw something familiar in his face. He held to the railing as he grasped for the memory.

"I'm Mark Pendleton." The man offered his hand. "We're in the same ward."

"Milt Greenlee." Milt took the hand, confused by the familiarity.

"I'm on your left," Pendleton explained with a smile.

Milt nodded. "Yeah. The bandage limited my vision." He relaxed and turned back to face the water. "Sorry if I haven't been very friendly."

"Don't worry about it. I was pretty surly when I first got here." Pendleton gazed out over the water. "Didn't like the idea of losing my leg. But I got used to it."

Milt glanced down, then realized what he'd done, so he forced himself to look back toward the ocean.

"It's okay." Pendleton reached down and pulled up his pants leg so that Milt could see his artificial leg. "Now that I have this, I'm beginning to feel more normal."

"Where'd you lose it?"

"Italy. Near Salerno. Shrapnel tore it up. Had to take it off in a field hospital."

"That must have been rough."

"The rough part was running through the surf straight into German guns." He shook his head. "Thank God I'll never have to do anything like that again."

Memories flooded Milt's mind. Boats churning in the water. Waves crashing into the obstacles that looked like giant versions of his sister's jacks, only these jacks were big enough for him to hide behind as bodies floated in on the waves, the water stained red with their blood.

The ear-splitting noise never stopped, even with his face buried in wet sand. Shells exploded all around. Machine gun fire came from every direction.

Run, his survival instinct had told him. But where?

Milt ordered his thoughts to stop. He wouldn't let himself think about that. Not now.

He squeezed his eyes closed and drew a deep, cleansing breath before re-opened them to gaze down at the swimming pool almost directly below.

I'm in the states. Safe. No more war. Not for me.

"Are you okay?" Pendleton asked. "You look kind of sick."

Beads of sweat dotted his face and trickled down his back. "Not used to this sun." He'd forgotten about the sunglasses he was supposed to wear. And he hadn't expected it to be so hot. He tried to turn toward the door and had to grab the railing as everything started to spin.

Pendleton got hold of him and helped him back to the wheelchair. Milt sank into the chair, grateful he hadn't collapsed.

Nurse McEwen wheeled a patient into the day room just as he looked up.

Pendleton pulled a chair up to the table and sat down. "I'll sit with you a while. Make sure you're okay."

"Thanks. I'll be fine. Just need to rest a bit."

"Sure. A little at a time. You'll get there."

Milt didn't want to talk about it. "You said you were at Salerno. What outfit were you with?"

"157th Infantry. Part of the Forty-fifth Division. What about you?"

"18th Regiment. First Division."

"Yeah? We were with you guys on Sicily." Pendleton shook his head and laughed. "What an experience. That was my first landing. Boy was I green. Thought it was gonna' be a cake walk."

Milt had watched the first wave land at Gela from the ship's deck. "Our unit was in reserve on that one. We went in later, after the beach was secured."

"You got lucky. Course the landing was just the start of it." He shook his head. "Sicily was sure no cakewalk."

"You're right about that."

Both men fell silent. Neither wanted to dredge up the memories.

After a brief pause, Pendleton stood. "I need to get some exercise. They want me to walk on this thing as much as I can."

"Sure," Milt nodded. "I'll stay here a while." He glanced over toward the desk. "Would you push me over there?" He waved his hand in the general direction. "I need to write my parents and I'm having trouble maneuvering this thing with only one hand."

"Sure." Pendleton pushed the chair to the desk. "See you later," he said over his shoulder as he left.

Milt gathered paper and pencil, then stared at the blank page. Words wouldn't come. Writing words on paper didn't work for him. Never had. He couldn't spell c-a-t and the only way he could write was to imagine drawing the letters, following the sample letters in his old classroom. He'd quickly learned to memorize those pictures, but when they were put together in words, they looked scrambled with letters appearing to be backwards or upside down. He'd worked so hard just to be able to struggle through reading the simplest sentences.

He had made himself write letters home when he was overseas. They were awkward scratches of misspelled words and stunted sentences. He'd never said much but that he was okay and that he loved them.

Just thinking of writing had his palms wet with sweat.

What could he say to them? That he was okay, would be okay, maybe.

The doctor had been pretty vague about his arm. He'd reminded Milt of a coach trying to convince some awkward boy with two left feet that he could play baseball when he knew all along the boy was hopeless. At least the eye doctor had been more straightforward. He could see, some. Would need glasses but no guarantee his vision would be any good.

A pitcher had to be able to see.

As for his head, the concussion's symptoms would fade. His head would stop swimming. The headaches should subside, in time. According to the doctor in England, the blow to his head should have killed him.

Would have if his helmet hadn't deflected some of the impact.

He should be grateful. But after over a month, he was tired of the pain and tired of sitting around. He wanted to get back on his feet, get on with his life, whatever that would be.

Guilt swept over him. He should write his family. Let them know...something. They would take care of him. He knew that much. They'd always stood behind him, even when he'd disappointed them. So now...

"Excuse me. Sgt. Greenlee."

Milt looked up into Nurse McEwen's lovely face.

Chapter 9

"I don't mean to interrupt your writing, but I couldn't help overhearing your conversation with Corporal Pendleton."

That heart-stopping grin had her struggling to keep her thoughts straight.

"Uh, that's okay."

Her face flushed with heat. She forced the words out. "Did you say you were in the First Division?"

"Yes, ma'am."

"In Sicily?"

"That's right."

"I'm sorry if I sound a bit odd, asking you these things." She fidgeted with her hands. Just ask him, she told herself. You'll never know until you ask. "You see, my cousin, Joe, Joe McEwen, was in the First Division....in Sicily."

"Oh, I see." The grin faded into thoughtfulness as his gaze shifted away, toward the open doors.

He thought he understood, but he didn't. She had to tell him, had to ask. Much as it hurt, she had to say the words. "He was in killed in Sicily." She hesitated, then forced herself to go on, before she had time to think too much. "Did you know him? He was in the Engineers. Lieutenant Joseph McEwen."

His gaze returned to hers. "I'm sorry," he murmured before he looked away again. "Sorry for your loss."

Annie didn't want his sympathy. "Did you know him?" she repeated.

He shook his head, just enough to answer her question. Her heart sank. She'd known it was a long shot.

"Do you know what happened to him? Where he was... killed?"

"No. We know next to nothing." She wrung her hands again. This time she didn't try to make herself stop. "That's just it. We don't know. I was hoping to find someone who knew him. Who knew what happened to him." Her family had been devastated by Joe's death.

"There were a lot of men in Sicily. The engineers were split up between the regiments."

"I see." She didn't even try to disguise her disappointment.

He grew quiet, staring off in space, lost in thought.

Her chest tightened. Maybe she shouldn't have brought it up. Maybe he wasn't ready to talk about all that.

Finally, he turned back to face her. "Didn't somebody write? His commanding officer?"

"No." She hesitated, unsure how much she wanted to share with a stranger. "Well, just the one letter."

He didn't say anything, but the question was written on his face.

"They sent a letter, an official one. All it really said was that he's...dead."

"Sometimes the commanding officer doesn't know what happened. Didn't know the man because he's new himself." He looked at his own arm encased in plaster.

"We lost a lot of good men."

"It's just that Joe meant so much to us." She brushed away a tear that had escaped her furious blinking. "To me." Her throat was so tight she couldn't say any more. She didn't want to break down and cry. Not here, not in front of a patient, this patient.

"If I run into anyone from the 1st, I'll ask about him."

He was being kind, and she appreciated it. She really did. But she wanted more. She wanted him to understand how important it was. Somehow, she hoped that this man with Joe's blue eyes was the man who could help her.

"Joe was more like a big brother than a cousin." She thought of the times he'd stood up for her, given her brotherly advice and just been there when she desperately needed someone to talk to. Like now. "I miss him so."

She looked into those blue, blue eyes. He didn't look like Joe. But there was something about him. Something that drew her to him.

She stepped closer, wanting to reach out and touch him. He must have sensed it because he pulled back and looked down at the paper on the desk.

"I'd better get back...and let you write your letter." She turned and took a couple of steps then whirled around. "I don't suppose you'd consider writing to my aunt and uncle? It would mean so much to them. To hear from someone who was there. Someone who could tell them what it was like." She held her breath, anticipating his answer.

"I...don't..."

"Please. It would mean so much...to me."

"Well," he hesitated. Then he looked into her eyes. "I don't know what outfit he was in. Where he was."

Her heart leapt with joy. He hadn't said no.

"He was an engineer." She moved closer. "I have his letters. His address will say what outfit he was in, won't it?"

"Yeah. That'll help." He hesitated. He hadn't really said he'd do it. But he was thinking about it.

"Whenever you feel up to it. It doesn't have to be right now."

"Nurse McEwen." The voice came from the doorway.

She reached out and touched his arm. "Thanks so much." Somehow, she knew he would. He just had to.

****

Milt sat at the desk, staring at the blank piece of paper, yet not seeing it at all.

Why didn't you speak up, you idiot? Why didn't you just say no, plain and simple? Now she expects you to write to them. To tell them about Sicily. To tell them about things you spent months trying to forget. Besides, I can't write. It's bad enough for my family to see my pitiful scribbles. I'm not going to embarrass myself attempting to write to strangers.

All thought of writing his parents vanished. Her face filled his mind, anxious, excited, sad.

That damn cousin of hers had been in the First and had gotten himself killed — in Sicily no less. On that scrubby, mountainous island where the natives tried to scrape a living out of the poorest soil he'd ever seen. Not that he knew much about farming, but Sicily had been nothing like the green hills of his home in Tennessee.

Africa had been bad enough. Their first combat. They'd muddled through and had somehow defeated the Germans, thanks to the armored and the artillery. He'd seen his first dead soldier there and he'd killed his first. In a machine gun nest with a grenade. Nothing so clean and brave as facing a man and shooting him before he shot you. No. He'd learned that war wasn't like that. It was messy and dirty and exhausting. It was freezing at night in a hole in the ground praying the artillery shells wouldn't hit you. It was sweating through your clothes while tramping through the desert until you either reached your objective or dropped in your tracks.

Luckily, he'd stayed on his feet and hadn't gotten hit. Then word came that the Germans had pulled out, back to Sicily and Italy. So, of course, the Americans had to follow them. Take Sicily first, the brass said. Then Italy.

"Mind if I get some paper?"

Milt jerked his head up. "What?"

"Paper. So I can write a letter. Like you're doin'." His fellow patient reached across Milt to the stack of blank white paper on the desk. "Don't look like you've got too far."

Milt looked down at the blank page. He let out a sigh. "Yeah. I know." He picked up the pencil and tried to write something on the page, but the paper moved. He maneuvered his casted arm as best he could, but he had trouble positioning it so that he could hold the paper still.

Over his shoulder the soldier chuckled. "I used to be like that. When I first got here. My arm was in one of those things and for the life of me I couldn't do a thing with it. Tried to write and ended up chasing the paper all across the table."

Milt wanted to sock the guy. He had enough trouble writing without some jerk making fun of him.

"Tell you what. You get one of them Gray Ladies to write it for you. That's what I did. They're nice old ladies. And they write all fancy."

"Gray ladies?" Was the man making fun of older women?

"Oh, that's just what they call them. Course most of 'em are older but not too old. They volunteer to help us out. You know. Do things for us. Bring us stuff. Like this paper. See how nice it is. No Army stuff. No sir. Nice, fancy stuff. Those Gray Ladies say nothin's too good for us war heroes."

Milt was no hero. But right now he was more interested in these ladies than in correcting the soldier.

"How do I find these 'Gray Ladies'?"

"Just tell the nurse you need some help writing your letter. She'll arrange for one of them to come by or maybe you'll have to go down to the lobby. Kinda depends. The nurse'll tell you."

Milt wasn't about to ask Nurse McEwen. He didn't want her to know...what? That he struggled to read and write. If she found out, like everyone else, she'd judge him.

And he didn't want that. He liked her.

A beautiful woman like that had asked him to do her a favor. Why had she asked him? Just because he was in the 1st Division, like her cousin. Pendleton had been in Sicily. Why didn't she ask him?

Writing to her family would mean he'd get to talk to her. Get close to her. Maybe it would be worth it,

58

dredging up all those memories. Especially if he could get help writing. As long as he had this damn cast on his arm, he had an excuse. That and the eye that made everything look blurry. He had a perfectly good reason to have someone else write for him.

He would wait until the nurses' shift changed. Then he'd tell the night nurse he needed help writing home. Maybe that way Nurse McEwen wouldn't find out.

He'd write his folks first. See how it went. Then maybe he'd think of what he could tell her family about Sicily. Not how he'd seen men die. No, he couldn't tell them about that. But maybe about the land and the people. Maybe if he forced himself to think about it, he could come up with a funny story or two. He'd seen some pretty weird things over there.

Chapter 10

Annie strode across the courtyard and skirted the center fountain. She hummed one of those upbeat songs that put a little lilt in her step.

After she met with Lt. Cushman, she would take the new sheet music down to the Canteen where she could run through it on the piano.

Her conversation with Sgt. Greenlee had lightened her mood. She'd actually found someone who'd been in the First Division in Sicily. Even if he hadn't known Joe, he'd been there. And he'd said he would write to her aunt and uncle. Well, he didn't actually say he would. But he implied it.

She shook the thought away. Be positive. He'd do it.

And any information Aunt Millie and Uncle Herschel could get would thrill them. Her father was another story. Nothing short of raising Joe from the dead would satisfy him.

She checked her watch and speeded up. Charlie Cushman would be waiting for her.

The fragrance of exotic flowers floated on the breeze as she rounded the corner. The palm trees swayed gently to their own rhythm.

She would never have guessed her first hospital assignment after her initial military training would be in a place like this. The Army had transformed the fabulous Breakwater Hotel, luxury retreat for the rich, into Ream General Hospital. On the outside it retained its luxurious resort-like atmosphere. Inside plenty of changes had been made.

Charlie Cushman leaned against a column on the outside colonnade, smoking a cigarette and gazing across the expanse of grass to where a group of off-duty nurses played volleyball.

"Lieutenant," Annie called.

He straightened and faced her. "Annie, thanks for coming."

She pushed past her discomfort at his familiarity and smiled. "Yes. I got your message to meet you here. Do you have my letter?"

"Oh, yeah." He rubbed his chin. "I almost forgot. Good thing you reminded me."

He glanced over his shoulder toward the shorts-clad women playing nearby.

"Then why did you want to see me?"

"You were a big hit the other day. You know that, don't you?"

"Yes." Pleasure washed over her at the memory of the applause, the smiling faces, the cheers. She didn't think she'd ever get used to all the compliments.

"The whole thing went over real well. Better than we expected." He dropped his cigarette and ground it out with his toe. "Thing is…I've been asked to put on another show. For a bond drive."

"Another show?" Annie's pulse raced.

"Yeah. And, of course, I thought of you for the singer."

"Me?" She detected something in his voice, something more than the compliments he'd heaped on her moments before. "I'd be happy to sing again." She hoped she didn't sound too eager.

"I was hoping you'd say that." He smiled in that know-it-all way of his. "Thing is we need to start rehearsing right away. It's gonna be in the Civic Center in town." His hand rested lightly on her forearm. "You think you can get away? I know you had trouble with the captain before. Missing work and all."

Despite her discomfort at his familiarity, her thoughts raced. "There was something said about rotating Lt. Bell off night shift. I could volunteer." Lt. Cushman didn't understand what she was saying. "If I'm working the night shift, then I am off in the daytime. I could rehearse whenever, and not miss my shift."

"But you gotta sleep." He squeezed her arm.

"I can be flexible. Sleep in between. It's not like we're going to be rehearsing all day every day." She wanted to pull her arm away, but she forced herself to focus on the positive.

"No. Nothing like that." He turned and steered her into the shade beneath the overhang. "I brought in some new fellows. We need to get them up to speed. Add some new numbers."

"I'll talk to the captain." She glanced back at the volleyball players, almost out of sight, and tried to free herself from his grip. He held fast.

"I was hoping to start right away. The show'll be in two or three weeks. As soon as they can get it organized."

Warning bells rang in her ears, but she ignored them. "You just let me know." She sounded more cheerful than she felt. "I'll be there." She thought of performing again in front of a crowd with a fabulous band seemed almost too good to be true.

"Okay." He grinned in triumph. "As long as you understand what's expected of you."

"Of course, I…"

His arm slid around her waist as he backed her up against the wall.

"Wh…what are you…"

His lips covered hers while his hands roamed to places they shouldn't.

Annie squirmed to free herself, but his hold on her tightened. Finally, she jerked her head to the side, dislodging his mouth from hers.

"What do you think you're doing?"

"You gonna play hard to get, huh?"

"Turn me loose!"

He held her against the wall with his body. His hands gripped her arms like vises. "You want to sing with my band, then you play nice. Understand?"

"No. I don't." How had she been so stupid?

"Fine."

He turned her loose so suddenly she almost fell.

"Have it your way."

She gasped for breath, trying to understand what he was saying.

"I'll find another singer. Someone smarter than you who understands how to play the game."

"Game?"

"You say you want to be a singer. Well, in this game, sister, you have to play nice if you want someone like me to help you up the ladder."

He grinned and shook his head. "You'll never make it in this business. Not 'til you want it bad enough to do whatever it takes."

He strode away while she stared after him, fighting back tears.

Stubborn defiance surfaced. Her father had said she'd never make it, too. But she'd show him and Lt. Cushman and everyone else. She'd make it on her own. She didn't need anyone.

Yet something inside her wondered if Lt. Cushman was right. Would she have to do things she didn't want to do, just to get a break as a singer?

After getting her emotions under control, she walked to the circle drive in front of the hotel where she hoped to catch a ride to the canteen. Lt. Cushman wasn't going to ruin her evening.

Two girls in Red Cross uniforms lounged against the fender of a staff car smoking. One of them was Margo Van Buren.

Before Annie could speak, Margo dropped the cigarette and greeted her. "Hi, there."

"Hi," Annie replied, nodding to both young women.

"You were swell the other day. That dress looked really good on you, better than it ever looked on me."

Despite being flustered, she remembered her mother's advice to 'smile and accept a well-deserved compliment,' so the raised her chin. "Thanks."

"We sneaked in the back to see the show," the other girl added. "You were definitely the best part."

"Reminded me of shows in New York."

Annie smiled at them both, certain she glowed beet red.

"I'm Alice Meriwether. I've heard you sing at the canteen."

"As a matter of fact, that's where I was going. Any chance I could bum a ride?"

"I can take you." Margo pointed to a jeep parked just beyond the circle. "Alice is waiting for Lt. Colonel Arkin."

"That'd be swell." Annie followed Margo and climbed into the passenger seat. "About the dress," she added. "I'll get it back to you as soon as I have it cleaned."

Margo started up the jeep and deftly turned it around. "Oh, don't worry about that. I doubt that I ever wear it again. Why don't you keep it?"

"I couldn't do that. It's much too expensive."

"Nonsense. I have plenty of them. And there's not much occasion to wear them with this war on. Not much of a social season, here or in Newport."

Annie still wasn't sure she could accept such a gift. She racked her brain for a reasonable excuse. After all, Margo Van Buren was rich beyond anything Annie could imagine, judging from her family's huge, luxurious estate.

Margo glanced over at her as they sped along the road. "Go ahead. Take it. I want you to have it. You were lovely in it."

Annie beamed. Not Charlie Cushman nor anyone else would stop her. Look out New York. Annie Laurie McEwen was on her way.

Chapter 11

The baseball game had just started, with Ream
General's team in the field, when Annie and her fellow
nurses, Kathy and Louise, arrived at the ball field.
Annie spotted Lloyd at the short-stop position between
second and third. He was bent forward smacking his
glove with his fist and watching the batter intently.

Already perspiring from the heat, Annie wished the
ocean breeze would pick up and cool her down. "Let's
find a seat. Looks like they've already started."

"How about over there?" Kathy pointed toward the
bleachers on the third base side of the field near the
home team dugout. The bleachers consisted of three
rows of wooden benches some of the men had nailed
together from spare pieces of wood to provide seating
for onlookers.

Other spectators stood and watched, some sat in
wheelchairs and others sprawled on the grass just
outside the foul line.

The batter struck out and the crowd cheered. Annie
and her friends took advantage of the lull as the next
player came to the plate to find a seat.

Two soldiers sitting on the bottom bench stood so
the three nurses could climb up and squeeze into a
space in the middle. Once seated, Annie looked around.

Sgt. Greenlee sat in a wheelchair near the end of
the bleachers. His bandaged head and casted arm

sticking out at that awkward angle made him easily identifiable.

She studied what she could see of his face. Absorbed in the game, he watched every move on the field. Letting him come had been the right thing to do. Just like many of the men, a sports event got his mind off his injuries and let him relax for a while.

Maybe it would be a good time to talk to him, here at the game. They could talk about baseball and then maybe she could bring up the subject of writing to her family…again. He hadn't been particularly enthusiastic about the idea the other day. And he hadn't actually agreed. Maybe today he would.

The batter hit a ground ball to the short stop. Sgt. Baker scrambled to scoop up the fast-moving ball, then he spun around and fired it to first base. His fast, fluid movement easily beat the runner. Annie cheered along with the crowd as the umpire called the runner out.

Watching Sgt. Baker's athletic prowess and the team's succinct movements warmed her heart like voices harmonizing to a lovely melody.

Sgt. Baker had not only pointed out how good he was, he'd taught her to appreciate the game of baseball. Much as she liked him, she'd tried her best not to get too close to the man.

"Don't get involved, no matter how nice or sweet or handsome they are," had been Annie's motto since joining the Army. Men meant trouble. Period. That included the male staff as well as patients. Yet somehow, she'd managed to get tangled up with Sgt. Lloyd Baker. She told herself the loveable guy with the heart of gold was like a brother, but the kiss he'd planted on her lips the day of the show had been anything but brotherly. She'd have to be very careful around him from now on.

Nope. No men in her life, not now. She'd focus on her work and her singing career. That was all she wanted. And if she played her cards right her singing career would take off and she would never have to return to Chattanooga. And she'd never have to deal with her father's plans for her future.

She'd watched him plot and plan Joe's life, as if Joe had been his own son instead of his nephew. Then the war broke out. Joe's college ROTC insured that he would go straight into the service when he graduated. Her father had merely adjusted his plans, saying that an officer with war service would enhance Joe's resume, make him even more certain to be elected, first to state office and then to Congress. Oh, yes. Her father had had great plans for Joe.

Now all he had left was the daughter he'd never loved.

A cheer for the Ream General team brought everyone to their feet. As the team trotted off the field, Sgt. Baker waved his cap in the direction of the bleachers.

A twinge of guilt crept into her heart as she waved back. She liked him a lot. But she wouldn't encourage him. She'd make sure he understood that they were not dating. Would never date. Not just because she was an officer and he was a non-com, but because she had no intention of getting involved with anyone.

Someone to her left shouted a derisive jibe as Camp Murphy's team took their positions on the field. Annie glanced around to find the offender. Sgt. Greenlee stood at the end of the bleachers leaning on his good arm. He watched the field, a hint of a smile on his face.

Sgt. Baker told her Sgt. Greenlee had played baseball before the war. Probably missed it. At least for now he could watch. Maybe Sgt. Baker would introduce him around. Greenlee hadn't been at Ream long enough to know any of the players. He looked like he wanted to be in the middle of it all, there on the bench discussing every detail.

At that moment, as if sensing that someone was watching him, he looked up and, despite the dark glasses he wore, their gazes met. She smiled and nodded to acknowledge him. He nodded in return. His lips formed a weak smile, but he looked a little odd to her, a bit distant. Pale and sweaty.

He ought to sit down. He's not used to being on his feet, especially in this heat.

****

She smiled at him, and he managed to smile back. He should thank her for putting his name on the list of patients to attend the game.

The pain in his head was worse today than since he left England, but he'd been so damned determined to get out of that hospital, he'd lied and said he felt fine.

If more exertion meant his head would hurt, then so be it. He wasn't going to lie in that bed from now on. He wanted to get out and watch a baseball game. Even if he couldn't play, he could watch.

He had spotted Nurse McEwen when she arrived with her two friends. She stood out, with that red hair and that classically beautiful face.

He wiped the sweat from his brow and held his hand up to shade his eye. Even wearing sunglasses, the

69

sun bothered him. What he needed was the broad bill of a baseball cap, if he could find one to fit over his bandages.

"First time in Florida?"

Milt turned to the soldier sitting on the bleachers to his right and reminded himself to be civil. "No. I trained at Camp Blanding."

"Hey, me too." The man grinned as if they were old friends. "I was at Blanding back in '43. When were you there?"

"In '42, with the First Division."

"Oh, that was way before my time. You must have been there when it was nothing but tents." The man turned back to watch the Camp Murphy pitcher warming up.

"Yeah. Tents."

Camp Blanding had been a lifetime ago. His few months there were a blur, one tough day after another. He'd enlisted after Pearl Harbor, and then he'd reported to Fort Oglethorpe for basic training. From there the newly minted soldiers had moved on to Fort Benning. By late spring he'd joined the First Division at Camp Blanding where the well-trained veterans made a man of him, to put it mildly. Yet his first days in North Africa erased any resentment for the rough treatment at Blanding. It had probably saved his life.

The crowd came to life when the Ream General team came up to bat. As the first batter warmed up at the plate, Milt studied the other players. Sgt. Baker was easy to spot swing a bat near the bench waiting his turn.

Milt had moved from the wheelchair, where he felt like a helpless invalid, to stand next to the bleachers. Here he could watch the game with one hand on the wooden structure to steady himself. The chair sat only two steps away. When he got tired, he'd ease back over and sit for a while.

Despite his pounding head, he wasn't dizzy. That was a good sign. To recover his strength, he needed to get outside and move around. He'd grit his teeth and endure the pain.

Sgt. Baker had been right. So far it had been a good game, with Baker fielding a line drive, then firing it to first for the out. Milt longed to stand on the mound assessing the batter, glancing at the base runners, then winding up to deliver the pitch. Something he'd never do again.

On the field the pitcher dug his feet into the dirt and massaged the ball, getting ready to deliver as soon as the batter was ready.

The lead-off batter came to the plate and the crowd grew quiet. The first pitch was a swing and a miss. Strike one. Next came a ball, high and inside, which the batter wisely pulled back from. One and one.

"So, who's favored to win today? Our boys or Camp Murphy?" the man beside him asked, interrupting Milt's concentration.

Just as he asked the question, the crack of a bat jerked Milt's head toward home plate. The batter slung his bat through the air and ran for first base. Milt's gaze followed the crowd's into the sky as the little white dot arched above the field.

The man in left field backed up as he gazed upward, then easily caught the high fly ball.

The crowd erupted in both cheers and jeers.

The first out.

The next batter was Sgt. Baker.

He took a couple of practice swings before the pitcher made his wind up and delivered the first pitch. It was way outside. Sgt. Baker stood there as the catcher reached out and caught it. Ball one.

Baker took another practice swing and then stood waiting. This one came fast and hard. Baker's swing connected. The ball bounced almost at the pitcher's feet then skittered past second base into the outfield. Baker raced for first and easily made it before the center fielder could scoop up the ball and shoot it to first.

The crowd stood and cheered Ream's first hit of the game.

Milt grinned with pleasure. He glanced over and saw Nurse McEwen standing and applauding with the rest of the crowd. Such a pretty girl, and she liked baseball.

The next batter came to the plate. Milt watched intently as the pitcher delivered his first pitch. Baker made a dash for second. As soon as the ball hit the catcher's glove, he was on his feet throwing it to second. But Baker was too fast for him, sliding into second base headfirst.

Milt cheered along with the crowd as Baker got to his feet and dusted himself off grinning from ear to ear.

"Boy, he's good," the guy beside him commented.

The batter connected with the next pitch and headed for first base. Baker tagged second and ran for third. The shortstop fumbled the catch, allowing the batter to make it safely to first base and Baker to reach third.

Milt focused on the new batter. "Knock him home," he shouted.

Two pitches later the bat cracked loudly, and the

crowd watched the ball sail through the air and out past the road which delineated the end of the field.

Home Run!

Everyone jumped to their feet screaming. Baker tagged home plate and turned to watch his teammates round the bases. By the time the home run hitter got there, the whole team gathered round cheering.

Wow! Three runs in their first at bat. And Sgt. Baker led it off. What an exciting game.

For the first time in a long time Milt felt joy...the old kind from when he was a kid cheering his teammates.

As the crowd settled back into their seats, a wave of weakness washed over him. His head swam. He grabbed onto the bleachers again and leaned in to steady himself. He wasn't exactly dizzy. Just weak.

"That was Joe Tennenbaum who hit the homer." The soldier sitting beside him was talking. "If he stay's hot, this ought to be a good game."

"Yeah. Looks like it," Milt managed.

Everyone looked toward the plate as the batter swung at a pitch. Another wild swing sent the batter back to the bench.

"Name's Shelton. Carl Shelton." The patient on the bleacher stuck his hand out.

Milt turned lose long enough to shake his hand. "Milt Greenlee."

He stood there watching the next batter. A tip foul and two strikes ended the inning.

Milt sighed, thinking he'd better sit down.

That's when he saw her again. Nurse McEwen went by following her friend. She sure was pretty.

He could feel the sweat trickling down his back.

No one else seemed to notice how hot it was. Maybe standing up for so long hadn't been such a good idea.

He turned and faced the chair only two short steps away.

Pushing off from the bleacher, he took one step. Then another. The effort caused his head to throb even more. He definitely needed to sit down before his legs gave way.

His head spun. He closed his eyes to stop it, but that didn't help.

"Are you okay?" he heard someone ask.

He opened his eyes. "Don't know." Strange, blurred faces stared at him.

He reached out to steady himself on the wheelchair. Someone grasped his hand but it wasn't enough to stop the sensation of falling. A thud reverberated through his body as everything went black.

Chapter 12

"I thought you were off for the day," Cassie commented.

Annie nodded. "I came in to check on Sgt. Greenlee."

"He's fine. We'll take care of him."

"I know. But I wanted to stop by."

Annie hesitated before going to Sgt. Greenlee's ward. After passing out at the ball field, he had come to and spoken to her. Overexertion and getting too hot had been her diagnosis. She needed to verify that she had been right and that he didn't have something more serious.

"Did Dr. B figure out what happened to the Sergeant?" she asked.

Cassie looked up from the chart. "He said that Greenlee shouldn't have been out in that heat. That he was too weak."

"In other words, I shouldn't have let him go to the game." She glanced down the hall toward Greenlee's ward. "I should have realized he wasn't strong enough to go out, especially when it's so hot."

"It's not your fault."

How many times had Annie heard that. None of the things that happened to people around her were her fault. But sometimes it was her fault, and she knew it.

Dammit. She'd tried to keep her distance and

remain purely professional in her dealings with Sgt. Greenlee. But something about him drew her to him. Those blue eyes conveyed his fears, his anxiety, his anger. Even with all the damage, his left eye was just as intense as the right. Or maybe it was the way his lips curved into that little smile, even when he didn't intend to smile, that drew her to him.

"I'll just go check on him."

Annie had only taken a few steps when Dr. Barenkowski emerged from another ward and strode toward her.

"Dr. B, I'm glad I caught you. How is Sgt. Greenlee? Has he recovered from his little incident at the ball game?"

"He'll be fine," the doctor kept walking so Annie hurried to stay at his side.

"Then it wasn't anything serious?"

"He fainted. That's all. Too much exertion. Too hot. I sent him back to bed where I expect him to stay for at least three days."

"Yes, sir." She wasn't about to mention that she'd been the one who'd okayed his outing.

Dr. B stopped at the nurse's station to talk to Cassie, clearly dismissing her, so she turned and went to Sgt. Greenlee's ward.

He lay on his bed with his eyes closed. His color was better. Hopefully, that meant he was okay.

She touched his arm and he opened his eyes, the blue a little duller than usual. "Hi," she said.

"Hi."

"The doctor says you will be fine. You just need to rest."

"Yeah. Rest. Tired of resting."

She smiled at his complaining. It was always a good sign when a patient complained.

"What are you doing here?" he muttered.

For some reason his grumpiness made her smile. "Don't get an attitude with me, Sergeant. I'm a nurse, remember."

He sighed deeply and closed his eyes. "I remember."

"Besides, I promised I'd come check on you."

"Yeah, sure."

Sadness and exhaustion. That's what she heard. "At least you got to see some of the game."

His lips turned up in that little smile, the one that looked like he was fighting it. "Yeah." Then he smiled for real and looked at her. "Thanks for letting me go."

"There'll be more games. You'll see."

"I used to play, you know. I'd be a pro…if it weren't for the war."

"You must really love baseball."

"I do." His eyes lit up. "That Baker. He's lucky. Getting to play while he's doing his bit."

"He's good. Not just at baseball. At his rehab job, too."

"I'll bet." His gaze moved to the ceiling, and she wondered where his thoughts were.

Annie knew she didn't need to burden him with anything else. He seemed down enough. She'd ask him about writing her family some other time.

"I'd better go. Let you rest." She turned and walked toward the door. Before reaching it, she stopped and looked back. He lay there with his eyes shut.

She had to get out of here. He was just another patient. Another wounded soldier to be taken care of.

Just because she had asked him to do her a favor didn't mean she had to fawn all over him. No. She needed to stick to her guns. She wouldn't get involved with anyone. And certainly not Sgt. Milton Greenlee.

****

Nurse McEwen left the ward without mentioning her request for him to write to her family. Yet he sensed her anxiety about it.

What had he agreed to?

Even if he got one of the Gray Ladies to write for him, he would have to dredge up memories of Sicily, memories better left buried.

But he hadn't been able to say no. When she talked about her cousin, he'd pitied her, and he instinctively wanted to help her.

So he'd promised her...well, he hadn't actually promised. He just hadn't said no. He'd let her believe he'd do it which was the same as a promise...almost.

Yet, he dreaded going back there, to North Africa and Sicily, where he'd learned what war truly was, where his friends screamed in pain, where he saw unimaginable horrors, smelled the putrid odors, and endured soul-numbing terror.

She said she wanted to know, said she wanted her family to know. But she didn't want to know what it was really like over there. No one in their right mind wanted to hear about that.

She thought she had seen war wounds, but by the time her patients reached a hospital in the states, they'd been cleaned up, sewn up, fixed up. They looked nothing like they did on the battlefield...covered with dirt, blood, their own excrement. And the dead ones. She never saw them. Never listened to them scream and

78

cry in agony as the life drained from their bodies. Never saw them lying where they fell, covered in flies, rotting in the hot sun.

Could he do it? He'd let her believe he would. He hadn't been able to say no, not to her.

That Gray Lady who'd written the letter to his folks was sympathetic enough. She'd readily accepted his fumbled explanation as to why he couldn't write it himself. The old gal had cheerfully accepted his pathetic excuse so she could to her bit to help the wounded.

He'd done that all his life. Made excuses. Gotten others to do things for him. Oh, he'd always done favors in return, if he could, but he'd never been truly honest.

He'd lied, cheated, finagled, joked, anything to hide the embarrassment of not being able to read without stumbling over every other word, of not being able to write a sentence without misspelling half the words.

He could still hear the names echoing through time…dummy, stupid, retard. Most had quickly learned to keep quiet or get punched. But he knew they still called him names behind his back. Girls giggled and whispered; boys snickered even when the teacher told them to stop.

He pulled himself out of those painful childhood memories.

He'd figure it out. Keep his promise. He had to.

Chapter 13

"Hold it still, will ya'?" Milt grumbled to the orderly holding the mirror.

"Sorry." To the man's credit he didn't return Milt's irritable attitude.

Milt struggled with the safety razor, determined to shave himself. Having only one hand made it more difficult than he imagined. And with the vision in his left eye so fuzzy, he had to squeeze it shut and strain his good eye to see his own face.

He dropped the razor into the basin and felt around his face to determine what he'd missed. The left side of his jaw was almost out of view, so he had to feel his way. His fingers detected the rasp of whiskers. A patch on the lower part of his left cheek.

Reaching down for the razor, his hand bumped into the orderly's.

"Here." The man smiled, an understanding smile, not a mocking one, as he fished the razor from the basin.

"Thanks." Milt took the razor. Using his fingers, he found the remaining patch of whiskers. A couple of swipes did the trick.

"What's your name again?" Milt asked as he handed the razor back.

"Kerry. Jim Kerry."

"Well...Thanks, Jim." Milt dipped the towel in the

water and scrubbed it over his face. "Thanks for your help." He looked the quiet man in the eye. "I have to learn to do this myself. You understand, don't you?"

"Sure. I get it." A smile lit his face. "You gotta know you can take care of yourself."

Milt sighed. "Sorry if I've been difficult." He knew he'd been a surly bear at times. Staying in bed for three days hadn't helped.

"Can't blame you. Not after what you guys have been through." Jim gathered up the shaving paraphernalia. "I'll get a wet cloth so you can get all that soap off your face."

At least he'd accomplished something. He'd shaved himself for the first time since…since leaving England for France. Since before they'd landed on that beach. Omaha they'd called it. Horror, that's what he remembered.

"Here." Jim stood beside him, a wet cloth in his extended hand and a dry towel in his other one.

Milt met his gaze. "Thanks." He meant it as much for the interruption as for the cloth. He wiped his face, feeling every stroke, then dried it with the towel.

"You want any aftershave?"

Milt nodded. "Sure."

Jim produced a bottle and Milt said, "You do it. But don't use much."

Jim rubbed the aromatic liquid across his face.

Someone called from the doorway. "Sgt. Greenlee."

"Over here."

The mail clerk came toward him. "Greenlee, you've got a telegram." He held out an envelope.

"Jim, would you open it for me?"

"Sure." Jim grasped the thin envelope, slid his finger under the seal and took out the single page.

Milt glanced around the ward. A telegram couldn't be good. And he didn't want to attempt to read it in front of these two.

Jim held out the telegram to Milt. "You want us to leave?" Jim asked.

"No." Milt blinked furiously. "Read it to me. I think I got some soap in my eye."

"Let me see." Jim bent down to look at his eye.

"Never mind that," Milt barked. "Just read it." He hated himself for being such an ass, but he couldn't read the damn thing. Maybe if he were alone, maybe he could decipher it. But a telegram meant something urgent, and he didn't have the patience to figure it out.

With a strange look on his face, Jim started reading.

"Mother and I will arrive on Saturday. Must see you for ourselves. Father."

Milt's breath caught in his throat.

No. They couldn't come here. Not now.

"Sounds like your folks are coming. Must be nice." The clerk rattled on. "Most folks can't afford to make a trip like that. Where they comin' from anyway?"

Ignoring the clerk's words, Milt queried, "Can I send a reply?"

"Sure," the clerk answered. He fished a pencil and paper out of his pocket. "What do you want to say?"

"Do not come. Please. Stay at home. I will write and explain. Just do not come here."

"You don't want to see your parents?" The clerk asked.

"Did you get down what I said?"

The man nodded.

"Then send it. Now." Milt screamed. He didn't care what the clerk thought. His job was to send the telegram, not make judgments.

He glanced over at Jim who had already turned and walked away.

Milt thought of facing his mother. His gut clinched. She would cry, and carry on, and fuss over him as if he were a baby. And his father. His face would be drawn tight with concern, but the man would say nothing.

No. He needed time. To prepare. To get himself ready before facing them.

His image in the shaving mirror filled his mind. Bandages on his head, scars across the side of his face. At least no one could see beneath the bandages where his scalp had been separated from his skull. He couldn't imagine his parents' reaction to that.

And what about his damn arm with no feeling in it? He didn't even know how long he'd have to wear the awful cast contraption. All the doctor would say was that after the bones healed, they'd be able to tell more.

No. His parents couldn't come. He couldn't face them. Not yet.

Surely his telegram would stop them.

Maybe he could place a long-distance telephone call. He'd ask the nurse.

****

Stella looked up as Annie approached. "I thought you were off tonight?"

"I am. I just stopped by to give this to Sgt. Greenlee. Then I'm off to the Canteen." Annie held up the folded paper. She'd written not only her aunt and uncle's names and address, but also her parents and a little about them, hoping it would help him compose his letter.

Stella shook her head. "Oh, he's been upset. Be prepared."

"Upset about what?"

"The way I heard it he got a telegram from his parents saying they were coming to see him. Seems that set him off."

"I wonder why?"

"He doesn't want to see them. He had the clerk send a telegram telling them not to come."

Annie wondered how she would feel under the same circumstances.

"He's been pretty irritable since he got here," Stella continued. "One of those who's mad at the world 'cause he got wounded."

Annie turned back to her friend. "He's always been nice to me."

"That's because he has a crush on you. Half the men here are in love with you."

"Oh, that's not true. They like me, yes. But they aren't in love with me."

Stella grinned. "Don't worry. Lots of patients fall in love with their nurse. And after that show you put on, well, that made you the one." She hesitated a minute. "Come to think of it, Sgt. Greenlee arrived right before your show. My guess is you made quite an impression right from the start."

"Don't be silly." But Annie wondered if Stella was right.

Annie turned toward Sgt. Greenlee's ward.

"See if you can calm him down," Stella called after her.

Annie nodded and continued.

How did Sgt. Greenlee feel about her? Maybe she could use his crush to put him in a better humor.

The patients had had their supper and were settling down for the night. Some were reading, others writing. Someone in the back had a radio on low.

Sgt. Greenlee lay on his side with his awkward cast pointing toward the ceiling. She didn't think he was asleep, but it was hard to tell.

"Nurse," the man in the next bed spoke. "I wouldn't bother him if I were you."

She smiled and nodded to acknowledge his advice. "It's all right."

When her gaze returned to the sergeant, his eyes were wide open. And from his expression she wasn't sure if he was happy to see her or not.

She leaned closer. "Hello." She tried for her sweetest smile. "How are you doing?"

"Umpth," he growled.

"I'm sorry to bother you, but I promised to bring you this." She held up the paper.

He glanced at it, then closed his eyes. The muscle in his jaw worked. Was he grinding his teeth to contain his anger?

One of the patients brought a straight chair and set it down beside the bed.

"Thank you," she whispered.

She pulled the chair close so they could speak quietly. There wasn't much privacy in a ward, but she wanted to make it seem like their conversation was between just the two of them. Maybe he would talk to her.

"I understand you heard from your parents."

That brought a sharp response. "So?" His right eyebrow arched high into his forehead. "What of it?"

He struggled to roll onto his back. Instinctively she reached out to him, but his defiant frown stopped her. She pulled back and held the paper with both hands, fighting the urge to wring it like a dish rag.

"I understand why you don't want them to come."

"You do?" He narrowed his eyes. "And why is that?"

"Why I understand?" She let out a little sigh. How could she explain? "Well...I wouldn't want my parents showing up here."

He waited, the question still written on his face.

"I just wouldn't want them around. And I'm not even injured." She waved her hand, vaguely indicating the room full of injured men.

"That doesn't explain."

She couldn't meet his eyes, so she looked down at the wrinkled paper. "They don't exactly approve of me...of my being an Army nurse." She chanced a glance up and caught those blue eyes squinted into a frown. "Actually, they don't approve of much that I do."

"Not even your singing?" Some of the sharpness in his voice had eased.

She smiled at his astuteness. "No. Not even my singing. At least my father doesn't approve of it. It was okay when I sang in church. But not on a stage. Not that 'swing' music."

"I don't like him already."

"Oh, he's a good man in many ways. We just don't get along."

She'd managed to calm him down and distract him.

Now she needed to get him to talk.

"So, why don't you want them to come?"

"Isn't it obvious? I don't want them to see me…like this."

"It could be worse."

"Yeah, I know." He bit back. "I know I'm lucky compared to some." Bitterness laced his words as his eyes roamed the room.

"Have you told them about your injuries?"

Those blue eyes focused on her intently. Finally, he answered. "No. Not exactly."

"Maybe that's why they want to come. To see what you won't tell them."

"Maybe," he mumbled.

"Perhaps if someone else explained," she ventured. "Kind of prepare them before they arrive."

"They're not coming. I sent a telegram." His fisted hand pounded the bed. "They can't," he muttered.

"I see." She wasn't sure what to say.

"I asked about calling them. Long distance. But the nurse said no. Said we couldn't make telephone calls from the hospital." He pounded the bed again. "If I could just talk to my old man. He would understand. He'd be reasonable about it."

"Sure, he would."

He must have heard the doubt in her voice. "No. You don't understand. He's always been very supportive." He relaxed his hand. "They all have."

Unlike her parents.

"It's just…my mother. She'll cry and make a fuss. She'll want to baby me and carry on." He reached out to her then. "I can't take that. Not now."

She took his hand in hers. "You're still struggling,

aren't you?"

He leaned back on the pillow and stared up at the ceiling. After a long silence he continued. "I don't know what I'm going to do. The doctors won't tell me how bad it's going to be. But I can guess."

"There are plenty of things you can do."

He smiled but it held no humor. "Yeah. I know."

A thought occurred to her. "Suppose I call your father? Explain a little, enough so he won't worry but will understand why you don't want them to come."

Before he could answer, she rushed on. "I'm going to the canteen. There's a telephone booth there. I could call from there. And then, you will feel better knowing they aren't coming, and they will feel better knowing why."

His shock dissolved into a soft smile. "You'd do that?"

"Well," she lifted the paper. "You're doing me a favor. It's the least I can do."

Chapter 14

Milt gritted his teeth and tried to stifle the groan as the nurse cut away the cast.

"I'm sorry. Do you want me to stop for a minute?"

"No," he muttered through clinched teeth. "Just get it over with."

"All right. I'll be as quick as I can." He closed his eyes and tried to think of something pleasant. Nurse McEwen appeared in his mind, her velvet voice soothing his pain.

With the help of an orderly, the nurse managed to remove the section of cast that covered his shoulder and upper arm along with the prop that kept his arm up and away from his body. Thankfully she was holding his arm steady because the muscles in his shoulder were so weak that he didn't have the strength to hold it up.

He moaned, involuntarily, as she slowly lowered his arm.

"Now let's get the rest of this off," she said cheerfully.

He avoided eye contact and nodded.

She was just doing her job. It wasn't her fault. Whose fault was it? The Germans? His own? Had he not gotten into a foxhole fast enough? Truth was, he didn't remember. Not anything after the patrol entered the woods.

"There. All done."

The section of cast around his midsection had come off with surprising ease, maybe because there hadn't been the swelling he'd had in his arm and shoulder.

He looked down at his arm. The flesh looked awful, at least what he could see of it. The worst was out of sight on the outer portion of his upper arm.

"We'll just clean this up a bit before taking you in for x-rays."

Cheerful and efficient. He'd give her that.

Soon the technician had taken pictures of his arm and shoulder and returned him to the cast room to be refitted with a new cast.

To his surprise his orthopedic doctor was waiting for him.

"I want to have a look at those x-rays before you put on the new cast," he told the nurse.

"Certainly, sir. I'll tell the x-ray technician you're waiting for them."

After the nurse left the room, Milt boldly asked the doctor, "Will I ever get the feeling back in my arm and hand?"

"That's a tough one, soldier." He moved closer and looked Milt in the eye. "It's hard to tell with a wound like yours. Nerves have been damaged. Will they heal?" He shrugged his shoulders. "We don't know."

"Well, at least you're honest."

"I try to be as honest as possible."

He lifted Milt's damaged arm and examined it while Milt watched. The doctor moved it up and down, then side to side. Despite the lack of feeling, it was clear to Milt that the arm was stiff and did not move properly.

"Is it always going to be stiff like that?"

"No. It shouldn't." He gently returned the arm to Milt's side. "We're going to put it back in a cast. For now. If you were going to be here for another month, say, I'd schedule you for surgery to relieve the stiff elbow. Return movement."

"They're shipping me out? Is that what you're saying?"

"You will receive your orders soon."

The nurse returned. "The x-rays are ready, sir."

"Good." He turned back to Milt. "Let me have a look at them. Then I'll come back and tell you what I think." He smiled sympathetically, and Milt nodded.

He tried to conjure up the image of Nurse McEwen in her evening gown, but instead his mother invaded his thoughts. He couldn't face his mother's fussing over him. He'd rather land on a German-occupied beach than have her hovering around treating him like a small child.

He'd worked so hard to gain his independence, establish himself as his own man. He'd faced up to his father, told the old man that he wouldn't be joining the family business because he was going to play for Nashville's minor league team. He'd never been any good in school, except in athletics. Nashville's team had scouted him as a pitcher opening the door to a career in baseball and independence from his family.

He'd played the one season, or rather he'd sat on the bench most of it. The coach had said he'd let him pitch more the next year...but then the war came along.

He didn't regret joining up. It was the right thing to do. And, once he'd gotten in, he'd liked it. Liked the men, the camaraderie, the physical challenges. His superiors had apparently seen something in him because he'd gotten promoted, first to squad leader then to corporal in North Africa. His sergeant's stripes had come in Sicily.

Sicily. The place haunted him. He pushed the memories away, deep inside.

Now with an eye messed up and his left arm essentially useless, careers in baseball or the Army were both out of the question. He'd have to return to Kerrville and live off the charity of his family.

The doctor returned to report that his bones were healing but were still fragile. And the flesh, or what was left of it on his upper arm, would require plastic surgery to cover where the muscle had been ripped away. He'd write up his recommendations. In the meantime, another cast would be put on his arm to protect it.

And that was it. Another cast. This one let his arm hang down by his side, bent at the elbow and in a sling.

Finally, the orderly arrived to escort him back to the ward. By the time he settled into his bed his shoulder throbbed, not to mention his head. He forgot to ask for painkillers when they passed the nurses' station, so he'd have to wait until they got around to checking on him. It wasn't bad enough to call the nurse, not yet anyway.

"Hey, Greenlee," Mark Pendleton strode into the ward. "I brought your mail."

"Thanks," Milt managed, squirming to get more comfortable. The new cast allowed him more mobility, but it would take some getting used to.

"I see you got a new cast," Pendleton sorted through Milt's letters.

"Yeah," Milt replied, not really in the mood for

Pendleton's company.

"One from England. Female hand." He wagged his eyebrows. "One of those lovely English lasses? Oops, no. WAC name of Greenlee. Your sister no doubt." He handed the letter to Milt and looked at the next one in the stack. "Another female hand." He looked up and grinned. "I can tell a woman's handwriting a mile away."

"That's nice. Now give me the rest of my mail."

"Not yet. Let's see now. This one's from someone named Kerr in Kerrville." He gave Milt a questioning look. Pendleton loved to tease him.

Milt impatiently responded. "That's my grandmother."

"Too bad." He handed the letter over to Milt.

"And last but not least." He hesitated. "From someone in Nashville. Looks female but I could be mistaken."

"Give it to me and maybe I can fill you in."

Pendleton reluctantly handed it over and Milt looked at the return address.

"Well?"

"It's from an old baseball buddy. Definitely not female. You struck out on that one."

"Oh." Pendleton wasn't that bothered.

Milt glanced at the letters, not really interested in reading any of them.

Pendleton eased closer and leaned down. "I heard something interesting," he whispered.

"What?" Milt couldn't help being annoyed at his friend. He wanted the nurse to bring the pain killers. Now.

"I heard that this hospital is closing. That it's

official."

"What do you mean, 'official'?"

"Rumor is that the owners of the hotel have been lobbying Washington to get their property back."

"Right now, I don't really care."

"As slow as Washington is, I figured the war would be over before they made a decision. But I was wrong. Decision has already been made. Our days in this place are numbered."

"That's probably why my doctor put off doing surgery on my arm. He said I'd be getting orders any time now."

"No kidding? The doctor told you that?"

Milt nodded, which only served to increase the pain in his head.

"Wonder what they'll do with us. I'd sure like to get closer to home."

"Not me," Milt heard himself mutter. He didn't want any closer to his mother. Not if it meant she'd be visiting all the time. And mothering him. No, she'd be smothering him. He couldn't take that.

Finally, the nurse arrived. When Milt told her about the pain in his head and shoulder, she shooed Pendleton away. After checking his chart, she produced two aspirin and suggested he take a nap.

Chapter 15

"It's about time you showed up," Stella whispered.

Annie's throat tightened. "I didn't know there was a meeting," she whispered back.

Captain Burrows must have noticed Annie's arrival. "Pass this back to Lt. McEwen." She handed a paper to another nurse who passed it around to Annie.

"Now, as I was saying," Captain Burrows continued, "although we don't have a date yet, we need to start making preparations."

"Do you know where we're going?" a nurse asked.

"Not yet. I'll give you your assignments as soon as I get them."

Annie scanned through the paper she'd been handed. The words "hospital closing" caught her attention. There had been a rumor. Even articles in the local paper debated the possibility. But she'd dismissed it as idle speculation. Now here it was in black and white. On official letterhead.

This was her chance to ask for a transfer to a hospital near New York City. Then she could spend every spare moment for the rest of the war in the city where the music she loved went out across the airways to the whole world. She'd meet as many people as she could and get her singing career on track.

Before Annie could ask about transfer requests, another nurse asked the question. "Can I request a transfer to a hospital closer to my home?"

Annie didn't want to be closer to home. She may have promised her mother she wouldn't volunteer for overseas, but she didn't want to be so close she'd be expected to visit often. Going home would dredge up all the pain from Joe's death, all the grief she'd buried deep inside.

"You can request a transfer if you wish, but I would prefer that you did not. You will be needed to care for our patients wherever they are assigned." Captain Burrows scanned the room. "Are there any more questions?"

The nurses and orderlies looked around but no one else spoke up.

"Good." The captain appeared pleased with the lack of response. "I shall be meeting with some of you as we make preparations for moving the patients."

She dismissed the group.

Annie stood for a moment lost in thought.

"So much for that," Stella said.

"What do you mean?"

"Follow orders and go where you're sent. That's what I go out of it."

"We are in the Army, Stella. I doubt any of these soldiers had any choice either."

****

Milt sulked. There was no other way to describe his mood or his actions. Reality had struck him hard, and he struggled to deal with what to do now, how to face a future with a horribly scarred face, an eye he could barely see out of, and a useless left arm.

Before he'd been blasted to hell...before his face had been destroyed...he had considered himself fairly good-looking. Not the most handsome, but good enough to attract pretty women who he'd charm with his likeable personality.

He hadn't been interested in any kind of permanent relationship. He'd long ago decided that if he ever married, it would be after he had established his independence in a career of his own. Otherwise, he had no intention of subjecting a wife to his inadequacies.

Now women wouldn't even look at him. They would turn their heads to avoid the horrid scars. If anything, they'd feel sorry for him, and he didn't want their pity.

His bad mood had been brought on by the skin graft they'd done the previous day. The cheery plastic surgeon had thoroughly enjoyed explaining the process while his nurse held a large mirror for Milt to observe. Viewing his mutilated face and head had been sickening.

They'd start on his scalp, the smiling doctor told him. Then, once that healed, they'd move on to the area around his eye, which might take several surgeries.

The doctor's interesting project was his face, his life. Didn't the man realize that?

After they took the mirror away, Milt tried to think of other things as they measured and poked. Eventually they'd done what they wanted, with him sedated while they cut skin from his leg and somehow attached it to his head.

He couldn't imagine what it would look like afterward. Like a patched tire. Or worse.

Chapter 16

"How you doin'?" Sgt. Baker asked as he approached Milt's bed.

Milt looked away. Coming up on his right side so Milt couldn't ignore him, Sgt. Baker continued his spiel. "Can't be that bad, can it? After all, you're here in sunny Florida, nobody shooting at you, just pretty nurses to take care of you. And, of course, guys like me who bug you to get out of bed and get some exercise."

The man was relentless. "Okay, okay." Milt stuck out his right hand and grabbed Sgt. Baker's hand. Using it for leverage, he pulled himself up to sit on the side of the bed.

"That's the ticket." Sgt. Baker took Milt's robe from the hook on the wall and held it for him to slip one arm into the sleeve. Then he draped it across his casted left arm, pulled the tie around, and tied it securely in front.

"Where are we going?" Milt asked.

"For a walk." Baker gestured toward the door.

Milt didn't much care where they went. He knew he needed to move around and get his strength back. Lying in bed feeling sorry for himself wasn't going to change anything.

After checking with the nurse, Sgt. Baker took Milt to the gym and informed him it was time he started working out. Milt thought he was kidding at first, but the sergeant was dead serious.

"Do you think those muscles are going to just reappear? You've got to work them."

"What can I do with this?" Milt nodded toward his cast.

"We're not going to work on that…yet. Right now, we're going to work on the rest of you. You've got two good legs, right? What about your abdominal muscles? Your perfectly good right arm? Looks to me like you've got lots to work on."

Milt nodded. The man had a point. Looking around the gym, he saw guys with no legs lifting dumbbells. Another with only one leg swung himself on bars. All around men with broken bodies worked to bring themselves back to something close to normal. Could he do less?

"Show me what to do."

Sgt. Baker grinned.

After some focused exercises, they stopped for a breather.

"When you get that cast off, we can start on the left arm."

Milt looked at what had become this lifeless object attached to his left shoulder, in the way and useless.

"I don't know about that. I can't feel my fingers. Can't move them." He looked away, focusing his gaze on a mat hanging on the far wall behind the basketball goal. It reminded him of the gym where he played high school basketball so long ago.

"You never know. I've seen things that could have been called miracles." He paused as if waiting for Milt to reply. After a few minutes of silence, he asked, "What does the doctor say?"

Milt recalled his last examination. "Not much. Wait and see. That sort of thing."

"They didn't amputate it so it can't be that bad."

"The bones are healing. But he said the nerves in my upper arm are damaged." Milt tried to force himself to sound positive. "Time will tell, I guess."

"Do you remember what happened?"

"Not really. Artillery shell, probably. Could have been a mortar or one of those damn rockets. I don't know."

"I'd say you're lucky to be alive after taking that kind of hit to your head."

"Yeah, maybe." Milt didn't want to think about it.

An image of a soldier, lying on the ground, half his head gone, came to Milt. The reality hit him like a line drive. He'd come that close to dying.

Baker touched his shoulder. "You made it. That's what's important."

"I guess I was lucky at that."

Sgt. Baker nodded. "Let's see if a little exercise will improve your attitude."

Milt smiled. Yeah. He needed a reminder now and then…that he was still alive, unlike many who'd died, who hadn't even had a fighting chance.

Someone turned on a radio. The strains of orchestra music filtered through the sounds of grunting and groaning and lightened the mood.

Milt gripped the small dumbbell for another set, his thoughts conjured up a beautiful red head in a nurse's uniform.

"What's with you and Lt. McEwen? You two seem pretty friendly." Milt placed the dumbbell back on the rack. He fought the inkling of jealously that crept up whenever he saw Sgt. Baker and Lt. McEwen together.

Sgt. Baker smiled, a dreamy far-away smile. "She's swell."

"Are you two an item?"

"Na," Baker shook his head. "She's too proper for that." His eyes twinkled. "No fraternization between officers and enlisted men. That's her motto."

He motioned Milt to the floor for some sit ups and leg lifts. Milt complied, trying to focus on the exercises.

"But I'm wearing her down," Baker continued. "She wants friendship. But I figure that friendship can work its way into something more, if a guy's patient."

Milt nodded. He'd like to be her friend. He doubted he'd ever be anything more.

He envied Sgt. Baker. A whole body, an athlete. Logic said that a woman would go for that before she'd consider a broken one.

Before the war he'd planned a life as an athlete, and then maybe, later on, a coach. A career like that would give him a way to support a wife and family. That plan had been shot to hell by the Nazi's. What could he offer a woman now? The charity of his family?

****

Back in the ward, a uniformed PFC approached Milt.

"Excuse me, are you Sgt. Greenlee?"

"Yes. I am," Milt replied. He wondered what the man wanted with him.

The soldier thrust an envelope in Milt's direction. "These are your new orders."

"Orders?" Milt growled.

The private held up his hand as if he needed to

defend himself. "I'm just delivering them." He glanced around the ward. "Lots of guys are getting them. This place is closing, you know. In a few weeks, we'll all be gone."

Dread crept up Milt's spine.

He stared at the envelope in his hand.

Oh, what the hell. He was still in the Army, and he had to take orders, like it or not.

"Do you want me to open it for you?"

Milt looked up. The PFC had disappeared, and Pendleton stood in his place.

"No. I can do it." Stubborn pride reared its ugly head. He'd had to accept plenty of help, and he would again, but right now he needed to do this himself.

He laid the envelope on the bedside table. His fingers fumbled to lift the flap and spread the envelope open so he could dump out whatever was inside. Two pages slipped out. He picked up one of them and tried to read the words, only he had it upside down. He put it down on the table beside the other page and turned them both with his one useable hand.

Identifying the first page, he held the orders up and read to himself. He'd never attempt to read aloud in public, not ever. Typed words were the easiest to read. Even so, he studied the words.

"…Two-week furlough…Report to Lawson General Hospital in Atlanta, Georgia…"

"Where're you going?"

Milton had forgotten that Pendleton was still there.

"I guess I'm going home. It says two-week furlough."

"And then where?"

"A hospital in Atlanta, Georgia."

Pendleton shook his head. "Sure hope I get to go home before I have to report to my new assignment."

Milt digested the news. Home. For two weeks. Dread settled in his gut.

Pendleton rattled on about getting closer to home, seeing his family and friends.

Milt didn't want to go home, didn't want to see his family, didn't want them to see him, not like this, not the horror he saw in the mirror.

He needed to get out of here, needed to get outside, needed to clear his head.

He tried to refold the letter but fumbled it. Pendleton quickly stepped in, folded it, and stuck it back in the envelope.

"Thanks," Milt muttered. He grabbed the envelope and stuffed it into the pocket of his robe. "Think I'll go for a walk."

"Sure."

Milt left the ward, taking the elevator to the lobby. Something made him walk toward the ocean, through the colonnade that led to the pool, then around it to the wall where he could see the waves crashing onto the sand.

Thunderheads accumulated over the water, matching his dark mood. The wind picked up, blowing the storm toward the shore.

Once he left here, he'd never see Nurse McEwen again. They would both leave this place and lose touch, like the guys he'd left over there in France. No. That couldn't happen. He'd talk to her, get her address, write to her.

He could use her cousin as an excuse. She'd asked him to write her aunt and uncle about her cousin. And he'd meant to. He just hadn't wanted to think about Sicily. And he hadn't wanted to ask someone to help him write another letter. Somehow, he'd put it out of his mind. Maybe if he wrote it now, maybe that would be how to stay in touch with her.

Lightning flashed from within the dark clouds. An idea sparked to life.

Her family lived in Chattanooga. That was on his way home. What if he stopped and visited with her family? If he made friends with them, then he could stay in touch with her. Then she wouldn't forget him. He'd be the man who talked to her family about her dead cousin.

That's what he'd do.

He wouldn't think about why he wanted to stay in touch with her, why it meant so much to him. Nothing could ever come of it. All he knew was that he couldn't lose touch with her. In the short time he'd known her, she'd become important to him, and he wasn't ready to let that go.

****

Captain Burrows sat behind her desk in her cramped, but neat office.

Annie tapped on the partially-open door to get her attention.

The officer looked up. "Yes?"

Pushing the door open Annie stood straight and saluted. "Lt. Annie McEwen requesting permission to speak to you."

After a half-hearted salute, Captain Burrows motioned for her to come forward. "What is it, Lieutenant?"

"Sorry to disturb you, ma'am. I just wanted a word

about the hospital closure."

"Yes?" The officer pursed her lips in an expression of impatience. "What do you want to know?"

"I read through the paper you gave us. I think I understand most of it." Annie hesitated then plunged ahead before she lost her nerve. "I'd like to put in a request for transfer to Halloran General."

"In New York?"

Annie nodded.

"You can put in a request, but we can't guarantee anything. Plans are already in place for transferring the staff to other hospitals." She held up her hand to let Annie know she wasn't finished. "Orders have already come through for some. Others will stay here long enough to get all the patients transferred."

"What about me?"

"Let me see." She pulled a folder from her drawer and leafed through it. "Here we are. You're going to Lawson General."

"Where?"

"It's in Georgia, near Atlanta. That's where a good many of our patients are going."

"But when?"

"Your orders are being cut as we speak." She closed the folder. "You may get a short leave to go home before you have to report."

Annie's gaze roved the room while her mind tried to process what she'd been told.

"I suggest you report to Lawson," the captain continued. "Then make your transfer request from there."

"Yes, Ma'am." Annie's gaze returned to the captain.

"There's going to be a lot of turmoil getting all the patients moved, getting the staff reassigned. The Army's been expanding Lawson. It's a more traditional facility than this one." She shook her head. "Commandeering a hotel may have sounded like a good idea at the time, but it really hasn't met our needs."

Annie just nodded.

"Lawson will be much better."

"When will I get my orders?"

"Tomorrow or the next day. You'll be part of the advance group so start packing."

"Thank you, ma'am." Annie turned to leave, barely remembering to salute.

Annie's mind swirled. Atlanta was a lot closer to Chattanooga...and to her family. Not good. She dreaded the thought of going home on leave even for a couple of days.

At least Captain Burrows had said she could put in for a transfer as soon as she reported to Lawson. New York was where she needed to be. And that's where she would go.

Chapter 17

Milt fingered the seams to get a feel for the ball. The last time he'd held a baseball had been in the spring back in England. A few guys had played an impromptu game in a field outside the village where they were billeted. He'd pitched and he remembered how good it felt.

He hesitated, unsure if he could even toss the ball.

"Take your time. I'm ready any time you are."

Baker stood a few feet away, patiently waiting for Milt to get up his courage.

Oh, what the hell.

He tossed the ball, underhand, trying to gage the distance.

Baker had to step into it, but he caught it.

"Good. Good." Baker strode the few paces and held out the ball. "Now, do it again."

It seemed silly. Tossing the ball like a little kid. But it felt right somehow.

After four or five tosses Milt tried overhand, and to his surprise the ball landed right where he intended. Baker hustled back with the ball, a grin on his face.

"Way to go. Gettin' the hang of it, aren't you?"

"Yeah. Seems like it's coming back."

"Want me to toss it back next time?"

"No. Not yet." Milt glanced away, to the other players and patients throwing and catching and swinging bats. "Maybe later."

"Sure. Whenever you're ready."

"Just get back over there and see if I can do that again."

Baker chuckled, running back to his position.

Focusing on his target, Milt threw the ball, harder this time. It was a little off, but Baker caught it easily.

That old feeling of satisfaction rose up from his gut. His cheeks spread as his teeth bared. Was he really smiling?

Baker grinned back. "Come on, throw it again."

Milt imagined himself standing on the mound again, bearing down on the batter, throwing so hard the ball whistled through the air right past the swinging bat, the satisfying whack when the ball hit the catcher's glove.

Whack! Right in the breadbasket. His smile broadened.

"Hey, look at Greenlee," someone called.

Baker brought the ball back to him. "Show 'em what you can do."

Milt nodded. He glanced to the side as if he were checking the bases. Several men stood watching. He concentrated on Baker's glove.

Whack! He shook his head in disbelief. He'd done it again. And the men were cheering for him. He turned to them and took a bow.

It only took a few more hard throws for the muscles in his arm and shoulder to start screaming. A reminder of how out of shape he was.

"I think that's enough" he told Baker, rolling his shoulder in answer to his protesting muscles.

"Sure. Don't want to overdo it the first time out."

Baker walked him to the sidelines where Milt sank onto the bench. Instead of sitting down beside him, Baker stepped around behind him and placed his hands on Milt's shoulders. The gentle yet firm massage relaxed Milt's aching muscles.

"This left one's really tight," Baker said while applying more pressure.

"Yeah. The Doc said it would be sore for a while after having my arm stuck up in the air like that for so long."

"I was surprised they put you back in a cast. Usually, when they take it off, they replace it with bandages."

"It's because I'm leaving. He didn't want me to reinjure it."

"Makes sense." Baker continued to massage both shoulders.

"Yeah." Milt laughed feebly. "He said they'd do some more work on it when I get to the next hospital. Don't know if he knew I'd be heading to Atlanta."

"That sounds like he thinks there's hope."

"Yeah. Maybe. I don't think he was too pleased with what he found under that cast. Course, he wasn't going to tell me what it was, but I could tell by the way he looked."

"Umm," Baker said.

"One thing I've learned about these Army doctors. They sure stay close-lipped. I don't know if they don't think I can take the truth, or they don't really know what they're doing."

"Oh, they know what they're doing. Most of them anyway." Baker stopped his massage and came around to face Milt. "And I don't think they think you can't

109

take it. It's just that every injury is different. And every patient is different. That's all."

Milt nodded. "I guess you're right."

"Hey, Baker," someone called from across the field.

Baker waved to the man, then spoke to Milt. "Stay and watch if you want. We can throw a few more later."

"If it's okay, I'd just as soon head on back to the ward."

"Sure. I'll check in with you later." Baker jogged across the field, dodging other players.

Milt stood and adjusted the baseball cap Baker had given him. The man knew his stuff, how to motivate men, get them out playing ball and back into life. He strode away from the field feeling more confident than he had in a long time. Funny what tossing a ball around could do for you.

Something white in the grass caught his eye. A stray ball. He leaned down and picked it up. Fingering the familiar leather, he looked around for someone to throw it to. The nearest man was further away than he could throw it. He squeezed the ball tight, feeling it in his hand.

He'd keep the thing. He could use it to exercise his hand and give himself something to hang onto.

****

Annie strode out of the surf and grabbed a towel, pleased she hadn't gotten her hair wet. She dried off and sunk down onto the sand beside Stella, who was stretched out on a towel soaking up the sun, a large floppy hat covering her face.

"Don't go to sleep in the sun. You'll get a terrible burn."

"I never burn," came from beneath the hat.

"Never say never," Annie joked.

Stella sat up and laid the hat to one side. "I want to get a good tan while I can. We'll be leaving here before you know it."

Annie watched the gentle waves wash up on the sand. "I still can't believe they're closing this place."

"That's the Army for you. Spend a fortune turning a hotel into a hospital. Then a year later, give it back."

"The rich folks want their hotel back so they can spend the winter here. I can't really blame them." Annie dug her fingers in the sand. "Have you heard anything more about where the nurses are going?"

"Nah! We'll be the last to know. That's how the Army works. One day the captain will hand us our orders and off we'll go."

"The captain told me I'm going to Lawson General in Atlanta, but as soon as I get there I'm going to put in a request for Halloran. I figure it can't hurt."

"Halloran, isn't that in New Jersey?"

"No. It's on Staten Island, right across from New York City. And New York is where the action is for a singer."

"You'll be working. How're you gonna be a singer?"

"On my days off I'll go into the city for auditions, maybe get an agent. I could work occasional jobs. At least I'll be close to the action. Not stuck so far away from everything. Then, when the war is over, I'll stay."

"Great plan if you get the transfer."

"Like I said, can't hurt to ask. They will be busy at Halloran with all the wounded coming back from Europe so they probably need more nurses." Annie tossed a shell into the surf. "I need to think about what is best for my career."

Voices drew her attention to the soldiers slowly running down the beach. Despite the sand, they kept a pretty good formation.

Annie and Stella stood and watched the recovering patients' progress.

Even before they came alongside the two nurses, the men began to whistle and shout at them.

"Dig those legs."

"What 'ya doin' tonight, sweetheart?"

Annie laughed and called back, "Sorry, I'm busy."

One grinning man waved furiously to get their attention, while another gave them a thumbs-up, then pointed from them then back to himself.

Stella giggled. "Oh, you guys."

The whistles and catcalls continued.

As the men passed them, one in the back did an about-face and headed in their direction until a fellow soldier grabbed him and drug him back into formation.

Annie and Stella nearly doubled over laughing at their antics.

"Don't you love the Army?" Stella laughed.

"Sure meet a lot of interesting fellows," Annie teased. "But I don't think I want to go out with any of that bunch."

After pulling themselves together, Stella took her watch out of her big cloth bag. "Time to go."

They donned their oversized shirts that served as beach cover-ups, gathered their few belongings and walked down the beach toward the stairs.

"Another one of your many admirers." Stella nodded toward the wall above the stairway.

Annie looked up. Sgt. Greenlee peered down at them.

"You gonna talk to him?"

"Of course," Annie replied incredulously.

"He's always looking for you or watching you, Stella grinned. "He's got a crush on you, just like I said." She lightly punched Annie's shoulder, grinning like a Cheshire cat.

They climbed the stairs that led from the beach to the hotel property. "I haven't seen you talking to him, so I thought maybe you had given him the brush off...gently, of course."

"No. He's the one who backs away. I think he's self-conscious about all those scars."

They fell silent as they reached the top.

Sgt. Greenlee waited, for once not shying away.

"Sergeant," Stella greeted him.

"Lieutenant," he replied. Then he turned to Annie. "Lt. McEwen, may I have a word?"

"Sure. No need to be so formal. We're all off duty now."

His gaze shifted to the water, the bill of his baseball cap shading his eyes.

"I'll see you later." Stella turned and walked down the path toward the nurses' quarters.

Sgt. Greenlee shifted his weight.

"You wanted to talk to me," Annie reminded him.

"Yes."

Their gazes met and held. Something in her stirred, something she'd worked hard to ignore. She didn't want to develop friendships with her patients, or her co-workers for that matter. She didn't want to get close to anyone. It was safer that way.

He finally found his voice. "I…I got my orders."

She nodded, trying to ignore the instant sense of loss.

"They're giving me two weeks' leave," he continued. "Then I'm to report to Lawson General Hospital in Atlanta, Georgia."

He stared at her, expecting a reaction, so she forced a smile.

"Leave will be nice. You can go home and visit your family." She kept her voice light, positive.

"Yeah," he muttered, then looked away.

"With the hospital closing we'll all be reassigned." She needed to fill the silence. "I'm going to request an assignment in New York. Get closer to the music business." She wouldn't tell him she was going to Lawson, too. Let him believe she'd be far away. Unreachable.

"There's something else." He again caught her gaze with those blue eyes, so serious and determined. "I…well, I never got a chance to write to your family. You wanted me to write them about Sicily and all."

It was her turn to look away. She swallowed to clear the lump from her throat. "I thought maybe it was too hard." She forced herself to look directly at him. "I understand. You don't have to. It was just a silly idea."

He held her gaze. "I meant to. I really did."

She nodded and exhaled, as if releasing her breath would relax the tension between them.

"What I wanted to ask…if it's okay, I mean…Well, Chattanooga is on my way home. I'll go right through there. I could stop. See your aunt and uncle."

Astonished, she burst out, "Would you? Would you

really do that?"

Her pleasure must have been contagious because he blossomed into a grin. "Yeah. Sure. Actually, it would be easier for me to just sit down and talk to them than to write a letter." His right hand motioned as he talked. That's when she noticed the baseball he held. "I always have trouble trying to figure out what to say in a letter."

"Of course. It's not like you knew Joe."

"If I meet them, in person, they can ask me questions. Things they want to know. How it was over there and all."

She pictured him sitting with Aunt Millie and Uncle Herschel, their maps and Joe's letters spread around them.

And her father and mother.

She jerked her head around toward the path Stella had taken moments ago. She didn't want him to see the dread that surely marred her face as much as it tightened in her gut. Her parents. He would meet her parents.

Her father would pounce upon him with his bitterness and anger while her mother would collapse into tears at the mention of Joe's name. Aunt Millie and Uncle Herschel were grieving. They'd lost their only son. But her father and her mother acted as if Joe had been their son, as if his loss piled another load of unrelenting grief on top of the one they had suffered before. The grief, according to her father, she had caused by not saving her little brother. Her father had somehow managed to blame her for Joe's death, just like he blamed her for Peter's.

"If you don't want me to visit them, I understand."

Sgt. Greenlee's words penetrated her emotion-fogged brain.

"Oh, no," she cried. "You don't understand. I do want you to talk to them. I just don't know how upset they'll get. It's been a while, and I'm sure you think they should have gotten over it, at least just a little, but..."

"I understand." His tone was serious.

She met his gaze again, those serious blue eyes piercing her very being. It hit her that he'd experienced loss, terrible, horrible loss. And he did understand.

"Yes," she nodded as she spoke. "Please, visit them. Talk to them." She hesitated a moment before plunging ahead. "And I'll go with you. I'm sure I can arrange it." Her mind raced. She was going to the hospital in Atlanta anyway. Why couldn't she get a few days off and go on to Chattanooga? Maybe even escort Sgt. Greenlee home.

"Sure. If that's what you want." His shock quickly transformed into that almost smile.

"When are you leaving?"

Chapter 18

Despite the early hour, the train station bustled with activity. Milt followed Lt. McEwen out onto the platform, grateful the trip from Atlanta to Chattanooga would be short compared to the long day they'd spent coming from Florida.

He didn't know how she had managed it, and he had no intention of asking. From the moment they'd left Florida she had been the efficient, business-like nurse caring for her patients aboard the hospital cars. She had apparently volunteered to escort a group of patients to the hospital in Atlanta, and she'd arranged for him to ride along. Both of them had stayed overnight at Lawson General, and this morning they would journey to Chattanooga where he'd meet her family.

Thus far she'd maintained her distance, after all she was a lieutenant and he a lowly sergeant. A nurse escorting her patient home, at least that was the official story. In truth, they would stay at her home in Chattanooga before she escorted him to Kerrville. Hopefully, once they boarded the train, she would relax her in-charge persona and they could get better acquainted.

In the station, the bandage on his head drew attention. People didn't notice his arm in a sling under his uniform jacket until they got closer. Then their stares went from the scars on his face to the cast on his arm, and the sympathy showed plainly in their concerned faces. Some averted their eyes, while others stared.

On the train up from Florida, he'd been on a hospital car with other wounded soldiers. They were all used to casts and bandages and missing limbs. Here, out in the public for the first time, he began to see how others saw him, broken, someone to be pitied.

As Lt. McEwen returned from checking their bags, an Army officer emerged from the crowd on the platform.

"Lieutenant," he said, touching his hat. "Don't tell me I am lucky enough to be on the same train as you."

"Sir?"

"I'm headed for Nashville." He jerked his thumb in the direction of the train they would board. "How 'bout you?"

"No. I'm sorry, sir." Lt. McEwen tried to step past the man, but he maneuvered in front of her. She stopped and faced him. "I am escorting a patient home, sir. I am sure you will be kind enough to allow me to fulfill my duties."

She glanced his way and Milt fought the urge to glare at the offensive officer who followed her gaze and eyed Milt standing nearby. For once he was glad to have the bandage around his head where the plastic surgeon had worked on his scalp.

"Oh, I see." The officer approached Milt, who straightened and saluted. The Lieutenant returned his salute and gave him the once over. Milt hoped he looked injured enough to require a nurse.

"Where'd you get it, Sergeant?"

"Normandy, sir."

The officer's face darkened. "Was it as rough as they say?"

Milt swallowed hard and met the man's gaze. "I don't know what they say, sir. My outfit landed and did our job. We lost a lot of good men."

"The Big Red One, huh." He indicated the patch on Milt's shoulder. "Yes, sireee. You boys did a hell of a job." He offered his hand and Milt shook it. "And they're still over there fighting. Somewhere in France, right?"

Before Milt could respond the officer turned to Lt. McEwen. "Can I be of any help?"

"No. Thank you, sir." She moved closer and spoke to Milt. "Shall we get on board?"

"Yes, ma'am."

The officer rushed ahead of them and called over his shoulder. "I'll get you seats, so you can sit together."

Milt grasped the handrail to steady himself and slowly climbed up the steps to board the train. He still wasn't used to the one-sided feeling he got, especially when trying to maneuver unfamiliar territory. The conductor must have sensed his unease and held out his hand to steady Milt if he faltered. With a sigh of relief upon reaching the top, he glanced back as the wrinkled face of the middle-aged conductor relaxed into an easy smile. Lt. McEwen, in full nurse mode, followed Milt up the steps.

He hesitated a moment before turning to go into the car and down the aisle, as always leading with his right shoulder to be sure he could see where he was going. He sensed Lt. McEwen's presence close behind him.

Passengers in various uniforms filled the seats. The

helpful officer stood farther down the aisle waving to get their attention. A young Marine stood just behind him.

"The Corporal here decided to give you his seat," the officer stated when Milt reached him.

"Thanks, Corporal." Milt nodded and then settled into the window seat the young soldier must have vacated, thankful his casted arm was out of the way.

The Marine Corporal settled in a seat across the aisle and two rows up in front of them beside an overweight, middle-aged woman. Guilt for ruining the young man's trip forced Milt to look away. He turned his head to peer over the seat, trying to locate the helpful Lieutenant, without success.

"Are you all right?" Lt. McEwen asked.

He straightened in his seat. "Yes, I'm fine."

He wanted so much to break through that strictly-business exterior and really talk to her in the short time they had together.

She settled her purse in her lap and leaned her head back against the seat.

"I guess you got the bags taken care of?" he asked, knowing it was a stupid question.

"Yes." She paused. "I just told the porter we'd be getting off at Chattanooga. I didn't want to confuse him."

He nodded and murmured, "Sure."

"We can check your bigger bag at the station. Then we only have to carry the small ones up on the mountain."

"The mountain?"

"Didn't I tell you?" She fumbled in her handbag. "My folks live up on Lookout Mountain."

"On top of the mountain?" he asked.

"Oh, don't worry. You won't have to climb the mountain."

She pulled out a small pad and pen and began making notes.

Just then the train lurched into motion. Milt leaned back and watched the busy station slide by.

"What are you thinking?"

Her words startled him. He turned to face her. "Everything has changed so…since I left."

"When was that?"

"1942. August. We sailed from New York, first to England, then to North Africa."

"Joe didn't go overseas until the spring of '43. I think he went straight to Africa, but I'm not sure. Uncle Herschel will know."

"He was a replacement, then." Their conversations always came back to her cousin Joe. But hadn't that been his plan? Use poor, dead Joe to get close to her?

He turned back to the window as the train picked up speed. He had to get used to the idea that he was here to talk about Joe and Sicily.

Even though his friendship with Lt. McEwen couldn't go anywhere, there could never be anything serious between them, he wanted to get to know her. He hadn't fallen for her. He was just a wounded soldier infatuated with his nurse, the beautiful nurse with the incredible voice. Who could blame him? He'd make the most of their short time alone together and enjoy her company instead of thinking of his family's reaction when he got home.

His scheme had gone much better than he expected. Visiting her family, getting to know them and thus having a connection to her, no matter where they were stationed, had been his plan. He'd never dreamed that she'd want to go with him. He still wasn't sure why she'd insisted, but he didn't care. He'd be spending the next two days with her. That was enough of a miracle.

For now, he'd let her be and just enjoy her closeness.

As they rolled through north Georgia nearing their destination, Lt. McEwen's demeanor changed. She became fidgety, nervous. Thinking ahead to his own homecoming, to his family's reaction to his scars, he understood, at least a little.

"How long has it been since you've been home?" he asked.

"Since I joined the Army Nurse Corps." She hesitated. "That's not true. I did go home after my initial training, but it was only for a couple of days."

"Kind of like this trip?"

"Yes." She cut her eyes his way and smiled.

"And that was?"

"Last November." She fiddled with the buttons on her sleeve.

That tidbit of information took a minute to sink in. "I'm sure your family has missed you."

"Yes. I guess." She fidgeted some more, and then she let out a long sigh. "Look. I need to tell you…about my parents." She turned in her seat to face him. "They can be…well, difficult."

He waited, knowing there was more and for some reason it was hard for her to say it.

After a long moment she continued. "You don't know what it was like after we got word that Joe had been killed." She glanced down at her hands in her lap.

"It was awful."

"I can imagine." How would his family have taken it if he'd been killed?

"Father was so…angry, broken…" Her voice trailed off.

What was she saying? "You mean Joe's father?"

"Oh, Uncle Herschel was heartbroken. So was Aunt Millie. Joe was their only son and they adored him." She looked at his face and she must have seen the question there. "But, you see, Joe was like a son to my father, too. And to Mother." She hesitated, returning her gaze to her wringing hands. He could tell it was hard for her to talk about. "Her health isn't good, so that made it harder. And Father, well…he is the type who wants to be in control. I'm sure that you've run into men like that. Anyway, he doesn't handle it well when he can't control things."

"I see." He didn't know what else to say. She obviously suffered from the loss, too, and it sounded like she hadn't gotten any support from her family.

She drew a deep breath. "Anyway, when we heard about Joe, I was finishing up nursing school, so I decided to join the Army Nurse Corps. I had to do something…for Joe. It's what he would have wanted me to do, I'm sure."

"And your father couldn't control that either."

"Exactly." She looked at him, gratitude shone in her eyes. The hint of a smile took his breath. "It gave me a chance to help soldiers, like Joe. I couldn't help him, but there were so many who needed help." She relaxed a little. "I'm doing my part, with the war effort. That's what Joe would have told me to do."

Earlier she'd said that Joe had been like a big

brother to her. He could hear her love and admiration for him in her voice. What she didn't say told him something about her, too. Her need to escape. He understood that. Wanting to get away from home, wanting to escape those confines, spread your wings and see what you could do, who you could be, on your own.

"What about your singing? Would he have wanted you to do that, too?"

"Oh, yes." Now she smiled, really smiled. "He always told me to follow my dream. Sometimes I thought he was the only one who really believed in me."

"I have a younger sister like that. Thinks the world of me. Hung on my every word. I hope I encouraged her the way Joe did you."

"Where is she? At home waiting for you?"

He chuckled. "No way. She's a WAC. In England. Works for some General in the Air Corps."

"So she's doing her bit, too."

"Yep. Said she had to help me win the war."

"How wonderful." They both laughed, but he knew his sister Katherine had helped him, more that she would ever know. Maybe Lt. McEwen wasn't so different from his sister.

****

When Annie called to let everyone know that she and Sgt. Greenlee were coming, Aunt Millie assured her that she and Uncle Herschel would welcome Sgt Greenlee. They were anxious for any information about Sicily. Millie said that Annie's mother had been her usual overly-emotional self. She didn't know how Annie's still bitter father would react.

Aunt Millie was a jewel. The glue that held them all together.

Would Sgt. Greenlee be able to share anything that would help them heal? He hadn't wanted to talk about it with her. She doubted he had talked to anyone about his experience. But he said he'd rather talk to them face-to-face than in a letter. Hopefully, that was a good sign.

While home, she would have to tell her parents she would be stationed in Atlanta, at least until she could transfer to Halloran. She dreaded that conversation and the fact that she'd be a short train ride away from home with no excuse not to visit more often.

"Hi there, pretty lady." The Army Lieutenant stood in the aisle beside her.

She forced a smile. "Hello."

He squatted in the aisle beside her seat so his face was on the same level as hers. "The name's Paul, Lieutenant Paul Stewart."

She kept her expression neutral but didn't speak.

"Well, I knew you were wondering." The man gave her one of those sleazy smiles slick guys use to pick up girls. "So now you can write my name in your little book there. And my address is 1699 Elm Street, Nashville. And don't worry. My parents will forward my mail to wherever I end up."

"Are you asking me to write to you, Lieutenant?"

"Of course. A beautiful woman like you can write me all you want. And it's Paul, remember?"

"I remember."

He grinned again. "I must have been overwhelmed by your beauty, 'cause I didn't get your name."

'Bull shit' was what she'd love to say to him, but she was much too polite. She just smiled and wished he'd go away.

"Won't you introduce yourself…and the Sergeant here?"

She glanced over to Sgt. Greenlee, who appeared curious as to just how she was going to handle the situation. Manners and military protocol trumped her desire to be rude and tell the lieutenant to get lost.

"Lt. Annie McEwen. And this is Sergeant Milton Greenlee."

"Well, it's really nice to meet you…both."

His triumphant grin turned her stomach.

"And where is such a lovely nurse stationed?"

Annie's eyes shifted down to her fidgeting fingers and then back up to meet the Lieutenant's gaze. "The Sergeant here is headed home to Tennessee. And I'm being transferred to Halloran General Hospital in New York." She kept her voice steady. It wasn't really a lie. She would put in for the transfer and it would eventually be approved. She hoped the misdirection would satisfy the over-anxious officer.

"Wow. New York, huh. After my leave I'm headed to Camp Monmouth, New Jersey. Maybe I'll make it to New York sometime and look you up."

Great. She should have told the truth.

"When will you head overseas?" Sgt. Greenlee asked.

At the mention of going overseas, the Lieutenant turned a little green around the gills. Was he all bluster after all?

"Don't know yet," the officer replied.

"Are you going home to see your family?" she asked.

"Yeah." His face perked up. "Got a two week pass

before I have to report." He placed his elbow on the armrest. "More training."

"What kind of training?" Sgt. Greenlee asked.

"Signal Corps."

"That's an important job, running those wires, so everybody can communicate."

"Yeah, I guess it is."

The sergeant's knowledgeable response changed the officer's attitude.

"If you don't mind me asking," the Lieutenant continued. "What was your job? When you got it, I mean."

Annie watched Sgt. Greenlee's face to gauge his reaction to the question.

His gaze shifted to the window. Then, after a long moment, he turned back to the officer. "I was leading a rifle squad. We were advancing through some woods, looking for the enemy."

His good right hand eased over to hold the injured left one, the one he said he couldn't feel. "In the hospital they told me I'd been hit by shrapnel, probably from an "88.""

"Jeez. I…You're the first real combat veteran I've ever talked to." The officer stood and reached across Annie. "I sure appreciate you telling me."

Sgt. Greenlee grasped the offered hand, and they shook.

"Good luck to you," The Lieutenant said.

"Thank you, sir. And good luck to you, too."

The more somber Lieutenant nodded. "Guess I'd better get back to my seat."

Annie waited a few moments before speaking. Finally, she asked, "Did it bother you to answer his questions?"

He glanced her way with that half smile of his. "I've got to get used to it, don't I?"

She nodded her understanding.

"When I get home, I'll get lots of questions. That's why this stop at your place will be good for me. Force me to talk about it." He looked down at his hand again. "Some of it, anyway."

"I don't want you to do anything that makes you uncomfortable."

He laughed, an ironic laugh. "It's all uncomfortable."

It sickened her to think of what it would be like for Sgt. Greenlee to go home and face his family and friends. She'd talked to his father briefly on the telephone. The man sounded calm and understanding, but that wouldn't make it any easier for Sgt. Greenlee.

"I really appreciate you doing this for me." She caught herself wringing her hands again. "I'll try to keep them from getting out of hand with their questions."

"Thanks."

"And...I've been thinking." She plunged ahead. "While we're there we can dispense with the formalities?"

That brought his gaze back to hers.

"What I mean is, maybe we can use our first names. You can call me Annie and I can call you...Milton? Would that be alright?"

He smiled, a real smile this time. "Sure. Sure, only call me Milt."

"Okay, Milt." Her heart raced like she'd climbed a steep hill and finally reached the top. Why hadn't she thought of it before? Too afraid? Afraid of getting too close, of getting hurt, of hurting him. But now that didn't seem to matter. They could be friends. Just friends, and it would be okay.

Chapter 19

At the train station in Chattanooga Lt. McEwen asked the older porter, "Are there any taxis available?"

"Yes'm. Some. Where you all goin'?"

"Up on Lookout Mountain."

The old man shook his head. "Won't get no cab to take you up there. Not less'n you got lots o' money."

"Then I guess we'll take the incline."

"Yes'm. The cabbie, he'll take you right there." He waved to an old vehicle parked nearby.

"Thank you." She pressed a coin into his hand.

"Yes'm." He looked at the coin and smiled. "Thank you, ma'am."

The graying driver loaded their bags as Milt gazed up at the huge mountain looming over the city.

"Is that where your folks live?"

"Yes. Up on Lookout Mountain," she said. "I guess gas is too scarce for the taxi to go that far."

They climbed into the cab's big back seat.

"Then how are we going to get up there?"

She smiled and his heart fluttered so that his breath caught in his throat.

"You'll see."

After a short ride they exited the cab by a small building with a sign that read "Incline Tickets." The adjacent, tree-shaded lot sported a handful of cars.

Milt paid the cab driver to prove that he could pay

his own way. She graciously accepted the cash he handed her for the tickets.

After purchasing their tickets, she picked up her worn leather bag. "I'm afraid we'll have to carry our bags from here." She paused. "Can you manage?"

"Sure." Milton grabbed the handle of the small, military bag with his right hand, grateful that it wasn't too heavy, and that Sgt. Baker had made him work out with weights.

Just then a loud, clacking noise captured his attention. A trolley like contraption emerged from the trees and clattered to a stop nearby. His gaze followed the tracks and cables up the mountain until they disappeared into the dense green foliage.

"It's an incline railroad," Annie explained as she led him toward the car. "It'll take us straight up the mountain."

He hesitated, unsure if he wanted to ride on the unusual vehicle built on an angle to match the steep mountainside.

"Come on," she urged.

They boarded through the lower end. Stair steps went up the length of the car with seats that faced them on each step. After taking a couple of steps, Lt. McEwen glanced back.

"Here, give me that bag." She reached toward him. "You'll need your good hand to steady yourself."

He hesitated, not wanting to appear weak. But when he took a step, and instinctively threw out his hand to grab the upright bar, the bag prevented him from catching it.

She eased closer. "Come on. Give it to me."

Those lovely eyes, crinkled into a soft smile,

assured him she only wanted to help. He handed her the bag.

As he slowly followed her upward, he watched her every move, memorized the shapely legs deftly negotiating the stairs, using the bags for balance by resting them on the backs of the seats as she climbed.

She chose seats on the top row just below the grey-haired driver. Other passengers boarded and climbed up toward them.

"Good to see you, Miss McEwen. It's been a long time." The aging operator tipped his hat in Annie's direction as he spoke. "You sure look pretty in that uniform."

"Hello, Bert." She flashed one of her prettiest smiles and a slight flush tinged her face. "This is Sgt. Greenlee."

The man nodded and extended his hand. "Nice to meet any friend of our Miss McEwen, especially one of our fighting men."

Milt shook his hand, grateful that the man didn't gawk at him like so many on the train had. "Nice to meet you."

"Bert's been hauling us up and down the mountain for as long as I can remember."

Lt. McEwen handed the man their tickets before he made his way down the stairs to greet the other passengers. She and Milt settled into their seats.

With their backs to the mountain, they'd be treated to a grand view out the glass panels in the roof.

Within minutes the vehicle lurched into motion. The cables alongside the track creaked and strained, pulling them slowly up the mountain. Between the overhanging limbs the city came into view and, as they rose, more and more of the panorama spread out before them.

After passing another car going down the mountain, the train's angle increased to a steeper incline, as if they were going straight up. Milt glanced up and saw stone outcroppings above them. The eerie sensation threatened to bring on a dizzy spell.

He returned his gaze to the treetops below hoping to quell the uneasiness. Smoke hung like a mist over the valley.

He glanced over to Lt. McEwen, who held her purse tightly.

"This is impressive," he commented, to hide his unease. "I never knew this was here."

Her gaze met his. "Yes. It was built years ago so the people who live up here could get up on the mountain."

The car slowed and then jerked to a stop.

Anxious to get out, Milt stood just as the car stuttered again. He grabbed for the seat back and the upright bar by the aisle to keep from falling. His mind expected both arms to respond. When they didn't, he lurched to one side. With extra effort from his functioning right arm, he compensated, gritting his teeth to control his anger.

Annie jumped up and grasped his upper arm. "Are you okay?"

"Yeah, sure," he grumbled.

She glanced past him to the driver. "That should be it." She released her hold. "We can get off now."

Milt nodded, then turned his back to her looking for the bags they'd stowed behind their seats. He still felt unsteady, but he was determined to hide it. He mistakenly glanced over his shoulder, down toward the bottom of the car where the other passengers were climbing upward toward him. The dizziness returned momentarily before he jerked his head around and forced himself to look up, a death grip on the upright bar.

"This way." Annie stood close, their shoulders touching. She pointed toward the top of the car only two steps up.

The driver moved down and reached for Milt's bag. "Let me help you with that." He flashed Milt an understanding smile and grabbed the smaller bag. "Just so you can get out."

Milt nodded. "Thanks." He let the man help him, yet hated that he needed it.

Out on the platform Bert deposited the bag beside Milt and then tipped his hat toward Lt. McEwen. "Bye, Miss McEwen. See you again soon."

She nodded and smiled. "Bye."

"You, too, Sergeant."

All Milt could manage was a nod in the friendly man's direction.

They walked past another small ticket booth and Milt breathed easier, happy to be on solid ground.

The air up here was cooler than down below. He wondered how high they were.

"This way."

He followed her along a tree-lined street that meandered and split following the uneven terrain. Houses lined the street, some barely clinging to the mountainside.

"It's not far," she said. "The walk will give us a chance to stretch our legs after sitting on the train for so long."

Milton followed in silence.

"Do you want me to carry that?"

"No. I'm fine." The case wasn't that heavy, but it strained his arm a little. He'd have shifted it to his other hand if he could have. Something else he'd have to get used to.

Annie's slow pace couldn't have been for his benefit alone. She appeared to be in no hurry to get home, judging from her eyes darting around and her fingers fidgeting with her purse.

Finally, she spoke.

"There it is. The big Victorian on the corner."

"Very nice." And really big. A two story with rounded turret and a porch wrapped around two sides. A low hedge and fence bordered the street with large trees spreading their limbs to shade the wood-frame structure that he guessed to be about the same age as his own home in Kerrville.

"My grandfather built it in the 1890's. As the oldest of five children, my father inherited it. We've lived here all my life."

"Guess your parents wanted a big family."

Annie's face flushed red, and she looked away. He realized, too late, that he shouldn't have made the remark. Maybe he should apologize.

"Yes, they did. But I'm the only one left."

Her phrase "the only one left" implied there had been other children. He didn't recall her mentioning any brothers or sisters when she was talking about her cousin. But he certainly wasn't going to ask, not now with her so nervous.

She strode ahead and pushed the gate open.

Together they made their way up the walk and across the wide porch. She hesitated momentarily before she turned the knob and opened the heavy, half-glass door.

"Hello," she called as she stepped into the dark entryway.

Milt stood in the open doorway unsure if he should follow her inside.

"Mother. It's Annie. I'm home." Her voice echoed in the wide half-paneled entrance hall.

An imposing staircase dominated the room, its dark wood railing turned in both directions at a landing halfway up. A huge grandfather clock stood in the center of the landing, its loud ticking echoing in the cavernous space.

Paneled, double doors were on either side of the stairs, shut tight.

A noise from deep within the house drew his attention to a hallway extending beyond the stairs.

"Hello," Annie called again. "Is anybody home?"

Footsteps hurried toward them. An older woman appeared.

"Miss Annie. Oh, Miss Annie."

"Mrs. Rice, hello. Where's mother?"

"Oh, she's upstairs, resting." The woman's soft face beamed with pleasure. "She got so excited about you coming home. Well, you know how she gets."

Her gaze fell on Milt still standing in the doorway. "Well, young man. Come on in." She eyed him curiously but didn't ask any questions. When he stepped inside, she moved past him and closed the door.

"Mrs. Rice, this is Sgt. Greenlee."

He set down his bag and extended his hand. She held it in both of hers. A soft smile lit her face. "Nice to meet you, young man."

Annie started up the stairs. "I'll go up and get Mother," she announced. "Take Sgt. Greenlee into the parlor."

"Yes, Miss Annie."

At the landing Annie hesitated, "And call Aunt Millie...if she's home."

"Oh, she's home." Mrs. Rice approached the double wooden doors on the right and pushed one back into the wall to open it. Then she pushed the other one open and led the way into the room.

Milton approached the darkened room where the bulk of heavy furnishings loomed in the shadows.

Mrs. Rice drew back the drapes at one of the windows. Sunlight streamed in, illuminating a portion of the room and revealing heavy, over-stuffed furniture, from well before his time. His mother would have remodeled with a more modern, up-to-date look by now.

Mrs. Rice pushed back the velvet drapes from two more tall windows to reveal a baby grand piano tucked away in a corner.

Mrs. Rice appeared at his side.

"There now." She clasped her hands in front of her. "You just make yourself comfortable, and I'll go get Mrs. Millie." Off she went, leaving him standing alone.

His gaze roamed the room for clues about the family.

Above the ornately carved fireplace, with roaring lion heads flanking either side of a thick wooden mantle, hung a portrait of a white-haired man holding a cane. He knew very little about Lt. McEwen's family. Or about her. They certainly didn't seem eager to greet

137

her.

"That's old Dr. McEwen. Herschel and George's father." The woman came to stand beside him before the portrait. "Annie's grandfather."

For a moment he thought Mrs. Rice had returned, but when he turned so that he could see her, another, shorter woman stood there.

A soft smile lit her care-worn face. "I'm Millie McEwen."

****

Annie tapped on the door and pushed it open when she heard a faint "Come in."

Her mother sat at her dresser attempting to fix her hair.

"Mother." Annie cautiously stepped inside the dim room.

The older woman turned. "Annie. Is that you?"

"Yes, Mother."

"Oh, Annie. Finally."

Her mother extended her arms, and Annie moved into the warmth of her mother's embrace.

When they separated, her mother's eyes gleamed with determination. "It's high time you came home. I need you here...to take care of me."

Annie had heard this before in every letter her mother wrote.

"I have explained it to you, Mother. I am in the Army. There is a war going on. They won't let me come home just anytime. And I can't stay here and take care of you."

"And why not?" Indignation poured out of the frail body. "I'm ill. I need you here to take care of me. Surely something can be done to get you out of that

138

horrid uniform and bring you home."

Annie shook her head, knowing nothing would convince her mother.

Picking up a comb, her mother returned her gaze to the mirror. "I'm sure your father could arrange it. He knows all sorts of people, important people." Her gaze met Annie's in the mirror. "He's already made inquiries, you know. Probably has it all arranged."

Fury roiled in Annie's gut. "He'd better not. He can't do anything if I don't want out of the Army." She paced across the small room and back to calm herself. She hadn't meant to admit that she didn't want to come home. And getting angry would only fuel her mother's tendency toward hysteria.

After a few moments of tense silence, Annie spoke again, using the calm but firm voice she used on her patients. "Mother, we have a guest downstairs. You should come down and meet him."

"Millie told me about the soldier you were bringing. Something about Joe and Sicily. She behaved like a child at Christmas. Quite disturbing."

"I'm escorting him home and he agreed to stop over and talk to Aunt Millie and Uncle Herschel." Annie stood beside her mother. "Come down with me, won't you?"

"Well, if I must." She returned the comb to the dresser, patted her breast where her favorite brooch graced the neckline of her dress and stood.

Annie held out her hand in a show of offering assistance, although she knew her mother was perfectly capable of walking. She wanted to tell her mother to be nice to Sgt. Greenlee...Milt, but she knew saying anything would be fruitless. Her mother was her mother, and she would never change.

Chapter 20

He and Aunt Millie, as she'd told him to call her,
sat in the parlor exchanging small talk about his journey
and about Annie. He liked Annie's aunt. She was easy
to talk to. She didn't gawk at his scars and didn't ask
about his wounds.

They heard quiet, feminine voices and footsteps on
the stairs. He started to stand, but Aunt Millie waved
him down as she hopped up and went to the door. A
moment later, Annie and a frail-looking woman that
must have been her mother appeared in the doorway.

"Oh, there he is. Your soldier," the older woman
commented to Annie, who turned slightly pink.

"He's not *my* soldier, Mother." Annie replied
firmly but avoided meeting his gaze.

At this point he rose to his feet expecting an
introduction.

Before Annie could speak her mother hurried
toward him, both her hands extended, her filmy dress
fluttering as she moved. "Oh, you poor dear." She
grasped his hand and patted it as she spoke. "Annie said
you'd been hurt, but I didn't realize your injuries were
so bad."

He forced a smile, trying to ignore her comment,
and looked into her eyes, Annie's eyes. The same hazel
color, the same finely arched brows. His stiffness
melted.

"My mother," Annie interjected. "And Mother, this is Sgt. Milton Greenlee. He's the one I told Aunt Millie and Uncle Herschel about. The one who was in Sicily."

"With Joe?"

Milt's gaze shot to Annie's face, not sure what to say.

"No, Mother. He wasn't with Joe. But he was in the same place, possibly near where Joe…" She looked away but couldn't mask her uneasiness.

Aunt Millie came to their rescue. "Yes, well…let's all sit down, shall we?"

"Yes, ma'am."

He settled back into the sturdy chair, as uncomfortable as it was outdated.

Annie's mother perched on one of the maroon velvet settees opposite Aunt Millie while Annie walked over and stood near the piano.

"Did you have a nice trip?" Mrs. McEwen asked. "I hope you weren't too uncomfortable what with…" She waved her hand toward him indicating his wounds.

"Yes, ma'am. The trip was fine." Milt had to turn his head to see Annie. He was unsure what she expected of him.

"Annie, dear, sit down." Mrs. McEwen patted the seat beside her.

Annie obeyed her mother's request, frowning.

"It'll be like a party. Having you here." She raised her hands and clasped then together. A smile lit her tired face. "We haven't entertained guests in ages." She turned to Annie, who was fidgeting with her hands again. "Isn't that right, dear?"

Annie looked up. "Yes, Mother." Her voice was flat, clearly uninterested in her mother's suggestion.

142

Milt caught her gaze and her face brightened. "Would you like something to drink?"

"That would be very nice," he agreed.

She reacted quickly. "I'll see what we have. Perhaps some lemonade."

That's when Aunt Millie took charge. "I'll get it. You stay here with your guest."

Relief rushed through him, and he mentally thanked her as she left the room. He wasn't sure how he would have made conversation with Annie's mother.

Mrs. McEwen glanced about and smoothed the stray locks escaping from the elaborate twists atop her head. Finally, her gaze fell on him. An odd expression on her face made him wonder what she was thinking.

"I suppose you are one of Annie's...patients." She spoke the last word with the slightest tinge of distain, as if he were untouchable, yet her refined manners would never allow her to say so.

"Mother!" Annie's exasperated expression accompanied a deep blush.

The older woman's unexpected comment caught him unprepared. He cringed and glanced down at his useless arm hanging in the OD green sling. Sucking in a deep breath to calm himself, he faced her and replied. "Yes, ma'am. She's a nurse at the hospital where I was treated." He hesitated and looked at Annie before continuing. "She's a very fine nurse."

The smile on the wrinkled face appeared strained. "Yes, well. I am sure she is." Yet her tone conveyed the exact opposite.

Annie's mother was clearly disappointed in her daughter's chosen path. She had probably expected Annie to marry well and join society, roll bandages rather than serve as an Army nurse.

His own mother would be disappointed, too. She had such high expectations for her children, especially her oldest son. Although his dreams had not been exactly what she would have chosen, she had supported him, knowing full well how his inabilities limited those choices. Now his athletic abilities were gone, destroyed by the war. What choices did he have left? Would she continue to support him?

The awkward silence was interrupted by the sound of the front door opening.

Mrs. McEwen stood and then took slow, deliberate steps toward the entrance. At the same time, Annie hopped up and slipped past her into the entrance hall.

"You made it," a deep masculine voice boomed in greeting.

"Oh, Uncle Herschel," was Annie's muffled reply.

"Herschel," Mrs. McEwen called from the doorway. "Come in, come in."

A tall, thin man came into view with Annie close behind him. Mrs. McEwen grasped his arm and pulled him into the room. "This is Herschel, my husband's brother."

"And my husband." Aunt Millie appeared in the hall behind them.

Herschel came forward with his hand extended. When Milt grasped it and shook, the older man introduced himself. "Herschel McEwen, Annie's uncle."

"Sgt. Milton Greenlee, sir."

Herschel pressed his lips together tightly and nodded. He had dark auburn hair with grey at his temples, bushy eyebrows and piercing blue eyes. The type of eyes that looked deep into your soul. Those eyes revealed the depth of the man's pain as he searched for the truth.

Aunt Millie announced, "Mrs. Rice is making the lemonade."

Herschel crossed to the fireplace, shaking his head when his wife motioned for him to sit.

"Once you get settled in a bit, we'll talk. Over in our sitting room." He motioned with his hand. "This room is much too stuffy and uncomfortable."

"Good idea," Millie McEwen took charge of the situation again. "We'll let you get settled first. Our sitting room is much cozier, better for talking. And that's where we have our letters and all."

"Mother, don't you need to consult with Mrs. Rice about supper?"

"She knows what we're having and what time we're having it," her mother protested. "Your father will be home soon. He assured me he would be here well before suppertime."

"Good." Annie sounded less than enthusiastic. "Does she know to set out the good dishes? You said yourself she's not used to having company."

"Oh, I'll talk to her. She won't do anything extra if I don't insist."

Relief clearly showed as Annie's face relaxed. She'd skillfully managed to get her mother out of the room which was a relief to him as well.

What would her father be like?

****

Aunt Millie steered him across the hallway to another set of double doors that led to a different world while Annie went to get the lemonade.

145

The lighter room with more modern furniture had soft green wallpaper and potted plants that gave it a garden atmosphere. Tall windows let in the light through their upper portions while wooden shutters covered the lower halves providing privacy and ventilation.

Millie seated him on a cushioned chair facing a floral chintz-covered sofa. Herschel sat opposite in a high-backed chair that appeared to be his normal place. Annie's mother, who'd quickly returned from the kitchen, scurried along behind and lighted like a bird on the sofa next to Millie, who affectionately patted her hand.

"Annie says you were in the First Division in Sicily," Herschel said abruptly.

"Yes," Milt hesitated, not quite ready to jump into his memories so quickly.

"Now, Herschel. Let the boy settle in, get to know us a little." Millie chided her husband firmly yet lovingly. She turned to Milt. "You'll have to forgive him. He's so anxious for any information."

"Yes, ma'am." Milt tried to smile and wished Annie would come back and help him. He'd forgotten how to talk to civilians, people who knew nothing about where he'd been or what he'd seen.

"The boy's going home to see his own family, isn't that right?" Mrs. McEwen spoke up.

Grateful, Milt replied, "Yes, ma'am."

"Where do they live?" Millie asked softly.

"In Kerrville, ma'am."

"That's not too far, is it Herschel?"

"No." Herschel appeared unhappy that his interrogation had been delayed.

Annie's voice came from behind him. "Here you are."

Milt turned to see her standing in the doorway with a tray of glasses and a pitcher of lemonade.

Millie jumped up and hurried toward her niece. "Oh, Annie, darling. Let me help."

Herschel rose, too. He moved out of the way while Annie deposited the tray on the low table by the sofa.

"Now, you just sit down, and I'll pour the lemonade." Millie took charge and directed Annie toward the sofa where she obediently sat next to her mother.

"Here you go, Sergeant." She handed him a glass making sure he had hold of it. "Or would you rather we call you Milton?"

"I go by Milt." He took a sip of the cool drink. Oddly, the tartness brought back thoughts of England.

"Not very sweet. Sugar rationing, you know. But cool and refreshing." Millie handed her husband the next glass.

Milt took a long drink that quenched his thirst. Then he carefully placed the glass on a small table to his right.

By now the ladies had been served and Millie had seated herself on the end of the sofa nearest her husband. All of them seemed a little anxious, anticipating what he might have to say.

"This certainly is a lovely home, from what I've seen so far. Annie said her grandfather built it."

Herschel glanced at his wife before anyone could answer. "Yes," he mumbled. "We McEwen's have lived here a long time."

"You said you were from Kerrville. Is that where

your family's from?" Millie asked.

"Yes, my father is in business there. Several businesses, actually. My grandmother's people, the Kerr's, founded the town."

She smiled. "That's good. My family is from down around Ringgold. In North Georgia. You came through there on the train."

She was trying to make small talk so Milt would feel more comfortable. He appreciated the effort. Unfortunately, their talk made him more self-conscious.

Annie sat stiffly beside her mother. Oddly enough, she appeared to be as ill at ease as he was. And even more unusual, her family was focusing all their attention on him, not the daughter or niece they hadn't seen in months.

"My boy, Joe …" Herschel hesitated and shot a quick glance at his wife before continuing. "Joe was in the engineers, with the 1st Division. Landed at…oh, somewhere in Sicily."

"Gela," Milt inserted.

"Yeah. That sounds right. Were you there?" His piercing blue eyes cut through Milt's meager defenses.

"Yes," he nodded. "I was there. But I didn't go in with the first wave. My regiment was in reserve, so we watched from the ship." He glanced around to find Annie and her mother listening intently.

Milt returned his gaze to Herschel's. "Joe was with the First Engineers, right?"

The older man nodded.

"They would have been attached to the 16th Regiment. He would have gone ashore with them."

The older man nodded thoughtfully before continuing. "In one of his letters, from North Africa, he mentioned mines. You know, land mines. Said they didn't get much training and had to teach themselves how to set them, disarm them, and all that."

Milt knew about mines. Knew what they could do. "I'm surprised information like that wasn't censored out."

Herschel nodded. "He said something about censoring his own letters 'cause his Captain had been killed. I guess he didn't figure that little bit mattered."

Officers did what they pleased, whereas, if he'd written about that stuff, it would have been cut out.

"You think that's what killed him?"

Milt shook his head. "Naw. He was an officer. The men would have handled the mines and he would have been overseeing them." He didn't mention that Joe could have stepped on a mine, or his jeep might have driven over one. He didn't need to add to what they were already imagining.

"Well, it worried me. Not training them like that. On something they should have known."

"Yeah, well. That's how it was sometimes." All fucked up. He couldn't tell these people about all the stupid stuff that went on, stuff that got men killed.

"We just want to know what happened to our boy," Aunt Millie said.

"Yes, ma'am. I know." How could he tell them that they probably didn't want to know what happened. That it would be easier not knowing than to hear of some of the horrible ways men died.

"When he talked about being an engineer, he talked about building bridges, roads, that kind of thing. Not mine fields."

"The engineers did fix bridges after the Krauts

blew them up. They repaired the roads where artillery shells left holes so big, they'd swallow a truck. They'd bring up their bulldozers and fill it in or cut us a new road, if need be."

"Then he wouldn't have been out there in front, getting shot at." Aunt Millie's voice rose with emotion. "Then what happened? How did he get killed?"

Milt glanced from face to face. He didn't have any answers for them. He wasn't there. He didn't know. What did they expect of him?

"Aunt Millie, didn't you get a letter? From Joe's commander?" Annie spoke in her calm, soothing, nurse's voice.

Milt appreciated her attempt to lower the anxiety level.

"Yes. I…uh…have it here, with his other letters." Aunt Millie got up and went over to a desk laden with papers.

"While you look for it, I'll take Milt upstairs. He looks tired." Annie stood and motioned for Milt to come with her.

"That's a good idea," Annie's mother chimed in. "George will be home soon. I'm sure he has questions, too."

Milt followed Annie out into the entrance hall. He wondered what her father would be like and if he would be any more intense than Herschel. The stress had him wondering if he did the right thing coming here.

When Annie told him she'd accompany him, he'd hoped to get closer to her, to talk to her and get to know her as someone other than a nurse. Instead, she'd been extremely quiet on the crowded train. And now she looked like she could jump out of her skin.

They had turned the landing before she spoke. "I'm sorry. That was kind of awkward."

"It's okay." He caught her gaze. "Families are always awkward."

"I bet yours isn't as bad as mine." They'd reached the second floor. She stopped in front of the first door on the right.

He stood beside her. "Your cousin's room?"

"Yes. It hasn't changed much since he left." She opened the door and went inside.

The room reminded him a little of his own except this one was neater and had a lot less sports gear.

Annie must have read his mind. "Joe was away at college before he went into the Army. He hadn't really lived here for quite a while. Aunt Millie still keeps it like he left it, though."

"Yeah," Milt said as he walked to the window and looked out over the treetops.

"The bathroom's right across the hall."

He turned to see her standing in the doorway. "Don't go." He crossed the room in long strides. "Where's your room?" After the words emerged, he wondered how bad they sounded.

She smiled. And Milt relaxed a little.

"I have my own floor. Up those stairs." She pointed to a narrower stairway almost hidden in the walls of the wider stairwell.

Milt wanted to ask to see it but decided not to. She might take it wrong, and he didn't want to scare her off just as she was becoming a little more friendly.

"Aunt Millie and Uncle Herschel are down this hallway. And my parents are over there." She pointed to a hallway on the opposite side of the stairs.

He looked around getting his bearings.

"I really appreciate your coming." Her soft voice was full of emotion. "You can tell them as much as you're comfortable with. They know it's hard. It's hard for them, too."

He could only nod.

She reached out and squeezed his hand. "Would you like to rest a little before supper?"

"I guess. Or maybe get some air, go for a walk to stretch my legs." Maybe that would be a way to get her alone.

"We could walk down to Point Park after supper. It's not far and there's a wonderful view."

He smiled at the invitation. "I'd like that."

Chapter 21

When Annie descended the stairs, her mother spotted her.

"Oh, Annie," her mother said. "Come help me. I need to decide how to arrange the seating."

Annie smiled. Her mother so longed for a social life yet lacked the skills to create the world she imagined.

"All you need to remember is to put Sgt. Greenlee next to someone he can talk to."

"And that would be you, of course." Ethel smiled knowingly. "He seems like a very nice young man." She led the way down the back hall. "A little quiet. And, of course, he has been damaged a bit, but that should all heal, shouldn't it?" She turned back to Annie for an answer. "Will the scars be too bad?"

"Mother, he's a patient. He was in the same division as Joe. That's all."

"Well, he might be a possibility for you. He's not a doctor, but his family is in business." She raised her finger and pointed toward Annie in that all too familiar gesture. "And young lady, you need to consider all your prospects. Otherwise, you will have to accept your father's choice."

"I know very well that you and father expect me to marry, but I am not ready for marriage. And right now I'm serving my country. Like Joe did."

"Don't use Joe as an excuse. I can understand your wanting to get away from Chattanooga. George may have a young man picked out for you, but I've told him you could very well find someone suitable in the Army." She said the word 'Army' like it was something nasty. "All the eligible young men are in service these days." The older woman stopped in her tracks before they reached the kitchen and turned to face Annie. "This young man, he's not an officer, is he?"

"No, Mother. He's a sergeant, not an officer." Annie tried to control her temper, especially with her mother. She didn't need to throw her into one of her spells, not now, not with Milt here.

"Well, nevertheless, his family is in business. That's something. Even with his injuries he could still amount to something. I'm sure your father can find out about them, before things progress too far."

"Mother. I'm not looking for a husband. And when I do it will be my choice, not yours or Father's."

"Well, you don't have to get so snippy about it. We're only thinking of what's best for you."

Annie shook her head and muttered, "I know. I know."

She went ahead of her mother into the kitchen where Mrs. Rice bustled over their evening meal.

The aroma of home cooking warmed her heart and made her mouth water. She hoped it would do the same for Milt, but having only one hand could make eating difficult.

"What are we having?" she asked Mrs. Rice.

"I've fricasseed a chicken for you. The potatoes are boiling. We've the green beans from the garden, tomatoes, and cucumbers. I'll mix up the cornbread as soon as Mr. McEwen gets here."

"Sounds wonderful. And the chicken, can it be cut with a fork?"

Mrs. Rice turned and gave her a quizzical look. "My fricassee chicken's so tender it falls off the bone," she insisted.

Annie smiled to reassure her. "I know. I'm just concerned about Sgt. Greenlee."

"Well, I guarantee my chicken will melt in his mouth." She nodded before turning back to the stove.

"She's made an apple pie, too. Do you think that will suit your young man?"

"He's not my young man, Mother," Annie retorted.

Her mother frowned and looked away.

"I'm sure he will love the pie." She went to her mother and slipped her arm around the older woman's shoulder. Her mother's hand reached out and tentatively slid around her waist. The two embraced. Annie breathed in her mother's unique, familiar scent. Perfume and powder, the same for as long as Annie could remember.

The telephone jangled in the hallway.

Her mother looked to Mrs. Rice who frowned but didn't say a word. Instead, she wiped her hands on her apron and hurried to answer the ringing telephone.

"McEwen residence."

Easing into the hallway, Annie wondered who would be calling. Perhaps someone for her father.

"Yes, sir." Mrs. Rice sounded very business-like.

"I understand, sir. Just hold on and I'll get him." She looked up as she placed the receiver on the table and whispered to Annie. "It's your father. He wants Mr. Herschel."

"I'll get him," Annie volunteered and scurried past Mrs. Rice who was picking up the receiver.

"Miss Annie is going for him now."

The door was still open to the sitting room, so Annie stuck her head in. "Uncle Herschel, Father is on the telephone. He wants to talk to you."

Uncle Herschel hurried down the hall with Annie on his heels. He took the receiver. "Thank you, Mrs. Rice."

She scurried back to the kitchen door where Annie's mother stood watching.

"Herschel here."

"Yes." He continued, turning to face the wall. "Yes, I know the place."

"What?" Annie whispered, but Uncle Herschel waved her away.

"I'll bring it. As quick as I can."

Both Annie and her mother descended upon him as soon as he hung up.

"What has happened?" Annie asked.

"He's had a flat tire. That's all. And the spare's flat, too." He turned toward the back of the house. "I have one I fixed in the garage. I'll have to take it to him."

"You mean he can't get home?" her mother asked.

He stopped and looked back at them. "He doesn't want to leave the car."

"But how?" she continued.

"I'll take the incline, then hitch a ride. Tell Millie where I've gone." He disappeared out the door.

Annie turned back to go tell Aunt Millie while her mother returned to the kitchen to tell Mrs. Rice supper would be delayed.

****

Since supper would be delayed, Annie suggested to Milt that they go for their walk before supper rather than after.

"Uncle Herschel said he'd be back soon," she explained as they went out the front door. "I think he's planning to spend the evening with you, picking every scrap of information from your brain."

She laughed when she said it, but Milt knew she sympathized with him.

"You needn't feel bad. I volunteered, remember?"

"I know. But I got you into it. I asked you to write to them."

He'd shrugged as if it were no big deal. He didn't want her to know how deeply it affected him, or about the nightmares brought on by dredging up memories better left forgotten.

"What about your father?" he asked.

She frowned and turned away. "I don't know." She looked over her shoulder. "I suppose he'll want to understand what happened to Joe."

The hot August day had cooled in the late afternoon.

"It's nice up here on the mountain."

She gazed off into the distance. "It's always cooler up here, cooler than down in town. And the views are amazing, don't you think?"

"Yes." He took in the beauty of the peaceful landscape. Ade and his other friends were fighting in Europe, probably in an equally beautiful landscape marred by armies with their bombs and artillery. He was lucky to be here instead of there. Despite his wounds, he would live. They might not.

"I thought you wanted to walk."

"Yeah, Sure." He followed her down the sidewalk. "Do me good."

After walking a block on the narrow street, she finally spoke again. "We'll just walk to Point Park and back. That's not too far."

"What's Point Park?"

"It's the park they made to commemorate the Battle of Lookout Mountain. It's where the mountain comes to a point." She made a gesture with her hands to illustrate.

He only nodded in reply as he walked beside her taking in her beauty. The fluttering leaves overhead and the bushes overflowing the fence nearby brought out the green in her hazel eyes.

She broke off a branch covered with tiny flowers from an overhanging bush and inhaled the sweet fragrance. His heart melted a little more.

Farther along, he saw the park. Stone towers, reminiscent of an ancient castle, stood as sentinels on either side of the arched entrance.

The iron gate swung aside easily to let them into the well-tended park. Pathways veered in either direction with one straight ahead that drew his eye to an enormous monument pointing to the heavens.

"I had no idea something like this existed." Awestruck, he wandered along the path, trying to grasp the implications of the scene before him. A memorial to a battle fought long ago, to the men who had died here.

"I like to come here sometimes. It's peaceful and quiet. A good place to relax."

"Do many people come here?"

"Some, but not many."

They reached the large stone monument and Milt read the inscription. He couldn't help but wonder if someday there would be memorials to the men who fought in Africa or to those who died in Sicily, like Annie's cousin Joe. And on that beach in Normandy. How could they not remember that? Where so many died just trying to get onto the land to save Europe.

"There's quite a view from up here," Annie continued. "You can see all of Chattanooga and the river." She pointed toward an outcropping of rocks down the slope. "Unless it's a still day and smoke fills the valley."

"Let's have a look." He headed downhill with Annie on his heels.

As he reached the rock formation, a panorama unfolded before his eyes. Mountains surrounded the valley below where the city nestled along the banks of the Tennessee River. The wide ribbon of water wound through the valley in a huge u-shaped curve.

"That's Horseshoe Bend," Annie said from somewhere behind him. "That's what they call that big bend in the river," she explained.

He turned to find her standing where the dirt path met the solid limestone.

"Come on," he motioned for her to join him. "Come tell me what I'm looking at."

"I...I don't like...getting near the edge." He detected a shakiness in her voice.

"That's okay," he assured her.

Chapter 22

He turned and looked out over the valley, and then he stepped closer to the edge to peer down the sheer drop to treetops hundreds of feet below.

"Don't" she squeaked. "Don't get too close." Her throat tightened until she thought she would choke. She wrapped her arms around her middle, holding on for dear life.

He glanced back at her, smiling. Then he turned back to the cliff's edge, so much like Joe, reckless and carefree.

When he eased to the side gazing out over the river, she squealed, "don't!"

"I'm all right. Don't worry about me." He looked down. "You know, there was a time when I would have scrambled down this cliff just for the adventure of it. But no more, not with only one arm."

He turned back to face her, sadness radiating through his gaze. She fought back tears. For his loss and for her own. Would she ever get over the terror? Could she ever go out to the edge without seeing the small body smashed on the rocks below?

His gaze returned to the panoramic view. He pointed to a boat on the river and shifted to the side as it rounded the bend.

His foot slipped.

Instinctively, Annie rushed forward and grabbed

him from behind. She pulled him backward away from the edge. Once he got his footing, he struggled to turn in her tight embrace.

"I wasn't going to fall," he insisted, irritation tainting his words.

She clung to him, shaking. He must have sensed her terror because he encircled her shoulders with his good arm.

She relaxed into the strength of his embrace. Blinking as tears streamed down her cheeks, she lifted her chin so she could see his face. The intense blue of his eyes conveyed comfort rather than distain.

He leaned closer and before she realized what was happening his lips gently brushed hers. She didn't pull away, so he continued more firmly and yet so softly. She felt herself letting go and kissing him back. Her need overwhelmed every other thought.

After an eternity of mere seconds, they broke the kiss and stared at each other, both in awe of what had just happened.

She trailed her fingers across the scars on his face. They somehow reflected the depth of his wounds, the pain he'd suffered. His vulnerability.

She couldn't do this. He was her patient.

She pulled away, putting distance between them.

"We shouldn't have done that," she murmured.

He drew a ragged breath. Did he understand?

The pain of rejection flashed across his face, and he looked away.

She contemplated the ground at their feet, wondering what she could say to explain. Yet she didn't understand it herself, so she turned and began the climb back up the hillside to the monument looming above them.

"We'd better head back," she commented over her shoulder.

****

She hadn't expected him to kiss her.

What was she supposed to do now? Sure, she found him attractive. Sure, she liked him. And, Lord knows, she appreciated him coming here, facing her family, talking about things he probably wanted to forget, just to help her, to help them, deal with Joe's loss.

But she had no intention of getting involved with Sgt. Milt Greenlee or anyone else.

Lloyd had kissed her. And she'd kept him at bay.

This...this was just a patient infatuated with his nurse. Nothing more.

Then why did she feel this way? Why did she feel this urge to throw her arms around him and kiss him again?

Her heart twisted inside her chest. How she longed for someone to love her.

No. She'd been there before. With Leroy. She'd wanted him to love her, and she thought that he did. Until he turned on her. Turned into a pawing, pushing, drunken monster.

She reached the monument. Her breath came in hard gasps both from the exertion and from the emotions she fought to control. The cool, hard stone beneath her fingers helped to solidify her resolve. She'd do the same thing she'd done with Lloyd. Stay friendly but make it plain there was no chance of anything developing between them.

"That's quite a climb," Milt panted, not far behind

her.

He dropped down to sit on the concrete apron at her feet.

She drew a deep, calming breath before joining him, careful to keep a distance between them.

"Milt," she started. "I…uh…I like you…very much."

Those intense blue eyes met hers. "But?"

She winced, knowing she had to continue. "But I'm not ready to get involved. Not with anyone." She clasped her hands in her lap to still her nerves. "I'm flattered by your interest…"

"I know. I know." He looked out across the valley. His lips pursed, then went flat. The muscles in his jaw worked as if he were chewing on his thoughts. Finally, he spoke, just loud enough for her to hear. "It's okay. I understand." Sadness and disappointment laced his words.

Annie hated hurting him.

"Well, after all, I am your nurse…"

"Not anymore," he interrupted her. "I'll be in a hospital in Atlanta. And you'll be going off to New York, right?"

The touch of anger in his voice sounded like the beginning of an argument. Did he want to argue? She hadn't corrected her lie about her new assignment, and she wasn't about to now. Right now, she needed to be firm and clear.

"Nevertheless, I have plans for my future. And I don't intend for anything to interfere with them. Not you. Not my parents. Not anyone."

He sat in silence. Good. Maybe that meant he was taking her seriously.

"I appreciate your coming here and talking to my family. I'd like for us to be friends…but nothing more. Do you understand?"

"Yeah. I understand."

He didn't look at her. Just stared at the twig he'd picked up. Guilt washed over her like a crashing wave.

"I'm sorry," she pleaded, hating the weakness in her voice. "I didn't mean to hurt you."

He nodded, and then he shot a stabbing glance her way. "I know you didn't. It's just something I gotta get used to."

He got to his feet and dusted off the seat of his pants. "Guess we'd better get back."

She stood and turned toward the entrance. When she glanced back over her shoulder, he was staring at the rocks below.

"Why are you so afraid of the cliff? You've lived up here all your life, haven't you?"

Her breath caught at the directness of his questions. Terror gripped her heart.

He looked at her then and his gaze cut through all her defenses.

She saw the rocks, the sheer drop below, an abyss of horror. She saw him falling. Heard her own screams and those of her mother as the small boy disappeared over the edge.

She turned away and began to walk, fighting the urge to run.

His footsteps sounded behind her. He grabbed her arm and stopped her.

"My little brother fell off one of those cliffs," she heard herself say.

She wrenched her arm free and ran...away from him...away from the horror of her memories.

Chapter 23

A door slammed and Annie stiffened.

"I don't know why he has to slam that door," Mrs. Rice complained.

"Never mind." Her mother raised her chin, thrusting her nose up in the superior manner she assumed as mistress of the household. "Go ahead and start the cornbread, Mrs. Rice. Mr. McEwen is home."

Annie glanced over at Mrs. Rice who shook her head in resignation.

"Come, Annie. You must greet your father."

Her muscles froze in dread of facing the man who had dominated her life. She couldn't move, couldn't speak, couldn't breathe.

Her mother tugged her toward the door and into the back hall just as her father opened the back hall door.

Annie grabbed the kitchen door frame, desperately needing something to hold on to.

He looked up, a little startled, but he quickly regained his composure. The same gruff, ogre figure from her childhood.

"Annie." He nodded as he grumbled her name, his tone and his frown clearly conveying his displeasure. "Herschel told me you were here."

"Dear," her mother spoke softly. "Isn't it nice to have our Annie home with us again?" She tried to take his briefcase, but he jerked it away.

"Humph," he grunted.

He stared at Annie. She could feel her heart pounding as his piercing blue eyes took in every inch of her. "Still wearing that uniform, I see. They haven't sent you packing."

She straightened to her full height, deflecting the insult. "No, Father."

Uncle Herschel came in behind her father. "I'm going to go clean up before dinner." He weaved his way around the three of them and proceeded toward the front of the house. Annie heard him speak to someone, presumably Aunt Millie, before his footsteps echoed up the stairway.

Her father opened the door to his study without speaking.

Her mother trotted along behind him into the room before he could shut her out. "The young man is in with Millie."

Unable to stop herself, Annie made her way the few steps to his door. A desperate need to please him overcame her fear as it always had when he came home grumpy. She became a small child again, eager for any crumb.

"He's injured," her mother continued. "Bandages on his head." Her hand went to her own head as if to demonstrate. "And his arm." She looked to Annie for help.

"He was wounded in Normandy," Annie added. "He's on his way to visit his family and agreed..."

"You told us all that when you phoned," her father interrupted. He deposited his bulging briefcase beside his desk and sank into the chair behind it. "Tell Mrs. Rice to get supper on the table. I'm famished."

"Of course, dear, of course." Her mother's hands fluttered in front of her as if the kinetic movement would propel her away more quickly. She hurried from the room to notify Mrs. Rice.

"I'll tell the others," Annie said as she turned to leave, too.

"I suppose Herschel and Millie have already started interrogating him."

Annie faced him. "Yes. They are anxious to hear what he has to say."

"No doubt Herschel will quiz him incessantly. Want to know every detail." Anger laced his words.

Was this visit so difficult for him? Was the pain of losing Joe still so fresh that he couldn't bear to talk about it?

"Don't you want to know…" She hesitated, searching for words. "…something about what it was like…over there?"

"What good does it do?" he growled. "Joe's dead. He's not coming back. Ever." He stared at the bookshelves across from his desk, frowning intently. She followed his gaze to a picture of Joe as a teenage boy eager to tackle the world.

Her father had pinned all his hopes and dreams on Joe. The sorrow at his loss joined with Peter's loss and festered inside the older man like an infected wound that would not heal. She hoped that learning more would be like opening the wound and letting the infection drain, so he could heal.

His fierce gaze met hers. "It's up to you now." He shook his head. "You, of all people, must fulfill this family's destiny." His hand curled into a fist. "You owe me that."

Annie leaned against the door frame so he wouldn't see how badly she was shaking. The man couldn't wait to attack her. He would use his most deadly weapon to get what he wanted.

"This…this crippled soldier you've brought home," he raised his hand along with his voice. "Don't think I don't know what you're up to. Playing on the family's sympathy, doing your good deed. Well, it won't work with me."

"Father, I…"

"No excuses. I don't want to hear them. What I want to hear is you agreeing to marry Brice Attwater. You can get out of that damn uniform if you want to. And you can go to Washington. He's invited you to come. So go. You two get together. He knows what's at stake, same as you."

Annie heard voices. "Can't we talk about this later?" She desperately wanted to run, to leave, to escape this overpowering torrent.

"Dinner will be served in ten minutes," her mother announced in the hallway behind her. "Annie, go tell Aunt Millie and that nice, young soldier."

"Yes, Mother." Annie gladly fled, to carry out her assigned task and to get away from her father and his unreasonable demands.

****

Although Annie's family treated him cordially, the tension around the supper table was palpable. Her father greeted him stiffly and made very specific inquiries about his injuries that Milt deflected as best he could.

Annie came to his rescue. "I'm sure that no one wants to talk about medical issues at the supper table."

And her mother quickly agreed.

Eating at their formal dining table proved less difficult than he anticipated. Annie had arranged everything within his reach and Mrs. Rice served his plate so that he didn't have to worry about passing the food-laden dishes. He focused on eating slowly and answering their questions.

Herschel made tactful inquiries about Milt's military service, where he'd been trained and when he had gone overseas, which led to Herschel's recounting of Joe's ROTC training in college and his subsequent training in the Army.

Millie listened intently but didn't speak. Instead, she let her husband take the lead.

When he and Annie returned from their walk, Millie had pulled him into their sitting room to show him pictures of Joe, from childhood to his graduation from college as well as his official photo upon becoming an officer. She'd also dragged out the letters he'd written them and the letter from his commanding officer notifying them of his death. She'd cried as she reminisced, her grief still raw and bleeding.

At the dinner table Herschel showed less emotion when talking about Joe, yet he too was obviously grieving.

Annie's father repeatedly inserted himself into the conversation with comments about Herschel's service in the Great War and his obsession with the military. Milt surmised that Mr. McEwen blamed his brother for Joe's loss because the father had encouraged his son to join the military where Mr. McEwen had wanted his nephew to pursue a different, safer path.

Milt took a bite of Mrs. Rice's apple pie and

groaned with pleasure.

"I haven't tasted anything this good since I left home," he commented.

Annie's mother beamed from across the table. "It's Mrs. Rice's best recipe. When we heard you and Annie were coming, she saved the sugar so she could make Annie's favorite pie."

"Well, it is excellent. The whole meal was wonderful. Really."

"I'll make sure Mrs. Rice knows you enjoyed it."

Annie glanced around the table. "If everyone is finished, perhaps we can continue the conversation in the parlor."

Her father frowned. "Nonsense. I doubt you women want to hear any war stories." He pushed his chair back and stood. "Herschel, we'll take the young man to my study. Then you can get all the gruesome details without having to worry about shocking the females."

Milt watched Annie. She covered her reaction to her father's comment pretty well, yet the strained set of her lips revealed something. He just wasn't sure what.

"You men go ahead," Millie spoke up from beside him. "We'll get the table cleared."

Pushing back his chair, Milt got to his feet. Annie gave him one of her sweet smiles from across the table. It almost looked like a silent apology.

Herschel approached his wife who had already started stacking up plates. "Are you sure? Mrs. Rice can do this."

She shook her head. "No. I...I can't listen. Not right now." She slipped her arm around his waist and gave him a hug. "You go on."

"All right," he answered, then turned his attention to Milt. "Come this way, young man."

Down the hall they entered a room where Mr. McEwen was already ensconced behind a desk, a cigar clinched between his teeth. Herschel directed Milt to an upholstered, high-backed chair while he seated himself on an overstuffed love seat.

"Close the door, Herschel," Mr. McEwen ordered.

"No reason to shut us up in here. The ladies aren't going to spy on us." He grinned at Milt. "And what if they do? We aren't going to talk about anything they couldn't hear, are we?"

"No," Milt shook his head. "I don't think so."

"Well in that case," Mr. McEwen rose and went to the window. "Ethel doesn't like smoke in the rest of the house." He raised the sash, allowing a slight breeze to waif through the room.

"Tell us about Africa, Tunisia. That's where Joe joined the First Division."

Herschel clearly wanted to know everything. Milt didn't know where to start, so he just plunged in.

"Tunisia was interesting. Not the sand dunes we expected. Hilly, rough terrain. Joe was in the Engineers, right?" Milt leaned back in the chair letting the memories surface. "I remember seeing engineers clearing mines. The Germans had different kinds of mines. Some anti-personnel, some anti-tank. They liked to lay them along roads, in a pass, anywhere they thought we would try to come through. When we came up on a minefield, we'd call up the engineers to clear them out." He stopped himself short. He'd almost told them about seeing an engineer blown up by a mine he was trying to diffuse.

Milt closed his eyes, the image vivid in his mind's eye. The suddenness. The shock. The gut-wrenching terror as the reality sunk in. The man was dead. Blown to bits right before his eyes.

These men might say they wanted to hear everything, but Milt was pretty sure they didn't want to know the gruesome details.

Herschel spoke up. "Like in that one letter Joe wrote. He said that he'd lost a man learning how to handle the mines. He couldn't say much in his letters after that, what with the censoring and all."

Milt nodded. When he first arrived in England, before they invaded North Africa, the brass pounded into them the orders not to write home with any specific information about what they were doing or where they were going. The officers made it clear that anything inappropriate would be cut out.

"His letters came to us all blacked out or full of holes," Mr. McEwen injected. "The first ones anyway."

"He learned what he could say and what to leave out." Herschel sighed. He pulled a pack of cigarettes from his coat pocket and held it out to Milt.

"No thank you, sir," Milt said. "Maybe later."

Herschel nodded thoughtfully as he withdrew a cigarette and lit it. "Except for that one letter where he talked about the mines, the rest weren't very informative. I always thought we'd talk about it when he got home." He stared at the smoking match, his thoughts far away.

Milt glanced from one man to the other before continuing.

"There was always the danger of our mail being captured. They didn't want the Germans to get any

173

information." He looked down and rubbed the arm of the chair back and forth to release the tension in his body. "We did the same. Went through any papers we found searching for scraps of information about their troops, supplies, where they'd been." He'd gone through pockets of men who were still warm and covered with blood. Worse were the ones covered with flies, deteriorating in the dry desert air. They'd only come across one group like that, still clothed and lying where they'd died. The locals hadn't gotten to them yet, hadn't stripped the bodies clean.

"We had to get to them quickly," he continued. "The natives stole everything they could get their hands on. It was unbelievable...the first time you see naked, dead bodies...soldiers stripped of everything."

"Bastards." Mr. McEwen spat out the word.

"What about the Italians? Weren't they fighting in North Africa?"

"Yes," Milt nodded, grateful to Herschel for pulling his mind away from images of death. "We didn't encounter many. The Germans ran the show. They had the tanks, the artillery. The Italians defended some of the fortified positions."

"So, Joe would have been clearing mines, then? Out in front?" Mr. McEwen inquired from within the cloud of cigar smoke swirling around him.

"Yes." Milton responded. "Some of the time." He watched Herschel's face, trying to gauge how to proceed.

"Herschel was in France in 1918. Trenches. Barbed wire and mustard gas. All that glorious bunk." Mr. McEwen's tone reeked with sarcasm. He stared at his brother with disdain. "Had Joe believing that going to war was some kind of heroic pursuit."

"You don't have to air your opinions in front of our guest," Herschel shot back.

"Humph. If he'd listened to me, he'd have been back behind the lines or better yet behind a desk. Safe and sound but still contributing."

"Just because you chose that path, didn't mean it was the right one for him. Joe wanted to be an engineer. And he would have been a good one, too."

Milton watched the angry exchange, driven by their mutual grief. He needed to pull the two men out of their growing anger, so he continued his tale. "The engineers kept the roads passable, too. When we got to Sicily, they'd fix bridges the Germans blew up in their retreat. Or build temporary ones. When artillery shells blew huge holes in the narrow roads, the engineers would bring up a bulldozer and plow a new section of road around the damaged part."

"Then the engineers were out front? Getting shot at?"

"Not all the time. We'd call them up when we needed them."

"We don't really know what happened to Joe," Herschel commented sadly. "The letter we got, it just said he was killed in the line of duty."

This was it. The question Annie wanted him to answer. But he didn't have any answers for them. "Sometimes the officers who write those letters don't know what happened themselves." The officers who had to write letters to families had a tough job, presented with a list of names, dead men they didn't even know, and having to write families about the death of their loved one. "They had to write a lot of letters."

175

Mr. McEwen stared across the room puffing on his cigar.

"Too many," Herschel said sadly.

Milt made Sergeant in Sicily. A battlefield promotion when Sgt. Iverson was mowed down by machine gun fire. He hadn't wanted the responsibility. Lives depending on his decisions. But he hadn't had a choice. Just like now. He'd agreed to tell them about Sicily, to dredge up memories and maybe, just maybe, he could help this family heal.

He'd written his friend, Ade Carlton, who was still over there fighting, before he left Florida. Maybe Ade could find someone who knew Joe. Someone in the engineers. Someone who could tell them more.

He hesitated, remembering Annie's admonition not to get their hopes up. He'd wait and see what Ade could find out before he said anything.

"I'll try to find out more, but I can't promise anything."

"How?" Annie's father demanded.

"I can ask around, talk to other wounded soldiers."

"And you'll let us know if you learn anything?" Herschel's face brightened at Milt's suggestion.

"Yes, sir. Of course. But it may take some time. After my leave, I have to report to a hospital in Atlanta."

"They're transferring you to another hospital. Why?" Mr. McEwen asked.

"Didn't Annie tell you? They're closing the hospital in Florida. Everyone is being transferred."

Chapter 24

"I want to show you something," Herschel insisted, getting to his feet.

"What on earth?"

"The map. The one of Sicily. It's still in our sitting room." He stood in front of Milt. "I took it down, but I want you to see it."

"Certainly." Milt stood, wondering what he was in for. "I'll be glad to look at it." He followed Herschel to the door where the older man stopped and looked back at Mr. McEwen.

"Come on, George. It won't hurt you to come over into our sitting room."

"Humph." Mr. McEwen stood and stubbed out his cigar.

They trailed Herschel down the hall and into the lighter, cheerier room. Millie, Annie, and Mrs. McEwen looked up from their interrupted conversation when the men entered.

"I want to show him the map," Herschel explained.

Milt stood uneasily as Herschel fished behind a small desk and brought out a surprisingly large map of Sicily mounted on a board and studded with pins and little notes.

"We can take it back to my study," Mr. McEwen said.

"Millie might want to hear this, too."

"Fine," Annie's father looked around at the anxious faces. "You go ahead. I've had enough." With that announcement he stomped out of the room.

Annie's mother jumped to her feet. "I'd better go, too," she said.

Millie and Annie exchanged glances and gripped each other's hands as if to say they were in agreement. Then Annie stood and quietly excused herself.

Herschel propped the map up on top of the desk it had been hidden behind and proceeded to explain to Milt all the markings. He had closely followed the 1st Division's movements in Sicily and had written dates and unit designations, both German and American.

Place names on the maps brought back vivid memories, some of friendly faces or interesting local landmarks, others of intense fighting. One triggered the memory of a nineteen-year-old kid. He'd been walking a couple of steps in front of Milt one minute, then the next, a deafening explosion blew him into the air. Machine gun fire started before the poor boy hit the ground. He lay only a few feet away, his lifeblood draining away, and no way to reach him without getting shot.

Millie touched his arm. "Are you all right?" she whispered. "This can wait if it's too much."

Milt met her gaze and nodded. "It's okay." He dare not tell her the real reason for his unease.

Herschel, caught up in the map and what it represented, didn't notice their exchange. Instead, he asked Milt to point out where he had been and locations where the engineers had provided support to his unit.

It wasn't easy for Milt to remember. He backtracked, scouring his memory for specific places and events.

"You have to understand," he explained. "Joe's outfit was most likely attached to the 16th, not the 18th." He looked to Millie for support.

"Herschel, Milt wasn't with Joe. He didn't even know Joe. He's just trying to help."

Herschel scrubbed his hand over his face. "I'm sorry. I get all worked up."

"It's okay. I understand."

Herschel looked him in the eye and for a second Milt thought the older man was going to argue with him, tell him he couldn't understand what it was like to lose your son. The man's gaze shifted to his wife.

Millie, as if on cue, spoke up. "Why don't you tell us some of what you remember about Sicily. What it was like. What the people were like."

Milt sighed in relief. "Oh, the people were nice. Friendly. Happy to see us…except when we destroyed everything they had." He smiled at the memory that popped into his head.

"There was this one dried-up, old woman. Little thing. Just fussing at us something awful. We couldn't understand what she was saying, but we got the message. We'd blown up her shed, if you could call it that. A little shack where she kept her goats." He shook his head. "They're so poor. It was a big loss to her. We couldn't stick around and rebuild it. So we left her there, still reading us the riot act in Italian."

Millie nodded. "Joe wrote us something like that. About how poor the people were. He felt sorry for them, I think."

Herschel frowned and looked back at the map. "They did appreciate it, didn't they?" The softness of his voice shook with emotion.

"Yes. Yes, they did."

The older man pointed back to the map. "I tried to trace Joe's movements, only the accounts in the paper were hard to follow." He paused as if remembering. "I wrote August 5, 1943, here by Troina. I'm pretty sure that was the date they said we took it."

Troina hit Milt like a punch in the gut. Memories flashed through his mind. Machine gun fire. Mortars and artillery shells exploding. Scrambling up a rocky hillside with bullets flying. Charlie falling, blood spurting as he tumbled on the rocks. After that Milt remembered staring down at the crumpled bodies of the Germans he'd just killed.

His breath came in short gasps. Someone faraway said his name.

He tried to shake off the images.

"Lemonade." A cool glass brushed his fingers and he grabbed hold.

"There. That should help."

Millie's face came into focus.

"We have this, too." Millie pointed to a bulky scrap book on a side table. "We started it when Joe went into the military."

Earlier when Millie had shown him Joe's pictures, she'd pulled out the scrapbook and said that they'd look at it later.

Milt sat down, picked up the book, and opened it. Snapshots of Joe and his friends during basic reminded him of his own training days. Herschel quizzed him about his experiences, questions about weapons and platoon strengths, armored support, and artillery barrages.

After a while, Milt needed a break and carefully extricated himself before he lost his patience. Too many memories raced around in his head. He needed to escape.

And he needed to find Annie.

****

This evening he'd talked more about the war than he ever had with anyone. Thankfully, Herschel and Millie let him take a break before the memories overwhelmed him.

Milt wanted to apologize to Annie for his behavior at Point Park. He hadn't meant to upset her. And he hoped she wasn't avoiding him.

Musical notes penetrated the closed parlor doors where someone played the piano. He tapped on the door and the music stopped. A couple of minutes passed, and he had almost decided that whoever was inside wanted to be left alone, when the door opened.

Annie greeted him, "Hello."

"Hi," he responded, trying to show his friendliest face. "May I join you?"

She hesitated for a moment, and then stepped aside to allow him to enter.

Now was the time, while they were alone, to apologize. He faced her. "I'm sorry…for earlier. I had no right."

"Don't let it worry you," she commented as she strode past him toward the piano. "It's all forgotten."

"Okay." He thought about how upset she'd been when she ran away from him. "I'm sorry about your brother, too. I didn't mean to pry."

She sat down on the piano bench. "You weren't prying. It's just not something that I talk about…ever."

He got the message. "Right. Understood."

He followed her to the piano knowing a change of subject was in order. "What are you playing?"

"Just some old songs. It relaxes me."

He leaned in to see if he could read the title on the sheet music. It was an old one he knew. Without thinking, he placed his right hand on the keyboard and fingered the melody. When he missed a note, he started over.

"Here, sit down." She scooted over on the bench so he could sit beside her. He ran through the notes again. "I didn't know you played," she said.

"I don't. Not really. Unless you count playing by ear," he quipped. "Can't read a note, but once I hear the melody, I can usually pick it out. Then add some chords."

He looked down at his useless left hand and shook his head. "At least I used to."

"Here. I'll play the bass and you do the melody."

He could feel his face flushing. "You sure?"

"I'm sure."

"Okay, here goes."

He played the melody as he remembered it and she added the chords just like she said. Then she began to hum along which helped him remember some of the parts he'd forgotten.

"That was pretty good," she said when they finished the song. "Want to do it again?"

She smiled and he'd do almost anything to see that smile. "Sure."

"Good. I'll sing this time."

She played a chord signaling him to begin.

Her velvet voice caressed the words, and Milt

almost lost his concentration. He shook himself to focus on the music and the notes his fingers were playing. The best way for him to keep his mind on the music, instead of the beautiful woman sitting beside him, was for him to sing along, too. So, as he played the notes of the chorus, his voice joined hers.

When he glanced up, her smile almost overwhelmed him. The moment was magical, sitting shoulder to shoulder, each playing, their voices joined in harmony. Milton had never felt anything so right.

"That was fabulous. You can really sing," she commented.

Her compliment made him blush. "It's not much. Just something I do sometimes, to pass the time."

"I'll bet you were the life of the party."

"I did try to keep the boys entertained," he admitted.

"And the ladies, I'll wager."

He nodded. No use denying it. He had been called a ladies' man in his time. Thoughts of what he looked like now dampened his mood. "Not anymore. Not with this mug."

"Oh, it's not that bad."

She meant to be nice, but he knew the truth. He could spot a false compliment a mile away. He'd much rather hear the truth, especially from her.

She must have sensed his darkening mood. "What else do you know?"

"Plenty, at least plenty of old ones. I don't know any of these new songs."

"Well, let's see. What about this?" She played the beginning of a familiar old song.

He nodded. "Yeah, I remember that one."

She reached up and shuffled through a stack of sheet music.

"I told you, I don't read music."

"Oh, I know. But it helps me remember all the words."

She placed the music on the stand above the keyboard, struck the opening chord, and then quickly sang through a few bars. "Refreshing my memory," she explained.

He joined her by playing a few notes and they both smiled.

"Okay, are you ready?"

"Ready."

The song began. He fumbled a little in the beginning, but, once he got going, they played and sang the entire song. By the end, both were laughing.

Across the room the door slid open, and Annie's father stepped into the room.

"Don't encourage her," he barked. "She's wasted entirely too much time on tomfoolery such as that."

"Father," Annie objected.

"Don't 'Father' me. I told your mother not to encourage you. Only wasting your time. I said no good would come of it and I was right. Wasn't I?"

"No, you weren't."

Annie's whole body trembled. "Sir, Annie's an excellent singer. Why, you should hear her…"

"I've heard all I want to hear. And I'll thank you not to interfere in family matters." He stood over them now, like a grizzly bear breathing down on them, ready to attack.

"Milt's our guest." Annie's voice shook.

"And this is my house." The older man glared at

his daughter. "You...you dare to bring this...this crippled excuse for a man into my house..."

Milt bristled at the insult. His hand curled into a tight fist held back only by his respect for Annie.

The older man's intense gaze bore into him. "You talk like you knew him. Like..." A wrinkled hand slashed through the air, barely missing Milt's head. "You didn't know Joe," he growled. "You couldn't hold a candle to that boy."

A fist landed hard on the piano, evoking a dissonant chord from the vibrating strings.

"Ughhh," Mr. McEwen half moaned, half growled. "I should have gotten rid of this monstrosity years ago, only your mother pitched such a holy fit every time I tried to. But one of these days, mark my words, this thing will be gone." He pounded his fist again for emphasis.

Annie stood, defiantly raising her chin. "I apologize for my father's behavior."

"Don't apologize for me. You're the one who disgraced this family, who insured that my name would not be carried on." He stepped closer to her as she backed away. "Then Herschel got rid of his son. Pushed him into the Army, into this bloody war. Didn't want him to be like me." The man suddenly jerked around to face Milt who'd gotten to his feet preparing to do what he could to defend Annie. "If he'd been more like me, he'd be alive today. Not dead in that God-forsaken country."

The man's eyes flashed, his face glowed red. He reeked of whiskey.

That didn't matter. What mattered was getting Annie away from his out-of-control temper before things got worse.

Milt took Annie's hand and pulled her toward the door.

"That's it. Drag her out of here. Take her back to that Army hospital where the soldiers can paw all over her. I know all about nurses in Army hospitals."

Milt turned back to face the man. "Annie's a good nurse," he insisted.

"Don't," Annie pulled him now. "He won't listen to anything when he's like this."

She was right. Milt recognized the anger, the lashing out. No one could reach him now.

In the hallway, Herschel and Millie met them.

"He's been drinking again," Herschel said. "We heard it, all of it."

"I'll go put on a pot of coffee," Millie said. "Annie, dear, why don't you come with me?"

"But Milt…"

"I'll be all right. You go ahead."

Milt glanced at Herschel who had pushed the door closed. "Best to leave him alone for a while. Let him calm down."

Milt nodded, then glanced down the hall where Annie and Millie had retreated.

What a mess. How could a father say such things to his daughter?

Chapter 25

Annie stood in the kitchen watching Millie make coffee. Mrs. Rice had gone to bed so the two were alone.

"How often..." Annie fought to control her voice. "How often is he like this?"

"Not often," Millie flashed a smile over her shoulder. "I imagine all this talk of the war and Joe has stirred him up again."

"Then he's better when I'm not around."

Millie left the stove and crossed the room to Annie. "Don't blame yourself."

"But I do. And he blames me...for everything." Annie blinked hard, fighting the tears.

"Here, sit down." Millie pushed Annie toward a chair, and Annie obediently sank into it.

Millie pulled up another chair and sat beside her. "Now you listen to me. It wasn't your fault that Peter died. And it certainly wasn't your fault about Joe."

Millie hesitated and Annie knew all the talk had upset Millie too. She took Annie's hand and continued. "Joe made his own decisions. He joined ROTC. Then he went into the Army. He wanted to." She sighed. "He wanted to serve, to help win the war."

It was Annie's turn to squeeze Millie's hand. "I know. It's just..."

"It's just that your father can't accept it. Oh, I

know how he felt about Joe. Like Joe was his son, not ours." She waved her hand around. "All this. This house. His other property. His plans for the future. All built around Joe."

Annie nodded. She knew. She'd heard her father talk. "Even though it wasn't what Joe wanted."

"Your father doesn't listen to anyone but himself. He gets these things in his head and there's no changing him."

"Except that Joe got killed." Annie added. "He can't change that."

"No, he can't. He can't accept it either." Her voice broke. "It's hard for all of us to accept."

"Oh, Aunt Millie." Annie reached out and hugged her aunt. Tears streamed down both of their faces.

After a few moments Annie spoke again. "I'm sorry. I thought it would help to have Milt come here and answer some of your questions. I was wrong."

Her aunt's head flew up. "No. You were right. It's what we need. To understand." She pulled a handkerchief from her pocket and dabbed at her eyes. "It's better to know than not know."

"Are you sure?"

"Oh, yes. Herschel, asking all those questions. Trying to picture in his mind what Joe went through. And me, just talking about Joe, remembering. Yes, it helps."

"And what about Father?"

"It'll help him, too. He has to face reality. Joe isn't coming back. Nothing he can do, nothing he can say, will change that."

Annie nodded.

The coffee started to boil, and Aunt Millie got up

to adjust it.

"And Mother?" Annie barely breathed the question.

"Ethel's in her own world."

Millie came back to Annie's side. "She deals with Joe's death the same way she dealt with Peter's. She pretends. She somehow fantasizes an explanation of what happened, where they are, and she just goes on."

"I was afraid Milt being here, all this talk, would upset her."

"Perhaps. But she's chosen to focus on the entertaining. Enjoys having a guest in the house. If we can calm your father down, then Ethel will be all right."

Annie stood and went to the window, gazing out into the darkness. She turned back to her aunt, glancing at the door to make sure they were alone.

"Did you ever hear anything from Joe's wife?"

Aunt Millie stared at her, a frown wrinkling her brow. Finally, she shook her head. "No."

"Did you write to her again?"

"We wrote several times," Aunt Millie spat out. "Not a word. The last letter was returned undeliverable." She turned back to face the stove. An uneasy silence filled the room. Finally, she spoke again. "Why would you ask about her?"

"I thought about trying to find her."

Aunt Millie whirled around. "What?"

"Just to talk to her. To try to find out more about Joe. About what happened in New York, before he left."

Aunt Millie stared at the floor in silence.

"Don't you want to know?"

She reached around and turned off the eye under

the percolator, then came over and sat down again. Annie followed suit and sat beside her.

Their gazes met and Aunt Millie took a deep breath before speaking. "We wrote to the Army, about Joe's life insurance." She looked down at her hands clasped in her lap. "They sent a letter saying that his wife had filed for it. She was the beneficiary, and they paid the money to her."

That meant the Joe had changed his beneficiary after he married. "Did they tell you where she was?"

Millie shook her head. "Herschel called them, after we got the letter. They wouldn't tell him anything. Said it was private. Said there was nothing we could do. The paperwork was all in order."

This fact only reinforced the family's belief that the woman had taken advantage of Joe. That some gold-digger had gotten a lonely soldier about to go overseas to marry her so she could get his money, his pay if he lived, his life insurance if he didn't. Somehow Annie didn't see Joe falling for someone like that. He'd been too sensible. But neither could she see him falling for a girl from New York City. Joe was a southern boy through and through.

Annie was the one who wanted answers. Joe had asked her to welcome his wife into the family. She'd let him down. She had done nothing to try to contact her, to get to know her, or to make her part of the family.

Her obsession with getting information about Joe also included trying to find his wife so she could keep her promise to Joe.

****

Late in the night a sound from downstairs woke her. Was Milt having a nightmare?

190

She couldn't go back to sleep, so she went down to use the bathroom. Outside Milt's door she heard his voice, calling out in his sleep, and she stopped to listen.

It sounded like he was telling someone to hold on. If he'd been screaming, like she'd heard in the wards, she would go in and wake him.

In a few minutes his voice died down, and Annie decided that she shouldn't be listening. The man deserved some privacy. So what if he had nightmares. Lots of wounded soldiers had nightmares. There was nothing she could do about it.

Hadn't she done enough already? Bringing him here. Exposing him to her family, to their thirst for information about Joe. Uncle Herschel especially wanted to know everything. And he'd continued to probe, for more and more, keeping Milt up until late into the night.

Poor Milt. After this he had to face his own family. Would it be worse? Or would they welcome him with open arms, grateful that he was alive?

When he suggested this visit, she had feared what her father might do. And for some reason she'd asked him to call her Annie instead of Lt. McEwen. The title had kept him at a distance. Yet in her own home she couldn't imagine him using her formal title.

It didn't mean anything. Only a change in form of address. It didn't mean that they were any closer. Did it?

She returned to her own bed and pondered.

She would remain true to her self-imposed rule about not getting involved with men despite the temptations she'd encountered from sweet, persistent Sgt. Baker, from Charlie Cushman's promises and his repulsive proposition, from friendly, steady Brice Attwater, her father's choice, or even from Milt whose blue eyes shown with pain and anguish revealing deep but invisible scars.

Her experience with Leroy all those years ago had hardened her resolve. Men weren't to be trusted, no matter how nice, how sweet, how helpful they seemed. Not even their vulnerability could convince her that they didn't have ulterior motives, that they didn't want more from her than she was willing to give.

Leroy's memory brought tears. Not just because he had been killed in the Pacific, but because she'd had such hopes, such innocent dreams. She'd soared with excitement with him and he'd encouraged her, fed her dreams until they'd blazed like a bonfire.

He'd taken her to that club, arranged for her to sing with the band, showed her that she could chase her dream of being a professional singer and someday achieve it. She'd be forever grateful to him for that.

But that vivid memory was always followed by the other. The one that ripped her insides out. He'd transformed into someone she didn't even know. Into this belligerent drunk groping her body and ignoring her pleas to stop. He'd pushed her into things she wasn't ready for, all the while saying she owed him because he'd taken her where she'd wanted to go, and it was his last night before leaving for military training.

He had hurt her so deeply, then he'd deserted her to face her father's wrath alone.

Later, when Leroy came home on leave, she'd refused to speak to him. Something she'd always regret. Maybe if they had talked…maybe…

But her thoughts couldn't go there. They hadn't

and he was dead. Lost on some island in the South Pacific.

She wished she'd told him that she had forgiven him. But had she? No. She wasn't sure she would ever truly forgive him.

One thing was for sure. She'd never let anyone hurt her like that again.

Still, here alone in her familiar bed, aching loneliness returned. At work she was always busy, always had a purpose, but with her family her uselessness cut like broken glass. Being unwanted and unloved by the ones who should love her the most left an empty hole inside her. A hole she knew would never be filled. Not by a man, and perhaps, not by an audience. But those moments up on stage, applause roaring, came closer than anything ever had.

Chapter 26

"I promise I will let you know if I find out anything. Anything at all." Milt's final words to Herschel and Millie rang hollow in his ears. They'd probably never know what happened to their son.

He didn't want to go home and face his family. At least Annie had agreed to accompany him on the short train ride to Kerrville.

Before the war, his family, as well as the whole town, had said Milton Greenlee was going places, going to make a name in the big leagues, going to be a famous baseball player.

Only the war had come. And he'd joined the Army. An opportunity to be a hero, he'd thought. How naive he'd been. How totally ignorant.

There hadn't been any heroes where he had been, just men fighting for their lives and the lives of their fellow soldiers. He'd gotten a medal for that day in Troina, for taking out that machine gun nest, but he'd only done what he had to do to protect his men.

He barely remembered that day in Normandy, just his rage from seeing his buddies shot up. In the citation for the medal, they'd said he'd gone out beyond the lines, taken out a dozen Krauts including some high-ranking officer. Exhausted, he'd crawled back behind a hedgerow for cover. Ade said they didn't know how he survived in the midst of the enemy. Now he wondered

194

if he did survive or if someone else came home in his place.

Why did going home feel like another landing on an enemy held beach? At least there he could fight back. He couldn't fight the onslaught of his mother's worry, her hovering, smothering attentions that made him feel like a helpless infant. What would she do when she learned how truly helpless he was, unable to use his left arm and half blind in his left eye, not to mention the horrid scars?

His hearing on the left side had returned, mostly, just as they said it would. They said his vision would improve and adjust to being dependent on his right eye. Yet he couldn't catch a ball thrown right at him. He would learn, Sgt. Baker insisted. But it was Baker's job to encourage him, to get him to try harder, even when the task was impossible.

And what about Annie? Would he ever see her again? After this, she would head off to New York, to her new assignment, to her new career.

After meeting her family, he understood why she'd been so nervous and preoccupied. She hadn't wanted to go home any more than he did. But, like a moth to a flame, she'd gone. And, by doing so, she'd given them some understanding, something to help them deal with their loss. And he'd been a part of that.

"I'm not very good at writing," he confessed, breaking the silence between them.

"You don't have to write," she assured him.

"I want to…to stay in touch," he explained. "I just meant that my letters may be short." He hesitated. "When I have something to tell you…about your cousin, I mean."

"I appreciate you telling my aunt and uncle that, but you don't have to. I know how hard it is to find someone who was there. I've been asking around ever since I joined the Army."

"I didn't say before." He looked down at his hand rubbing his thigh back and forth as if the motion could calm his nerves. "I have a friend, over there, still fighting." He looked up into that angelic face, marred with worry. "I wrote to him, before we left Florida. Asked if he could find anyone who might have known Joe in Sicily."

Her eyes widened, softening the tight worry lines. "Do you think he can find someone?"

"If he can talk to some of the engineers, then maybe." He wanted to see her smile even if he had to make promises he couldn't keep. "Sure. He should be able to find someone." If he's still alive. He hated to think that his friend might be dead, but he knew enough about the battlefield to be realistic.

The side of her mouth quirked up in a half smile. "You didn't tell my aunt and uncle that, did you?"

He shook his head, caught in the empty promise.

"I appreciate you not getting their hopes up. I really do." The smile broadened. "You know it's a long shot, don't you?"

"Yeah," he admitted. "But it's worth a try."

Her hand covered his, stilling the back-and-forth motion. "Thank you." Her voice was a husky whisper, emotions threatening to break through.

He nodded in response and wished he could will his other hand to move, to take hers and hold it. Instead, he sat, impotent, unable to return her gesture.

****

He'd told her about writing his friend. The least she could do was to come clean about Joe.

"I have a confession to make, too." she stated, avoiding eye contact.

"What?" His tone revealed his apprehension.

"I didn't tell you everything about Joe." She plunged ahead into uncharted waters, hoping he didn't feel betrayed by her withholding information. "He was married."

She chanced a glance at his face to gauge his reaction. He stared straight ahead, his expression unreadable.

"You see," she continued in a rush. "He met a girl in New York City, just a few days before he shipped out. And they got married."

He turned and those blue eyes met hers. "Okay. It happens. Guys are lonesome, going overseas. Don't know if they'll come back."

"Exactly." She nodded, grateful he understood. "She knew all that, and she was nice to him and convinced him to marry her."

"Maybe they fell in love."

"In love? In just a few days? No." She shook her head emphatically. "Not Joe. He was smarter than that. He wouldn't have fallen for some…some," she hated to use the language her father had used, but in this case it fit. "Some floozy."

"Did you meet her? Did someone tell you that about her?" He looked away. "I've seen the type of girl you're talking about." His gaze returned to hers. "I've also seen soldiers fall head over heels for a girl the first time they laid eyes on each other. Anything is possible."

"I don't believe in those quickie romances. Just because we're in a war doesn't mean people change their behavior."

Milt shrugged.

"Anyway," she continued. "None of us met her. He wrote Aunt Millie and Uncle Herschel, and he wrote me. He told us about meeting her…and marrying her." She grabbed his hand and held it tightly in both of hers. "How could he do that? How could he fall for some…some girl from New York City? Someone he barely knew?"

How could she explain? Milt hadn't known Joe. Hadn't known how proud he was of his southern heritage. How he loved the genteel ways of southern women. He had described the kind of girl he was looking for, a soft-spoken Tennessee girl who could cook southern style. He wouldn't settle for a fast-talking New Yorker unless he was really, really lonesome.

"You never know." He looked down at her hand in his.

She followed his gaze. Self-conscious at holding his hand, she pulled away and cleared her throat.

"Well, anyway, my aunt and uncle tried to contact her. They wrote several times, but she never answered. Not even after he died."

"Oh," he responded.

"Aunt Millie told me that they contacted the Army and found out that she collected his life insurance money." She drew a deep, calming breath before continuing. "So, it seems that all she cared about was the money. She's probably already found her another poor sucker."

"I'm sorry." He sat quietly, not offering any further comments on love.

"Me too."

Yet the feeling still nagged at her. In his letter Joe asked her to make his wife feel like part of the family, to get his parents to accept her. Did he really want her to find his wife? Or was it her own morbid curiosity?

Joe had been a good judge of character who wouldn't have fallen for some obviously cheap gold-digger. No. Either the woman was a very good actress, or something was very wrong. And Annie needed to know which.

Chapter 27

"Miltie." his mother's excited voice called out just as he stepped down from the train.

She ran up to him and threw her arms around him, almost knocking him over. "Oh, son. My dear son."

He struggled to get his balance. "Mother…"

"Don't crush the boy," his father chided from behind her.

His mother released her hold. She pulled back and looked him over, smiling like a kid with a new toy. The smile quickly vanished as she took in the bandage on his head, the scars, and the cast on his arm. "Oh, you poor thing. My poor baby."

He focused on his father and forced a smile. "I didn't expect both of you to come."

"On an occasion like this?" His father took the suitcase from the conductor, but his gaze never left his son's face. "Our son coming home from the war? We should have arranged for a band and a parade."

He could hear the strain beneath the forced cheerfulness.

"Oh, no," Milt protested, pulling his good hand free from his mother's grasp. The very thought of so much attention made him cringe. "I couldn't handle that."

He caught a glimpse of Annie. She stood back a few feet from them and watched the family reunion unfold.

"There's someone I want you to meet." He nodded in her direction.

On cue Annie moved closer, that captivating smile on her face. Her beauty hit him like a line drive slamming into his glove. He froze in place unable to speak.

She must have sensed he was off-balance, because she extended her hand to his father.

"Hello. I'm Lt. Annie McEwen, Milt's...I mean Sgt. Greenlee's nurse."

"We didn't realize he needed a nurse to bring him home." His mother's voice wavered with concern.

"His doctor thought he should have an escort," she smiled reassuringly as she shook his father's hand. "He made it fine, though. I'm sure he could have done it on his own."

Milt appreciated how tactfully she handled his parents. Now it was his turn to explain.

"It was Lt. McEwen's family that I visited in Chattanooga. She was kind enough to volunteer to escort me the rest of the way home."

"Thank you for watching after our boy," his father said.

His mother took Annie's hand in hers. "Yes, my dear. Thank you for being so kind." She then transferred her attention back to him. "We'd better get you on home. You must be tired."

His father reached for the small bag Annie held. "Let me take your bag, too?"

"Oh, this is Sgt. Greenlee's." She smiled. "I'm catching the next train back to Chattanooga, so I didn't bring one."

"That'll be hours, won't it, James?"

His father pulled out his pocket watch and nodded. "Yes. Almost four hours, if it's on time."

"Well, you can't wait here." His mother placed her hand on Annie's back. "You just come along with us. Have lunch. Visit a while. We'll get you back in time to catch the train."

"Of course," his father agreed. "Run along and get in the car. I'll just tell the ticket agent to expect you back."

They loaded into his father's sedan. His mother climbed into the back with him, so Annie got in the front.

"How was your trip?" his mother asked.

"Fine." He gazed out the window at the familiar buildings.

"And your stopover in Chattanooga? Did the Lieutenant's family appreciate your visit?"

Milt detected the slightest tinge of disapproval in her voice. "Yes. It went fine. They were very nice and seemed grateful to hear what little I could tell them."

They drove through town toward the big house on the hill.

"Did you ever get that spur built?" His father had worked incessantly to get the railroad to build a spur to the factory to facilitate loading and unloading freight away from the station where passengers had boarded for almost a hundred years.

"Yes, we did. I thought I wrote you about that."

"Maybe you did. I don't remember." So much was a blur.

He took in his small hometown as they drove down Main Street with its assortment of store-front businesses. The sturdy brick building that housed the Greenlee Shoe Factory stood back toward where the railroad ran almost through the town itself. They passed the Methodist and Baptist churches on opposite sides of the street. A mixture of homes stood beyond the churches. More houses of varying size littered the hillsides surrounding the narrow valley.

Just visible down a side street, the sprawling three-story boarding house his aunt ran stood across the street from his grandmother's home. Beyond there the street climbed to the hill-top cemetery where his ancestors rested, both from before his time and the more recently departed, still overseeing the town and its rising and ebbing fortunes.

The town probably looked like a small village to Annie. He'd never thought about what this little town looked like to a stranger. Probably small and provincial, especially to a girl who grew up in Chattanooga.

His father made the turn into the drive that wound its way up the hill. His father liked to say that from his front porch he could oversee all his business interests. And they were many. James Greenlee owned at least half the town and employed most of the workers.

Milt's grandfather had come to Kerrville at the turn of the century. He'd purchased the then booming lime business with its mines and kilns and coopers. By the time his father took over, the lime business was in decline, so he'd transformed the old warehouse into a shoe factory, purchased and rejuvenated downtown real estate, joined the bank's board of directors, and invested in various other enterprises. One of the few who had funds during the depression, his father had bought up farms and businesses in foreclosure.

Some in town resented the Greenlee's. But others, who stayed on as tenant farmers, appreciated having a place to live and work. During those lean years, a few local businesses stayed afloat thanks to private loans from his father. Milt had learned that having money in a small town was a mixed blessing, especially for a boy growing up.

As soon as his father opened the car door, the piercing cry of a baby reached his ears. He hadn't expected the cry even though he knew his older sister, Suzanne, and her children were living here.

Inside the back hallway, the screaming filled the house.

"What on earth is the matter?" his mother asked Suzanne who stood holding the squirming, squalling child.

"Oh, he's mad because I won't give him his bottle. But it's not time."

His mother reached out to take the unhappy child. "Where's Josie?"

"She went to change Sammy's clothes after he wet himself…again. I don't think he'll ever learn."

Milt absorbed the unfamiliar scene. He'd never been around babies and hadn't thought about how loud they could be.

Suzanne finally noticed her brother. "Oh, Miltie." She came over and threw her arms around him in what felt like a genuine, heartfelt hug. "Welcome home." She released him.

She gave him a once-over like she was taking an inventory of his injuries and comparing what she saw to what she'd been told. "Are you all right?" she asked.

"Sure," Milt answered. "I'm fine." But he was

anything but fine. Her perusal made him want to squirm like the infant his mother held. At least the child had calmed down, distracted by his grandmother's cooing baby talk.

"Here he is," announced his father.

Milt turned just in time to see the small boy running towards them.

"That can't be Sammy." When he'd gone overseas the boy hadn't even been born.

"That's Sammy all right," his father replied. "And the unhappy one in your mother's arms is Dalton."

Although his mother had managed to quiet the baby, he looked like he could resume his loud protestations at any moment.

"Master Milton. So good to have you home."

Milt spun around to see Josie's smiling face. The woman had worked for his family for as long as he could remember. He gave her a one-armed hug, which was the best he could do. "Josie." He wanted to say more but his throat had tightened with emotion.

She patted his back. "Our little boy back from the war."

He pulled away and nodded.

"And now we have two more little boys. Fine little boys." She stepped past him and took the baby from his mother's arms. "Now what's the matter, little man. Are you hungry?"

"He saw his bottle. And, of course, he screamed for it," Suzanne explained. "You need to put those where he can't see them." She turned to her brother, as if she owed him an explanation. "It's better to keep them on a strict schedule."

"Yes'm." Josie headed toward the kitchen. "Come

on, Sammy. We'll get you something, too."

The small boy followed her through the kitchen door. Milt marveled at Josie's way with children.

Suzanne called after her. "They get not one bite to eat until it's time. It's all written down on their schedule."

"Yes'm," Josie repeated.

Suzanne's gaze found Annie still standing in the open doorway. "Who's this?"

Milt turned around. He held out his hand to beckon Annie forward. "This is Lt. Annie McEwen. She brought me home."

Annie extended her hand to his sister. "This is my sister, Suzanne. And those are her kids." He looked around to find his mother.

"Nice to meet you," Annie said.

"She's his nurse." His mother stood behind him so he couldn't see her face, but he could hear the concern in her voice.

"Can't we just go in and sit down?" he asked. He hated having to explain everything over and over.

"I'll take your bags up to your room," his father said.

"That's all right. We can take them up later."

"But you must be tired, Dear. Don't you want to rest after that train ride?" his mother interjected.

"No, I'm fine." Milt tried to be patient, but he could see it would be a challenge.

As he followed his father down the hall, he glanced back over his shoulder just in time to catch his mother's pained look before she shook her head and turned away. Her pity was palpable. And he hated it.

He hated being helpless and he hated being pitied.

Annie didn't see him as helpless, didn't pity him. Maybe she wasn't interested in him the way he was in her, but she did treat him as an adult. Even her slightly crazy family had treated him as an adult, though a damaged one. Why must his mother treat him like a child?

****

"Have a seat," Milt's father insisted.

The room felt cozy. Large and well-used, yet cozy. The furniture was modern and comfortable in warm, relaxing colors with splashes of bright here and there. Family photographs lined the mantel and adorned tables around the room. A large ash tray stood beside the chair Mr. Greenlee settled into after making sure his son was comfortable.

Milt's mother sank into the cushioned couch beside her. "We'll have some lunch shortly. Just some sandwiches. Nothing fancy."

"That sounds nice," Annie replied.

"We've planned a welcome-home dinner for Miltie tonight. We'd love for you to stay." She patted Annie's hand as her gaze drifted toward Milt.

The lady obviously doted on her son, maybe a little too much.

"I'm sorry, but I must get back," Annie said.

"Lt. McEwen has to go back to her family," Milt explained. "Then she's being reassigned."

Annie's head jerked around to face him. She hadn't corrected the story she'd told the Lieutenant on the train, so Milt still believed she was going to New York. She should tell him the truth, yet the lie created a distance between them she needed. It was cowardly to tell a lie rather than the truth. It wasn't fair but leading

207

him on wasn't fair either.

Suzanne paced restlessly. Her gaze darted from Milt to her mother, then back. "I'll go check on the children," she finally said before leaving the room.

"Check on lunch, too," Mrs. Greenlee called after her.

"So, son, how long will you be home?" Milt's father asked.

"A couple of weeks." Milt's awkwardness intensified around the family he'd been away from for so long.

"That's not very long. But I suppose it will be long enough to look around. I want to show you the factory and the machine shop we've set up."

"Sure, Pop." Milt didn't sound very enthusiastic.

"Andy should be home soon," his mother interjected.

"Isn't he in school?"

"Only mornings. He comes home at lunch then goes to the factory." Mr. Greenlee beamed with pride.

Annie wondered how many siblings Milt had. He'd mentioned a sister overseas in the WAC's and Suzanne here. This Andy must be his brother.

"Olivia is coming in from school for the weekend," his mother added. "We'll all be together." She beamed.

"Except for Katherine," Milt spoke up.

"Well, of course." Mrs. Greenlee turned to Annie. "Katherine is our other daughter. She's in England."

"In the Women's Army Corps. I think I told you about her."

"Yes," Annie nodded. "You did."

Just then a voice came from the back of the house. "Is he here?"

A teenage boy burst into the room.

Milt stood as the boy ran towards him. Pushing aside Milt's offered hand, the boy grabbed him into a bear hug. "Oh, man. It's swell to have you home."

That gorgeous grin spread across Milt's face. "Kid, you've grown up on me."

The two separated. "Sure, I have." A matching grin lit up the younger face. "Good to have you home."

Suzanne appeared in the doorway. "Della say's lunch is ready."

The happy family group, all talking at once, moved in a single direction.

"We've been eating in the breakfast room for some time now," Mrs. Greenlee offered in way of explanation. "I hope you don't mind."

"Of course not," Annie replied. Why would she mind?

"Lunch around here is simple fare. Sandwiches, potato salad. That sort of thing."

They'd made their way into a fair-sized room dominated by a round table laden with food. Smells and sounds emanated from the kitchen nearby.

Mrs. Greenlee sat on Milt's left, his damaged side, and his father sat to his right. Mrs. Greenlee pointed Annie to the seat on her other side.

Had she noticed Annie's feelings toward Milt? Or was she being merely polite?

Annie watched the family interact, fascinated by the warmth between them.

Mrs. Greenlee discretely filled Milt's plate, a sandwich neatly cut in half easily held in one hand, potato salad, and slices of tomato. The cook placed a glass of iced tea by each person's plate. She too exchanged comments with family members as if she were one of them.

Suzanne divided her attention between the baby sitting in a wooden highchair pulled up near the table on one side of her and the small boy they called Sammy on her other side. He sat on a box in a regular wooden chair and could barely reach his plate. Andy, on the other side of Sammy, ignored the boy. Instead, he inhaled his food while maintaining a constant stream of chatter.

"You should see the girls' softball team. They've got the league wrapped up this year. Thelma Atchison's batting 340. Can you believe that? You'll have to come watch them play."

"Wasn't she the little blonde who lived out on Raymond Road?" Milt asked.

"That's her. Only she's not so little anymore."

"How'd the boys team do?"

"Rotten. All the good players joined up. They don't even have that league you played in anymore. Nobody left to play."

Mrs. Greenlee leaned over toward Annie. "I can't believe he's home," she whispered. "We've prayed for this day and now he's here."

Annie washed down a bite of chicken sandwich with the tea and smiled. "I'm happy for you."

"How long will they keep him in the hospital?"

"I'm not sure. I expect he'll have to undergo some more procedures." Annie forced herself to look directly into the concerned face. "They don't really tell us nurses what's planned for each patient. That's the doctor's job."

"But they will take good care of him?"

"Yes, ma'am. They will."

Milt turned in his chair so he could look at them, apparently aware that they were talking about him.

"I'll be fine, Mother." His words were confident, but his tone implied his impatience.

The older woman smiled and patted him on the arm. "I know you will, dear."

Mr. Greenlee took over the conversation and told of Andy's work in the factory. From there the conversation drifted to local people, who'd married, who was sick, who'd died.

Annie marveled at the dynamics of this large family. They all had different interests, yet they got along. No, they more than got along. They loved each other.

She'd never experienced anything like it and couldn't help wondering if this is what her father had wanted. A big family. If her mother had been able, would Annie have been one of many siblings vying for attention while supporting each other at the same time? Would there have been this loving feeling around the table in her house?

She'd never know. She was the only one left and her father didn't want her.

She watched Mrs. Greenlee pick up her youngest grandchild and cradle him in her arms.

Five children of her own and already two grandchildren.

Her own mother would dote on grandchildren-or would she? Would she fear they would take from her the attention she craved? Her father would take charge of them. He'd run their lives from the day they were born, scheming and plotting to get what he wanted. No.

Her family would never have been like this one. No matter how many children had lived.

Soon after lunch, Annie said goodbye to the Greenlee family. Milt followed her out to the car.

"Thank you, for everything," he said quietly.

She took his good hand in hers. "Thank you. For talking with my family. I know it was hard."

"No. It was okay." He paused looking at the ground. "I'll let you know if I hear anything. I'm no good at writing but…"

She squeezed his hand. "Sure. We'll be in touch. One way or another." Somehow, she knew she'd see him in Atlanta. She just couldn't bring herself to tell him. Not now. Let him think she'd be gone, far away. Unreachable. Then maybe this nurse-crush thing he had going would fade.

"You'll have to send me your new address when you get to New York."

She nodded and stared straight ahead. Her plans hadn't changed. And there was no room in them for a man. Not now. Not ever. Yet somehow, she didn't feel the conviction she once had. And that scared her.

She climbed into the front seat. Before she closed the door, she reminded him, "Don't forget to contact your doctor right away and give him the orders for changing that bandage."

Chapter 28

His father led the way to his old, familiar room and placed his suitcase beside the bed. Memories of a different person in a different time flooded back.

"It's pretty much the way you left it. Your mother had Josie clean it and put fresh sheets on the bed." He pulled open a drawer in the chest. "Your old clothes are still here. You look like you might be able to wear some of them." He pushed the drawer closed.

Milt fingered the baseball and glove on the desk. A pang of sorrow clinched his gut.

No more baseball. Never again.

"Son," his father broke into his memories. "If you need any help, your mother…"

"No," Milt barked. "I don't want her waiting on me…like I was a child."

"I know." But he didn't sound like he understood.

Milt looked his father in the eye. "I want you or Andy to help me. Not her." It wasn't a question of if he needed help. He still struggled to dress himself with one hand, and bathing would be more difficult in a house without a shower.

He suddenly felt extremely awkward. He'd gotten used to it in the hospital with an orderly or another patient always nearby to help. And even letting Annie help him had seemed normal somehow. Yet here in his own home, his pulse pounded from the awkward embarrassment.

His father nodded. "All right. If that's what you want."

Milt turned away. He could still feel his father's gaze, feel the questions. He had to change the subject.

"Where's Andy, anyway? Did he leave?"

His father sighed as if resigned to the distance his son had created. "Yes. He's probably already gone down to the factory. He usually spends the afternoons there."

"From your letters I take it he's doing well." Milt turned to face his father, leaning back against the dresser for support. "Already running the factory."

His father smiled at that comment. "He's not really running it, not yet. I have a manager for that. But Andy's really taken to the business. Got a good head for figures, that boy."

Milt nodded. "I'm glad." His younger brother would be able to take over the family business. Something Milt would never be able to do, even if he wanted to.

His father went to the door. "You get some rest before dinner. And tomorrow, I'll take you around. Show you what we've got going on."

"Okay," Milt nodded. When the door shut, he let out a sigh and closed his eyes. He was tired. So tired.

He picked up his bag and moved it to the corner by the dresser, letting it fall to the floor with a thud. Then he stretched out on the familiar mattress. In the quiet dimness he allowed his mind to drift back, into the past. To a time when his biggest worry was getting to practice on time.

****

Annie arrived back in Chattanooga in late afternoon. She went by the hospital where she had trained to be a nurse and visited with old friends before heading back up the mountain.

The setting sun cast deep shadows across the street as she climbed up the steps from the incline and walked slowly toward her home.

She'd needed to stay away today, needed the distance and the reminder of her independence. She was no longer a child but so often, in that house, she felt small and helpless.

The light was almost gone when she pushed the gate open and strode up the walk. A whiff of cigar smoke told her she wasn't alone, although she couldn't see her father in the shadows. She tensed and focused on reaching the door, not wanting an encounter with him.

"It won't work." Her father's voice boomed out of the darkness.

She stopped abruptly. "What?"

"Your scheme. Bringing that soldier here. All shot up. Try to make us feel better...about Joe."

He wasn't drunk, thank goodness. Yet his voice bore his disdain for her.

How could she respond without antagonizing him?

"Is that the best you can do for a boyfriend?" he continued. "You think because he's only half a man he won't hurt you?"

She stiffened. Her teeth ground together to stifle a smart reply, refusing to rise to the bait. After long seconds she allowed herself to speak.

"Milt is...was a patient, a friend. He was in Sicily, and I thought Uncle Herschel and Aunt Millie would like talking to him. So they would know what it was like there…for Joe."

"He didn't know Joe," her father spat out.

"No, but…"

"You thought someone like that could take Joe's place. Well, he can't. No one can."

She didn't dare say that Joe took Peter's place, not to her father, so she remained silent.

"Joe's gone. Period." He hesitated a moment before muttering, almost to himself, "Just like Peter."

Her throat tightened. She didn't want to go there, didn't want to dredge up those awful memories from that awful day.

She forced herself to breathe and forced her thoughts into the present.

His footsteps moved closer, but he remained in the shadows, his cigar smoke drifting in a cloud beneath the porch roof.

"This big house. Humph. What a waste." He stepped out of the shadow only a few feet away. "We planned to fill it with children. Boys, full of life, running up and down the stairs, playing games in the yard." His voice trailed off and he took a puff of his cigar before continuing. "But Ethel couldn't do it. Couldn't give me the sons I wanted. That frail, empty-headed woman couldn't even watch over Peter. Let you chase him over that cliff."

He loomed over her like he had at seven years old. His ominous presence accusing her of causing her brother's death. She wanted to melt into the porch, to disappear into nothingness, bearing the weight of his disapproval.

"So now I am left with only you." His voice was

quiet but lethal.

She couldn't look at him, couldn't meet his eyes.

After a moment of staring at her, he turned and took a few steps, as if, this time, he needed to put some distance between them.

"So now, there is no one to carry on the McEwen name. No McEwen males to carry on the line. No legacy for the future."

She steeled herself. "I'm going in." She took two steps and turned the knob. The heavy door swung inward. She half expected him to say something more, some cutting, hurtful remark as she made her escape, but he said nothing.

He'd already said enough.

She hurried up the stairs to her room, not wanting to see anyone. She eased the door shut and flung herself across the bed, letting the tears she'd been fighting come until they built into heart-wrenching sobs.

The only one left. The one they didn't want. The one they'd never wanted. Neither of them. Not her father nor her mother. She wanted to get away from this place, to go back to work, to sing, and forget what he'd said, forget the hurt deep inside her.

****

Aromas from the kitchen drifted up to the second floor. Milt's stomach growled in anticipation. He made his way down the ornate wooden staircase, his fingers sliding along the smooth surface of the banister. On the landing he grasped the newel post like he'd done so many times before. Below in the foyer the pendulum on the big wall clock swung back and forth, each tick marking time. A feeling of contentment settled around him. It was good to be home.

In the formal dining room, his sister Suzanne put last minute touches on the table.

"Doing it up fancy, I see," he commented.

She looked up. "Yes. In honor of your homecoming. Mother's had a special meal prepared. All your favorites."

He walked around the table. "Good. I'm starved." He counted the places and mentally did a head count. "Who's coming besides the family?"

"Grandmother Kerr."

He nodded his understanding. "I guess it is a special occasion."

"Don't start," his sister warned.

"I'm just surprised Father would agree to it. Have they called a truce?"

"Something like that." She glanced around the room as if looking for something. Her gaze settled on the sideboard where a serving tray rested. "There it is," she murmured to herself.

"When do we eat?" he asked.

"That's what I want to know."

Milton whirled around at the sound of another familiar voice. "Grandma!" He hurried to her outstretched arms.

"My boy." She hugged him. "So good to have you home."

"Good to be home." And he really meant it.

She reached up and gently touched the left side of his face, just below the bandage. "My poor boy."

He looked away. "It's okay. Don't worry about it." But the spell was broken. He pictured himself the way she must have seen him and inwardly cringed.

"Mother, you're here."

His mother's voice came from behind him. He turned his head enough to see her coming from the kitchen carrying a bowl. Suzanne followed with another.

"Perfect timing." She placed the bowl on the table. "Miltie, go tell your father that dinner is ready. He and Andy should be in his study."

"Sure thing." He was grateful for something to do to escape from his grandmother's pity.

He made his way to his father's sanctuary, as the older man liked to call it. Through the partially open door, Milt heard voices. He tapped on the wood and peeked inside. A ledger lay open on the desk in front of his father. Andy stood looking over the older man's shoulder.

His father looked up. "Dinner must be ready."

"Yes. Mother sent me to tell you."

Closing the book, he stood.

Andy stared at Milt.

Uneasy under his younger brother's close scrutiny, Milt averted his gaze.

What did he see?

The ugly cast encasing his useless left arm, that had been hidden under his coat, was now exposed hanging in the OD green sling. His shirt sleeve had been cut away at the shoulder to accommodate the cast on his upper arm.

To break the awkward silence Milt blurted out, "So, Andy, how was your afternoon at the factory?"

"Okay," Andy stammered. "Same as always."

"I'm hoping you two can spend some time together," his father intervened. "You haven't seen each other in…what…two years?"

"Longer," Milt said. "More like two and a half."

Andy moved closer and gave Milt a good once-over. "I...uh...didn't want to ask you before, in front of Mother, about your injuries...I mean. They told me you were hurt, but nobody would say exactly what..."

"Yeah, I know." Milt tried to keep it light. "Just a bum arm," he patted his left arm with his right hand, feeling the plaster encased object as if it didn't belong to him. "And this." He pointed to his bandaged head.

Part of him wished the bandage extended over the left side of his face, hiding the whole ugly mess. That would be far better than facing the stares and the pity.

His brother, just like everyone else, was curious about how he got hurt and how long it would take him to recover. If the scars would remain red and angry or fade in time. He didn't have answers for any of their questions, not now, maybe never.

"We'd better get in there. Your mother has no patience for latecomers." His father herded them out of the study and closed the door behind them.

Andy took the lead, glancing back over his shoulder as he went.

Tension coiled in Milt's gut knowing that every member of his family would be watching him. Oh, they'd be discreet about it, but they would watch his every move nonetheless.

Milt took the place his mother indicated on his father's left. Andy sat on his left between Milt and their mother, who sat at the other end. Grandmother Kerr and Suzanne sat across from him. Milt noticed that his maternal grandmother had been seated next to her daughter rather than beside his father who had never gotten along with her. Tonight, they seemed to be tolerating each other.

Della, the cook, placed a platter of ham slices in front of his father's place. "I'll get the bread and you'll be all set," she smiled and nodded at Milt. "So good to have you home."

"Thank you, Della. It all looks great." Della had been their cook for years. He'd often thought of her when his mother sent cookies. Other men's mothers baked for them. He always knew that Della was the one who produced his goodies. He reminded himself to make a point of thanking her.

"Here son, let me fill your plate." His father reached for Milt's plate.

"No," Milt stopped him. "I can do it." Too late he realized how sharp he sounded. Before he could rephrase his father nodded.

"All right. I just wanted to help."

"I'm sorry." Milt felt the eyes on him. "I'm used to doing things for myself, that's all."

"Certainly." The older man covered the awkward moment by reaching for a bowl of mashed potatoes Suzanne held out for him.

Milt stabbed a piece of ham with his fork and placed it on his plate. Then he reached out and lifted the heavy platter with his right hand, grateful for the exercises Lloyd had insisted on, and passed it to Andy. His mother said something, trying to get a conversation going, as they passed the food around. Milt tried to follow what they were saying but he quickly saw that he needed to focus on the dishes or he'd end up dropping something. He carefully took each dish, placed it on the table by his plate, spooned some of its contents onto his plate, then picked the dish up and passed it on.

So far so good. No mishaps.

He reached out for his glass of tea and took a long sip.

"Milt." Andy's voice broke through his concentration.

Milt turned to face his brother. "Yeah?"

"I asked you if you wanted the butter." Milt sensed his brother's irritation.

"Oh…I guess I didn't hear you." Although the hearing in his left ear had returned, he still had trouble sometimes. He had failed to mention this to anyone in his family. Another short-coming to get used to.

Milt reached across with his right hand and took the butter dish. Having an immobile left arm encased in plaster made the motion a little difficult. It was much easier when they passed him things from his right. He glanced around to see if anyone noticed. They all appeared to be concentrating on their food, but he knew they were keenly aware of his every move.

Just eat, he told himself. Get through this meal. It'll get easier once they get used to you.

"How long will you be home?" His grandmother's question drew his attention away from his fears.

"I have a two-week furlough. Then I report back."

"Will you be going all the way back to Florida?" She continued. "Don't they have any hospitals closer?"

"Actually, I'll be reporting to a hospital in Atlanta."

"In Georgia?" his sister asked, her interest piqued by the mention of her husband's home state.

"Yep." His gaze returned to his plate. He grabbed the cornbread muffin, intent on buttering it before it cooled. He glanced at his knife, then at the butter dish and realized that he couldn't hold the muffin and butter it at the same time. If he cut it, he'd have to place it on his plate, then pick up the knife, cut the muffin in half and try to spread butter on it one-handed. He wasn't ready for that. No. He'd eat the cornbread without butter.

He bit into the warm bread. It was delicious. No one in the Army, or anywhere else, made cornbread like Della.

"Do you want me to butter that for you?" His mother pushed her chair back and started to get up.

"No," he almost shouted. "I...I'd rather eat it like this." He looked around at all the faces staring back at him and forced a smile. "Not used to eating so much rich food, not in the Army."

His mother settled back in her seat and eyed him suspiciously. Thankfully she didn't say any more.

He continued to eat, slowly, tasting the potatoes, the vegetables. He cut the fresh, ripe tomato slice with his fork and carefully took a bite, savoring its taste. The Army didn't serve homegrown tomatoes, either. He avoided the thick slice of ham in the center of his plate, knowing he couldn't cut it. He loved ham and his mother knew it. She'd had Della cook it just for him. He didn't want to hurt either of their feelings by not eating it. Yet he couldn't bring himself to ask someone to cut it up for him.

It had been one thing to have someone cut up his meat when he was in the hospital where there were so many who needed help. He'd been one of the more able-bodied patients compared to ones who'd lost both arms, or the ones whose faces had been blown away.

Those guys would be eating through straws for a long time, until the doctors could rebuild their faces. So, Milt's injuries seemed like they weren't so bad.

Right here, right now with his family looking on, he felt like a freak.

He put his fork down and drew a shaky breath.

"Are you all right, son?" his father asked.

Milt fought the urge to scream at him, at all of them. Instead, he slowly shook his head.

"I...I'm not that hungry." He pushed his chair away from the table. "Please, excuse me."

As he stood, his napkin dropped to the floor. Rather than pick it up, he glanced at his father's worried face, desperate for understanding.

Then he strode out of the room without looking back.

Chapter 29

His father found him under one of the maple trees he'd helped plant when he was still in knee pants. He stood with his head only inches from the young tree's spreading branches, gazing out over the town below and wondering what he would do when he came home for good.

"Your mother said to tell you that she left a plate for you in the icebox. In case you get hungry later tonight."

Milt turned to the older man. Even in the darkness, the worry lines creased his face. "I'm sorry I walked out."

"No harm done. We know it's hard for you. You've been away for a long time. You've seen a lot and done a lot since you left us." He reached up and snatched a small branch, examining the leaves.

Milt stepped out into the moonlight, swinging a stick he'd picked up earlier. "I really made a mess of things, didn't I?"

"Oh, it was just dinner. They'll get over it."

"I don't mean that. I mean this." His sweeping gesture indicated his left side. "All I was ever good at was athletics. Baseball. Basketball. Track. What am I going to do now?"

"You'll figure it out. Things will work themselves out, you'll see."

"Ha." Anger bubbled up again. "That's easy for you to say. You're so smart, so good at everything you do." He took a swing at the tree trunk, hitting it with a whack.

"Son…" The calm voice expressed his concern.

"I know I should be grateful to be alive. And I am. It's just…if I were like other guys, who don't have to struggle to read or to work the simplest arithmetic problems, then it wouldn't matter so much."

"I know you counted on playing ball. But there are other things you can do."

"What? I haven't just lost the use of my arm, you know. My eye's never going to be right." He paced back and forth to calm himself. "I can't even catch a ball. I've tried. I couldn't be a coach, if that's what you're thinking. How could I teach kids to play the game if I can't do it myself?"

"There are other things."

"Yeah, sure. Go into the business. What could I do? Stand around and watch people work? What about all the paperwork?"

"That's what secretaries and bookkeepers are for." His father sounded like he'd had enough of Milt's pity party. "Now I don't want to hear any more of this. Things will work out. You just have to believe that."

His father placed his hand on Milt's shoulder. The little boy in him wanted his father's arms around him. Wanted…no needed, to hear those words…That it would be all right, somehow. Instead, he stepped away, out of his father's reach, denying himself the comfort he didn't believe he deserved.

"Do you have any idea how worried we were? How afraid?" His father closed the distance between them. "Every time the telephone rang or the mail arrived, how we feared what they would tell us?" His breath stuttered, preventing him from going on. After a moment he continued slowly. "When that telegram came, they took it to the house. Your mother couldn't bring herself to open it, so she called me at the office, practically hysterical. I rushed home, certain that it would say you were dead." His voice shook. A sob escaped, and he covered his mouth with his hand.

"When I read the word 'wounded,' we rejoiced. Do you understand that, son? We praised the Lord that you'd been spared."

His father swiped at the tears on his cheeks.

What an ungrateful bastard I am.

Milt hung his head, unable to look at his father. He moved close, put his arm around his father's shoulder, and muttered, "I'm sorry."

The older man sighed and then drew his son into his arms. Milt had never seen his father so emotional.

Several moments passed before they separated, and his father resumed his speech.

"So now you see, it's just a matter of working out the details. The most important part is settled. You are alive. And you are home."

"You're right," Milt nodded his agreement. He forced himself to look his father in the eye. "Thank you."

With a smile, his father patted Milt on the shoulder. "Let's go in, shall we?"

****

Clayton rolled to a stop in front of Brooks Drug Store.

Milt turned in the worn seat of his family's old

227

pickup truck so he could face the aging man. "Why are we stopping here?"

"Mr. Greenlee's office." The old man pointed in the general direction of the drug store.

"Here?" Milt turned back to stare out the window. "Isn't his office over by the feed store?"

"Nope. Moved over here…"

When he hesitated, Milt faced him again, waiting for an answer.

Clayton rubbed the graying whiskers on his wrinkled face. "Must have been last summer. June, maybe."

"Oh," Milt nodded. The man who'd worked for his family all his life had aged since he'd been gone. More than he'd noticed until this very moment. "Okay, then." He reached over and patted the aged hand gripping the steering wheel. He climbed out and glanced around, then he leaned down and gazed through the open window of the truck. "Thanks for the ride, Clayton. I'll get a ride back with Father."

"Yes, sir," Clayton replied, his grin revealing straight, white teeth.

Milt watched the old truck drive away then directed his attention to the drugstore. Youthful memories flooded his mind. He pushed open the door and the old familiar sights and smells engulfed him in the nostalgia of his lost youth. He shook it off and strode down the aisle toward the soda fountain.

"Milton Greenlee." A voice rang out from his left side.

Milt turned just in time to see Mr. Brooks, the druggist, hurrying toward him.

"Well, I'll be," the man exclaimed. "I heard you

were home."

"Yes, sir," Milt tried to smile and be cheerful.

Mr. Brooks grabbed his hand and shook it. "Glad you made it back, son." He held Milt's hand in both his and squeezed. "We were mighty worried."

"Yes, sir." Milt nodded and attempted to extricate his hand.

"We heard it was rough over there." Mr. Brooks shook his head slowly, frowning. "Such a shame."

A flush of self-consciousness rose within him. His chest tightened and Milt pressed his lips together to prevent saying something he shouldn't. After all the comments he'd endured on the train ride, he refused to take out his frustration on someone who'd been his friend.

"You remember the Ames boy, William? Just got word. Plane went down over Germany." Mr. Brooks shook his head and looked away, finally releasing Milt's hand. "Terrible, just terrible."

Milt didn't remember the boy, but he hated to hear of anyone lost in this war.

Before Mr. Brooks started asking him questions, he needed to get out of here. He glanced around. "Clayton dropped me off here. Said Father had moved his office...."

"Upstairs," Mr. Brooks interrupted. "Last year. After he bought me out."

"Bought you out?"

The graying, bespeckled man nodded. "Saved my life. That's what he did."

Milt couldn't imagine what Mr. Brooks was talking about.

"I'd gotten myself in a mess. All through the

depression I'd held on by the skin of my teeth. So much out on credit, you know. No way to collect." He shook his head back and forth as he spoke. "Mortgaged the building to the hilt. Then things began to pick up. Thought I'd made it. Started adding stock. But what with the war and rationing and…well, I just got in too deep."

"I'm sorry to hear that." Milt couldn't imagine Kerrville without Brooks Drugstore.

"That's when your father stepped in. Made me a proposition." He smiled then and glanced around the store. "He offered to buy me out. But wanted me to stay on and run the store, just like always."

Milt thought the man was going to cry.

"Saved me. That's what he did. Don't know what I would've done. I'm too old to start over in some other town. Work for someone else. I was just beside myself. So, you see? That's why I say he saved me."

"I'm glad." Milt glanced around again, looking for a stairway leading upstairs.

"Here I am carrying on when you're looking for your father's office." He smiled and patted Milt on the arm. "Go back out, down on the right there's a stairway. It leads up to his office. Takes up the whole second floor."

"Where the dentist office used to be, years ago?"

"That's right. Only James fixed it up real nice."

"Thanks."

"You go on now." Mr. Brooks waved him on toward the door. "And give him my best."

Milt nodded and waved as he hustled out of the store before the druggist thought of something else to tell him. He easily found the stairway. A plaque on the wall beside it read "Greenlee Enterprises."

The long flight of stairs climbed upward, illuminated by wall lamps and a small window at the landing where he paused to catch his breath and marvel at the things his father would do to keep this town going. At the top, a door, with a similar plaque mounted on it, opened into a nicely furnished reception area. A well-dressed middle-aged woman sat behind a small desk. When Milt entered, she looked up from her paperwork. Recognition flushed across her face, followed by a self-conscious smile. "Why, young Mister Greenlee…" Her voice faltered. "Why, uh, Mr. Greenlee said you'd be stopping by."

Milt filled in the rest for her. "But you didn't expect me to look like this?" He regretted his words as soon as they left his mouth.

She blushed a deeper red. "I…uh…"

"I'm sorry," Milt injected. "I can't seem to get used to the way people stare at me, as if I were some freak, or something."

"Oh, I'm the one who should be sorry. I certainly didn't mean to treat you like…well, unkindly."

Milt looked away, searching for some way to extricate himself from the uncomfortable situation.

"I'll just let Mr. Greenlee know you're here." The woman disappeared down a hallway.

I should have been more friendly. Asked her name. Something.

He heard footsteps approaching. Milt forced himself to smile as he turned to greet his father.

"Son. I see you found us." His father's face said he was genuinely glad to see his son. He held out his hand to usher him down the hall. "Mrs. Littleton, I don't want anyone bothering me right now. You understand."

"Yes, sir." The woman eased behind her desk.

Before she could resume her seat, Milt spoke. "Mrs. Littleton, thank you."

She smiled and nodded.

Milt hoped she didn't despise him. He wasn't sure why he cared, except that she worked for his father, and she lived in his hometown, and he didn't want to make enemies, not because he was a thoughtless ass. He reminded himself that he might very well be working with these people unless he found some other way to make a living.

****

After showing him around the offices where Greenlee Enterprises managed its many business interests, James Greenlee escorted his son on a tour of his small-town empire. Their first stop was the old lime quarry. A handful of men still extracted limestone from the gaping pit as engines hummed pumping the ever-present water from its depths.

James explained that he would have closed the whole thing down except for the demand for lime brought on by the war. The old process was terribly inefficient, and he could not justify the investment it would take to modernize.

"What you are seeing is the end of an era. When the war's over, I plan to shut it down for good."

Milt couldn't be sorry. He had only bad memories of the short time he'd worked down in that hole. The time here had served its purpose, though. He'd buckled down and studied, worked hard at the lessons his tutor gave him. And he'd thrown himself into every sport played at the local high school. Yeah, this place definitely straightened out a defiant, rebellious teen.

Milt noticed activity in the old cooper shop and asked his father about it.

"We've converted it to woodworking. I managed to get a small subcontract to provide wooden dowels for a plant in Nashville. It's not much. But it keeps a few men employed. Not sure what we'll do with it after the war." He laughed and slapped his son on the back. "Maybe you can come up with something."

Milt shook his head, dodging his father's implication that he would be here working for his father, a family charity case.

From the quarry, the two drove to the sprawling, two-story brick building that housed the Greenlee Shoe Factory.

Milt followed his father through the factory, walking on oiled wood floors with whirring machines lined up on either side. Some were connected to contraptions that hung from the wooden ceiling. Women stood at every machine, intently focused on their work.

He knew next to nothing about the operation here. He'd never cared what went on in the factory. Now he needed to pay attention. This might be his future.

A middle-aged man greeted his father with a handshake. His father introduced the man as Charles McElroy, the factory foreman. McElroy led them through the noisy machinery to an area where the finished boots were being packed into boxes.

Milt picked up a familiar combat boot and fingered the smooth leather. This one was a high, lace-up model worn primarily by airborne troops. He pictured the airborne soldiers marching in England with their pants tucked into the tops of their laced-up boots and bloused out, looking smart and tough. A regular infantryman like him would have gotten himself beaten up if he had dared to wear boots like that.

McElroy and his father spoke of production schedules and contracts while Milt wandered around observing the many, hard-working women.

A young woman dressed in overalls with a scarf tied around her head approached him.

"Milton Greenlee. Is that you?" she exclaimed.

The voice sounded familiar, but he struggled to identify her.

"Don't you know me? It's Janie. Janie Duncan."

The smile she flashed, along with her voice, brought back a memory of a pretty blond he'd dated in high school. She'd put on weight and dressed in work clothes he didn't recognize her. She continued to talk as he tried to overcome his embarrassment.

"I'm Janie Harris now. My husband, Ralph, is in Missouri, at Leonard Wood. He's an Army trainer there." Her voice betrayed a nervousness Milt didn't understand. "So he won't...uh...He won't have to go overseas."

"It's good to see you, Janie." He smiled but knew it must look forced. "It's been a long time." It dawned on him that she was close enough to get a good view of his scarred face.

"I'm really glad you made it back...okay...um, alive, I mean." She continued to stare awkwardly at his injuries. He glanced around and caught other faces gawking at him. Some quickly turned away when he faced them. Others didn't bother.

Through the roar in his ears, he barely heard

Janie's words, "Gotta get back to work," as he self-consciously moved away from her.

He turned into an aisle between machines and noticed two young girls, their heads together, giggling behind upheld hands. They were laughing at him.

Shame crept up his spine, bringing a chill to his flesh despite the heat. The walls closed in. His chest tightened, and he couldn't seem to get enough air into his lungs. Suddenly he felt like he was standing there naked in front of all these staring faces.

Telling himself to remain calm, he made himself turn away, back to where his father stood, still talking to the foreman. Beyond them he saw a door, its window glowing with sunlight. Without a word, he strode toward the door.

"Milton?"

He heard his father's voice, but he didn't stop, not until he'd thrown the door open and stepped outside onto what appeared to be a loading dock. A man looked up from the boxes he was stacking. Milt ignored him. Shaking with panic and shame, he made his way to a set of stairs. Down on the bare earth, his long strides took him across the open lot where several trucks were parked. A wooded area lay beyond the open space.

By the time he reached the shade of the trees, his breathing had almost returned to normal. He reached out and leaned on a sturdy tree trunk, taking one deep breath after another.

He'd never been able to stand being laughed at. It was bad enough that they stared at him like he was some kind of freak, but to laugh at him, like…like they'd laughed when the teacher forced him to read in front of the class. Little girls, giggling, making fun of his stammering. The boys he could silence with his fists. But not the girls. They had been cruelest of all.

He wasn't sure how long he stood there before he heard his father's voice.

"Son, are you all right?"

Milt turned to face him. "Yeah. I'm okay. Just had to get out of there." He looked down at the weeds growing at the base of the tree. "Sorry." He'd embarrassed his father, something he should never have done.

"It's all right."

There was worry in his voice. And questions he wouldn't ask.

"I know they don't mean to stare. But...all those people...gawking at me like some..."

"They are glad to have you home. Safe."

"But I'm not safe," Milt snapped at his father. "I'm not well. I'm all messed up."

His father placed his hand on Milt's shoulder. He didn't say a word, but his pinched face spoke volumes. His father felt sorry for him. Milt pulled away. He didn't want pity. Not from anyone.

After a few moments of silence his father suggested they go back inside.

"Andy's upstairs in the office," he explained. "I promised we'd come see him."

Milt agreed to go along. He had to try, had to make an effort, even if he'd rather go back home and lock himself in his room.

Chapter 30

Annie reported to the Nursing Director at Lawson General Hospital and received her new assignment, the neuro-psychiatric ward. She had discovered her knack for dealing with these patients in the short time she'd spent with them in Florida, so it was no surprise that Captain Burrows recommended her for the assignment.

Maybe it was the years dealing with her mother that gave her a certain amount of empathy for patients suffering from mental problems.

After returning from Kerrville to Chattanooga, she had spent only one night at her home. She could have stayed longer, but her discomfort with her parents led her to tell them she had to report back. The Army didn't mind that she arrived early. They promptly put her to work.

As the days passed, she ran into several familiar faces, nurses from Florida or from her training days. She heard Sgt. Baker's name mentioned and decided to avoid him. He'd learn soon enough that she was at the same hospital. And she had no doubt that he would look her up when he did.

****

Barney made his way through the sage and tall weeds sniffing for game. Milt ambled along trying to keep the beagle in sight but not really concerned. He'd circle back eventually to trot along by Milt's side.

He'd brought his .22, not sure why, since he had yet to try to shoot it one-handed. At some point he would. He'd wanted to get out in the woods, alone, forget everything and enjoy Mother Nature.

He reached the crest of the hill where the overgrown field gave way to a stand of trees. Barney returned to his side, those gentle brown eyes seeking direction. Milt pointed to the right along the ridge and the dog took off in a run.

How many times had he walked this familiar ground with his dog, hunting rabbits and squirrels? And sometimes with Clayton or his sister Katherine tagging along.

Memories flooded back with each tree and every little dip or protruding stone. Memories of a past life gone forever.

He heard Barney barking. A rabbit, he guessed.

A huge old oak marked the spot where he veered to the left and made his way down into a deep hollow. His destination lay far below where a spring flowed from beneath a stone outcropping.

He scanned his surroundings as if the enemy might take a shot at him at any moment. Survival instinct. That awareness had saved him more than once.

Climbing down proved more difficult than he remembered. A tree that must have fallen during his absent years blocked the way at one point. Poor eyesight on his left hampered his progress, too. On the steep part, his useless arm forced him to hold on with his right hand even though his natural instinct was to use his left on the more convenient handholds. Another disappointing reminder of how he would have to adapt in his new life.

A movement in the woods below caught his attention. He squatted to make himself less visible. He brought the rifle up and awkwardly pointed it in the direction where he'd sensed someone in the underbrush.

He'd taken the point, out ahead of the others searching for Germans. Now that he'd found them, where were his men?

A shot rang out!

He searched for the source. Seeing nothing, he scrambled up the slope, back toward his buddies.

His foot caught and threw him off balance. He tried to catch himself with his left arm. It gave way as if it wasn't there. He sensed himself falling, tumbling down hill, through bushes and rocks.

Aughh!

He slammed into a tree that stopped his downward trajectory.

His heart pounded. He lay there gasping for breath.

Where was his weapon?

The German patrol. They'd find him unless his buddies got there first. Panic seized him.

His hand searched for his knife. He came up empty. Nothing.

How could he defend himself?

Someone stood over him.

A German soldier.

No. He didn't wear the German helmet.

A dog barked.

A face came closer. A boy.

"You okay?"

No German accent. No uniform.

A dog licked his face.

His left arm wouldn't move, so he used his right

hand to push the mutt away.

He blinked. "Barney?"

"Here, I'll help you up." The boy grabbed his arm, the good one, and tugged.

Milt struggled to his feet and leaned against the tree trunk. Looking around, he tried to get his bearings. The woods. The hillside. The spring bubbling down below.

"Who are you?" the boy asked.

"Milt…Milt Greenlee."

"Greenlee, huh. You must be the one who come back from the war."

"Yes," Milt nodded, flustered at being so disoriented.

After a tense moment, the boy rubbed his hand on the side of his pants, then extended it.

"I'm Georgie Gates." He spoke confidently as the two shook hands. "We live on the old Jones place." He jerked his head to indicate the direction. "I usually squirrel hunt up around here. Mr. Greenlee said he don't mind."

"I'm sure he doesn't." Milt suspected that the boy's hunting skills put meat on the family's table that they otherwise wouldn't have. "I used to hunt in these woods, too."

After checking himself over, Milt determined that, except for a few bruises, no harm had been done. "I sure would like to have a drink of that cool water."

The boy grinned then. "Sure 'nuff. I'll give you a hand."

With the boy's help, Milt made it down to the spring.

The familiar beauty of the cool, clear water

rewarded his efforts, just the same as he had pictured it so many times when he'd needed a safe haven to go to in his mind. He loved this spot; loved the green beauty of the moss and ferns growing near the water; loved the gray of the rocks in their natural, unplanned state; weathered by time; loved the cool, clean water emerging as if by magic into the crystal-clear pool.

He squatted down and scooped up a handful of water. It dripped from his fingers as he lifted it to his mouth and slurped up the refreshing liquid. No water anywhere tasted this good.

The boy joined him, getting down on his knees and immersing his face in the cool water.

That's when Milt noticed the other dog, the one Barney sniffed as he wagged his tail like they knew each other. It must be the boy's dog.

Milt sat for a minute, taking in the natural beauty. Exhaustion and aching muscles made his decision. He glanced up the hill, the way he'd come, then turned back to face the boy. "I guess I'd better be heading home." He got to his feet and smiled at the boy who reminded him of his own youth. "It was nice to meet you, Georgie Gates. Maybe we'll run into each other again sometime."

"Sure thing," the boy nodded.

Milt took a few steps up the slope. His muscles screamed in protest. He must have groaned because the next thing he knew the boy was at his side, firmly holding his arm.

"I'll just help you up to the top. Sure hate to see you take another tumble," the boy said.

Chapter 31

Each night, Milt's father helped him undress and bathe in the big tub. He promised his son that when he returned, there would be a shower in the bathroom to make bathing easier.

Milt fought to overcome his shame at being unable to do for himself.

One night, when his father had to return to the factory after supper due to an accident, he suggested that Andy could help. Milt insisted that he could manage, but Andy seemed so eager to be of help that Milt relented.

The sixteen-year-old couldn't hide his shock when he saw the scars on Milt's shoulder.

"I...I didn't realize it was so bad," the boy commented.

Milt sighed. "It's okay if you want to go. I can manage."

"No, no. I didn't mean...I can help you. I want to help you." The boy's eagerness broke down Milt's objection.

"Just help me climb into the tub. Then you can come back later and help me out." He hadn't decided whether to let Andy massage the shoulder before helping him dress, as his father had been doing. If he skipped a day, the muscles could tighten again.

When his brother returned, Milt explained what he

needed. Andy surprised him by how quickly he caught on.

"How much longer will you have to have this cast?" Andy asked.

"I'm not sure," Milt replied. "The doctor said when I get to Atlanta, they're going to operate on my arm again. Says that will free up my elbow, so it will straighten out." He shook his head. "I don't know if it will work or not."

"You mean, even without the cast, you can't straighten your arm?"

"No." Milt sighed. Might as well tell him the truth. "I haven't been able to feel that arm since I got hit. They took the cast off in Florida. And my arm was stuck, bent at the elbow." He looked at his arm, tried to visualize the flesh under the plaster. "I guess after they operate, it will just hang down instead of being in a sling all the time."

"You think you'll ever be able to feel anything?"

"To tell you the truth, no. I guess I'm reconciled to not being able to use it ever again."

"So, if the feeling came back, it'd be kind of like a bonus."

Milt laughed at the boy's enthusiasm. "Yeah, I guess so."

After a few minutes of massaging, Andy spoke again. "I sure wish I could go into the Army. Go over there and fight."

Anger flashed. "Don't say that. Don't even think that." Milt faced his little brother. "Be glad you're not old enough."

"But I'm missing out," the boy argued. "This is the biggest thing that will ever happen. And I'm missing it."

"Don't be an idiot. You're not missing anything. There's nothing fun or glorious or heroic about it. And don't you let anyone tell you any different."

Andy stared at his older brother. Milt wasn't sure if Andy understood what he said or not. He drew in a deep breath and tried to settle his raging emotions.

"It's bad, Andy. Real bad. Seeing men blown to bits, men you know, friends. Knowing any minute, it could be you."

"Did you kill anybody?" Andy's voice was quiet and so very young.

Milt stood and turned his back. He wasn't going to talk about this, not now, not ever.

"What's it like? To kill someone?"

Milt grabbed the pack of cigarettes from the nightstand. His hand shook as he struggled to remove one. The shaking traveled up his arm, engulfing his whole body.

The pack dropped to the floor. Andy moved toward him to pick it up, but Milt put his hand up to stop him.

Struggling to find his voice, Milt blurted out the words. "You'd better go."

"But we're not finished. You don't have your pajamas shirt on."

Milt turned and took the three steps to the door. He forced his fingers around the cool, metal knob and turned it. The door swung open. "I'll manage."

It seemed an eternity before Andy moved. As he eased through the door, he gave Milt a look that sent pain stabbing into his heart. Confusion, anger, disgust. He didn't want his brother to hate him. Didn't want him to think he was some kind of freak from another planet.

But maybe he was. Where he'd been only a few months ago had been as foreign to the people here in Kerrville as the moon would be. There was no way they could understand.

Andy was so young, so innocent. He had no idea. And even if Milt tried to explain, he would never understand. No one who hadn't lived through it could ever understand.

The nightmares came again that night. Murderous machine gun fire. In the open. No cover. He clung to the earth, fingers digging in the hard ground. Bullets flying around him. Screams for help from his buddies. He tried to crawl to one of them, but something held him back. He turned his head and saw Lt. Mead lying across his legs, a bullet hole in his forehead. He kicked himself free as rounds riddled the lifeless body. Screams for "Medic!" sounded nearby but he was paralyzed, unable to move. The sound of a mortar overhead…

Milt jerked awake gasping for breath, damp with sweat.

A soft knock. "Son, are you all right?"

Anxiety was evident in his father's voice.

"I'm okay," Milt called. He didn't want his father to see him, still shaking from the vivid images. And he didn't want to explain.

"Go back to bed," he said, trying to keep his voice strong. "I'm okay."

****

Milt tried to ignore the tension at breakfast. His mother was quiet, not asking the prying questions he expected. His father was all business.

After breakfast, Milt wandered into the music

room. He lifted the cover on the piano keyboard and ran his fingers over the cool ivory.

Annie invaded his thoughts as she had so often since he'd been home. He wondered what she was doing. Probably on her way to New York. Would he ever see her again? He closed his eyes and pictured her, smiling and singing.

He sat on the bench and fingered the keys, at first randomly. Then he began to pick out a tune, one they'd played together at her house, when she'd laughed, with him, not at him. He'd surprised her with his musical abilities, limited as they were. She'd even complimented his singing voice. For a few minutes he'd felt whole, like he had something to offer her, like she accepted him as he was.

The bubble had burst too soon.

"I wondered who was in here."

Milt looked up. His sister, Olivia, stood in the doorway. "Where'd you come from?"

"Got in last night," she answered as she came closer.

He returned his gaze to the keyboard, uncomfortable under her scrutiny.

"Sounds like you're mooning over some girl."

Her words punched him in the gut. How did she know what he was thinking?

His instinctive reaction was to shake his head. "No," he muttered.

She laughed, that silly little laugh he remembered from childhood that said she didn't believe him.

He decided to change the subject. "How'd you get here? There's no train that late."

"Alfred. He's a friend from school. 4-F 'cause of

his bad leg. Broke it in an accident when he was a kid."

She shuffled through a stack of sheet music on top of the piano. Halfway down the stack she pulled out one and plopped down on the bench beside him.

"Play this one," she ordered.

Milt glanced at the title and tried to remember how it went. "Hum it for me."

She met his gaze, and then nodded. Good. She remembered. She started humming. Soon he joined her, the tune coming alive in his mind. His fingers followed, finding the keys to match the melody in his head. Once he had the melody, his mind added chords, never even looking at the music. But without his left hand he could only play the melody. At least he still had his gift.

He'd never been able to learn to read music. Trying had been harder than learning to read words. But the sounds from the piano keys spoke to him. He could hear the music and found the right keys to replicate the sound. His mother called it "playing by ear." He called it his gift. Something to make up for his other deficits.

Now immense gratitude rose within him...that he hadn't lost this, too, not completely.

When the song ended, Olivia gave him a hug. "I'm glad you're home," she whispered.

He nodded.

She pulled him from the piano bench and gave him the once-over.

"Not bad," she commented. "I definitely know girls who would go for you, even with all this." She waved her hand toward his damaged left side.

"Oh, no." He turned away shaking his head.

"Mother thinks you need to get out. Socialize."

"No. What I need is to be left alone." He started

toward the door.

"Don't go," she pleaded. "I won't…"

He looked at her.

"I'm sorry." She stepped closer. "I'll forget all that. I promise. Can't we just sit together? Maybe play some more songs. Like we used to."

He softened, remembering the little girl who'd looked up to him. She was so much younger. They'd never really spent much time together. But she'd loved to hear him play.

"Okay," he nodded, returning to the piano bench. This was his little sister, and his leave was almost gone. He could spare a little time for her, pretending nothing had changed.

Chapter 32

Lawson General Hospital reminded Milt of an Army post, with single-story, wood-frame buildings, lined up in typical Army fashion, organized in rows as if men's wounds could be put in some kind of order.

In one of the identical buildings, the orderly assigned him a bed, one of many lined up in the ward occupied by broken men, the bandages or casts testifying to their injuries. He saw no familiar faces.

Knowing this would be his home for months to come, Milt introduced himself to the men around him. By the time he'd unpacked, an orderly walked through the ward announcing that all ambulatory patients would report to the mess hall. The men who weren't already dressed pulled on robes over their pajamas and headed for the exit. Milt followed.

The next day, as ordered, Milt reported to Captain Wilson, an orthopedic surgeon with an excellent reputation, who already had him scheduled for surgery on his left arm.

For once the Army didn't have him waiting. The surgeon called it a minor procedure to allow the joint to move. Milton called it useless. He still had no feeling in most of his left arm and hand. Try as he might to move his fingers, nothing happened.

Captain Wilson's vague words held a hint of hope, that with time and therapy the nerves might heal. He might regain some use of the limb. Even as Milt felt himself grabbing onto the glimmer of hope offered, he warned himself against the inevitable disappointment. He knew full well that a life as an athlete was not within the realm of possibilities.

His plastic surgeon, who turned out to be Captain Fairchild, inspected his handiwork and laid out his plans for future surgeries. Then, an ophthalmologist looked at his eye and recommended he be fitted with glasses. Milt doubted it would help clear the blur. He'd just have to live with whatever they could do for him.

He headed back to his ward, a bit dejected.

"Sergeant Greenlee, how was your leave?"

The cheerful and familiar voice brought Milt's head up. Sgt. Lloyd Baker stood a few feet away.

"Baker," Milt exclaimed, grabbing the man's extended hand. "How'd you know I was here?"

"Oh, I've been on the look-out for you." A wide grin lit up the boyish face. "I saw the list of transfers. Made note of the ones coming to Lawson."

"Then there are others?"

"Yeah, sure. Several." He leaned closer. "I'm gonna make sure you are assigned to me. Hope you don't mind."

"That's swell!" Milt felt better about his new home already.

Baker pulled out a pack of cigarettes. "Want one?" Milt shook his head and Baker proceeded to light up.

"Someone else you know is here." Sgt. Baker blew smoke out of the side of his mouth. "A nurse." He raised his eyebrows as if to taunt Milt, but Milt didn't bite.

"Lt. McEwen," Baker announced.

Milt's heart stopped.

Sgt. Baker laughed. "I thought that would get your attention."

Milt gulped and forced his gaze away from Baker. He'd already revealed too much. "I…I thought she was going to a hospital in New York."

"Well, she didn't. Captain Burrows sent her here instead."

"That's not fair." Milt remembered Annie's excitement about going to New York.

"Nothing's fair in the Army. You ought to know that."

"I know. I know." Milt walked on, unable to remain still. As much as he wanted to ask where she was and had Baker seen her, he steeled his nerves and kept his back to his friend.

Baker seemed to take the hint. After a short silence he said, "Well, I just thought you'd want to know."

"Yeah, thanks." Milt forced himself to turn back, carefully concealing his excitement. "Maybe I'll run into her sometime."

"Yeah, maybe. Anyway, how's that arm doing? Still no feeling?"

Milt rubbed the fingers on his left hand. "Doc's got me scheduled for surgery to loosen up the elbow. They'll leave off the cast. Let it heal a while. See what happens."

"That sounds hopeful."

"He said sometimes the nerves heal themselves and the feeling gradually returns."

Baker dropped his cigarette and ground it out with his shoe. "Sounds like we'll be working on it soon enough."

****

Milt sat on his bunk in the open barracks, his thoughts on Annie.

When she got into his father's car to go to the train station, he'd wanted to kiss her goodbye, just a peck on the cheek, but she'd become distant, as if they were strangers again. Up on the mountain, she'd pushed him away after their kiss, acted as if it hadn't happened. He'd gotten the message to keep his distance, to remain strictly friends, no more. Yet she'd been warm, almost joyous, when they'd sung together at the piano. Was it her father's anger and obvious disapproval of him? Or was her interest strictly in gaining information about her cousin?

The orderly, delivering mail, dropped a small bundle of letters on Milt's bed.

"Looks like your mail's catching up with you, Sergeant," the clerk commented before moving on.

Milt untied the string and scanned the return addresses one by one to determine who had written him and which one he wanted to read first.

His once monthly letter from Aunt Winnie with an update on local gossip and family news, that probably had been written before his leave, judging from the postmark. A letter from his mother, again written just before he went home on leave. Those could wait. Two came from his sister Katherine. She must have time on her hands these days. He'd read the oldest one first.

The last letter was from Sgt. A. Carlton, and the APO address of the 1st Division.

Milt's hand shook as he tried to open it one-handed without destroying the envelope. Images of his buddy crouched in a muddy fox hole scribbling a letter filled his mind. A quick prayer went up for his friend's safety as he pulled the two small sheets of paper out of the crumpled envelope.

He struggled to read his friends handwriting. Judging from its condition, the letter must have been written in the field. It was addressed to Lawson General, so Milt knew Ade had received his letter inquiring about Joe McEwen.

From Ade's vague references Milton guessed that the division was fighting somewhere in eastern France. There were no details for the censor to black out.

After carefully reading the letter twice Milt deciphered the most important details about Annie's cousin. Ade had found an engineer who knew Lt. McEwen. The engineer said that the lieutenant had been shot by a sniper and died instantly. Ade gave the name of the engineer and said that the man promised to write to Milt with everything he remembered about the dead officer.

This letter gave him an excuse to approach Annie. Even if she didn't want to see him again, she'd want the information about her cousin.

****

Annie finished up her paperwork. The night nurse had arrived a half-hour before, and they'd gone over the patient's charts with Annie holding on to the last two so she could make her final notes for the day.

The men in her ward suffered from more severe combat fatigue than she'd seen in Florida. Their physical wounds were mending nicely, but their minds remained on the battlefield, still living the terror.

As she emerged into the cool evening, she breathed deeply to clear the stale ward air from her lungs. She'd requested a piano for the day room, hoping that music could reach some of the more difficult patients, but Captain Burrows had been skeptical. Annie had decided to approach the Red Cross to see if they would provide the piano.

In the meantime, she had her own problem to consider — Brice Attwater.

He'd called the night before to say he was home on leave and wanted to see her. She couldn't very well say no. They were friends and, even though her father was determined that she should marry Brice, that shouldn't keep her from seeing the man. She'd made it clear to every other man who'd shown any interest that she was not available. Surely, she could do the same with Brice. After all, her father's wishes weren't necessarily Brice's wishes.

Engrossed in her thoughts, she bumped into a soldier.

"Excuse me," she muttered, as she quickly side-stepped the man.

"Annie."

That voice. She looked up into the soldier's face.

"Milt…Sgt. Greenlee." She hadn't expected him.

"Lieutenant." He straightened and saluted.

As she returned his salute a little shiver ran through her. He looked rested.

"I… uh…Sgt. Baker told me you were here…at Lawson."

Oh, so that was how he found her. "Yes."

"Sorry you didn't get to go to New York."

"Yeah, well…" A group of soldiers walked by, thankfully interrupting the explanation she didn't want to make.

She motioned for him to walk with her. "I was going to my quarters, to change." She forced a friendly smile. "I'm meeting someone for dinner."

"Oh, I see."

He maneuvered himself so she was on his good side, and they walked a little way in silence.

"I got a letter," he blurted out.

"What?"

"From my friend, Ade. I told you I wrote him." He glanced up and caught her gaze. "He talked to an engineer who knew your cousin."

Her breath caught and she stopped in her tracks. "What did he say?"

Although she was desperate for any information about Joe, she gazed into his eyes, surprised at how much she had missed him. Yet the gulf between them loomed wide. She'd intentionally kept her distance. Now she had to abide by her decision.

He dug out a wrinkled envelope from his shirt pocket. "Here, you can read it."

She examined his guarded expression. Those blue eyes bore into her, an arching brow issuing a challenge.

She took the envelope and glanced around, conscious of being observed in a public place.

"You can take it back to your quarters. Read it there." He sounded distant, resigned to his status as a patient of lower rank, who wasn't supposed to fraternize with her.

She hesitated, fingering the paper. "I…uh…I'm not sure I can." She started to walk again. They'd almost reached her building. "No. It's your letter. I'd rather you be with me when I read it." Why had she said that?

They stopped at the foot of the steps leading into

her quarters.

"Okay," he nodded. "But we'll have to find a place…"

"Annie." Brice emerged from the building. "I've been waiting for you."

"Brice, how nice," she managed as he quickly descended the steps.

"Who's this?" Brice inquired.

Milt snapped to attention before Annie could think. He executed a quick salute. "Sgt. Milt Greenlee, sir."

Brice casually returned his salute. "At ease, soldier." He glanced from Annie to Milt, clearly wanting to know what was going on between them.

"Sgt. Greenlee has been making some inquiries for me. About my cousin." She gave Brice one of her sweetest smiles. "You remember Joe, don't you?"

"Of course, I do. Damn shame to lose him." Brice glanced over at Milt, expecting further explanation.

Before Milt could say anything, Annie held up the envelope. "He brought this to show me."

"What's that?" Brice asked.

"A letter from a friend of mine. He's still in Europe fighting."

"His friend found someone who knew Joe. Who knew what happened to him." Annie's voice shook. She gripped the envelope tighter, afraid of what was inside.

"Well, what did happen to him?" Brice sounded impatient.

"He was shot by a sniper," Milt announced.

"What!" She hadn't expected such a blunt statement. As the information sunk in, weakness almost overcame her. "Oh, poor Joe."

The warmth of Brice's hand on her shoulder lent

her strength, but it was Milt's gaze she sought.

"I'm sorry," he said, in a softer tone.

"Well, that's certainly unexpected news." Brice moved closer and slipped his arm around her shoulder.

"You can hang onto the letter. Read it for yourself."

She nodded and looked down, fighting tears.

"I'll let you know if I hear anything else."

Then Milt faced Brice and saluted again. "Sir."

She looked up and caught his gaze.

"Ma'am."

Brice returned his salute, and she made a feeble effort before watching him until he disappeared around the corner of another building.

"Poor fellow," Brice commented. "Nice of him to help you, though."

"Yes," Annie agreed, not wanting to discuss Milt with him. "I'll just be a minute. I'd like to freshen up a bit."

"Of course."

They climbed the few steps, and he opened the door for her.

"Have you been waiting long?" she asked.

"Only a little while. The train arrived about three. One of the nurses said I could wait in here." He indicated the small sitting room intended for guests of the opposite sex.

"Yes." She held out her hand toward the sitting room. "Well…just a few more minutes, then we can go."

He nodded, smiling in that sweet, smug, possessive way he used when he wanted something. Anxiety crept up her spine like a spider. Did he want her? Was her father right?

For now, she intended to read Milt's letter before she did anything else.

Chapter 33

Milt's reconditioning program resumed soon after his arrival. The team of rehab specialists, with Sgt. Baker in charge, rotated between patients depending on who was available.

After his arm had sufficiently healed from the surgery to free up his elbow, they added physical therapy on his arm to his regime.

One day a big man in his thirties approached. "Sgt. Greenlee?"

"That's me."

The man offered his hand, so Milt shook it. "I'm Lew. I'll be working with you today."

"Fine. That's fine." Milt looked the man over as he studied some papers on a clipboard. Definitely an athlete like Baker. But older. "I haven't seen you around."

Lew looked up and smiled. "I've been on special assignment." He put down the clipboard. "Let's get a look at that arm."

He helped Milt strip down to his undershirt revealing gauze wrapping. Lew gently grasped his arm and slowly manipulated the elbow.

"Does that hurt?" Lew asked.

Milt tried to tamp down his disgust. "Doesn't that paperwork tell you anything?"

Lew's gentle eyes conveyed infinite patience. "You

tell me. What do you feel?"

"I can't feel anything…from just below the shoulder down." He reached around with his right hand and encircled his upper left arm with his fingers. "It stops here, where the worst scarring is."

Lew's hand covered his. When Milt pulled his hand away Lew gently touched his upper arm. "Tell me when you can't feel it."

"I feel it there." Milt waited. "There. That's where I lose it."

Lew raised Milt's arm and felt underneath with Milt nodding to indicate he could feel Lew's touch. As his hand descended, Milt told him "Now it's gone."

"Okay," Lew responded cheerfully. "We'll work on strengthening your shoulder and keeping the arm nice and limber, so the muscles don't atrophy."

"You think the feeling will ever come back?"

"I don't know. But the doctors must think there's a chance or they wouldn't bother with therapy."

"Makes sense," Milt nodded. He liked Lew's positive attitude. "I just wish I knew. I don't want any false hope. I mean, if it's going to be like this from now on, I'll have to get used to it."

"Tell you what. For now, let's think it's going to get better. Maybe not back like it was, but better. You think like that and do the work and see what happens."

"Okay." Milt liked this guy.

"Meanwhile, we'll get the rest of you back in tip-top shape."

As they worked Milt distracted himself with conversation. "You from around here? You've got a southern accent, but I can't quite place it."

Lew laughed. "Yeah. I grew up in North Carolina.

Been living in Chicago. Thought I'd lost some of the accent but now that I'm back down south it's come back."

"I'm from Tennessee. Small town called Kerrville."

"Yeah. Baker told me. Told me you played baseball, too."

Milt nodded. "Not anymore." He hated to think of what might have been. Lew gave him that look like he expected Milt to tell the story, so Milt continued. "I went to spring training with the Nashville's minor league team. Spring of '41. They put me on as a reserve pitcher. Didn't play much that season. Then…" He shrugged. They both knew what he meant. The war changed his plans.

"That's a tough break."

"I thought I'd go back, after the war was over. But with this." He shook his head. "I can't play like this."

"You'll find something else."

"Yeah." Milt thought of his father's shoe factory. He'd always have a job there, whether he was any good at it or not, but he'd wanted more. That's what hurt so. That he'd never reach his dream of playing in the majors. Of being a baseball star.

"You know, baseball's a wonderful life. But it's not for everybody. It's hard startin' in the minors and working your way up. You gotta want it, but you also gotta have luck and lots of it."

Milt nodded. "Well, obviously I don't have the luck."

"Oh, I don't know. You survived, didn't you?"

Lew's words brought a wave of guilt. He was right. How many of his friends had died? They'd all had dreams they'd never have a chance to fulfill.

They continued to work through the cycle of exercises in silence. As they finished up, Sgt. Baker appeared.

"How you boys doing?" Sgt. Baker slapped Lew on the shoulder.

"Oh, we're becoming fast friends," Lew replied.

"Has this old coot been telling you baseball stories?"

Milt wasn't sure what Baker meant. "Sure. We talked about baseball."

Baker looked from one man to the other. "Oh, I get it. Lew here didn't introduce himself, at least not properly."

Did Baker mean the older man's rank of Corporal?

"Sgt. Milton Greenlee, I'd like you to meet Lew Applegate."

Baker grinned as he said the name. It sounded familiar, but Milt wasn't sure where he'd heard it.

"Oh, come on. Chicago. Major Leagues."

The light bulb came on. "You're *the* Lew Applegate? The famous baseball player?"

Lew nodded, a sheepish grin on his face.

Milt grabbed Lew's hand and shook it hard, like they'd just met instead of spending the last hour together. "I am honored, sir. To meet such a great player."

"Don't call me 'sir.' I may be older than you boys but I'm not that old."

"But how?" Milt looked from Lew to Baker and back. "What are you doing in the Army?"

Lew laughed. "My wife asked the same question."

"Good old Uncle Sam," Baker injected. "He got

drafted."

"But I didn't think they were drafting older…uh, no offense Mr. Applegate."

"Call me Lew. Nobody calls me Mr. Applegate."

"They're drafting just about everybody these days," Baker said.

"But you were just named batting champion."

"That was in '43. Got drafted that November." Lew looked over at Baker. "Lucked up and got in this outfit. Army seemed to think us athletes could help get you boys back in shape."

"Yeah. I don't know how I got in," Baker interjected. "A little semi-pro ball and coaching a girls basketball team doesn't quite stack up to all the professional athletes and college players."

"We'll have to introduce Greenlee around. There's a guy who played a couple of seasons in Brooklyn. Nice fellow. Not sure he's got the staying power. Have to find out after this war's over." Lew looked at his watch. "I gotta go."

He turned to leave then glanced back over his shoulder. "Baker, don't forget about tonight."

Baker flushed crimson. "Uh, sure. I won't forget."

Lew grinned. "See you boys later."

Milt watched him walk away. "Wow! I can't believe I met Lew Applegate."

"Oh, you'll be seeing a lot of him."

Milt grinned. "Yeah, I will, won't I?"

"He's swell. The nicest guy you'll ever want to meet."

"We used to get some of the Chicago games on the radio. The announcer was always talking about Applegate. Sounded like Chicago loved him."

"Yup. They still do." Baker walked Milt toward the exit.

"By the way, what was that about tonight?" Milt asked.

"Oh, his wife's set me up to meet this girl she knows." A tinge of color returned to his face. "Their landlord's daughter."

"That's great. But why the hesitation?"

"He showed me her picture. A real beauty. I mean bona fide beauty contest winner." He shook his head. "Way out a' my league."

"Not necessarily. Love's funny, you know." Milt slapped him on the shoulder. "The way you're reacting I'd say you've already fallen for her."

"I don't know about that. But I am nervous about meeting her." Baker waved to someone across the room then turned back to Milt. "Speaking of love, have you seen our favorite nurse lately?"

Milt shook his head. He didn't want to tell Baker about going to her quarters to show her the letter from Ade. She'd sent him away rather than read it in front of her officer friend. He wasn't sure why.

"I know how you can hear her sing."

"How?"

"She's on a radio show on Monday nights. This show about the hospital and the recovering soldiers. They've got a little dance band and Lt. McEwen sings with them."

Milt's heart raced with excitement. He could see her again and hear her sing. "Where do they do the show?"

Lloyd laughed. "I thought you'd never ask."

"Well?"

"As a matter of fact, Lew is scheduled to appear on the next show. How about tagging along to give him moral support?"

Chapter 34

Annie headed back to her quarters after her shift, glad to find her room deserted, giving her the opportunity to read through Ade Carlton's letter one more time, alone. The difficult-to-read handwriting had probably been written hurriedly and in less than optimum conditions. She scanned over the words. Her pulse raced every time she read them.

"*Lt. McEwen was hit by a sniper. Shot in the head. He never knew what hit him.*"

The words swam on the page as tears slipped down her cheeks. The vivid image of her beloved Joe with a bullet in his head wrenched her soul. A sob caught in her throat. She closed her eyes and shook her head trying to erase the horrible picture that came back every time.

"Are you okay?"

She hadn't heard her roommate return.

She nodded and swiped at the tears. "Yes. Yes. I'll be fine."

"Don't you need to get dressed?"

"In a minute."

Her gaze returned to the letter. She blinked until the words came back into focus.

"*Wazinski says he wrote to McEwen's wife after McEwen was killed and told her what happened. How the sniper got him. I gave him your name and address*

*and he said he'd write you with everything he could
remember. Maybe we'll get lucky and the Krauts will
let up long enough for him to write you."*

Annie digested the information. This man knew
Joe. Wrote to his wife. The woman had known what
happened to Joe but didn't communicate with his
family.

The letter provided answers but also created more
questions.

"I wish I knew where she was," Annie muttered.

"What did you say?"

She looked up, realizing she'd spoken out loud.

"Oh, nothing."

Joe's wife. Another reason she had requested to be
assigned to New York. Now that her transfer had finally
been approved, she'd be able to look for her.

Joe had told them so little about the girl he'd
married, the girl from New York City. Looking for her
in the big city would be like looking for a needle in a
haystack, but Annie fully intended to try. She might
come up empty-handed or she might get lucky.

Meanwhile she'd stop in Chattanooga on her way
north and show the letter to her family. At least it was
some new information.

Would this Wazinski write to Milt? He was still
over there fighting. He or Milt's friend could die any
day. Or they could already be dead.

The thought sobered her. This war had taken or
damaged so many men. Joe wasn't the only casualty of
this war.

****

Milt, along with Lloyd and his new girlfriend,
followed Lew and his wife into the sound stage at the

Atlanta radio station. They were ushered down to seats in the front row.

Looking around, Milt saw Annie sitting on stage with the band. His breath caught when their gazes locked.

A man spoke with Lew about when he would be brought onstage for his part.

"This is Sgt. Milton Greenlee. He's the one I told you about."

When he heard his name, Milt's attention shifted to Lew and the man from the show.

"Sgt. Greenlee, I am honored to meet you. It will really boost the show to have both of you on air today."

Milt nodded and wondered how he had let Lew talk him into this. His desire to hear Annie sing must have clouded his judgment.

"I'll come get you just before you are to go on. And you'll just go right up those steps." He pointed to the side where a small stairway led up to the raised stage. "Then over to the microphone where our announcer will introduce you."

"That sounds easy enough." Lew wasn't the least bit nervous.

"Of course, it is. Just speak into the microphone and talk to the audience. Don't think about the radio program at all."

After the man left, Lew elbowed Milt. "I know you're nervous." He pulled some note cards out of his pocket and passed them to Milt. "I wrote these up for you."

Milt glanced at the cards as Lew continued. "Always helps me when I have to speak in front of a crowd of people. Just glance down and read a word or two. That usually jogs my memory enough to keep me going."

Milt could make out a few words. 1st Division. Europe. War bonds. The rest ran together in a jumble of shapes. He'd never be able to read them.

"I thought you were going to do the talking."

"You never can tell how these things will go. Just follow my lead and it will be fine."

Fine. A lot he knew. Milt wished he'd never come. He'd only humiliate himself...in front of Annie...in front of all the people out there listening.

Suddenly everyone came to life as the show started.

The band struck up a tune, then the announcer introduced the show.

Thank goodness they started it off with Annie singing. Listening to her lovely voice relaxed him a little.

Before she finished her number, the man appeared and directed him and Lew to go up onto the stage.

He moved automatically, following Lew. Annie stepped away from the microphone and the announcer took her place. She passed behind him and he felt her touch on his back. He glanced over his shoulder and caught her reassuring smile.

What would she think after he made a fool of himself?

"Ladies and Gentlemen. We are honored and pleased to introduce to you our special guests for the show. Someone all you sports fans will be thrilled to meet. And he's brought with him one of the hospital's most illustrious heroes. It is my honor to introduce to you the famous baseball player, Mr. Lew Applegate."

The audience applauded as Lew stepped up to the microphone.

"Thank you so much. It is an honor to be here in Atlanta and to be speaking to all of you today."

"Mr. Applegate…"

"Call me Lew."

"Well, Lew. How does it feel to be on loan to the Army?"

"I tell you, it's great. I'm working at the hospital, Lawson General Hospital, right here in Atlanta, Georgia, with a great bunch of guys. We're working with our wounded soldiers who've come home from battling overseas."

"We understand that a lot of you athletes are helping these soldiers get back in shape after being injured."

"That's right. We're helping them get back to normal life. And speaking of that, I've brought with me one of those soldiers. A decorated hero who was wounded in France, Sgt. Milton Greenlee."

Lew poked Milt and motioned for him to step up to the microphone. Milt hesitated. The announcer nodded for him to move closer and out of the corner of his eye he could see the other man waving his hand.

Milt stepped closer to the announcer.

"Sgt. Greenlee, we understand that you were awarded the Silver Star for valor. Is that right?"

"Yes, sir," Milt said.

The radio man waved his hand and mouthed "Speak louder."

"And you also received a Bronze Medal and a Purple Heart?"

"Yes, sir." Milt tried to speak louder but his voice

shook.

Lew waved a card in front of him. Milt glanced over and met Lew's gaze. Lew gave him a quick nod and a weak smile that must have been meant to reassure him.

"Can you tell us a little about your experiences overseas, Sgt. Greenlee?"

Sweat slid down the side of Milt's face. He'd rather face a Kraut machine gun than stand here in front of this microphone. He couldn't look out at the audience, and he couldn't seem to make himself speak.

"I think the Sergeant here is a little nervous," the announcer said, trying to smooth over the situation.

Milt met his gaze trying to apologize silently.

"Maybe Lew can fill us in."

Lew leaned in close to the microphone. "Milt here's not used to speaking like this. But he did a great job over there battling the Germans." He took the cards from Milt's sweaty grasp and read them silently. "Sgt. Greenlee served in the 1st Division, 18th Regiment, in North Africa, in Sicily and in France. He got the Bronze Star in Sicily. Then in France, where he was wounded, he got the Silver Star for bravery and the Purple Heart."

"Well, that is certainly an impressive record, Sergeant."

"Thank you, sir." It was all Milt could say.

"Didn't the 1st Division land on D-Day?"

"Yes, sir. On Omaha Beach." Did they even know what that meant? No one out there could have any idea.

He glanced around. Faces stared at him.

Panic engulfed him. He needed to get out of here.

Then he saw her, that sweet, reassuring smile. She nodded, ever so slightly.

271

His tension eased. He drew a deep breath.

Lew spoke again. "We have many brave soldiers wounded in battle. And more returning every day. They need your support, your encouragement."

"Thank you, Lew, for the work you are doing at the Army hospital. And thank all the others who work there helping our soldiers recover."

"It is an honor, sir."

"Thank you. Mr. Lew Applegate, All Star Baseball great. And Sgt. Greenlee, decorated hero, for appearing on our show today."

Lew's hand rested on Milt's shoulder as they made their way off the stage.

As Milt sank into his seat, he leaned over close to Lew. "I'm sorry."

"Don't worry," Lew whispered. "You did fine."

Milt wanted to sink down to the floor. The eyes of the audience were on him, even as an officer from the hospital took the microphone and started talking about some program to help returning soldiers. While the man droned on, Milt braved a glance at Annie. She was looking at the man at the microphone, but within a few seconds her gaze shifted his way. A sweet smile graced her lips. His heart pounded.

All he really cared about was what she thought. No one else mattered.

Chapter 35

Annie held on to the free-standing microphone as she sang her number. Ironically, it was the same song she'd sung the first time she saw him. And somehow the words seem to fit. Had she found a dream?

Milt sat in the audience, down front where he and the baseball player had retreated after their spot on the show.

She focused on her song and on the man, who'd been through so much, the man who'd found out about Joe, the man who got nervous speaking to an audience. A brave man, nonetheless.

When her song, the last one of the show, ended, some people in the audience jumped to their feet, clapping and whooping. Sgt. Lloyd Baker, as well as Milt and Lew were loudest by far. The ladies with them, her nurse friends and a couple of doctors stood applauding. All that noise went out over the airways and sounded like a much larger audience, which pleased the producer immensely.

Annie took her bows as the "on air" light went out. The voice of the announcer in the sound booth took over with his spiel, thanking everyone for listening and signing off so the next show could begin.

The band members behind her congratulated each other on another good show. Turning, she thanked them, complimented their playing, and tried not to blush when they raved about her singing. She was lucky to be on this show and she knew it.

"Sure sorry to lose you," the piano player, who doubled as band leader, called to her as she gathered up her music.

"Thanks. I'm off to New York. Wish me luck," she answered.

"You'll do swell."

"You were great!" Sgt. Baker's familiar voice sounded close behind her.

Annie spun around. Both Lloyd and Milt stood there grinning.

"You were really good," Milt said. "Your voice is so beautiful." Milt appeared more relaxed than he'd been onstage.

"Thanks, boys." She flashed a big smile and glanced around looking for her friends.

"How about having a cup of coffee with us?" Lloyd asked. One of his sheepish smiles hid something.

What were they up to?

She waved to Rose and Susan. "Actually, I was planning on going out with my girlfriends. Sort of a farewell party."

"Farewell?" Milt said.

The circle expanded to include her fellow nurses. "My transfer came through. I'm leaving in a few days."

Lloyd took charge. "There's a little cafe just down the block from here. We can go…"

"Excuse me." One of the band members held up his trombone case, indicating he wanted to get by.

They moved back, and she became acutely aware of her shoulder against Milt's broad chest. She steeled herself, trying not to react to his presence.

Milt leaned closer. "We can all go." His deep voice reverberated in her ear.

All she could do was nod in response.

"Annie, dear. You were wonderful."

Her head jerked around. Brice stood nearby resplendent in his dress uniform. His shiny First Lieutenant's bars brought the enlisted men to attention.

"Brice. What are you doing here?"

He stepped closer and hooked his arm through hers. "I just made it in time to hear your last number. You still have that lovely voice. Isn't it nice of them to let you sing on the radio?"

A little annoyed, she muttered "thank you" to his 'not quite' compliment. "Why are you here? I thought your leave was over."

"Oh, no. Not yet." He grasped her hand, with his arm still wrapped around hers, and turned her away from the group. "I decided to go through Atlanta on my way to New York so I could see you again."

Annie gulped at the mention of New York. He'd told her he'd been reassigned to Ft. Dix as a supply officer in charge of loading ships destined for Europe. He'd asked for the duty in hopes of being sent overseas. But he also knew she had put in for a transfer to New York.

Rose and Susan chatted with Sgt. Greenlee, Sgt. Baker and the unknown girl who'd been sitting beside Baker earlier. Corporal Applegate and his wife stood nearby.

"Brice, I want you to meet a famous baseball player."

Annie steered Brice over to the group. "Everyone, this is my friend, Lt. Brice Attwater."

The enlisted men quickly snapped salutes which Brice returned rather informally.

She eyed Lloyd. "Sgt. Baker, will you introduce your friends?"

Lloyd brightened. "Of course." He turned to Lew. "This is Corporal Lew Applegate and his lovely wife."

"Mr. Applegate. It's a pleasure." Brice reached out to shake hands. "And Mrs. Applegate." He nodded to the quiet woman holding on to Lew's arm. "What made you leave baseball?"

Lew shrugged. "Uncle Sam called."

"You're pretty well known. "Old Aches and Pains," isn't it."

Lew grinned sheepishly. "That's what they call me. I guess 'cause I get hurt so much."

"Always has been accident-prone," Mrs. Applegate said.

"But still a fine player."

"This is Sergeant Milt Greenlee," Lloyd continued.

"We've met." Brice nodded but didn't offer to shake his hand. "Sergeant."

Lloyd pulled the girl who'd been sitting with him out from behind Milt. "And this is Patsy Fairchild." She gave a little wave.

Annie smiled at her and wondered where Lloyd had met this petite beauty. "I'm Annie McEwen."

"Pleased to meet you," the girl murmured.

"And these two are my friends, Rose and Susan."

Brice nodded. "Ladies."

"We're all going out for coffee." Susan blatantly batted her eyes at Brice. "You can bring your handsome friend."

"Well…" Brice's gaze met Annie's. From the look

he gave her she knew he didn't want to go. She squeezed his hand.

"Sure, we'll come," Annie told her friend.

Brice nodded. reluctantly agreeing.

She looked him in the eye and acted as if she hadn't sensed his reluctance. "It'll be fun."

****

Milt reported to the gym for his exercise class. His eye doctor had just fitted him for glasses. He didn't like the idea, but the doctor assured him that it would improve his vision. He was mulling it over when Lloyd and Lew approached.

"Greenlee. We were looking for you," Lloyd said.

"Yeah? What for?"

"Wondered if you'd be interested in helping out. We're putting a team together."

Milt looked from one to the other. "A baseball team?"

"Yep," Lloyd replied. "We're getting some boys together, boys like you, who used to play baseball. We thought a friendly game would help with their recovery."

"What can I do? I can't play. Not with this bum arm."

"Sure, you can. There are others who've lost legs and arms. They're all going to give it a try. So can you."

"All right. But I'd probably be more useful coaching or handling the equipment."

"That reminds me." Up till now Lloyd had done all the talking. Now Lew took over. "How about going with me to round up some equipment?"

"Sure. What do you need?"

"Just about everything. The hospital has next to nothing. Not enough to field a team, much less two." Lew grinned and Milt knew the man had something up his sleeve.

"Okay. What?"

"I thought maybe you and I could go around to stores, schools, and such and ask for donations. You know, benefit wounded soldiers and all."

"And you want me to be the wounded soldier."

"Well, you are the decorated hero and you're an ex-baseball player. That'll make a great sales pitch."

"Okay, but only if you lay off the hero stuff. I'm just a wounded soldier who used to play."

Lew slapped him on the back and grinned. "You'll do just fine."

Lew then blew his whistle to signal the class that it was time to start.

Lloyd still stood near Milt as the men lined up for their warm-up exercises.

"Did you see Nurse McEwen before she left?"

Milt shook his head. "Nope. Didn't get a chance. Last time I saw her was after the radio show."

"Don't worry about that guy Attwater. She's not interested in him."

"Well, she's sure not interested in a guy like me," Milt insisted.

"Don't be so sure."

Milt took his place in line and followed Lew's lead in the exercises.

He knew that Annie liked him. But she had no intention of dating him much less getting serious. No. She was a sensible girl. She could see that Milt had nothing to offer her. And she sure wasn't romantically inclined toward a cripple with only one arm and a scarred face when she could have any whole, handsome man she wanted. Besides she didn't know about his other inadequacies. That would really push her away.

He'd been surprised when she'd said her transfer to New York came through and even more so when she said she planned to look for Joe's wife when she got there. With so little information he doubted she'd find anything.

Meanwhile, he'd focus on getting stronger and learning what he could do with only one arm. He could learn from the other men who were glad to be alive even with missing limbs. At least he'd made it home and he didn't have face the possible death Ade and his other friends faced every day.

Chapter 36

Annie's travel orders allowed her time to stop in Chattanooga and visit her family, which gave her an opportunity to show Uncle Herschel and Aunt Millie the letter from Milt's friend in person. Although she dreaded it, they deserved to know how Joe died.

She arrived on Saturday morning unannounced.

From the front entrance, she heard her father and Uncle Herschel arguing in her father's study. To avoid getting in the middle of their dispute, she climbed the stairs to look for her mother.

She knocked on her mother's bedroom door.

"Mrs. Rice?" a weak voice answered.

Annie pushed open the door. "It's me."

"Annie!" Her mother's hands flew up and the afghan slid from her lap.

Annie crossed the room and wrapped her arms around her mother's frail shoulders. When she let go, she reached down and retrieved the colorful afghan her mother had crocheted.

"This is lovely. You always make the prettiest things."

"Oh, it's nothing. Something to pass the time." Her mother pointed to the other chair. "Sit down." Before Annie could get seated comfortably, her mother continued. "When did you get home? We didn't know you were coming, did we?"

"No. I decided at the last minute."

"Oh, it's so nice to have you so close."

"I heard Father and Uncle Herschel downstairs. They seemed to be having a disagreement, so I didn't disturb them."

"Oh, they're probably arguing politics or maybe something about the house. I don't know. They can't seem to agree on anything."

"Where's Aunt Millie?"

"Working. Always working. I keep telling her that place is going to blow up and with her in it."

"Have they had explosions? Munitions can be very dangerous."

"Of course, they have. But only little ones. One day…well when it happens, I hope Millie is not there." She looked away as if gazing into the past. "Can't lose anyone else."

"Where's Mrs. Rice?"

"She should be around somewhere. She might be off doing the shopping. Or she might be out in the garden. She grows vegetables, you know." She stared at Annie for a moment then an idea lit her face. "You must be hungry. Of course, you are."

She flung the afghan aside and pushed herself up to her feet.

"That's all right, Mother. I can find something for myself."

"Nonsense. I'll go down with you and we'll find something for both of us. How's that?"

Her mother's smile warmed Annie's heart. The older woman had been listless for so long that Annie had wondered if she would ever show any animation again.

Down in the kitchen Annie's mother pulled out bread and crackers. Then she rustled around in the refrigerator and set out a hunk of cheese, a jar of jam, and some eggs.

"Surely we can make something out of all this."

Annie covered her mouth to keep from laughing. "Yes. We can make something." She reached up and pulled a plate out of the cabinet. "Maybe I'll just have a jam sandwich."

"There's milk, too." Her mother turned back and extracted a bottle of milk.

"That's fine," Annie said. Her mother had always been helpless in the kitchen, so her efforts to feed her daughter on short notice touched Annie's heart.

"So, what do we have here?" Her father entered the kitchen with his usual gruff manner. Uncle Herschel followed him. "This is unexpected."

Annie tried to smile in greeting. "Hello."

"There must be some reason for you to grace us with your company." Her father's words dripped with sarcasm. "And Ethel, what's come over you? Preparing food. So unlike you."

"Mother thought I might be hungry."

"She never thinks that I might be hungry. Do you, my dear?"

"Why, I'll be happy to find you something, too." Annie's mother flitted around the kitchen opening cabinets as she searched for more food. "I'm sure Mrs. Rice…"

"Yes. Mrs. Rice will no doubt be home soon. At least I can count on someone to feed me."

"George, let's go…" Uncle Herschel tried to distract her father to no avail.

"I'll just…" her mother muttered, a lost look on her face.

"You'll just what?" His voice rose as his face flushed. "Good for nothing woman," he muttered.

"You shouldn't say such things," Annie interjected. "She's doing the best she can."

"How would you know? You ran off. Left us to fend for ourselves. Didn't care anything about the rest of us. You should have stayed here and taken care of your helpless mother instead of leaving her to Millie and Mrs. Rice. Isn't that what daughters are for?"

Annie gritted her teeth and made herself stay silent. No one ever argued with her father and won, especially not her. He loved hurting people and he knew just where to strike.

Her father stood there glaring at her and her mother.

"George, let's go see if we can find that handy man. See if he's got that window fixed."

Annie silently blessed Uncle Herschel. Now she prayed her father would listen to him and leave.

"Hmph." Her father turned and stomped out of the room.

Her mother sighed as she sunk down into a chair.

Her father's angry words still rang in Annie's ears. He'd implied that she didn't come home unless she had a specific reason, and he was right. She'd intentionally stayed away. And the only reason she'd come home this weekend was to tell them what she'd learned about Joe.

She looked over at the frail woman fumbling to open the jar of jam.

"I'll do that," Annie said.

"It's just that it hasn't been opened in so long. The

283

lid's stuck."

Annie took the mason jar and strained to open it. Finally, the ring twisted off and she removed the disk, revealing about two-thirds of a jar of strawberry jam. She held it up and sniffed in the luscious aroma. The Army never served homemade strawberry jam.

"That's been in there since the last time you were home. No one eats it but you and Joe. Remember...." She dabbed at a tear slipping down her wrinkled cheek, and then, she looked up and smiled at Annie. "It sure was a good thing we put up so much of it...that year we had the bumper crop...now when was that...'41, or was it '42?"

"I don't know." Annie shook her head. If her mother started to reminisce, she could go on forever.

Annie quickly spread the jam on two pieces of bread and took a bite from one, before crossing to the cabinet.

"When will Aunt Millie get home?" She reached for a glass.

"Oh, sometime in the afternoon. I lose track of time."

"Before supper?" She poured about half a glass of milk and then returned the milk bottle to the refrigerator.

"Oh, yes." Her mother followed her every movement. "Now sit down and eat."

Annie sat and took another bite of the scrumptious yet simple meal.

"Why do you ask? What do you want with Millie?"

"I have something to tell them."

"Then he was right." Her mother's disappointment was clear. "That's the reason you came home."

"Not the only reason." Guilt crept up Annie's spine. She wanted to deny their accusations, but she couldn't. She hadn't wanted to come home. Had dreaded the thought of it. But she couldn't wait any longer. They deserved to know how Joe died.

And she had to tell them of her transfer to New York, that she'd be further from home, and she didn't know when she'd be back.

Hours later, Annie faced Uncle Herschel and Aunt Millie with the letter from Milt's friend Ade Carlton in her shaking hand. She read the words, blinking back tears. Their gasps caused her to pause momentarily before she finished reading.

They all sat in silence for a while after the initial shock at learning that Joe had been killed by a sniper. Aunt Millie sobbed into Uncle Herschel's chest as he stared into nothingness.

Finally, Herschel got to his feet and perused the map of Sicily still propped up against the wall where it had been when Milt was here.

"Makes sense that they would shoot the officer. They were probably in a defensive position, and they wanted to slow us down as much as they could. By taking out the officer in charge of the engineers, that would delay getting the road fixed and hold up the Americans' advance."

Annie listened without making any reply. She knew her uncle was trying to work things out in his mind, like he'd been doing since the news of Joe's death. Only now he knew a little more about what happened.

"You'd think Joe would have known they'd have snipers. Would've stayed behind cover instead of exposing himself."

"Milt said there wasn't much cover, at least not much vegetation. He said it was dry and rocky." Annie stopped herself from saying any more. She didn't want them to talk about the possibility of another letter, from Wazinski, with more information.

"Still…" He turned back to the map. "They would have been near Troina. Isn't that what Milt said?"

"Yes," Annie confirmed.

While Uncle Herschel searched the map, Aunt Millie turned to Annie. "Sgt. Greenlee's friend sounded like he was happy to hear from him…to know he was alive. They must have been worried about him, not knowing whether he lived or died, I mean."

"Yes." Annie had read the letter so many times she almost had it memorized. Yet she hadn't thought about how Milt's friends had reacted after he was hit. Milt said he didn't remember what happened. If he was carried away, bleeding and unconscious, his friends must have thought he was as good as dead.

"Here it is," Uncle Herschel announced. He kept his finger on the map as he turned to face them. "Probably needed to take it to get to Messina…over here." He pointed to the tip of Sicily closest to Italy.

"Remember Milt said that Troina was on top of a mountain, kind of like this one." Uncle Herschel nodded so she continued. "He said there weren't as many trees, but in places the mountain was almost straight up like here on Lookout Mountain with very rocky, rough terrain."

"Like Lookout Mountain? Yes, I remember him saying that." Uncle Herschel stepped closer, soaking up her every word.

"He said he didn't think it was as high, but when they got to the top they could look out over the valley where they'd come from, kind of like we can look out over Chattanooga."

Herschel nodded. "The Germans were above them, on the high ground. Like the Confederates firing down on the Yankees when they attacked up the mountain."

"Yes." Annie could see the light of understanding on his face. Aunt Millie covered Annie's hand with her own. Her aunt understood, too, but her face revealed the pain she felt imagining her son's death.

The stark reality sounded so harsh she wanted to soften it somehow. "Milt told me that from up on that mountain they had a beautiful view of Mt. Etna. The big volcano on Sicily. He said it was huge with snow up near the top, even in August."

"That's where Joe is buried. Somewhere in Sicily. With strangers. So far away with no one to care for his grave."

Annie patted her aunt's hand to comfort this dear woman who'd lost her only son.

****

Uncle Herschel went to get her father and mother to tell them about Joe's death while she waited with Aunt Millie.

Her father came in grumbling, as usual, with her mother following quietly.

"Annie brought us this letter…from a friend of that young man…" Uncle Herschel said.

"Sgt. Milt Greenlee," Annie interjected.

"Yes, Greenlee. Anyway, the letter says that he talked to another man who'd been in the Engineers with Joe…in Sicily." Uncle Herschel looked at his wife, who held a handkerchief to her mouth to contain her emotions. "This man…he was with Joe, when…"

"Go ahead. Spit it out. He was with Joe when he was killed. Is that what you're trying to say?" Her father could be so blunt and so impatient. He couldn't just sit back and listen, let Uncle Herschel tell it at his own speed.

"Yes. That's right."

"So, what did he say? What happened?"

"Joe was checking a road the Germans had blown up, to determine what they had to do to fix it."

"That was his job, wasn't it?"

Herschel nodded and looked away, toward the map. "The Germans held the high ground. Joe's outfit was trying to take it. Blowing up the road would have slowed them down."

"What are you trying to say, Herschel?"

Her father never let up. He pushed and pushed. Never understood how other people felt. Never saw their pain.

"He was shot by a sniper. Never knew what hit him."

For once her father was silent.

Her mother let out a forlorn cry and collapsed into Aunt Millie's arms.

Annie's chest tightened and deep inside her heart squeezed so hard she thought it would stop beating. She absently wiped tears from her cheeks. She didn't mean to cry. Didn't know when the tears started.

Aunt Millie touched her knee. Annie looked up and met the other woman's gaze. Tears streamed down her face, too. Her handkerchief crumpled in a ball in her other hand.

"Damn!" Her father's curse jerked everyone's attention back to him. "Damn idiot." His face flushed red with anger.

They all stared in shock.

"I hope you're satisfied." Her father shook his fist at Uncle Herschel. "It's what you wanted, isn't it? Send him over there to get his head blown off. When I could have used my influence. Gotten him a desk job in Washington where he'd have been safe. He'd have had a future."

He stomped around, his gaze roaming from Uncle Herschel to Aunt Millie to his wife and finally settling on Annie.

"Humph," he roared. His steely blue gaze bore into her like an icy sword, his hatred so strong she could taste it.

Finally, he turned and stormed out of the room, leaving a wake of anguish behind him.

She'd been right to dread her father's reaction.

That night her mother went to bed with a severe headache. Annie assumed her father was in his study, but she certainly wasn't going to look for him. All she could do was hope he settled down by morning.

She knew that the bearer of bad news often bore the brunt of someone's grief and anger, but she wished that she wasn't the one always on the receiving end of his.

She hoped he'd said his piece, that her sleepless night full of thoughts of her family's collective misery was the end of it. But the next morning he rounded on her like he hadn't done in years.

She had just sat down at the piano and started to play through a song she had recently learned when the heavy door slid open, and he appeared.

"Good morning. I didn't realize that you were up and about."

"I haven't been to bed."

Annie took a deep breath and turned around to fully face him. "I'm sorry that the news was so upsetting for you. It was upsetting for everyone."

"How long have you had that letter?"

"I had to wait until I had some time off. I didn't want to try to tell you all over the telephone."

"But you and your boyfriend had plenty of time to talk about it. Didn't you?"

"I told you…he's not my boyfriend. He's been very kind to write and get his friend to find someone who knew Joe. You should be grateful."

"Grateful?" He moved closer to her. "Why would I be grateful? That Joe's dead? That he was stupid enough to walk right out in the open and get himself shot…in the head no less?"

"How could you say such a thing. Joe didn't mean to get shot."

"No. What did he mean to do? Be a hero? Go over there and come back with a chest full of medals? He got all that from Herschel. Couldn't see what a wimp Herschel was. That's cause Herschel never told him the truth. That he was a coward who got himself shot in the leg so he could go back to Paris and have a good time. Maybe that's what Joe thought. That he'd get wounded and sent home like that shot up boyfriend of yours."

Annie tried to calm herself. She'd heard similar things before. She knew how out of control he could get. "Father, I know you are hurting. You don't need to get all upset like this."

"Hurting. What do you know about it?"

"I'm a nurse. I have patients who have been through a lot and who get upset and it's my job to calm them down."

"Calm them down. Ha. You worthless excuse for a daughter. I thought when you went to nursing school that you would learn something. That your guilt at what you did to your brother … how you let him die…had spurred you to learn how to take care of people. So you could take care of your mother. And, God forbid, me. But no, you traipse off and join the Army. Go gallivanting around the country wearing that uniform and sidling up to any man who'll pay you any attention.

"You prey on those poor, crippled soldiers who think you care about them. But I know different. You don't care about anyone but yourself. You're still trying to make some kind of celebrity out of yourself. Trying to convince people that you're this big, fancy singer.

"I heard you telling Millie about singing on some radio show in Atlanta. Like Atlanta is some big city and you are some big star with her own radio show. Well, Atlanta's no bigger than Chattanooga and you're no more a big star than I am.

"You're just plain ol' Annie McEwen who daydreams instead of doing what she's supposed to. How many men have you let die, huh? Or do they let you anywhere near really sick ones. I bet not. Why, you couldn't take care of a dog, much less a man."

Annie wanted to shrivel up and die right there. If she could disappear into the cracks of the hardwood floor, she'd gladly do so to get away from him. This horrible man. This man she couldn't get away from no matter what she did. Even hundreds of miles away she had to fight to keep his words out of her head.

She forced herself to move, past him, out into the hallway. She glanced up the stairs. No. She wouldn't go hide in her room. She wasn't a child anymore.

Instead, she turned toward the door.

"Where do you think you're going, young lady?"

She didn't look back, didn't answer him. She opened the door, stepped through it, and pulled it shut behind her. Then she put one foot in front of the other…down the walk and out onto the sidewalk.

She saw nothing. She just walked.

Chapter 37

New York proved more exciting than she remembered. The military personnel crowding the city added to the bustle.

After high school her mother brought her to New York to make the rounds of agents and producers, but a teenaged singer with limited experience drew little attention. In the evenings they'd delighted in numerous Broadway shows and the show-biz bug had bitten her big time.

Now older and wiser, she made a list of talent agents and band leaders to see when she got leave to the city. She hoped her confidence and determination would get her an audition.

She was wrong.

The first agents wouldn't even take her name. "Get some experience," they told her. And contacting any of the band leaders proved impossible without an introduction, like the letter from Charlie Cushman she didn't get. Continuing her search, she visited the next agent on her list. Although nicer, he turned her down saying "Come back after the war."

Making her way back to the train station, she spotted a sign, "Singer Wanted" in front of a small "club." Desperate, she went in. The place appeared a bit dingy and more of a bar than a club.

"Can you start tonight?" the owner asked.

Annie quickly agreed, eager to prove her abilities. She tried out the piano. Without sheet music she'd have to sing the songs she knew by heart.

Customers slowly filtered in. When the owner signaled her to start, she played the piano and sang an old familiar ballad. More people arrived and the liquor flowed. She doubted anyone could hear her for the loud talking and laughing from the inebriated customers. The language got rougher as the evening progressed. Annie became more uncomfortable.

A couple of drunks approached her, pawing her, and making indecent comments. She turned them down flat, but they persisted, even trying to kiss her. She called for help from the owner who stood nearby. He only laughed at their antics.

Annie had had enough. She walked out, both disgusted and a little afraid the drunks would follow her. She vowed she'd never work in a place like that again.

Hurrying away, she wondered if working in joints like that was what people meant by "paying your dues."

****

On her next weekend pass into the city, Annie decided to search for Joe's wife instead of visiting more agents.

She gave the taxi driver the only address she had, a run-down apartment building in Manhattan, and talked to the superintendent and his wife.

"We get lots of people in and out. Can't remember everybody, especially not two years back," the man said.

When Annie mentioned that Carlene had married a soldier, the woman laughed. "So many of those boys in and out. We had a bunch of show girls in here back then. Lots of soldiers came to see those girls." She paused. "Seems like one of those girls talked kinda like you."

"Was her name Carlene?" Annie asked.

"I don't know. Could've been."

"You called them show girls. Do you know where they worked?"

The man smiled. "That bunch she's talking about worked at Radio City Music Hall." His wife eyed him. "I know 'cause they said I could come see 'em dance. Said they could get me a free pass."

This exchange made Annie plan a visit to Radio City Music Hall.

"Annie, this was a great idea," Flo said following the Usherette down the aisle.

"Thanks," Annie said.

Two other nurses followed in the semi-darkness. They all settled into their seats waiting for the show to begin.

As soon as the movie started, Annie eased out of her seat and headed backstage. The Rockettes would perform after the movie. While the dancers were getting ready, she talked her way into the dressing room, saying she was a friend of one of the dancers. Excitement buzzed as everyone prepared for their performance. She longed to join them, to step out on stage and sing.

Annie explained her mission to one of the girls. "I'm looking for my cousin's wife, Carlene. She used to work here, about two years ago."

The dancer shook her head. "Never heard of her." Then she turned. "You might try Elsie over there. The one with the coal-black hair. She's been here the longest."

Annie made her way through the crowded dressing room to where the woman sat applying makeup.

"Are you Elsie?" Annie asked.

The girl eyed her in the mirror. "I'm Annie McEwen. I'm looking for my cousin's wife who I think worked here a couple of years ago. Her name was Carlene."

"I don't know." She leaned in to straighten an eyelash. "The name doesn't sound familiar."

"She might have had a southern accent, like me." Annie was desperate for any information.

"No. I've worked with a couple of southern girls. One called Nancy and the other…let me see, something like Jasmine or Josie. Definitely not Carlene."

"Would anyone else remember her?"

"Nope. I break in all the new girls. Have for over four years now. I'd remember if she'd danced with us."

A pang of disappointment sliced through Annie. What now?

"Maybe you should try some of the other dance halls."

Discouraged, Annie made her way to the lobby. Rather than return to the movie she perused the modern art in the elaborate art deco space and debated her next move. A uniformed employee walking toward the office area caught her eye.

Annie approached her. "Excuse me."

The usherette stopped. "Yes. Can I help you?"

Annie flashed a friendly smile. "I hope so. Have you worked here long?"

"Yes. Almost three years. Why?"

"Well...I'm Annie and I'm trying to find a relative. You see we've lost track of her and while I'm stationed nearby, I'm trying to find her."

Despite the quizzical look on her face, the thirty-something woman said, "How can I help?"

Relieved, Annie continued. "She used to work here. Her name's Carlene. Do you remember her?"

"Carlene? Hmmm."

"It would have been about two years ago. She married a soldier." Annie heard the desperation in her own voice.

"There was a girl, worked as an usherette for a while. Might have been her." She eyed Annie as if trying to access how much to say.

"The soldier she married was my cousin. He was killed in Sicily."

"Oh, I'm sorry." She gazed across the lobby as if conjuring up some memory. "She was a pretty little thing. Wanted to get into show business." She turned back to Annie. "She fell for this soldier. Handsome fellow in his uniform. I warned her off. Told her soldiers were trouble. Leave you high and dry."

"Was that Carlene?"

The usherette nodded. "I think that was her name."

"Do you know what happened to her?"

The woman shook her head. "I was off for a while. Had to take care of my mother after her operation. When I came back, she was gone."

Annie sighed. Another dead end. "Thanks for your help."

"Sure thing." The woman turned to walk away.

"Could you ask around? See if anyone else remembers her?"

"Sure."

They exchanged contact information, but Annie had little hope of hearing anything more.

****

Milt stared at the pages in front of him, struggling to decipher the words scribbled there. Obviously written in the field, Wazinski's atrocious handwriting ran together in a series of scribbles. Ade's writing wasn't the best, but his friend's inclination to print made his letters much easier to read. This was impossible: at least it was for Milt.

He'd always struggled to read. If he worked at it, he could read printed words, especially if he could take his time. Handwriting was incredibly difficult. His tutor said everyone wrote differently and that's what made it harder for Milt to read. Over the years he'd become familiar with his family members' handwriting, probably because all of them knew about his problem and took great care in their writing. His sister Katherine even typed her letters.

But this thing from Wazinski…he'd only been able to pick out a few words.

Much as he hated to ask for help, Milt resolved to find one of the Grey Ladies to read it for him. Maybe he could even find someone to transcribe it. His father's secretary could decipher any handwriting, no matter how bad. Worst case, Milt could take the letter home and get her to type it up.

He would tell Annie about the letter, once he knew what it said, not on the telephone though. He could never read it to her. No, she deserved to read it herself.

The letter provided the perfect excuse for him to go to New York and see her in person. Question was, when? His doctor had him scheduled for another skin graft. He'd shoot for after that. Give it time to heal.

He scanned the letter again, picking out words he thought he recognized. He was pretty sure about one very important word, "baby." Annie would definitely want to know about that.

Chapter 38

Milt made his way from the platform to the huge lobby of Grand Central Terminal. Annie's wire said to meet her in the Servicemen's Lounge.

Wandering among the people, he searched for an information booth where he could get directions. He glanced up at the enormous War Bonds display then up at the ceiling high above. A sign on the balcony caught his eye. Its bold letters announced, "Service Men's Lounge."

Annie sat alone at a table, a cup of coffee in front of her. She glanced up when he stood beside her.

"Hello," he said.

A lovely smile spread across her face. "Hi there."

He slid into a seat opposite her, where he could take in all her beauty.

"How was your trip?" She eyed his left arm in a sling.

"Fine, fine." He followed her gaze. "This is just to protect my arm on the train. Had a skin graph a couple of weeks ago. It's still healing."

"Still no feeling?"

He shook his head and stared at the table between them. The scar might look better with the new skin, but the arm was as useless as ever.

"So, what's this about a letter? Your telegram said you'd gotten one."

Grateful for the change of subject, Milt looked up and gazed into her lovely face. "Yep. I got a letter from Wazinski. You remember? The guy Ade said knew your cousin Joe."

"What did he say?"

Milt reached into his inside pocket and withdrew the envelope. "It's in here."

She slowly reached for it, her fingers shaking.

"His handwriting was hard to read, so I had one of the Grey Ladies type it up."

She laid the pages on the table between them. "Is it bad?"

He wouldn't lie to her. "No. Not so bad. Interesting, I'd say."

At that she met his gaze. "What do you mean?"

"Just read it. Okay?"

****

Annie hesitated. She remembered the last letter, the one that told of Joe being shot in the head by a sniper. That horrid image came to her again. The image that wouldn't go away.

Would this letter do the same? Create horrible images she couldn't forget?

She began to read and understood what Milt meant about the handwriting. She was too anxious to know what he had to say to decipher it herself, so she switched to the typed copy.

My name is John Wazinski, and I'm a Sergeant in the 1st Engineers. I was assigned to drive for our commanding officer, Lt. Joe McEwen, in Sicily. Your friend said you were trying to find out what happened to Lt. McEwen so you could tell his family. He said too that you were in Sicily at the time, so you know what it was like.

We were near Troina supporting the 16th. They called us up cause the Krauts blew up a road. One of those where the road winds around the mountain. Rough terrain. No cover. I warned the Lt. to be careful out there walking around trying to figure out what we had to do to fix the road. I heard the shot. Saw him drop. A sniper. Up above us. The infantry got on it and scrambled up the mountain after him. I went out and got the Lt. and put him on the jeep. And carried him back to the CP. They got him in the head. He was dead instantly. You can tell his family he didn't suffer any.

The Lt. was a good guy, and we were sorry to lose him. I wrote to his wife after he was killed. They had me go through his things to send back to her and I found her picture, so I sent that back to her. I felt real bad for her with a baby coming and all.

Annie stopped reading, stunned. She looked up at Milt who nodded.

"Baby," she squeaked.

"Yeah, I know. That's the stunner." He rubbed his head where the bandage had been removed and scars ran across his close-cropped scalp. "You didn't know, did you?"

"No." She shook her head and then looked down at the letter again. "I don't understand. Why didn't he write and tell us?"

"Maybe he didn't have time."

"But he was killed in August. He left in…March." She mentally counted. "She would have been five months…"

"You have to remember how slow the mail is when you are in the field." Milt sounded like he'd already thought this through. "When I was in Sicily, I got mail that was two months old."

"But surely she would have told him sooner than that. I mean…" How could she voice her fear that the baby might not be Joe's? Why had the question immediately popped into her head?

"Go ahead and read the rest of it," Milt urged.

She found her place.

I felt real bad for her with a baby coming and all. Lt. McEwen had just gotten her letter telling him a couple of days before he was killed. I remember how excited he got. Told anyone who would listen. He'd started a letter to her. I found it in his things and sent it to her. All I remember about her was that she was a pretty young girl with dark hair. I think her name was Carla or something like that. The address he had was in care of a person called "Packard." I remember because it put me in mind of the car. Anyway, it was on some "Bush" street in Brooklyn New York. I never heard anything back from her. Thought I might look her up if I ever get back home. Lt. McEwen sure was good to me.

Hope this helps.
Yours truly,
John Wazinski

Annie put the letter down and sighed. The weight of Joe's loss enveloped her again hearing this man, this stranger, talk of Joe with such familiarity. They'd apparently been close, yet he could speak so objectively about a man he'd seen killed.

She looked up at Milt and wondered how many men he'd seen killed.

"It's not much to go on, is it?"

"What do you mean?"

"If I'm going to try to find her, he hasn't given me much information."

"Then you are going to try to find her?"

"I have to. Especially now. If there's a baby, I have to…to know if it's Joe's."

"You don't think it is?"

"I don't know what to think. She didn't answer any of our letters. She just disappeared. Why would she do that?"

Milt shook his head and looked away. "I don't know."

Chapter 39

After they left the restaurant where they'd eaten dinner, Annie asked, "Do you feel like walking?"

"Sure," he replied.

Annie's comfort with this sweet, kind man surprised her. She could talk to him, and he didn't tell her she was wrong or shouldn't feel something. He listened.

And, best of all, he didn't paw at her like other men had.

A cold wind whipped around the tall buildings, making her shiver. She pulled her cape more tightly around her. At the corner, she noticed the entrance to a park.

"Let's walk in the park?" she suggested.

"Sure." He looked both ways. "Wonder what time it closes? Or if it closes?"

"I don't know. Come on." She stepped off the curb and hurried across the street.

Milt caught up with her just as she reached the other side. "Glad I grabbed this overcoat. Down in Georgia, I didn't need it."

As they followed the walkway into the park, she glanced at Milt. "You sneaked up on me."

"What do you mean?"

"Being nice to me. Helping me look for Joe's widow. I know what you've been doing."

305

He slipped his arm through hers. "Has it worked?"

She didn't reply, yet it pleased her that he asked.

After a few minutes she said, "I haven't had very good luck with men." She shouldn't have said that. He might get the wrong impression.

"Maybe your luck will change."

One eyebrow raised in question; she eyed him.

He must have realized how he sounded. "I, uh…what I meant was that…uh…I'm sure you'll find someone."

Rather than reply she let him stammer on, as a blush spread from his neck to his cheeks.

"I…I mean…there are plenty of nice guys around."

She fought the giggle threatening to emerge. "Well, if you're trying to woo me, you're not exactly saying the right things."

"Me?" He looked away.

She waited.

Finally, he faced her. "Was I that obvious?"

She nodded. Then , she tugged his arm and began to walk.

"I had a boyfriend once. His name was Leroy. We were still in high school, but he made me feel so grown up. He took me to this club, and they let me sing with the band. Just a little three-piece band, but to me it was so exciting."

"Weren't you underage?"

"Yes. But that was part of the thrill. Knowing that I wasn't supposed to be there yet being treated like I belonged."

He nodded as if he understood.

"I was having such a good time that I didn't realize how much Leroy had been drinking. On the way home he almost ran off the road. I told him to let me drive even though I'd never driven before."

She glanced up to see Milt's reaction to her tale. Despite his frown he remained quiet.

"Anyway, Leroy pulled off the road. But instead of letting me drive, he got...well, he made improper advances." Let him imagine the rest because she couldn't say any more about that part of it. "I managed to get out of the car, and I started walking down the road. He came after me but about the time he caught up with me another car came along. They stopped. Two men. I didn't know who they were, but I guess they could see that I was trying to get away from Leroy. I told them I needed a ride home. And they took me home. To my father."

This time he stopped and looked at her with such an intense expression, as if he were trying to see inside her and really understand.

"What did your father do?"

She forced a smile. "Well, you met my father." She pulled her gaze away from his. "He was angry. At me. At Leroy. He forbade me from ever seeing him again." The pain from long ago erupted in a sob. Her fist covered her mouth to stifle it.

He pulled her close, saying nothing, just letting her know he was there for her.

Finally, she continued. "He didn't have to do that. I had already decided not to see him again, not ever again. I'd trusted him. Cared about him. And I thought he cared about me." She stared past Milt's shoulder into the darkness remembering the panic, the sense of betrayal, the way he'd man-handled her, trying to force her to do things she didn't want to do.

"I was so humiliated." She jerked back to face Milt. "He didn't rape me, if that's what you're thinking." She shook her head back and forth still trying to understand what had happened herself. "He just changed so fast. He wasn't the boy I knew. He was someone else. Someone who shoved me down and kissed me when I didn't want to be kissed, like he could force me to do what he wanted, to be what he wanted. And when I didn't, he got angry and …"

Milt pulled her close again. He didn't say anything. He just held her. And she let him. She stood there just letting him hold her, feeling his one strong arm around her shoulder, protecting her from the memories.

"What's funny is that's the way my father acted. With anger. Always trying to force me to do what he wanted. Never caring what I wanted." She drew a deep breath and pulled away from him. "It took me a while to see that. Joe was the one who made me see that Leroy was a lot like my father. That that was why I was drawn to him." She met his eyes then. "Does that make sense?"

"Yes. It does."

"I made up my mind then that I wasn't going to get mixed up with anyone."

He nodded.

She waited for him to respond, to tell her he was different, that he was the man for her.

"Annie. I don't know if I'm the man for you or not." He had an odd look on his face, one she couldn't read. "I want to be." He looked away. The silent seconds ticked away. Finally, he spoke again.

"I want you to be happy. I want you to find whatever it is that makes you happy. I'd like for it to be me. But I've got problems, too. I don't know what I'm going to do with my life. With my limitations. I'll probably have to go back home and work for my father…and my brother. That's not much to offer someone like you."

"What do you mean, someone like me?"

"I mean a beautiful, talented woman who wants a life in a city like this, singing on a stage with a band, on the radio, making records, touring around the country." He shook his head. "I couldn't ask you to give up that dream."

"Sometimes I think it's just a dream and that's all it will ever be."

"No. That's not true. You are too good. You'll make it. I know you will."

She couldn't help smiling at that. He believed in her. It meant so much to hear him say it. To have someone who really believed in her.

"You sound like Joe. He was the best at cheering me up when I got down."

He answered her smile with one of his own. Such a nice smile. It lit up his whole face. Even in the dimness she could see his eyes crinkling and sparkling behind the frames of his glasses. At first, she hadn't liked the glasses, but she'd grown accustomed to them. They made him look older and wiser, not the angry young man she'd first met.

A cool breeze blew up under her cape and she shivered.

"You're cold. We'd better get back to your hotel."

"Not before we do one more thing." She put her arms around him and pulled him close. Then she leaned her head back so she could look up into his eyes.

He smiled down at her. "What?"

"This." She kissed him, gently at first, feeling his firm lips against hers.

He was holding back, waiting for her. And she wanted more than just a chaste kiss. She wanted the passion she'd seen in the movies. But she didn't know how. She'd been afraid for so long, afraid of being pushed into something she didn't want. Now she was pushing for what she did want. So, she followed her instincts, did what felt right. And he did, too.

He kissed her like no one had ever kissed her. His own passion, as bottled up as hers, unleashed in a scorching kiss that made her toes curl.

When they separated, both were breathless.

The question on his face pierced her heart. "I'm…"

Her fingers covered his lips. "Don't. Don't say you're sorry."

His expression relaxed. "I won't…if you won't."

A smile strained her cheeks. "No, I'm not sorry. It's what I wanted."

She hooked her arm through his. A smug sense of accomplishment rose in her chest.

"Now we can head back."

They walked along in silence. Annie relived the kiss in her mind. He had easily eliminated her fear. Maybe finally telling someone about Leroy, someone who listened and didn't criticize, had dissipated the fear, and allowed her to express her true self.

Then, she shook off the unfamiliar feelings. For now, she would stick to her plans and focus on her career. Maybe later she'd think seriously about Milt and how much she'd enjoyed his company.

****

"Brrrr. It's cold."

Milt chuckled to himself. "I've been through much worse than this."

"Really. Where?" She frowned in such a pretty way that he couldn't help but smile.

"Well, in England and in North Africa. Now that was cold."

"In North Africa?"

"Yeah. At night it gets really cold, and the tents we slept in didn't offer much protection from the elements."

"I thought Africa was hot, not cold." She snuggled close to him and grasped his hand.

"Well, it was. Very cold."

They walked in silence for a few minutes.

"Do you think maybe Joe met her at Radio City Music Hall?" Annie blurted out.

Surprised at her sudden change, Milt thought back to their previous conversation. Over dinner she'd told him about her search thus far. "He could have. That usherette you talked to claimed she remembered Carlene."

"But she didn't know what happened to her."

"I know. It's something, though."

"Yeah," she nodded.

"Wazinski's letter gives us some clues." He squeezed her hand. "She was living in Brooklyn with an aunt named Packard when she wrote to Joe about the baby."

"I still can't believe it. A baby."

"I know." He paused. "I haven't a clue how we go about finding someone in Brooklyn."

"They have a separate telephone book for

Brooklyn. I say we start there. We can look for all the listings for Packard. There can't be that many."

"You mean you want to go find every Packard in the book?" Milt dreaded the thought of reading a phone book. Annie couldn't know how all the letters and numbers ran together and scrambled themselves when he tried to read something like that.

"If I have to, yes."

Milt's stomach churned. "When…do you want to do this?"

She pulled away so she could look him in the face. "Why not now?" she beamed.

"Now?"

"I'm sure they have lots of phone books at the train station."

"Why not wait until morning?" Milt asked. He racked his brain for an excuse. "I'm pretty tired."

"I'm sorry. I forgot you just got here."

Milt slipped his arm around hers. Much as he wanted to spend more time with her, he wouldn't tonight. "Yeah. I'm bushed."

Chapter 40

The next morning, they hired a taxi and made their way to Brooklyn with a list of addresses to find. First on their list were the addresses on Flatbush Avenue.

Milt had managed to be late when he met with Annie at Grand Central Station. He'd found her pouring over a large telephone book with a list already started. Once again, he had avoided the arduous task of reading, and once again, he'd deceived Annie. Guilt mixed with relief.

The first address on Annie's list turned out to be a dead end. No one answered the door and the superintendent, though not very cooperative, told them the elderly tenant had been hospitalized.

At their second and third attempts, the occupants had never heard of a girl named Carlene.

Their fourth try turned out to be a brick, multi-story apartment building on a corner. They climbed the stairs to the second floor and rang the bell for the apartment on the list.

A stout, dark-haired woman answered the door, frowning at the two of them. "Yes?"

Milt took the lead. "Good morning, ma'am. We are looking for Mrs. Packard."

"That's me." Her eyes narrowed. "What do you want?"

"My name is Milt Greenlee and this…" He

gestured toward Annie who smiled sweetly. "This is Annie McEwen."

He looked for any sign of recognition in the woman's face. A slight frown creased her brow.

"We are looking for Carlene McEwen," he continued. "Is she by any chance your niece?"

"What do you want with her?"

Jackpot! They'd found the right place.

"She was married to Annie's cousin, Lt. Joe McEwen."

"That sorry son-of-a-gun," the woman exploded. "Left Carlene high and dry."

"He was sent overseas," Annie defended her beloved Joe.

"She should never have gotten involved with that louse. Took advantage of her, then left."

"We know it must have been hard on her," Milt said, trying to calm the irate woman.

"Hard? On her. On us. He didn't care that he left her all alone with no way to support herself."

"He loved her," Annie said. "He wrote me and told me about her, about how much he loved her."

"Bunk! He took advantage of her, I tell you." Bitterness strained her voice. "Seduced her. Left her with child to raise." Her hard gaze bore into Annie. "If he had loved her, he would have waited."

Milt had to defuse the situation, or they wouldn't learn anything. At least in her ranting she'd confirmed the existence of the child.

"Maybe we could come in and sit down and talk calmly."

"No, you don't." She pushed the door to shut it.

Milt put his foot in the door to keep it open. "If

you'll just let us talk to Carlene."

"Carlene's gone," she announced, while shoving the door against his foot.

"What?" Annie gasped. "Where did she go?"

"I'm not telling you a thing. She's better off not having anything to do with you or your good-for-nothing family."

Milt thought of the unanswered letters and wondered if Carlene had ever seen them.

"Just give us her address and we'll leave you alone."

"I told her he was no good. And his family was no good. Any man who would treat a girl the way he did is scum in my book."

"Joe was a good man. It's not his fault that he got killed over there. And it's not my aunt and uncle's fault either." Annie was near tears.

"Just her address. That's all we ask," Milt pleaded.

"No. I'll not do one thing for that sorry so and so. Now leave me alone."

This time she pushed hard on the door, smashing his foot. Milt jerked his foot back and the door slammed. The lock clicked and the chain rattled. The woman was taking no chances.

Milt looked over at a frustrated Annie and shrugged.

She swiped at the tears streaming down her cheeks. "What do we do now?"

"I don't know." He put his hand on her shoulder and turned her toward the stairway. They descended in silence. On the street they stood looking in one direction and then the other.

"Maybe some of the neighbors know where she

went," Annie said.

"Yeah. Only how do we know which ones to ask?" He glanced back at the building they had just left. "Can't exactly go door to door. Mrs. Packard's neighbors would probably be as hostile as she was."

"Surely Carlene had friends. Someone she talked to."

Milt's every step reverberated through his foot. Mrs. Packard had nearly crushed it. Add that to the exhaustion from tossing on the flimsy cot that passed for a bed the night before, he searched for a place to sit for a while and rest.

A drug store across the street caught his eye. "What do you say we get a cup of coffee or maybe a sandwich?"

****

A lunch counter took up one side of the drug store. Behind it a young woman stood chatting with a couple of teenagers drinking sodas.

Annie and Milt passed the two youngsters and sat on stools further down.

The waitress approached. "What can I get you?"

"I'll have coffee," Milt said. "And can I get a sandwich?"

"Coffee for me, too, and a piece of pie. Whatever you have." Annie added.

"Sure."

The girl plunked empty coffee mugs in front of each of them, turned and reached for a pot of coffee sitting on a burner. As she poured the coffee, she slid a typed menu in front of them.

"You want cream or sugar?"

Milt shook his head and concentrated on the menu.

Yes, please." Annie nodded to the waitress.

The young woman fetched a little cream pitcher and a sugar dispenser.

"Give me a ham sandwich with mustard," Milt said.

"Sure thing."

The waitress quickly returned with a slice of apple pie and placed it in front of Annie. Then she moved farther down the counter and began preparing Milt's sandwich.

"I wonder if she knew Carlene. She's about the right age."

Surprised at his comment, her gaze shifted to the young woman slathering mustard on two slices of bread. "I don't know."

"I'm going to ask her. Might strike out but you never know."

When the waitress returned with his sandwich, he spoke up. "We are looking for someone who used to live around here."

The girl's bored expression disappeared. "Who?"

"Her name is Carlene. She lived with the Packard's, down the street."

"Oh, sure. I remember Carlene. She's been gone a while, though."

Annie couldn't believe their luck. "Do you know where she went?"

The waitress eyed them both suspiciously. "Why are you asking?"

"She was married to my cousin," Annie blurted out.

"Her husband's family…" Milt nodded toward Annie, "has been trying to contact her."

"You mean she really was married?"

The question wasn't what Annie expected.

"Yes. My cousin, Lt. Joe McEwen, met her while he was on leave, and they got married. Then he shipped out."

"Lt. McEwen was killed in Sicily a few months later," Milt added.

The girl stood with her mouth open. Finally, she said, "Oh, my gosh."

Her gaze roamed the store as if she was looking for someone. "I feel so bad. I never believed her. I just thought it was a story she made up to explain the baby."

"It's true," Annie assured her.

"Mrs. Packard wouldn't tell us how to find Carlene. Do you know?"

"That old battle axe. She's awful. I always felt sorry for Carlene, having to live with those people. Her husband's almost as bad as she is."

"Can you help us?" Annie pleaded.

"Wait just a minute." The waitress headed down the counter to help a newly arrived customer.

"Do you think she knows anything?" Annie asked.

"Beats me. Guess we'll find out when she comes back." Milt picked up the sandwich and took a bite.

He had devoured half his sandwich when the waitress returned.

"I guess we should introduce ourselves. I'm Sgt. Milt Greenlee. And this is Lt. Annie McEwen."

The waitress nodded. "I'm Rebecca."

"You said you knew Carlene?" Annie asked.

"Yes. I did." She looked over toward her newest customer. "I went to school with her."

"Then you must know her maiden name. We know

it wasn't Packard."

"Oh, no. She just lived with the Packard's. Her name was Tyler, Carlene Tyler," Rebecca said. "She came here to live with them…" She hesitated. "Eighth or ninth grade, I think."

Annie had finished the pie, so Rebecca took the plate.

"Must have been ninth," Rebecca continued. "I remember her coming into Mrs. Arndt's class."

"Why did she come here? And where did she come from?"

"I think her parents died in a house fire. Old Mrs. Packard was her aunt, so she came to live with them."

Milt turned up his cup and drank the last of his coffee.

"Do you know where she went?" Annie asked anxiously.

Rebecca offered Milt more coffee before answering. "No, sorry."

Annie's gaze dropped to her own coffee cup and covered it with her hand before Rebecca refilled it. Milt had advised her to just let people talk rather than bombarding them with questions, but she found it hard to hold her tongue.

"You see, after high school, she'd moved out. Into the city. She wanted to get away from them." Rebecca nodded toward the Packard apartment. "And she had the idea that she could be a dancer in one of those Broadway shows."

"Then she comes back one day saying she was married to some soldier, and she was going to have a baby." Rebecca shook her head as she spoke. "No one in the neighborhood believed her, least of all the

319

Packard's. That old woman had a fit. Talked about Carlene something awful."

Annie ached for the poor girl.

"Carlene had a ring. And one time she tried to show me a letter she got. But I didn't believe her, I'm ashamed to say. I had no idea she was telling the truth."

"Then she left?" Annie asked.

"Yes. After she had the baby. Guess I couldn't blame her after the way everyone treated her."

"Was it a boy or a girl?"

"A little boy. And the cutest thing."

"But you don't know where she went." Milt came back to the critical question.

"No."

Annie blinked away tears as she met Milt's gaze. "We'll never find her."

He patted her hand. "Don't give up. We'll keep looking."

"I wish I knew. I really do. I feel so bad."

Annie couldn't think. It was like her brain had choked up as much as her throat.

"Is there anyone else around here who knew her? Someone she might have confided in?" Milt asked.

"No one I can think of." Rebecca looked down the counter again. She frowned and shook her head. "Maybe someone else from school," she offered. "I could ask around."

Annie pulled a handkerchief from her bag, afraid she'd start crying for real. "My aunt and uncle have written several times. The last letter was returned undeliverable. They've never seen Carlene or their grandson."

She'd gotten her hopes up when the girl said she

knew Carlene. They'd come so close. But it wasn't to be.

"Thank you for your help," Milt told the young woman.

"I'm sorry I couldn't do more. Is there somewhere I can reach you? If I do find out anything?"

"Oh, yes, I'll give you my name and address so you can write me directly." Annie fumbled in her bag and came out with a pen and paper.

"Do you know where Carlene came from when she moved here?" Milt asked.

"Oh, that's what I meant to tell you," Rebecca said.

Annie perked up. Maybe Carlene had family back where she came from and maybe that's where she went.

"She came from somewhere down south," Rebecca continued. "Like you. That's one reason she had a hard time fitting in."

"Was she from Tennessee?"

"Could have been. I don't remember. Some of the guys teased her about being a hillbilly." Rebecca smiled. "I don't think she liked it, but she kept quiet. Kept to herself. That's why I never could see her on the stage. She was too shy."

Annie handed her address to Rebecca.

"She did say one thing before she left," Rebecca said. "That she was going to take her little boy home. And the way she said it I thought she meant back where she came from. It wasn't long after that that she left."

Annie wondered where Carlene went.

Milt fished some money out of his pocket and put it on the counter.

Out on the street Annie turned to him.

"We still don't know where she is," she

complained. "Back home somewhere in the south could be anywhere."

"At least we know she has a little boy. And we have a pretty good idea why she didn't reply to the letters."

"Yeah. That horrible woman didn't give them to her."

They walked a little way and then Milt announced, "I have a surprise for you."

Chapter 41

"I wish I had an evening gown to wear," Annie commented, as they rode the elevator to the roof of the hotel where Milt had made reservations. A couple in lovely evening attire rode up with them; the lady wore a long flowing gown and the gentleman a tuxedo.

"You are just as beautiful in your uniform as you would be in an evening gown."

She appreciated him saying so even if she didn't believe him. He'd seen her in that gorgeous gown Margo Van Buren had loaned her. Given her, actually. But it was packed away in her room near the hospital.

"You are sure they said it would be okay?"

"Yes. Military people are expected to wear their uniforms."

"And you don't think anyone will say anything about our ranks?" As soon as she asked, she wanted to pull the words back, but she couldn't.

"It'll be fine," Milt said with a tinge of irritation in his voice.

She hated to say such things, but she didn't want him to get in trouble.

They stepped off the elevator into an elegant hall decorated with gilt framed paintings and a sparkling glass chandelier.

The Maitre d' took Milt's name, checked it against his list, and removed the velvet rope that barred the entrance to the night club. Bowing slightly, the Maitre d' said, "Welcome." If you will, please follow this gentleman to your table."

They weaved their way through the crowd, following the waiter to a tiny table on the far side of the room. Milt allowed the waiter to pull out Annie's chair and seat her rather than doing it himself. She understood, but the waiter didn't and gave Milt an impatient stare. Milt appeared perfectly normal standing there in his dress uniform with his left arm at his side. No one could tell until he was expected to use it and couldn't. She'd gotten used to it and rarely noticed until something like this happened and she was the only one who understood what was going on.

The waiter presented them with menus, small, beautifully printed ones enclosed in leather binders.

She looked up from hers to see that Milt had laid it on the table. He'd barely looked at it.

He met her gaze and frowned. "Did you want something to eat?"

She shook her head.

"Good. Cause I hadn't planned on eating here. Too expensive. If you are hungry, we can get something afterward."

"That's fine." The butterflies in her stomach weren't conducive to food.

She looked back at the menu. It only offered drinks and hors d'oeuvres. Hardly enough if they had intended to eat here. And Milt would have known that if he'd actually looked at the menu. Another of his odd behaviors.

"Do you want a drink?"

"Yes," she smiled. Maybe a glass of wine would

settle her excitement.

When the waiter returned Milt said, "We'll have some wine."

"Yes, sir. May I ask what you wish?"

Milt looked over at her. "Do you have champagne?"

"Sir. The menu…" He picked up the menu from in front of Milt, opened it and placed it right in front of him. "What we have is here. If you will choose one, I will be happy to…"

Milt slammed his fist down on the table. "Just bring us a bottle of Champagne. And not too expensive, either."

"Yes, sir." The waiter quietly backed away from the table.

She'd never seen him behave like that, getting angry at the waiter when he never once looked at the menu. Her father came to mind, but she quickly pushed the thought away.

"You didn't have to be so short with him," Annie said. "He was just trying to be helpful."

"I don't see why they have to put all that fancy stuff in there. Why can't they just tell you what they have?" Clearly agitated, he glared at her. He must have seen the concern in her face. "I'm sorry. Overseas we had to take whatever we could get. I'm not used to all this fancy stuff."

"It's all right," she assured him, hoping to restore his earlier good mood. "I'm really happy you brought me here tonight. I haven't been to a night club in ages and never one like this."

"I knew you'd like it."

He fidgeted in his seat and then stood. "Excuse me

a minute, will you?"

She nodded and he hurried away.

After Milt left the Maitre d' approached the table. "Ma'am. Is everything satisfactory?"

"Oh, yes. I'm sorry if my friend was short with the waiter. He was wounded overseas, and he is a little uncomfortable. He won't make a fuss, I promise."

"Very well. We are always proud to have members of our armed forces with us, especially heroes who have been in battle. I noticed the many ribbons on his chest and the…"

"Oh, he's a hero all right." She didn't want to bring attention to Milt's scars. "He served in North Africa and Sicily and France. That's where he was wounded."

"I see," he nodded.

"After he arrived at the hospital, the General presented him with a medal for heroism in Normandy. He landed with the invasion forces." Annie laid it on thick, thinking that they would be more tolerant of the behavior of a war hero.

"It is an honor to have such a man with us. Thank you, ma'am, for telling me."

Just then Milt appeared.

"Sir, the lady has been telling me of your heroism. It is an honor to have you with us."

Milt gave the man a look that clearly indicated his dissatisfaction with the term hero.

"Thank you," Annie said as the man withdrew. She breathed a sigh of relief.

"What did you tell him?" Tightly controlled anger colored his words.

"Just that you fought overseas, and you were wounded and got a medal."

He glared at her. His jaw clamped tight.

The waiter brought the champagne, opened the bottle, and poured it in their glasses. He then faded away without a word.

Milt remained silent. Grateful, Annie hoped to avoid an unpleasant scene.

The band members came out and took their places. She sipped her champagne and focused all her attention on the stage. The famous band leader appeared to a roar of applause. He waved and then he brought the trumpet to his lips and began to play. From the first note, the music swept her away. His masterful playing stirred her soul and transported her into another realm.

Listening on the radio or recordings couldn't compare to hearing a live performance. His undeniable talent filled the room.

After two numbers the band leader introduced a girl singer who performed in the next number. Her voice, accompanied by the band, filled the huge space.

Annie imagined herself on stage with a famous band singing her heart out. She believed, given the chance, she would be as good as others she'd heard. All she needed was a chance.

After another couple of tunes, the band leader came to the microphone and spoke.

"Ladies and Gentlemen. I have been told that we have with us tonight a genuine war hero who was wounded fighting with our boys in France." The spotlight roamed around the audience. "Sergeant Greenlee, won't you stand so we can all give you a round of applause?"

Annie waved her hand, which quickly brought the spotlight to their table. She jerked it down when she saw the expression on Milt's face. He was gritting his teeth and frowning. Was he fighting anger or was embarrassment flushing across his face?

"Come on Sergeant. Stand up for us."

Milt reluctantly got to his feet and gave a little wave. The audience burst into applause.

"We want to thank you and all our boys fighting overseas."

The applause died down and Milt sank back into his chair. The trumpet blasted a series of notes to begin another song.

Milt stared at the table, his breathing tightly controlled. The muscle in his jaw flexed. Watching his reaction, Annie regretted telling the waiter about his war record.

****

Milt's heart pounded in his chest, adding to the throbbing in his head. He desperately wanted to get away from these people staring at him like he was some freak.

How could she do such a thing? Attention was the last thing he wanted. He wasn't a hero. The things he'd done…had to do, were horrible, not heroic. The ones who died were the heroes. Not him.

Several men from nearby tables came over and shook his hand. He forced politeness, yet inside he wanted to run. Trapped in this crowded room with everyone looking at him, he fought back the urge to hit something or someone.

The run-in with the waiter had been bad enough. He couldn't read the menu. One glance and the words had all run together like gibberish, completely undecipherable. If his head hadn't been pounding, maybe he could have handled it better. He could have kidded around like he usually did to avoid being put on the spot.

Couples moved onto the crowded dance floor. Could that be an escape?

He leaned over to Annie. "Let's dance."

Surprise flickered across her face before she nodded.

On the dance floor he took her left hand in his right, leaving his useless arm to hang by his side. She placed her right hand on his left shoulder, and he reveled in her gentle touch.

The tension in his body began to relax with this beautiful woman so close and the music flowing around them. Maybe this closeness would revive last night's romantic mood.

Despite all his discomfort, watching Annie's face as she listened to the famous bandleader made it all worthwhile. She was in heaven and that was enough for him.

Chapter 42

They returned to their table and sipped champagne without speaking.

The band continued to perform alternating instrumentals with songs by the lovely singer. How Annie wished she was the one up there singing. She imagined herself wearing fancy clothes, standing in front of a fabulous band, and serenading the audience with a beautiful love song.

The bandleader announced their final song before taking a break. Annie almost cried. She didn't want the show to be over, not yet.

The waiter approached. Annie glanced at Milt and shook her head, hoping he'd understand that she didn't want him to order another bottle of champagne.

"Excuse me," the waiter said. "It is requested that you come backstage. The band leader is anxious to meet you."

Before Annie could speak Milt said "I don't really think…"

"Yes," she practically shouted. "We would love to."

"But…"

She shot him a sharp look. "Yes, we will," she said emphatically. It might be her only chance to go into the behind-the-scenes world of a night club during a performance.

He frowned but said no more.

She pushed her chair back and the waiter quickly moved to hold its back as she stood. "Come on."

"I'll just wait here."

"No, you won't."

"Sergeant, they specifically asked to meet you."

Triumph welled up in Annie's chest. She grinned and held her hand out to him.

He got up slowly, but he did get up, and they followed the waiter.

Back stage another man led them to a dressing room with a gold star on the door.

The band leader greeted them with a beautiful woman at his side. He shook Milt's hand and then introduced his wife, Betty.

She reached out to take Milt's hand. "So good to have you with us."

"Ma'am…" Milt blushed at the attention from the glamorous blonde. "I…I, uh…"

"We are so pleased to meet you," Annie pushed Milt forward.

"Come in and sit down." The band leader directed them to a plush couch.

Milt took a seat. "It's an honor to meet you…both."

"The honor is all ours, isn't it Harry." Betty grabbed Milt's hand again. "I never miss a chance to talk to our men in uniform, especially the real heroes like you."

"Oh, I'm not a hero, ma'am. I just did what I had to do."

"They gave you a medal, didn't they?"

"Well, yes. But there are plenty of guys over there

who deserve medals."

She gave him a big smile and patted him on the shoulder. "I'm sure there are."

She then turned to Annie. "And who is this?"

"Oh," He flushed red again. "This is Lt. Annie McEwen."

"You're a nurse, aren't you?" Harry asked.

"Yes, sir. But I'm also a singer. I love your band. I dream of singing with a band like yours someday."

The famous band leader smiled, and Annie could almost see him thinking that he'd heard that before. "Maybe someday," he said.

The singer who performed with the band appeared in the doorway.

"There's who you should talk to if you want to be a singer," Harry said.

Annie smiled at the newcomer.

Betty made the introductions.

"Nice to meet you." The singer's gaze slid to Milt. "So, this handsome soldier is our war hero."

Milt blushed. "I'm no hero."

A man burst into the dressing room. "Harry, we need you. Terry's got a problem."

"Sure." Harry faced Milt. "Sorry. I'll be back in just a minute."

Milt nodded as the famous band leader left.

Betty gestured for the singer to join them on the large, overstuffed sofa. "The Lieutenant here wants to audition for your job."

The singer laughed, then waved her hand. "Oh, I'm not making fun of you, Lieutenant. It's just that I had to beg Harry to let me sing with him."

"Yes. Harry told her if she wanted the job that bad,

he'd give it to her, but he wouldn't guarantee how long it would last."

"I thought he meant how long I would last," the singer responded.

Annie tried to laugh along but she didn't understand. "What did he mean?"

"Oh, honey. Keeping a band like this going costs a fortune. Here in New York is okay. He can perform and record. But on the road, oh brother, do the bills pile up."

"So, I'll stick around for a while, or I'll take off if I think I can get a better deal."

"Don't worry, honey. Harry knows how it is."

Annie wanted to ask how she would go about getting an audition, but she doubted her query would go over well.

Milt, who'd hung back listening, spoke up. "So how would a girl like Annie get an audition with a big-name band leader?" He directed his question to both women. "She's a swell singer. Surely somebody could use her."

Betty faced Milt, giving him one of her signature heart-stopping smiles. "Harry could introduce her around. Spread the word, so to speak. Of course," she turned to Annie, "She'd have to be as good as you say."

"Oh, she is."

"And then there's that uniform."

Annie looked down at herself. She'd almost forgotten what she was wearing. "I could change. That wouldn't be a problem." Although she had no idea what she would wear.

"I don't mean you'd have to change clothes. I mean you'd have to fulfill your obligation to your country. We're still at war and you are an Army nurse."

"Of course, I'd have to stay in the Army…until the war is over. But then…" Her gaze roamed from one to the other. "Then I want to sing."

"I tell you what, sweetie. You look us up after the war and we'll see what we can do."

"Thank you." Chill bumps ran up Annie's arms.

"Now, Sergeant. Come sit over here by me and tell me all about your adventures overseas. Where were you wounded?"

Milt moved slowly across the room and sat beside the beautiful woman. Annie knew how he hated to talk about the fighting and especially about his wounds. Much as she wanted to be here, she wondered how badly he wanted to leave.

After a few minutes of questioning and Milt's abbreviated answers, Betty decided she'd go see what had happened to her husband.

After she left the room, the singer spoke. "This all must seem kind of a crazy to you."

"Yes, I guess."

"Do you really want to be a singer?"

"Oh, yes." Annie focused on this talented young woman who actually seemed to be interested in her.

"Learn all you can about this crazy business. Then sing all you can. If you stay with one band too long, you can get stale. You have to be able to change when the music changes. I want to have a long career, but I also need to work. This job came along, and I saw it as an opportunity to sing with a great band. I'll move on when I see a better opportunity. So, you see, you always have to be moving, changing as the music business changes."

Annie had never heard anyone talk about singing as a business. The joy of singing and her love of music had spurred her towards a career, along with the freedom it would give her. She'd never thought much about it as a job, a way to make a living.

"You have to really want it to succeed in this business. And you have to put up with a lot of crap, especially at first."

"I think I know what you mean." Annie remembered her experience in that dump of a club.

"Everyone has to decide exactly what they're willing to do to succeed in this business."

Before Annie could ask more questions, Harry rushed back into the room with Betty close behind.

"Sorry folks. We've got a problem. Something I've got to deal with." He held out his hand. "It was good to meet you." They shook as Milt mumbled something back.

Then Harry turned to Annie. "Good luck. Hope it all works out for you."

"And remember to look us up after the war," Betty added along with one of her killer smiles.

Another man came in. "I finally got hold of Charlie. He's tied up with another gig."

Milt took Annie's hand and pulled her out into the hallway. The room full of glamorous people faded into the background.

"Let's get out of here," he said.

She followed him out of the club and down to the street.

"Did you enjoy the band?" Milt asked.

"Oh, yes. It was great. Thanks for bringing me." She hesitated. "Sorry about all the attention. I know you were uncomfortable."

"That's okay. As long as you had a good time."

"I had a wonderful time," she exclaimed.

At the end of the block, he stopped. "I don't know about you, but I could eat something. How about we duck into one of these all-night places?"

"That sounds swell."

Chapter 43

Milt steered Annie away from the bustle of the bar to the back of the restaurant where they could have some privacy. She slid into a big, round booth and he slid in beside her.

They ordered and settled back to wait for their food.

"We've had a pretty good day, haven't we?" he commented, more relaxed than he'd been in the night club.

"Yes." Annie smiled remembering. "Thank you for everything. I couldn't have done it without you."

"Sure, you could. I just came along to keep you company."

"You've done more than that. I couldn't believe you asked them how I could get an audition."

Milt chuckled. "I was going to ask Harry to let you sing, right then and there."

"You wouldn't have?" The very thought mortified her, but it also secretly pleased her.

"Yeah. I would have if I'd gotten the opportunity. Might as well swing for the fence."

She glanced down at her hands. "Do you really think he would have liked me?"

"He'd have loved you."

Annie couldn't contain her excitement. "And I would have loved singing for him and that band of his."

The idea apparently excited Milt too, judging from his expression. She almost leaned over and kissed him, but the waitress arrived with their food.

Her stomach growled from hunger at the luscious smells. She immediately dug in.

Milt nibbled on his fried potatoes and watched her eat.

"Aren't you hungry?" Annie asked.

"Not very." He took a bite of the hamburger, not taking his eyes off her.

She liked the way he looked at her, as if drinking her in. His warm gaze spoke volumes, said he thought she was special, someone he wanted to be with. No one else looked at her the same way, with the same intensity, with the same longing.

Before long Annie finished her food. She dabbed at her mouth with the napkin. "That was good." She reached over and covered his hand with hers. "I've had a wonderful time tonight. Thank you."

"I had a good time, too." He slid closer and wrapped his good arm around her shoulder. "And the night's not over."

"What do you have in mind?" She leaned in to where she could feel his breath on her cheek. Her gaze slid up and drank from the depths of those incredible blue eyes.

"Are you...going to kiss me?" she asked.

"If you want me to."

She blinked. Uncertainty flashed before she nodded ever so slightly. "I think so," she whispered.

Her lips parted in anticipation. Her heart raced and desire flared deep within. *Take it slow.* He must have read her mind because he tentatively brushed his lips lightly against hers. Touched, then touched again.

She leaned toward him, wanting more, so he gave her more.

He tasted so sweet, so right.

Her arms slid around his neck, and he pulled her body closer. She noticed the absence of his other arm. She wished she could fix it, wished she could make him whole.

Suddenly their kiss ignited pent-up emotions. His mouth devoured hers, his need matching hers.

From somewhere nearby, someone cleared their throat.

Reluctantly he released her ànd turned to see the waitress standing over them.

Once she had their attention she said, "Will there be anything else?"

Annie flushed hot.

"No," he shook his head. "That's all."

The waitress placed the check on the table and took their plates away. Her smug expression told Annie that the woman had enjoyed breaking up their little tête-à-tête.

Annie moved away, only a few inches, but enough to let him know that she wasn't going to let him kiss her again. Not here, in such a public place.

"I guess we'd better head back to the hotel." She picked up her purse, scooped up her nurse's cape, and draped it over her arm before she slid out of the booth. "I'll just stop in the lady's room before we leave."

Milt nodded. She disappeared into the hallway at the back.

Once alone the singer's words came back to her.

What am I willing to give up for a singing career?

Love? A family?

She liked Milt a lot. Loved it when he kissed her. But did she want him more than singing on stage with a big band?

By the time she came out of the ladies' room, he had paid for their meal. Together they pushed through the door and into the cold wind whipping between the tall buildings.

The temperature had dropped. She pulled her cape tight around her body and, after buttoning his overcoat, he wrapped his arm around her again.

He shivered.

"Are you cold?"

"Just thinking of Ade and the other guys over there, sleeping in foxholes with only a thin blanket and a shelter half. On the radio they said the weather has turned cold over there. And if the First Division is near the Siegfried Line, the fighting must be fierce."

"That's in Germany, isn't it?"

"It's the fortifications along the border." He shivered again. "Let's see if we can find a cab," he suggested.

After an eternity that was probably only a few minutes, they flagged down a passing taxi and crawled into the warm interior, hoping to get their blood flowing again.

Annie told the driver the address of her hotel.

"Can you take the long way?" Milt asked.

"Sure thing," the man replied. "I can swing through the park if you want."

"Sounds good," Milt answered, pulling Annie closer.

They snuggled together in the warmth. His mouth

found hers, and they kissed like the night would never end. To her amazement, she wanted him as much as he seemed to want her. Desire hummed between them like the electrical current that lit up the city.

Is this what I want? What about my singing career?

After long moments, she pulled away. "We have to stop."

He tried to kiss her again, but she pushed him away, torn between her career and a relationship with Milt.

"This isn't going to work...between us."

Milt didn't respond. She met his gaze and saw anguish.

"I...I'm sorry."

The cab came to a stop.

"Sorry folks," the cab driver announced.

Milt pulled away from her and looked out. Despite the steamed-up windows, the lights of the hotel shown only a few feet away.

He turned back to Annie who'd straightened up in the seat. Their gazes met in a silent apology. Neither wanted it to end.

The driver got out and opened the door. It was late and he obviously wanted to go home himself.

Milt got out, then turned and offered Annie his hand. When she took it, his somber expression had her wondering what was on his mind.

Chapter 44

Cold wind swept away the warmth from moments before. They huddled near the hotel doorway.

"Milt…" Annie started.

"Yes." He tilted her chin up, desperately hoping for another kiss.

"I'm sorry if I've led you on."

"What?" *Is she really doing this?*

"I've really enjoyed being with you, but…"

"But what?"

"Don't you see? It'll never work out." She forced a smile. "You and me, I mean."

He stood in frozen silence, afraid of what she would say next.

"I want to be a singer. Have a career. And to do that I'll have to work…very hard. I won't have time for anything else."

An ice pick stabbed his heart. He couldn't speak. He could only stare into nothingness.

She touched his face so he would look at her. "As much as I like you…I have to make a choice."

Doesn't she see that I'm head over heels in love with her?

"Singing is all I've ever wanted," she continued. "All I ever dreamed of."

"I know," he muttered.

He could see her dream so clearly, yet she couldn't

see his. All she saw was him standing in her way. This cripple, scarred, half-man who had nothing to offer but his love.

She sighed. "Thanks for understanding." She turned toward the door. "You can come in the lobby…and get warm before you leave."

"Okay." He followed her, his heart shattered.

Before they reached the front desk, someone called, "Annie."

"Brice. What are you doing here?" Her surprise told Milt she hadn't expected to see the officer who hurried toward her.

"Looking for you. Where have you been?" A strange urgency tinged Lieutenant Attwater's words.

He glanced over at Milt. Their gazes locked. Recognition registered on Attwater's face. He not only recognized Milt, he realized that Annie was with Milt. The officer's freshly-shaven jaw flushed, and muscles worked as he ground his molars together.

"Sergeant. What are you doing here?"

"Brice, you remember Milt, I mean Sergeant Greenlee." Annie's shaky voice added to Milt's discomfort.

"I certainly do." Attwater's sarcastic reply ramped up the tension. "He's your friend from Atlanta."

"Actually, he's from Tennessee, but he's assigned to the hospital in Atlanta."

Lt. Attwater turned his anger from Milt to Annie. "What I want to know is what he's doing here…with you?"

"He's helping me look for Joe's widow." Attwater's eyes narrowed so she continued, clearly uncomfortable. "I asked him to help me." She didn't

343

mention the letter.

"Not exactly appropriate to be associating with an enlisted man, is it?"

Annie straightened up and faced him. "I believe that is my business, Lieutenant."

Good for you. Stand up to him.

"Why are you looking for me anyway?" she continued. "Does my father have you checking up on me now?"

The color drained from Attwater's face. His expression morphed from angry to dead serious.

"Annie, is there somewhere we can talk...alone?"

She looked from Attwater to Milt and back. "We can talk right here. There's no reason Sgt. Greenlee can't hear whatever it is you have to say."

God, he loved her.

The officer reached out for her hand, but she withdrew it and continued to glare at him, waiting for an explanation.

"It would be better if we were alone."

"Like I said, it can't be anything that personal. We can talk right here."

Attwater turned to Milt. "Sergeant, would you mind? It really is important that I speak with Annie right away."

"Sir, I believe the lady expressed her opinion. I suggest you do as she says."

Attwater sighed. He looked at Annie with such pity that Milt feared what Attwater was about to tell her would hurt her badly.

"Annie," Attwater placed his hand on her shoulder. "There's no good way to tell you this."

Her expression morphed into an anxious frown.

Her brow wrinkled and lips flattened as she held her breath.

"It's your father. He's had a stroke. A bad one."

She gasped. Her hand flew to her mouth. "Father? A Stroke?"

Attwater moved close enough to encircle her shoulders with his arm.

"It was sudden. No one expected it."

"No," she objected. "It can't be."

She glanced at Milt. He tried to move closer, but Attwater pulled her into a protective hug. He glared at Milt daring him to interfere.

"I'm so sorry," Annie. He wanted badly to hold her and comfort her himself. Instead, he forced himself to refocus on Attwater.

"How did you get word?" Milt asked.

"My father called me. They couldn't get in touch with Annie. Her superior officer told them she had come into the city so Herschel asked my father to contact me to see if I could find her."

Milt nodded as he processed what Attwater said. "So, her family wanted you to find her."

"That's what I said." Attwater ground out.

"Mother. What about Mother?"

"I don't know," he told her. "If you want, we can call."

"Yes. Oh, yes, Brice. Please call. I need to talk to her, make sure she's all right."

"There's a phone booth here in the lobby. I'll just…" Attwater looked around.

Milt saw his opening. "Go ahead. Place the call. I'll stay with her."

Clearly Attwater didn't want to leave Annie with

Milt, but he reluctantly nodded and released her. He shot Milt a warning glare before heading for the telephone booth.

Milt stepped closer to her. He wanted badly to put his arm around her, but he didn't dare. Not with Attwater only steps away.

"Why don't you sit down?" Milt led her over to a bench. She sank down onto it. Milt perched on the edge beside her so he would not appear to be too familiar.

"I can't believe it…" She blinked furiously.

"I know, I know."

She looked directly at him. "My father…he's…he's…never been sick." Tears now streamed down her cheeks. "What will Mother do?"

Milt rubbed her arm, up and down, up and down. He didn't know what else to do or what to say. How would he feel if he'd just been told his father had had a stroke?

Suddenly she threw herself at him and sobbed against his chest. His arm instinctively went around her, holding her as her grief poured out.

"What are you doing?" Attwater demanded in a harsh whisper.

Milt looked up to see the officer looming over them, glaring at Milt with such venomous hatred that it gave Milt a start.

The man sat down on Annie's other side, took hold of her shoulders, and turned her around to face him. "The operator is placing the call," he assured her in a calm, caring voice. "We'll have to wait until it goes through. Then you can speak to your mother or at least to your aunt or uncle."

"Thank you." She swiped at her wet cheeks.

Attwater quickly produced a handkerchief for her, and she blew her nose.

Milt stood, unsure what to do next. He wanted to help her, but there didn't seem to be anything for him to do. Attwater wanted him to leave, but he wouldn't desert Annie in her hour of need.

While Attwater comforted Annie, Milt took a seat nearby and watched.

This was the man her father wanted her to marry. An officer with a responsible, safe position handling supplies for the Army. He had family connections and would probably get a good job after the war. The man had everything a young woman could want in a husband. And he seemed to care for Annie.

The telephone in the booth across the lobby rang in that insistent way it had when you were waiting for it to ring. So sudden and yet final.

Attwater hurried to answer it. Annie watched him, and then she rose slowly. She glanced at Milt. He stood and walked with her, close but not touching, across the open space.

Attwater stepped from the booth with the receiver in his hand.

"It's your aunt."

Annie took the receiver and stepped inside the booth.

Milt watched her as she talked. Tears flowed into the wadded handkerchief gripped tightly in her fist. She stared at the wall beside the telephone to avoid eye contact with either him or Attwater.

When he glanced over at Attwater, Milt was surprised to find him staring back at him.

"As soon as she gets off the phone, I think it would

347

be a good time for you to leave."

"Why?" Milt asked.

"Why? Because she is upset. She needs to get her things together while I make travel arrangements. You'll be in the way."

"Maybe I want to go back with her."

"No. That would be an intrusion on the family."

"You're not family."

"My father and Annie's father are very close friends. Annie and I grew up together." He glanced back at Annie before continuing. "You are just a patient she met who could help her find out something about Joe. You've done that now. It's time you moved on."

Milt's temper flared. "Look, just because I'm not an officer doesn't mean I can't have feelings for her."

"Feelings. You think you are anywhere near good enough for her. Never mind your rank or that you're from small town nowhere. Look at you. Look at the scars all over your face that you're trying to hide behind those hideous glasses. What about that arm of yours? The one that just hangs there. No telling what kind of damage that uniform is hiding. Why would Annie want a shot up piece of crap like you?"

Milt saw red and lunged for the jerk despite his fancy officer's uniform. Attwater dodged and caught hold of Milt's bad arm. When he wrenched it back, incredible pain shot through Milt's shoulder, radiating through his back and up his neck.

Milt's vision blurred momentarily.

Annie's voice rang out from somewhere behind him. "Stop! Stop!"

It took a second to register that she was talking to Attwater, not him.

"Let go of him."

"He took a swing at me," Attwater growled as he released Milt's arm.

"Milt, are you all right?"

He grabbed his upper arm with his right hand, trying to somehow release the muscle spasm. "I'll...I'll be fine."

That's when she turned on Attwater. "How dare you. He's been wounded and still isn't fully recovered." She glanced over her shoulder at Milt.

"It was my fault," Milt confessed. "I did take a swing at him."

"And what did he say to provoke it?"

Milt couldn't help smiling at that. She knew the man pretty well.

"All right. I said some things I shouldn't have said," Attwater admitted.

"Then both of you apologize and shake hands."

Milt knew when to follow orders. He stuck out his hand. "Sorry, sir."

To Attwater's credit he grasped Milt's hand and muttered, "Yeah, me, too."

Chapter 45

She had to leave. She had to tell Milt goodbye. She had to go home. In her head she understood. But her heart was screaming "No!"

"You need to go upstairs and get your things. I'll go with you to the hospital so you can make arrangements there." Brice took charge, like a good officer.

"He's right, Annie. You need to go," Milt said, in that gentle tone of his. "Your family needs you."

She met Milt's gaze. "Yes, I know." Yet she couldn't move.

Milt gave her a weak smile. "We've done what we could. And you have some news to share with your family."

"Yes. Yes, I do have that."

He took her hand. Brice stepped forward as if to object.

"Goodbye, Annie," Milt said, squeezing her hand.

"Goodbye." She blinked back tears. "Thank you."

Milt nodded and released her hand.

He faced Brice. "Sir."

"Sergeant."

And then he was gone. Out the door into the darkness.

****

Milt barely remembered the trek back to his hotel.

Once inside, the heat assailed him. He hadn't realized how cold he'd gotten.

He'd tried to hold the image of her face in his mind, but Brice's countenance kept intruding. Just as Brice's words echoed in his ears.

"...scars all over your face...those hideous glasses...that arm of yours...that just hangs there...Why would Annie want a shot up piece of crap like you?"

Brice was right, of course. He was a "shot up piece of crap." That's why she'd pushed him away. Oh, sure, she said it was because of her career. But Milt knew better.

Milt punched his pillow. It felt so good, he hit it again and again.

"Hey, what's going on over there?"

Milt had forgotten about his roommate. "Sorry," he ground out.

"I gather you had a bad night." The man sat up on his bed and faced Milt. "You wanna talk about it?"

"No," Milt shouted, fury bubbling over.

"Okay, okay." The man held up his hands. "Just wanted to help."

Milt tried to control himself. "Sure."

He fumbled in his bag and pulled out the baseball he carried with him all the time. Gripping it in his right hand, he massaged the hard sphere, the smooth leather, the rough seams.

"Do you know if there's a gym or someplace a guy could go to work out, maybe throw the ball?"

"I don't know," his fellow soldier replied. "Maybe the YMCA. But I doubt it's open in the middle of the night."

A good physical workout would stem some of this smoldering anger. Years past, when his whole being had raged with anger at his inability to read, he'd turned to running and then to throwing the ball. That's how he'd developed such a good fast ball. Throwing ball after ball, expelling anger with every pitch. Controlling it had gotten him noticed by the pros, got him a chance at a career in baseball. Now all that was gone. No career, no nothing.

But he could still throw the ball. Lew and Lloyd had made him practice, plus they'd pushed the strengthening exercises to get him back in shape.

"How could I find out?"

"I guess you could go downstairs. Get the clerk to call the Y."

Milt woke up the night clerk, got him to call. The YMCA did have a gym. It opened at 6 am. Milt would be there when it opened. He'd work himself into exhaustion if that's what it took to get her out of his system, even for a little while.

****

Milt rode the subway toward Brooklyn. The workout had calmed his anger, but it hadn't gotten Annie out of his mind.

She's better off without me, he kept telling himself.

He didn't want to see her go, but he knew it was best. He might not like Attwater, but the guy cared about Annie. She needed someone to care about her.

She didn't need him...not with his scarred face and his useless arm. And that wasn't the worst of it. The thing she didn't know about him was the pièce de résistance, as the French would say. His difficulty reading made it impossible for him to give her any kind of a life, especially not the life she deserved.

No. No matter how much he loved her, she was better off without him. She was better off with a man like Attwater.

Milt entered the drugstore, and his gaze took in the lunch counter, searching for Rebecca. She wasn't there so he wandered around the store looking for baseballs. Near the back he spotted Rebecca talking to another young woman.

As he approached, she looked up. "Oh, Sgt. Greenlee. We were just talking about you."

"You were?" Milt smiled at the two pretty girls.

"Yes," Rebecca gushed. "I had no idea you'd be back today."

"Thought I'd check in with you again before I left town."

"This is Sandy. Sandy Blaine. She knew Carlene in high school."

"Hi, Sandy."

Rebecca looked around. "I'd better get to work. The manager's giving me the evil eye."

She laughed as she headed for the lunch counter, so Milt figured she wasn't in that much trouble. He and Sandy followed her and took seats.

"Did you want something?" Rebecca asked.

"Yeah, I do. Give me another one of those ham sandwiches. And some coffee." Milt turned to Sandy. "What about you? I'm buying."

"Well in that case, I'll have a chocolate sundae." Sandy's grin told him it was a special treat for her.

While Rebecca prepared the food, Milt asked Sandy, "How well did you know Carlene?"

"Not very well. Nobody did. She kept to herself."

Sandy gazed into the mirror on the wall behind the lunch counter as if looking into the past. "She was different. I guess because she came from the south and some people made fun of her. And she'd lost her parents. I felt sorry for her."

Rebecca placed the sundae in front of Sandy. "Just a minute on your sandwich."

"Did Carlene ever talk about where she came from?"

Sandy licked her lips. "Not really."

"What did she talk about?"

"She liked the movies. Went all the time." Sandy took a big bite.

"What kind of movies?"

"Musicals. Those Busby Berkley dance numbers. She loved those." She looked away again. "Guess that's where she got the idea she could perform on Broadway. Be in one of those chorus lines."

Rebecca brought his sandwich. "Mustard, right?"

Milt grinned at her. "Yep."

She poured his coffee. "Didn't you say yesterday that Carlene worked at Radio City Music Hall?"

Milt nodded as he chewed.

"I never knew that," Sandy said.

"As an usherette," Milt added. "Someone remembered her."

Rebecca moved down the counter to wait on some other customers.

Sandy finished her sundae, deep in thought.

"And she really was married to a soldier? And he was killed?"

He nodded. That's another lead he could pursue. Find out where they kept marriage records.

"We didn't believe her," Sandy confessed.

"It's understandable. I mean, you never met him."

"No, but still…" Sandy faced him. "When she did talk, she'd tell wild tales. It was hard to know what to believe."

"What kind of wild tales?"

"Well, like the time she came to school saying she'd met this famous movie star."

"Oh."

"She said she went to the theater and waited at the stage door until he came out. Then just introduced herself and asked for his autograph."

"Maybe she did."

"Did what?" Rebecca stood in front of them.

"I was telling him about Carlene getting that famous actor's autograph."

"She had a signature in a little book, but we thought she'd just made it up."

"You couldn't even read it," Sandy added. "Anybody could have written it."

Milt saw the manager out of the corner of his eye. "How about giving me the bill?" He said it loud enough to be heard by the nosy man.

"Are you sure you don't want anything else?" Rebecca asked.

Milt grinned. "How about one scoop of that ice cream. Strawberry."

Rebecca smiled and quickly moved to get the ice cream.

Sandy's gaze followed the manager who had turned toward the other side of the store. "He doesn't like us hanging around talking."

A dish of ice cream appeared in front of Milt. "And

here's your bill, sir." Rebecca smiled like a Cheshire cat. "I just remembered something."

"What?" Sandy asked.

"Remember that first year Carlene was here? In Mr. Hansen's geography class?"

"Yes." Sandy's face blossomed into a big smile.

He swallowed the mouthful of ice cream. "What happened?"

Rebecca started, "We were studying Europe and Mr. Hanson had this big map in front of the class." She looked from Sandy to Milt. "He pointed out all these places on the map. And then he asked if anyone had been to anywhere in Europe."

Sandy took up the story. "Some guy in the back spoke up and said he'd seen London Bridge. Several people laughed at his joke. Mr. Hansen stayed serious and asked again."

"I remember Carlene's face. I was sitting in the next row over," Rebecca explained. "She raised her hand, and when Mr. Hansen nodded, she spoke loud and clear. 'I was born in Paris.'"

"No one had ever heard her say anything in class before," Sandy said. "And in that southern accent, too."

"When everyone laughed, she smiled like she was pleased with herself. She went on to say, 'And I've been to Milan.' Only she said it with a long 'i' and Mr. Hansen corrected her saying it was 'Meelan'." Rebecca shook her head. "Poor girl. Everyone was laughing so hard, and Mr. Hansen couldn't get the class to settle down. That's when she blushed red as a beet. She finally realized she'd messed up and everyone was laughing at her."

"Kids ribbed her for weeks," Sandy said. "Maybe

that's why she stayed quiet after that."

"Can't blame her." Milt knew that humiliation. He'd been teased enough for stammering when he tried to read. The girls had been the worst. He could give a boy a hard look and he knew Milt would take care of him on the playground, with fists if necessary. But he had to take it from the girls.

Sandy's story gave Milt an idea. "She never said where she came from?" he asked.

"No. Never." Rebecca answered. "At least not to me."

"Me either," Sandy said.

Milt pulled out his wallet and put cash on the counter, enough to cover the cost plus a generous tip. "Keep the change."

Rebecca's eyes went wide. "Uh, thank you."

He stood. "I'd better get going before you get in trouble."

"Oh, don't worry about him."

"Annie...I mean, Lt. McEwen gave you her name and address, didn't she?"

"Yes," Rebecca nodded.

"If either of you think of anything else, you can send it to her. She had to return home due to a family emergency, but they'll forward it to her."

Sandy stood, too. "I'll walk you out."

Milt waved to Rebecca. "Thanks so much."

Outside Sandy spoke. "I hope you find her."

"So do I," Milt took her hand. "You've been a big help."

"Tell her I'm sorry...for not believing her."

"I will."

Chapter 46

Annie slept most of the way back to Chattanooga, a fitful sleep with dreams of hospital beds, her parents, Milt, and strangely, Brice.

At home she found Mrs. Rice attempting to manage her mother who refused another dose of the sedative the doctor had given her right after her husband's stroke. Upon seeing Annie, her mother's whimpering escalated into hysterics. She insisted Annie take her to the hospital to be with her husband.

"I'll take you if you settle down." Annie held her mother's hand and glanced up at Mrs. Rice. "Maybe the doctor can give you something to calm you but not knock you out."

Mrs. Rice nodded her approval.

"I don't want any medicine," her mother insisted.

"You can't go to the hospital unless you calm down."

Eventually the older woman agreed. Mrs. Rice got her ready while Annie contacted the family doctor.

At the hospital they found her father semi-conscious. After a few moments, Edith's pleading voice roused him.

"What…you doing…here," he mumbled out of the side of his mouth.

Edith smiled. "We've come to take care of you."

His gaze moved beyond Edith and rested on Annie.

"So…you've come." He blinked a few times. "To watch…me…die."

Annie moved closer. "No, Father. I've come to see you get well."

"Humph."

Annie ignored her father's foul mood, as she had so often in the past. Rather than making her angry, she pitied him in his helpless condition.

The doctor came around soon after Annie and her mother arrived. As he left Annie caught him in the hallway.

"How is he…really?"

The doctor frowned, and for a moment, she wondered if he would tell her anything.

"The stroke was bad…as you can see from the paralysis on the left side. We'll work with him. Perhaps be able to restore some function."

"But not all?"

"No. He's going to be an invalid." He met her gaze as if assessing her. "You know what that entails."

"Yes," she nodded. "Constant care."

He didn't have to say the words to know what he was thinking. She was a nurse. She would resign from the Army, come home, and take care of her father. It didn't matter that her father hated her, didn't want her around. In her head she could already hear his constant taunting and ridiculing. No matter what she did, it would never be good enough.

But she couldn't leave him to Aunt Millie and Mrs. Rice. They didn't have the nursing skills. And her mother would be a challenge for them all.

That night she sat by her father's bed. Uncle Herschel had taken her mother home, and since she'd just arrived, Annie volunteered to stay the night so the others could rest.

It seemed like such a long time ago since Brice took her to the train station after leaving Milt at the hotel and Brice's unexpected announcement.

"I know this is not a good time," he'd said.

She'd expected him to kiss her or make a declaration of love. Instead, he'd said, "I've been reassigned."

"What do you mean?"

"I'm shipping out. Going overseas. I'm not sure if I'll be in England or France."

"But why? You're in supplies or something, aren't you?"

"Yes. It's called Quartermaster. They need people on the receiving end, too." He looked down again. "I…uh…sort of volunteered to go."

"Volunteered?" She couldn't believe he would put himself in harm's way. Not after all the maneuvering his father had done to make sure he stayed safely in the states.

"Don't worry." He smiled, pleased at her reaction. "I won't be in any danger. The Germans are on the run. This thing will be over by Christmas. Overseas duty will look good on my record."

Now she understood. Always thinking of his future in politics.

"I know that sounds bad to you. Even if I didn't go, I'm proud of my service." He threw his shoulders back and stood tall. "I've worked hard to help win this war by keeping the troops supplied. No one appreciates what all it takes back here. They only think about the guys over there."

"I know. I'm sorry."

He grasped her shoulders. "I hate leaving…with things like they are. I won't be able to see you for a long time."

She melted into his warmth, into his strength. She didn't want him to leave.

He'd kissed her then. A soft, gentle kiss on the cheek. A goodbye kiss.

"Take care of yourself over there," she'd said as tears pricked her eyes.

He'd smiled then. "I will. And I'll write as soon as I get my new address."

Now, sitting in the dark, she missed him. Missed his steady presence. Despite her father and his manipulations, she could imagine being married to Brice. A man like Brice would take care of her, would be nice to her and not be angry with her all the time. He wasn't at all like her father.

What made her think about marriage? Was it her vulnerability? Or something more?

****

Annie arranged for Mrs. Rice to take her mother to the hospital. They would sit with her father while she met with Uncle Herschel and Aunt Millie. It wasn't fair to them to wait any longer to tell them what she had learned about Joe's wife.

"What's this about? You wanting to talk to us?" Uncle Herschel asked.

"Please sit down." Annie waved them toward the sofa. "I need to tell you what I found out…about Joe."

They both eyed her curiously but followed her direction and sat on the sofa side by side.

"While I was in New York I spent some time

trying to find Joe's wife."

"That was a waste of time," Uncle Herschel muttered.

"Now, Herschel, let Annie tell us what she has to tell."

Annie looked from one to the other. She let out a sigh and sunk into the chair opposite them. "I didn't find her, but…"

"See, I told you."

"But I did find where she had lived, and I learned that she had worked at Radio City Music Hall as an usherette."

"She's long gone though, isn't she?"

Rather than respond Annie took the letter from her purse and handed it to them.

Surprised, the two began to read.

"Milt…Sgt. Greenlee's friend found a man who knew Joe, who was with him when he died. That letter is from him."

Annie watched them read. When Aunt Millie exclaimed and covered her mouth, Annie knew they had gotten to the part about the baby.

"How…how is this possible?" Aunt Millie asked as Uncle Herschel reread the letter.

"I know it's a shock. It was to me, too."

"Why didn't he tell us?" Uncle Herschel asked.

"Best Milt and I could figure, he was killed before he had a chance to write you."

Aunt Millie cried into her hands. "Oh, my Joe."

"Milt and I went to Brooklyn and searched for the Packard's. It took a while, but we found the aunt Carlene lived with."

Aunt Millie wiped her eyes with her handkerchief.

"What did she have to say?"

Annie couldn't help but smile at the memory. "Not much." She met her aunt's gaze. "She was something else. She got very hostile when we mentioned Joe."

"But you talked to her?" Uncle Herschel asked.

"Briefly. She wouldn't let us in. She admitted that Carlene had lived there and that she had a baby. She also said that Carlene was gone. She wouldn't say where."

"How do we find her and the baby?" Aunt Millie looked from Annie to Uncle Herschel.

"I don't know. We did get some more information from a girl who went to high school with Carlene."

"A friend of Carlene's?"

"Yes. Rebecca, the girl who knew Carlene, told us that Carlene's maiden name was Tyler and she was from somewhere in the south. She had a southern accent. Her parents died, and she was sent to live with her aunt in Brooklyn."

"Where was this friend?" Aunt Millie asked.

"We talked to Rebecca in a drug store near where Carlene's aunt lived."

"What about this aunt?" said Uncle Herschel. "You said you talked to her?"

"Briefly," Annie admitted. "She got very angry. Milt and I both think she's the reason Carlene didn't answer your letters. That awful woman probably never gave the letters to her."

"Why would she do that?"

"I don't know. She seemed to think Joe had taken advantage of Carlene. I don't think she likes the Army very much."

"Then she didn't tell you anything?"

"Well, not much." Annie smiled. This was the good part. "What she did tell us is that Carlene had a baby. Joe's baby."

Both her aunt and uncle sat in silence for a moment, then they looked at each other. Finally, they turned back to Annie.

"Are you sure?" Uncle Herschel asked. "I…I mean, that it was Joe's?"

"Yes." Annie looked down as she wrung her hands in her lap. "Don't you see. It's in the letter. She wrote Joe to tell him about the baby."

"Then why didn't he tell us?" Anger flared in her uncle's voice.

"I'm sure he meant to. He got her letter not long before he was killed. He probably didn't have time to write before…"

Uncle Herschel jumped to his feet and walked across the room shaking his head. "No! No, it can't be. It was too long after he sailed." He spun around to face Annie and Aunt Millie. "She lied to him. He'd been gone too long."

"I thought that, too. But then I thought that she probably wanted to be sure before she told Joe. And Milt told me that their mail often got delayed for months and then they'd get a bundle."

Aunt Millie got up and went to her husband. "I know it sounds farfetched, but maybe…"

"You just want to believe it."

Annie stood and faced them. "The girl we talked to had known Carlene. They didn't believe she was really married. They thought she just said that because she got involved with some soldier and got in trouble." Annie stood and faced them. "The way they described

364

Carlene, she wasn't the type to run around with men. I don't think she would lie to Joe, not about something like that."

Aunt Millie drew Uncle Herschel back to the sofa. "Go on. Tell us everything you found out."

Annie resumed her seat and her tale. "Well, the baby explains why Carlene's aunt was angry with her. There was probably lots of gossip that she had to endure. And the girls said she was a horrid woman who treated Carlene badly when they were in school. Carlene had left her aunt's home after high school. She moved to Manhattan and got a job at Radio City Music Hall. That's probably where she met Joe."

"I always wondered how Joe got mixed up with a girl from up north." Aunt Millie looked from Annie to her husband. "What you said about her being from the south. It makes sense. She was probably homesick, just like Joe."

"Did you talk to anyone else? Maybe someone who worked with her?" Her uncle still sounded skeptical.

"No. We didn't find anyone else. If we'd had more time, maybe we would have."

Annie thought of Milt, alone in the city. He'd helped her when he didn't have to.

"Her aunt didn't say where she was?"

"No. She actually refused to tell us where Carlene is living now. I don't know if it was because she didn't know or she didn't want us to know."

"Why would she keep it from you?"

"You didn't meet that woman. I felt sorry for Carlene having to live with her. She probably refused to tell us out of spite."

"Oh, how awful." Aunt Millie said.

"Milt was hopeful that we might find Carlene. But I don't know. She told her friend she was going home. We just don't know where home is."

"Where is Milt now?"

"He came to New York on leave. I imagine he's on his way back home for Thanksgiving."

She thought about the last time she'd seen him, about how she'd rejected him and how hurt he'd been.

Then Brice showed up and everything went topsy-turvy. She hadn't really said a proper goodbye. And she might never see him again.

Chapter 47

A few days later while Annie sat with her father, the doctor came in, and after examining the elder McEwen, informed Annie that the family should make arrangements for her father to go home.

"We've done all we can for him here," the doctor said. "You can continue the exercises at home where I am sure he will be more comfortable."

"Of course, doctor," Annie replied. She hadn't expected to take her father home so soon. He still seemed so helpless. But then, based on what the doctor had said, her father would be helpless. His left side remained paralyzed and there seemed no hope of him regaining its use. The exercises would merely keep the muscles from stiffening and make it easier for her to manage him.

The thought of caring for her invalid father for an indeterminable amount of time almost doubled her over. The pain in her gut masked the heartache at losing her dreams. No singing career. No taking care of wounded soldiers. No life. Nothing.

Her father stirred. She swiped away a stray tear and eased closer to his side.

"Where'd…doctor…go?" he grumbled.

"He'll be back." she assured him. "You drifted off, so we let you rest. Sleep is good for you. It'll help you to heal."

"Humph," he groaned. "Can barely…move…talk."

Annie plastered a smile on her face, determined to at least appear cheerful. "The doctor says you can go home soon."

"Home?" He glared at her.

"Yes. We'll get everything set up so we can take good care of you."

He eyed her with that look of disdain. Painful memories made her look away and busy herself straightening his sheet.

"So…you…going to…do it?"

"What?"

"Take care…of me?"

She stood up straight and tried to smile. "Yes." She dreaded making the commitment. "I am. Not alone, of course. I'll need help."

"Humph." He tugged at the sheet she'd just straightened. "Guilty conscience."

She bristled at his accusation. "No. It's my duty. Besides, I'm a trained nurse. It's only logical that I should stay and take care of you."

"You don't…give a damn…about me…never have."

"That's not true. Maybe we haven't gotten along so well…" She turned away from him and eased closer to the window that overlooked a courtyard.

"Damn…understatement."

She whirled around to see him flailing around in the bed, trying to turn himself over. She hurried to his side. "Let me…"

"Get away." He tugged at the sheet again. "Why…the hell…should I…want you…of all people…to help…me." He gasped for breath.

Her temper flared. "Because I'm all you've got."

He stilled.

After a pause, he gritted out, "Fine."

She stepped closer, pulled the sheet back and slid her hands under his body. Using all her strength, both physical and emotional, she lifted and pulled until he rested on his side.

"There. How's that?"

"Humph."

Turning away, she shook her head. What did she expect? Gratitude? From her father? No. He would never change, and she had to accept that reality.

Annie circled the bed and settled in the upholstered chair where she could keep an eye on her father as he dozed. A book lay on the floor next to the chair, so she picked it up and began to read. Yet her mind wandered back to her time with Milt. Back to that taxi ride where they'd snuggled close and shared kisses.

She slammed the book closed. *Don't think of that. Don't think of him. You made your decision.*

Her father groaned in his sleep. She wiped away the tears.

No. Her decision had been made for her.

****

Milt journeyed to Kerrville for the traditional Thanksgiving family get-together. He struggled to put thoughts of Annie out of his mind. After all, he'd lost her. He had never really had a chance with her, just a stupid fantasy.

The blanket of melancholy that surrounded Milt on the train ride home continued to envelop him as he wandered the familiar family home. The cold, rainy weather didn't help.

During the Thanksgiving meal, Milt caught his father's questioning gaze more than once. Afterward, the older man invited Milt into his study.

Milt sank into the old leather chair in the corner while his father settled behind the desk.

"Son, do you want to talk about it?" his father asked.

Milt avoided his gaze. "About what?"

"Whatever is bothering you."

Milt took hold of his useless left hand and massaged it, wishing for his baseball to squeeze away the tension. "Nothing's bothering me," he replied. "At least nothing that anyone can do anything about."

"You mean your injuries?"

"Yeah," Milt blew out. "What else?" Maybe the letter he'd written to Ade, returned with "deceased" written across it. Or the doctor's assessment that the nerves in his arm weren't going to heal. Or Annie saying it wouldn't work between them.

"Well...Did something happen on your trip to New York? Didn't you go up there to help that nice nurse find a relative?"

"Yeah, sure. That went okay." Milt didn't want to talk about Annie. Not now. Not ever.

"I see." His father leaned forward and took out a cigar. "Do you want one?"

Milt shook his head. He'd never acquired a taste for cigars, unlike his little brother.

As his father went through the ritual of lighting the cigar, Milt debated how much to tell him. Maybe the basics would satisfy the older man and get him off Milt's back.

"I took a letter to Annie...I mean Lt. McEwen.

From a guy overseas who knew her cousin. Turns out his wife had a kid."

His father's eyebrows raised. "She didn't know?"

Milt shook his head. "The family hadn't been able to contact the wife. We used the information in the letter and found the wife's aunt. She wouldn't talk to us, but we went into a nearby drugstore and the girl behind the counter had known the wife. But we didn't find her."

"Nurse McEwen must have been disappointed."

"Yeah, she was." Milt straightened in the chair, ready for the conversation to be over.

"So that's not what's got you down?"

Milt was tired of the third degree. "Look at me. Don't you think I've got plenty to get me down?" He stood to leave.

"You're right. But you've got to accept what's happened and move on."

"Move on? That's rich." He stared at his father. "What am I going to move on to? Have you got me a job lined up? Doing what? Sitting behind a desk shuffling papers?"

His father stood, too. "What do you want to do?" Tightly controlled anger simmered beneath the surface.

"I want to play baseball," Milt shouted.

"Well, I'm sorry, Son, but that is out of the question." His father drew a deep breath. "What's the next best thing? Surely you have some ideas."

Milt looked away, fearing his father would see the tears welling up in his eyes. He'd known, since England, that baseball was out, that his injuries meant he'd never play again. He just hadn't been able to imagine anything else.

Pacing around the room, he let his thoughts tumble out. "I went with Lew to get people to donate equipment…baseball equipment to the hospital so we could make up a team and play. Lew said I was good at talking people into giving us stuff."

"Like what?" his father gently asked.

"Bats, balls, gloves. We even got a uniform company to make us up some uniforms." Milt smiled at the memory. "'Course they were donating to the wounded soldiers because they felt sorry for us…for me." Milt faced his father. "That's why Lew wanted to take me along. So they'd see somebody who'd been all shot up."

"Who's this Lew fellow?" his father asked.

"Lew Applegate. I thought I told you about him."

His father shook his head.

"You know, the famous baseball player in Chicago. At least he played until Uncle Sam drafted him."

"Lew Applegate!" the older man exclaimed. "That's amazing. I had no idea."

"Yeah. Lew's a great guy." Talk of Lew cheered Milt. The man might be famous, but he'd become Milt's friend.

"Someone like that could be a real asset. Get your foot in the door."

"What do you mean?"

"Well, at one time you mentioned coaching. He could help you get into that."

"I don't know. In coaching you've got to get out there with the players. All I can do is throw the ball. I can't even catch it."

"You're too down on yourself. Think more positively. You know the game. Know what needs to be done. That doesn't mean you have to do it yourself."

"I don't know. Maybe." Milt wasn't convinced, but maybe it would get his father off his back. "I'll think about it."

His father placed his hand on Milt's shoulder. "That's the spirit."

He made his way out of the study thankful to end the conversation. Milt hadn't told him all of it. The certain knowledge that he would spend his life alone.

The deep ache from knowing how Annie saw him…as a cripple, as a lost cause, someone she didn't want to be with, resurfaced. And why would she? A beautiful woman who could have anyone she wanted. And a handsome Lieutenant her father would approve of her marrying, a man who had a real future ahead of him, not some second-rate, make-do job earned by pity alone. No, for Milt women were beyond his reach. He'd have to accept loneliness as a way of life.

****

Annie hurried down the hallway, ticking off in her mind all the things she still had to do before her father came home. She'd put off interviewing the night nurse. After all, her father would want a say, and the poor woman might not be able to tolerate his foul moods. The bed and medical supplies had been delivered this morning, and although she hadn't had a chance to itemize everything, she could do that after he got home.

The other thing she had to remember was to send a telegram to her superior officer and find out what she had to do to get herself discharged from the Army. Caring for her father would be a full-time job, not to mention trying to keep her mother on an even keel.

Nearing her father's room, she heard elevated

voices and immediately sensed an argument.

"Stupid woman," her father shouted just as Annie stepped inside the door.

"I'm sorry," her mother whimpered.

Annie rushed to the bed and found the whole side of it wet where her mother had spilled water, evidently trying to give him a drink.

"Calm down," she soothed. "It's all right." Annie patted her mother's shoulder while easing the older woman away from the bed.

Her father's face glowed red, his eyes bulged. She eased closer hoping to calm him, too. "There, there. It's only water. We'll get it cleaned up in no time."

A nurse appeared.

"We'll have to change the bed. Probably change him, too," Annie ordered.

The nurse came closer, "Thank you, ma'am. I'll take care of it." She glanced over at Annie's mother. "If you will just take your mother out, and I'll get this all taken care of."

"Yes, of course." Annie wasn't in charge here. Soon enough she'd have to take over, but for now she'd let the hospital staff deal with it.

"I was only trying to help," her mother whined as they eased out into the hallway. That was something else she'd have to get used to. Her mother's constant whining.

"It's all right, Mother. They do this kind of thing all the time."

"How will we manage? At home, I mean?" her mother asked.

Annie slipped her arm around her mother's thin shoulders. "We'll manage just fine."

An orderly hurried into the room with an armload of linen. Within only a few minutes, the nurse emerged.

"I'll call the doctor. Get something to calm him down. He doesn't need to get so agitated in his condition."

"Yes. I understand," Annie replied. "Thank you."

Annie knew her father didn't need to be upset. But she also knew her father. The man always managed to stay upset over something. Had for years. She'd have to placate him to keep him calm.

"Mother, why don't you go down to the cafeteria and get us both a cup of coffee?"

"Oh, yes. I'll do that." The older woman set out on her mission. Annie hoped she'd remember the coffee.

Back in her father's room, he squirmed in the bed, trying to get comfortable. Annie eased closer to help with the clean sheets.

"Damn woman," he muttered.

"It'll be fine," she soothed, hoping her tone would calm him.

"You…" he said. "You gonna…do…"

"I am going to take care of you," she assured him, patting his hand. "Isn't that what you've always wanted?"

"Wanted?" Drool slid from the side of his mouth. She grabbed a cloth to wipe it away. "I wanted…my son."

"I know." She needed to distract him.

"Do you?" He tried to push her away. "Your fault."

Annie wasn't going to argue with him, not now. "We'll get you all settled down when we get you home. It'll be much better. You'll see."

"Humph."

Keep calm, Annie told herself. Let him settle down.

Hopefully, the nurse would return with a sedative before her mother came back with the coffee.

"Brice...you see him?"

"Yes. He told me you were ill and that I should come home."

"Good boy."

"Yes, he is." Maybe if she let him talk and agreed with him, he'd settle.

"You...you marry him?" He slurred the words but not enough for her to not understand him.

"We can talk about that later."

"No...Now!" His face flushed again.

She eased closer and wiped his brow.

"Ugh." He waved her away.

"The nurse is going..."

"You...promise...me," he interrupted her in that familiar booming voice.

"What?" She needed to calm him down before his blood pressure went through the roof.

"Marry...Attwater."

She tried to force a smile. "Why, he hasn't even asked me."

"I...I'm...telling...you."

"All right. I will. I'll marry him. If that's what you want."

He drew a ragged breath. "Promise," he whispered.

Annie gulped. She'd always kept her promises and he knew it. He was trying to trap her into something she wasn't sure she wanted.

"Promise," he said, louder this time.

"Okay...yes, I promise." The words rolled off her

tongue and she immediately wanted to pull them back. What was she agreeing to? Could she renege later...when her father was stronger?

"Good." He visibly relaxed.

"Now, you need to rest. The nurse will bring you something to help you sleep."

Her father eyed her suspiciously.

"What I...wanted...always."

"I know. You've always wanted me to marry Brice."

He nodded.

She wouldn't tell him that Brice had gone overseas. It would upset him too much. Perhaps she'd tell him later, after they got him home.

The nurse came in with a pill for him. She wrestled him to a sitting position so he could swallow it just as her mother plunged through the door with two cups of coffee.

"Get it while it's hot," the older woman announced.

Her father coughed loudly and choked on the pill. The nurse pounded his back and almost immediately he vomited up the pill and water all over himself.

Annie stepped forward to help. That's when she saw the traces of blood.

"Get me some help," the nurse ordered.

Annie rushed down the hall, thinking of what she'd seen. She called to the nurses and orderlies before turning back to her father's room.

The scene she returned to was surreal. The nurse held her father as he jerked violently. Her mother wailed as she pressed herself against the wall, coffee spilled at her feet.

The medical staff rushed in, and someone pushed Annie and her mother into the hall.

A doctor appeared, then another.

It all happened so fast. One minute she was talking to her father and the next a doctor told her he was dead.

Chapter 48

When he mentioned going to Paris, Tennessee, to search for Carlene, Milt never expected his father to volunteer to drive him. The older man had said it would be a chance for him to spend some time with his son, but Milt suspected his father knew he couldn't drive with only one hand, and if he took the bus, it would be a long, arduous journey.

On the drive Milt admitted that he wanted to get the commitment he'd made to Annie and her family off his shoulders. He didn't tell his father everything, not that he'd fallen for Annie or that she'd rejected him. He just let the older man think he was fulfilling an obligation to the family of a dead soldier.

Once he located Annie's cousin's wife, Milt told himself, he could put that part of his life behind. Write it off as a wounded soldier's infatuation with his nurse. Nothing more.

In Paris the two men visited the Post Office, hoping the employees would be as helpful as those in Kerrville, even though Paris was a larger community.

An older man waited on customers at the only open window. Milt stood patiently behind a middle-aged woman mailing a package overseas to her son. The postal clerk obviously knew the woman and took his time with her package.

When the woman walked away, Milt stepped up to

the window.

"May I help you?"

"I hope so. I am looking for a young woman by the name of Carlene McEwen. Her maiden name was Tyler and I was told she had moved back to the area after being gone for some time." Milt hoped he'd given enough information to find out her address without arousing too much curiosity and the gossip that naturally followed in a small town.

"Carlene McEwen, you say?"

"Yes. Carlene Tyler McEwen."

The old man scratched his head. "There used to be some Tyler's lived out on the east side. That was a few years back." He looked around then said, "Hold on just a minute."

The man retreated into the inner workings of the post office. Milt could hear low voices but couldn't understand what they said.

The man returned. "Have you got a few minutes, young fellow?"

"Yes. I suppose so." What did the man want him to wait for?

"Well, you see, one of our carriers used to live out that way. He might remember the family you're asking about."

"Good."

"Course, he hasn't gotten back from his route yet. Might be a half hour or more. If you can wait."

"Sure. I can wait." Milt looked around. "Is there some place I could get a cup of coffee?"

"Over 'cross the way. Willie's Cafe." The man pointed toward the opposite side of the street. "They'll take care of you. Then you can come back. Maybe

Alton will be back by then."

Milt and his father returned to the Post Office thirty minutes later and spoke with an older man named Alton Gregory, who said he knew the Tyler family. He asked Milt a lot of questions, why was he looking for Carlene, what was his connection to her husband. After a while, he seemed satisfied and promised to ask around among the people who had known her as a child.

When they left the Post Office, it was late afternoon. Milt and his father checked into the nearby hotel Mr. Gregory recommended.

They returned to Willie's Cafe for their evening meal. Milt and his father sat at a table mulling over their options.

"If Mr. Gregory doesn't come up with anything, where else can we ask?" Milt asked.

"The people at the bank didn't help. They said they couldn't give out information on their customers."

Mr. Greenlee stopped when the waitress took their dirty plates. After she left, he resumed. "We can go to the Court House tomorrow. They have records of property sales, wills, things like that."

"How long will take to know we're looking in the right place?" Milt asked as his father sipped coffee.

"Long enough to cover all the bases. Even if it turns out to be a dead end, you want to believe you did all you could, don't you?"

"Yes," Milt nodded.

Was this a wild goose chase? After all, it was only a hunch that this was Carlene's hometown and that she would come back here. She could have gone anywhere.

A young woman pushed through the door of the cafe. Her gaze roamed the small establishment. After a moment's hesitation, she walked straight toward Milt.

"Are you the one looking for Carlene Tyler?" she asked when she reached their table.

Surprised at her straight-forwardness, Milt nodded. "Yes."

"Why are you looking for her?" Her hostile tone wasn't exactly friendly.

"I'm helping her husband's family look for her."

Still the unfriendly face. "What do they want with her?"

The girl reminded Milt of Mrs. Packard's sour demeanor. "She's their son's widow." He'd have to tread carefully, especially if this was Carlene standing before him. "They tried to contact her after Joe's death. They wrote but she never answered."

Her gaze shifted to the window. Milt tried to read the myriad of emotions on her face.

At that point Milt's father intervened. "Won't you sit down?" He motioned toward the seat beside him.

She hesitated.

"I'm James Greenlee," he held out his hand.

She nodded, still wary. Finally, she shook his hand.

"And this is my son, Milton. He was in Sicily, same as Joe."

Her gaze darted to Milt, uncertainty still evident.

"I didn't know Joe," Milt quickly added. "But I was there at the same time. And I was in the 1st Division."

She stared at him.

"I can order you something…while we talk." His hand went up to get the waitress' attention.

The girl hesitated and then she quietly sunk into the chair, avoiding their gazes.

When the waitress arrived, Milt asked, "Is coffee okay?"

"Just water," she murmured.

Milt glanced up at the middle-aged woman just as she pulled her order pad from her apron pocket. "Would you bring the lady a glass of water?" He glanced over at the girl. "What kind of pie do you have?"

"Tonight, all we've got is apple and chess."

"Bring us three pieces of apple pie."

"Comin' right up."

The waitress disappeared and Milt studied the girl sitting across from him. She was pretty, but her face showed a weariness. She probably didn't get much sleep. A widow with a small child, alone in the world.

"Joe's parents have been trying to find you."

Her head shot up. "No, they haven't." She blinked, realizing she'd practically admitted she was Carlene. "You don't know anything."

Milt waited for her to continue.

"Who are you anyway? And why are you here? None of this is any of your business."

Milt fought a smile. "You're probably right. It shouldn't be any of my business. But Joe's cousin…your cousin, asked me to help her find you."

"Why?"

"If you mean, why me, because I was in the First Infantry Division, same as Joe. And I was in Sicily at the same time as Joe."

Her eyes brightened. "You said you didn't know Joe."

Milt shook his head. "No. I didn't know him." Her sadness returned so he continued his explanation. "I wrote to a friend of mine who found an engineer who knew Joe, who was with him when he died."

Her eyes filled with tears. She blinked them back with determination.

The waitress plunked saucers laden with pie in front of them along with forks and a glass of water. "Will that be all?"

Milt's father spoke up, "I'd like some more coffee, if you don't mind."

When the waitress was out of earshot, Milt leaned forward. "That engineer wrote to me. He told me about your aunt in Brooklyn and he told me about…about your baby."

Her gaze met his, filled with fury. "That is none of your business."

"It's your family's business."

She swallowed hard. "What was his name? This engineer who wrote you."

"Wazinski."

She nodded. "He's the one who wrote me."

She took a sip of the water. Milt thought she was trying to calm herself. He waited for her to speak again.

"He said Joe was happy about the baby." She met his gaze again. "But Joe never got to write me and tell me."

Milt nodded.

"He knew it was his." Her voice pleaded with him to believe her.

"I know. But your aunt didn't, did she?"

"No. She said Joe wouldn't believe it. She said awful things about me."

Milt shook his head. "I know. We met her…in Brooklyn. She's a dreadful woman."

She almost laughed at his comment. Then she

384

stopped. "We? Who is we?" She glanced at Milt's father who shook his head.

"Me and Annie McEwen, Joe's cousin."

The waitress returned and refilled the coffee cups.

"She was looking for me?" Carlene asked after the waitress left.

"Yes. Annie asked me to help her when I was in the hospital in Florida. Then she was transferred to a hospital on Staten Island."

"Staten Island?"

"Annie is an Army nurse. She joined the Army after Joe was killed."

"Oh." She toyed with the pie, then took a bite.

"When I got Wazinski's letter, I took it to her in New York."

"Joe told me about her. Called her his little sister."

Milt cut into his pie. "From what she told me, they were very close."

She thought for a few minutes as she consumed the pie. "You said they wrote to me. Joe's family. I never got any letters."

"They wrote. I saw the letters with "Undeliverable" printed across them." He hesitated before plunging ahead with what he thought had happened. "My guess is that your aunt sent them back because she didn't want you to see them."

She frowned. And then she nodded. "She wasn't happy that I'd married Joe. That I had his child." She met his gaze again. "I would never have gone back there if I'd had anywhere else to go. When I got the insurance money, I left. Came here."

"Didn't Joe give you his parent's address? You could have gone to them."

She chewed on her lip before answering. "He did. But I lost it. I was too ashamed to ask him again. Then it was too late."

"Well, I can give you their names and their address. Herschel and Millie McEwen. They live on Lookout Mountain above Chattanooga."

"Joe told me they lived on a mountain, but I didn't remember where." She pushed the empty plate away. "You must think I'm stupid."

"No. I think you are a young woman who fell in love with a soldier. And, sadly, he was killed, leaving you alone with his child."

She sat in silence.

"I'll give you the names and addresses of your in-laws' and Annie's. Then you can write them, when or if you want to."

"Won't you tell them where I am?"

"Not if you don't want me to." Milt wasn't sure about making such a promise. It would be hard to face Annie and not tell her what he knew. Then he remembered that he wasn't going to see Annie. He wouldn't have to lie to her.

Besides, in his gut, he believed this young woman would contact the McEwen's. It might take her a little while, but he was sure she would.

"What are they like? His parents."

"They are very nice people." Milt thought back to the time he spent with the McEwen's. "They loved their son very much. Herschel asked me all kinds of questions about Sicily. It was like he wanted to know every detail of his son's life."

"And his mother?"

"A sweet woman. Hardworking and caring. She

works in a munitions factory, and she takes care of her sister-in-law, Annie's mother."

"Does she live with them?"

"Yes. Annie's parents and Joe's parents live in this big house high up on the mountain. It's not out in the middle of nowhere. It just sits there overlooking Chattanooga, part of the city yet high above it."

"And Annie's parents?"

Milt looked away. He'd almost forgotten about Annie's father, about his stroke.

"Is something wrong?"

"Uh, no. Sorry. It's just that Annie's father had a stroke recently. I'm not sure how he's doing."

"I'm sorry. It must have been hard on her."

"Yes....Actually I haven't seen her since it happened." He glanced to his father, who had been listening intently. "I expect she's still in Chattanooga taking care of him." Guilt at not telling his father tightened his gut. Now he'd have to explain.

"Were you wounded in Sicily?"

"No. In France. Normandy. The First Division landed on D-Day. I got hit a few days later."

"But you lived."

He could hear her thoughts. Unlike Joe, he had lived. "Yes."

She had accepted him and what he told her. He sensed that she wanted to know Joe's family, but fear of more painful rejection stood in her way. How well he understood that fear.

Before parting, she asked Milt and his father to come to her house the next day and meet her son. They happily agreed.

****

Annie made her way downstairs. The house was quiet without her father's overbearing presence.

The inviting smells of coffee and bacon lured her toward the kitchen where she found Mrs. Rice cooking a big breakfast for her mother, Uncle Herschel, and Aunt Millie.

"I was about to come up and get you," Aunt Millie said.

"Good morning, Miss Annie," Mrs. Rice chimed in. "I haven't cooked your eggs yet. Do you want one fried like you always used to like?"

"Yes, that would be nice."

Annie took her place at the big round table. One seat was conspicuously empty.

"Mother, how are you feeling this morning?"

Her mother looked up with a strange, far-away look in her eye. "I'm fine." Her thin, forced smile couldn't hide the deep lines that creased her face, lines Annie hadn't noticed before.

"Good," Annie replied.

Mrs. Rice placed a plate in front of her. The sunny-side-up egg and two strips of bacon stared up at her and her stomach suddenly rebelled. Annie pushed the plate away.

"Maybe I'll just have coffee."

"Nonsense," Aunt Millie injected. "You need to eat something. You've barely eaten since you got home."

Annie appreciated her aunt's concern. "Maybe a biscuit."

"And some eggs and bacon." Aunt Millie could be an unrelenting force when she put her mind to it.

Unexpectedly, her mother chimed in. "Do as Millie says, dear."

Annie looked at her fragile mother and tried to remember how many times this slip of a woman had stood up to her belligerent father...for her, for her only daughter, and drawn his anger onto herself. That's how her mother had protected her.

"Yes, Mother," Annie answered. Then she pulled the plate back, took up her fork and began to eat. Aunt Millie placed a buttered biscuit on the side of her plate and beamed in triumph.

Not long after breakfast, the funeral director arrived with a box full of flower cards and the guest book from the funeral parlor. All these reminders overwhelmed her mother, so as soon as the man left, Mrs. Rice took her mother up to her room to lie down.

Annie stood outside her father's study, fighting the sense of helplessness. She had no idea what to do next.

Aunt Millie's hand rested on Annie's shoulder. "Come away from there. We'll get in there later. Clean it out. But it's too soon." She pointed Annie toward the front of the house.

She welcomed her aunt's intervention. She wasn't ready to face her father's ghost quite yet.

"Come into our sitting room with me." Aunt Millie steered her into the bright, cheery space and insisted she sit down.

"Tell me about New York."

The question shocked Annie back into the present, into reality. "What do you mean? I already told you what we found out about Carlene."

"Tell me about that soldier. Milt."

The old familiar ache settled in her chest. Milt. She'd pushed him away. She hadn't realized at the time how much it would hurt. She'd been too caught up in herself and her singing career. Then Brice had showed up with news of her father's stroke. She'd dismissed Milt as if he meant nothing to her.

"There's nothing to tell. He helped me find Carlene's aunt. That's it."

"That's all? Nothing else happened between you?"

"He did take me to a night club to see a famous bandleader. We went backstage and met him."

"That sounds nice. Like a date."

"Oh, no. It was nothing like that." Annie thought of the taxi ride. "He just knows how much music means to me. He knew how much I'd enjoy hearing such a great band."

She had to put Milt out of her mind. After all, she'd promised her father that she'd marry Brice, just like he'd planned for so long. Brice was right for her. Kind and considerate. Of course, Milt was kind, too. But he'd said himself that he wasn't the right man for her. That he had nothing to offer her. They both knew it wouldn't work between them, despite the fact that he was a great kisser.

Funny how her singing career had faded into the background. She seemed to have accepted the idea of marriage. Why? Had singing lost its appeal? Or had her father changed her mind for her?

She needed to think. They'd buried her father. His overpowering personality could no longer control her life. Yet what he wanted for her was still there, in her mind. Was her desperation to get away from him why she'd decided on a singing career? Was it really what she wanted?

Chapter 49

The next morning Milt took a taxi to Carlene's house while his father went to meet a business associate.

At the door several toddlers eagerly greeted him. Carlene explained that she took care of the children while their mothers worked making blimps in a nearby defense plant. Her patience with the little ones amazed him.

She introduced her son, Joey, a bright-eyed two-year-old who reminded him of his sister's boy. When Joey reached for him, Milt picked him up with his good right arm and the small body snuggled against him. Then, as quickly as he'd reached for Milt, Joey squirmed to get down. Milt placed him on the floor and the boy joined his friends at play.

Milt had not spent much time around small children. He'd hardly seen his sister's kids when he was home. He watched with fascination as the four toddlers played. Distinct personalities emerged almost immediately.

What would his child be like?

He'd never thought about having children, about having a family. All his life he'd wanted to get out on his own. Now he found himself longing for the belonging only a family could give. Only he'd never have a family of his own. Instead, he'd be the bachelor uncle who got shot up during the war.

After sitting where they could watch the children, Carlene began. "Tell me about them, Joe's parents and his cousin."

Milt forced a smile. He'd wondered all night what he would tell her. "I actually only met your in-laws once. I spent a day and night at their house. I was on leave from the hospital, going home to see my family. Rather than write to Joe's parents, I offered to stop in Chattanooga on my way home and talk to them."

"Where's your family?"

"Kerrville. It's a little town about halfway between Chattanooga and Nashville."

She nodded, but he doubted she'd ever heard of it, so he continued with his story. "Annie went with me. She'd been my nurse. Anyway, in Chattanooga, I met her parents and Joe's parents."

"What did you talk to them about?"

"Mostly about the fighting in Sicily. Joe's father had a map of Sicily where he'd followed the Allies progress."

"Did you tell them what Wazinski said?"

"That was before I got the letter from Wazinski." He reached down and grabbed a block from the floor and squeezed it, wishing he'd brought the baseball he usually had with him.

When he returned his gaze to hers, he found her watching him closely. "Don't mind me. Nervous habit."

"How badly were you injured?"

"I got hit on my left side." He pointed to his face and then to his arm. "Head, arm. I still can't use it." He indicated his left arm. "Can't see too well out of the left eye. They tell me I might regain some sight and some feeling in my arm, but I don't think so."

"But you're alive...home."

The deep sadness told him she was thinking that Joe didn't come home.

"I'm sorry."

"For what? For surviving?" She jumped up and turned away.

Little Joey sensed his mother's distress and began to whine. Carlene picked him up.

"Don't feel guilty. I'm sure your family is grateful to have you home, regardless of your injuries. I know I'd love to have Joe back, even as an invalid."

Milt's chest tightened. He did feel guilty that so many others would never come home. He'd never met Joe, but he had witnessed the devastation his death caused.

"Would you excuse me for a minute? He needs changed."

"Sure," Milt nodded.

Milt watched the other children until Carlene returned and placed Joey on the floor with them.

"When I change one, I usually check them all." She gently checked each child, her voice soft and reassuring. "Pete, you're doing really good today. Do you want to go potty while I change Suzie?"

She took Pete by the hand and carried Suzie in her arms. "I won't be long."

Although still small, the boy was obviously the oldest of the four. The third boy suddenly jumped up and ran to Milt.

"Hi there, big boy. Did they run off and leave you?" The boy stood at his knee staring up at him. Joey followed so Milt had two little boys standing in front of him. He had no idea what to say to them. Thankfully, Carlene returned with the other two following along behind her.

"All of you, back to playing. Don't bother Sgt. Greenlee."

He wanted to say that they were no bother, but truthfully, they made him uncomfortable. He wasn't sure why. Maybe the way they stared at him.

"You told me his father wanted to know about the fighting. What about Joe's mother? What did she talk about?"

"She's the one who showed me the letters. She showed me pictures and talked about Joe growing up. I think Joe's father felt guilty that he'd encouraged his son to join the Army. His mother, too, to a certain extent. Annie's father gave them a hard time about it. He'd tried to discourage Joe from joining the military."

"Joe said his uncle tried to run his life."

Milt chuckled. "Yes. I'm sure he did." He thought of how the man had tried to run Annie's life and how Annie had defied him.

"Why do you think that's funny?"

"Because he did the same with Annie and she stood up to him, just like Joe did. Annie really loved Joe. She looked up to him."

"And you did all this, talking to them and coming to find me, for her."

Her words took him by surprise. Of course, he'd done it for Annie. She'd asked him and he'd done it.

"Are you in love with her?"

Milt stared at Carlene. What could he say? He couldn't deny his feelings. But he couldn't voice them either.

After an awkward silence, he looked away. "I made her a promise and I keep my promises."

"Why don't you want to admit your feelings for her? It's so obvious."

His neck and face heated. To fight his self-consciousness, he focused on the little girl's blonde curls bouncing as she spoke to her doll. His grip on the block relaxed, and he found his voice.

"She deserves someone better than me." He met her gaze. "She's beautiful and talented and smart. She needs someone who can give her a good life. You'll understand how special she is when you meet her."

She didn't respond, and he assumed she didn't agree. But it didn't matter. That's the way things were.

He reached into his pocket and brought out a piece of paper. "I've written down all the names and addresses. The McEwen's, Annie's, and mine. Just in case you want to contact me. I'll be happy to provide moral support, even go with you to meet them, if you want."

She took the paper and stared at it.

"Take your time. Whenever you're ready."

"Do you think they really want me? Or do they just want Joey?"

"They will be thrilled to have both of you in their lives." Milt had no doubt the McEwen's would welcome her with open arms. He knew Annie would have told them what they found in Brooklyn, the aunt, the friends. They now had a better understanding of why Carlene had not contacted them.

Carlene folded the paper back up, seemingly satisfied with his answer.

She stood. "I have to fix the children's lunch.

You're welcome to stay and eat with us. I'm afraid it won't be much."

"Sure," Milt said, unsure when his father would pick him up.

****

"McEwen Residence."

Milt cringed. He'd hoped that Aunt Millie or Mrs. Rice would answer the phone. Instead, it was Annie. He didn't want to talk to her, but what could he do?

"Hello, Annie. This is Milt…uh…Sgt. Greenlee."

"Milt, how nice to hear from you."

A forced cheerfulness permeated her voice. Had he made a mistake calling?

"Nice to hear your voice, too." He paused. "How is your father?"

Silence. Had he said the wrong thing?

"My father passed away," she said finally.

"Oh…I'm so sorry. I didn't…"

"There's no way you could have known. He had another stroke. We were getting ready to bring him home and then…Well, it was quick. He was gone very quickly."

"I'm so, so sorry." He didn't know what else to say. After another moment of silence he asked, "Your mother. How is she?"

"She's…She's holding up. Not real well, but she will, in time."

"Yes. I'm sure it was a shock. To all of you."

"Yes."

Silence again. Milt had to tell her. That's why he'd called long distance and now he stood here ticking away the expensive minutes.

"I found Carlene."

"What?"

"Joe's wife, Carlene. I found her."

"Where?"

"In Paris. Paris, Tennessee. Something one of the girls said made me think of it."

"The girls? In Brooklyn?"

"Yes. After you left, I went back and talked to Rebecca again. She introduced me to another girl who had known Carlene. Anyway, after I came home, I went to Paris and found her."

"And the baby?"

"Yes. Cute little boy. Carlene's keeping children for women who are working."

"Oh….What's she like?"

"She's nice. Hesitant at first. I think her aunt had convinced her that Joe's family didn't care anything about her."

"You set her straight, didn't you?"

"Yes, of course. I told her that your family tried to get in touch with her, that I'd seen the returned letters. I think she's afraid that Herschel and Millie only want the child. But I told her that they would welcome her into the family."

"Of course, they will."

"Anyway, I wanted to let you all know. I gave her your names and addresses. Left it up to her to contact you…when she's ready."

"Do you think she will?"

"Yes. I'm sure of it. But it might not be right away."

Annie went quiet again. Finally, she said "Thank you. I'll tell Uncle Herschel and Aunt Millie."

"Good." He hesitated. "Well, I'd better go."

"Milt...I'm sorry. About us. It just wouldn't have worked out."

His chest contracted like being squeezed in a vise. He didn't want to hear this again.

"Besides," she continued. "I promised my father I'd marry Brice. That's what I'm going to do."

"Yeah," he muttered. "I understand." He tried to breathe. "Uh...I have to go."

Before she could say anymore, he hung up and slumped against his father's desk. Getting shot hadn't hurt this much. Nothing had ever hurt this much. He should never have fallen in love with her, but how could he not? She was so beautiful in so many ways. Too beautiful for a crippled mug like him.

Chapter 50

"What do you think?" Milt had just gone over his ideas for manufacturing baseball bats in his father's woodworking shop and cleats in the shoe factory.

James Greenlee rubbed his knuckle against his chin, frowning. "I see what you're getting at." He looked at Milt. "We will have to convert from combat boots to something else. But cleats? Who would we sell them to? Shoe stores aren't going to want them."

"Lots of people play sports. We could ask around, find out who supplies the Vols and Vanderbilt." Milt wanted badly to convince his father. "It'll take a lot of work, but I'm willing to do it."

"We'd need to determine what constitutes a good pair of cleats. That means getting a pair and taking them apart. See how they're made." His father paused. "Then we'd need to make a prototype."

Milt thought through the possibilities. "I've got a pair upstairs. You could start on them."

His father smiled. "Okay. I'll keep an open mind and you keep working on it."

Little Sammy appeared in the open doorway. "Papa, Papa."

Suzanne hurried to catch the boy. "Mother says to come eat your supper."

The elder Greenlee held out his arms, and the small boy ran to him. Scooping him up, he said, "All right.

Let's go."

Milt followed them into the dining room where his mother fussed over the table settings. She looked up. "Miltie, will you go out and get Andy. He's doing something to that old car."

Milt cringed at the old nickname. It sounded so childish. But rather than complain to his mother, he headed out the back door.

His younger brother had his head under the hood of an old '32 Nash.

"Supper's ready," Milt announced.

"I've almost got it." Andy straightened and wiped his hands on a greasy rag.

"Good. But for now, you'd better wash up."

While the two were alone, Milt decided to recruit his brother's support for his proposals. "I've just been talking to Father. About the factory."

"Yeah?" Andy went to a metal wash bowl set on a shelf by the outdoor faucet.

"Yeah. I suggested that after the war, we convert to making cleats instead of Army boots." Milt waited for his brother's reaction as he watched him fill the basin with water.

"That's an idea." Andy sounded non-committal. Milt hoped that meant he was keeping an open mind.

"I know the shoe factory is yours…well, not yours exactly, but that's where you've been working the most. So, I wanted to run it by you. See what you thought." His brother had put in a lot of hard work at the factory. And he'd shown more interest in the business than Milt ever did. Would Andy welcome him and his ideas into the family livelihood?

Andy scrubbed his hands and arms up to his

elbows without saying a word. He rinsed off in the basin and then grabbed an old towel hanging on a nail.

"Does this have anything to do with you not being able to play baseball anymore?"

Milt had to give his brother credit. He cut right through to the heart of the matter. "Yeah. I guess it does. Since I can't play, I've been trying to figure out how I could stay connected to it somehow."

Andy only nodded. He hung the towel up and turned toward the back door. "We'd better get inside."

The entire family gathered around the dining room table. Milt ignored the small talk and focused instead on passing the dishes and filling his plate. He didn't want to drop and break any of his mother's china. She placed such store in pretty things and she was making a real effort to overlook his disabilities.

"Pop, Milton's got a great idea for the shoe factory." Andy's enthusiasm surprised Milt. He'd hoped to win him over, but he hadn't expected him to get behind his idea so quickly.

"I know," his father replied. "He told me about it earlier."

"We could go around to the high schools, talk to the coaches. I bet we could stir up lots of interest that way."

"Yes, that's true, but first we will have to make sure we can make them."

"Miltie," his mother spoke up. "What are they talking about?"

Milt cringed at her use of his childhood nickname...again. He'd long outgrown it, but his mother persisted in using it. "Oh, it's just an idea I had about making cleats."

401

"Cleats. What on earth for?"

"Mother," his father intervened. "It's not a bad idea. We're a small manufacturer. Maybe if we create a niche for ourselves, we can keep the factory going and make a little money."

"But what does Miltie know about the shoe business?"

Milt wanted to crawl under the table. He knew she meant well. She just didn't understand how her words and that tone of hers made him feel small and stupid.

His father must have seen his reaction. "Milton has some very good ideas. And he's going to investigate the possibilities." He paused and their gazes met. Milt silently pleaded for his father to understand.

James Greenlee shifted his gaze to his wife. "And another thing, Mother. I think it's high time you stopped calling Milton 'Miltie'. He is a grown man and should be treated as such."

His mother flushed crimson. "Why…why I…" Her gaze shifted to Milton. "I never meant anything. It's…it's just a term of endearment. You know that, don't you?"

"I know, Mother. But Father's right. I'm not a child anymore." He glanced around the table. "My friends call me Milt, and that's what I prefer. Milt or even Milton. But not Miltie. Not anymore."

Suzanne's mouth curved into a smile as her gaze darted from Milt to their mother and back.

His mother nodded. "If that's what you want, then that's what we'll do. Milton."

He smiled at her choice of names. After all, she'd always insisted that they use the more formal "Mother" and "Father" instead of "Mom" and "Dad."

"Thank you, Mother."

Chapter 51

"Yeah, we were stuck in Des Moines for a week when the bus broke down."

The balding, middle-aged man had talked for the full hour-and-a-half Annie had been waiting.

"What'd you do in a place like Des Moines? I mean, it's gotta be pretty dull," his friend responded.

"Not for me. I can always scare up a good time when I need to." He elbowed the other man in the ribs and looked over at Annie before continuing. "You know what I mean?" Then he laughed.

Annie tried to pretend she hadn't heard him, but in the small waiting room she couldn't help but hear.

What am I doing here?

Annie had lost track of the agents she'd talked to. Ten, maybe twelve. And none had given her the least bit of encouragement. "Come back after the war," most had said.

She actually looked forward to going back to the hospital. The wounded men appreciated her efforts to help them. Whether she was directing the chorus or singing for them, or simply listening to their fears, it was rewarding.

Do I really want to live this life? On the road all the time with the likes of these characters?

Finally, nearing the two-hour mark, she was summoned into the office. Before she could say anything, much less sing a few bars, the agent said, "Sorry. Can't use you."

"But why? You haven't even heard me sing."

"Look, Lady. Singers are a dime a dozen. An' I'm not putzin' around waiting for the war to be over before you can even start. So beat it."

Flushed with embarrassment, Annie turned and marched out of the office.

"Hey, girlie. You can come sing for me anytime," the balding man offered. "We could make beautiful music together." He leered and laughed, his meaning clear. Half a dozen others laughed along with him.

Annie almost ran out the door. The thought of that filthy man's hands on her turned her stomach.

Later, in her quarters, Annie found a letter from Brice, the first since he went overseas.

She hesitated. She'd promised to marry Brice, only she'd promised her father, not Brice. She'd have to write back, tell him what she'd done.

She might as well see what he had to say.

Dearest Annie,

We made it safely across the Atlantic and are getting settled in. I can tell you I'm in the French capital, for now. Use the above address to write to me and tell me how your father is doing.

Should she send him a telegram? After all he'd done, Brice deserved to know about her father's death.

I have to admit that I was a coward. I should have told you before you left New York, but I just couldn't bring myself to say the words. Somehow, it's easier writing them.

I fell in love with a girl I met in Washington. Her name is Cherry. And I've asked her to marry me. I

405

know you'll love her.

Annie blinked before re-reading that last bit. Brice. Marrying someone else. After she'd promised her father. She threw the letter on the bed.

Fire blazed within her.

How could he? The slime ball. He'd as good as lied to her.

He'd been so possessive…in New York…and even before that, in Atlanta…like he owned her…expected her to marry him…to carry out their fathers plans of uniting the families.

Beneath her anger at Brice, a sense of relief bubbled up.

She didn't have to marry Brice.

A lightness filled her.

She was free. Free to do what she wanted to do, not what her father wanted.

But what did she want?

She'd pushed everyone away. She never believed that Brice or Lloyd or Milt really wanted her. Had really cared for her. No. She hadn't let them care for her. She'd used her talk of being a singer…of singing with a big band and touring the country as a way to keep them at a distance.

To keep from getting hurt.

Her eyes burned with unshed tears. The lump in her throat threatened to choke her.

She fumbled in her dresser for a handkerchief as tears streamed down her face.

What will I do now?

The tears became sobs as she sprawled across the bed and buried her face in the covers. No one wanted her. She was alone and she'd always be alone.

****

Milt drew back and threw as hard as he could.

Whack!

The baseball slammed into the padded wall. A sense of satisfaction had him reaching for another ball. Focusing on that one spot, he wound up and threw again.

Yes! Even closer.

"Good throw," Lew commented from somewhere behind him.

Milt gritted his teeth and reached for another ball. "Yeah. I've been practicing."

He threw again. This time it was further off.

Milt reached down for another ball and found the bucket empty.

"I'll gather them up for you," Lew said.

He walked over and started picking up baseballs. Milt followed with the bucket.

"Your aim would be better if you weren't so angry. Control takes concentration."

The man was perceptive. "Right now, I'm working on power, not accuracy."

"It goes together. Power's no good if you can't get it over the plate."

Milt turned back to the spot he'd designated as the pitcher's mound with the bucket full of balls, determined to keep throwing until his arm fell off.

"What do you say we go outside onto the field. I'll get some guys to catch and field, and you can show me what you can do."

Milt stared at him for a moment. Why not?

"Okay. You're on."

Out on the ball field Milt strode to the pitcher's

mound. Lew recruited Roy from the rehab team to catch, and two amputees to field any balls Lew hit.

"Throw a few warm-up pitches," Lew called from the side-line. "Roy, give him a good target."

Roy held the catcher's mitt up in the strike zone. Milt focused on the mitt and threw his first pitch. Roy managed to catch it even though it was way outside.

"Shit!" Milt's anger at himself for the bad pitch did little to help his confidence.

"Keep going," Lew encouraged.

Milt bent down and grabbed another ball from the bucket. This time he took his stance, one-handed and awkward as it was, and drew a deep breath. He looked over his shoulder at the catcher's mitt and focused on its very center. Another deep breath, then he let loose.

The familiar whack as the ball hit the glove gave him a sense of satisfaction. Only a few inches off. Definitely a strike.

"That's it," Lew called. "Now do it again."

After two more pitches, one wild and inside, Lew announced he was ready to bat.

"Aren't you afraid I'll hit you?" Milt asked.

"Naw. I'm not afraid of you. I've faced much worse." Lew chuckled as he took his place in the batter's box.

After a few practice swings, Lew gave Milt a slight nod.

Milt readied himself again, focused on the catcher's mitt and threw as hard as he could.

Lew connected with his first swing, sending the ball sailing toward the outfield.

Milt watched it go, amazed that his friend connected with a solid hit. Of course, Lew was a professional at the top of his game before the war started. Why did it surprise him that the man could hit so well?

An hour later, despite his exhaustion, Milt felt better than he had in a long, long time.

"Thanks," he told Lew.

"What for?"

"For believing in me. For pushing me to come out here and do this."

"It was time." The two men gathered balls. "Whatever motivated you to really throw that ball, like you were doing inside, you need to hang onto it. Use it."

Milt nodded, his thoughts going to Annie and what he'd never have.

"It's that nurse, isn't it?"

"No!" Milt barked. Then guilt at yelling at his friend made him apologize. "I'm sorry. It's just not something I want to talk about."

"Ok," Lew agreed. He slung his bat up on his shoulder as they walked toward the door.

"That's not one of our bats, is it?" Milt asked.

"This? Oh, no. This one's mine." He swung it down caught the end with his other hand. "Have to have my own bat. It's got the right weight, the right feel to it. Makes a big difference at the plate."

"Do all the big leaguers have their own bats?"

"Some do. Most have a favorite. Length. Weight. Grip."

Milt's mind raced. "Remember I told you I was going to talk to my father about converting his woodworking shop to making bats?"

"Yeah, I remember."

"Don't suppose I could talk you into being an advisor. You know a lot more about bats than I do."

Lew stopped and faced him. "What exactly do you mean? Do you want an endorsement? An investment? What?"

"I want your expertise. Heck, if you want to endorse something after we get up and running and actually have something to sell, I'd love to have that, too?"

"But not money?"

"No. My father can handle the cost of getting everything going. We could actually pay you. I mean, it would be worth it. And then if you want to endorse our product, we'd pay you for that. After all, you're the big-league ball player. Being able to use your name would get sales for sure."

"Well, Milt, I'm flattered."

"Will you do it?"

"I need to think about it. We'd have to figure out how much time it'll take. Things like that."

"But you like the idea, don't you?"

"Yes, I do," Lew smiled. "I think you're onto something."

Chapter 52

Annie returned from putting her things away. Animated voices filled her aunt and uncle's sitting room. Through the half-open door, she took in the scene. Aunt Millie sat on the couch talking to Carlene. Uncle Herschel held a small child, Joe's child, while Annie's mother looked on.

Her mother turned when Annie entered.

"Annie, oh, Annie," her mother cried. The older woman hurried to greet Annie as if she hadn't seen her only minutes before.

The two women embraced. Annie relished her mother's warm hug and her smiling face.

When they separated, Aunt Millie called., "Annie, come sit with us."

Her aunt pointed to Carlene beaming with pleasure. "I still can't believe she's here. Joe's wife." Tears of joy slid from her eyes.

Annie smiled at the obviously nervous girl. "I'm so happy you came."

"Me, too." Carlene sighed as Annie sat beside her. "Milt said you were the one searching for me," she continued.

Annie flinched at the mention of Milt, followed by a creeping finger of jealousy. This woman had seen him, talked to him, made friends with him.

She forced herself to smile and make some kind of

answer. "I knew Aunt Millie and Uncle Herschel wanted to find you, and I was happy to help."

"You did more than that," Aunt Millie countered. "We'd practically given up. But our Annie here wouldn't quit. She was determined to find you."

The small child left Uncle Herschel and climbed into his mother's lap.

"Hello there," Annie said.

Carlene beamed. "Joey, can't you speak?"

Annie took the child's hand. "Can we be friends?"

The boy's wide eyes stared up at her. They were Joe's blue eyes. Her throat tightened at the thought. Joe had come home.

Annie's gaze remained fixed on the small child who ducked his head and curled up in his mother's arms.

"Come on, Ethel. Let's see if we can find some lemonade and cookies." Aunt Millie steered Annie's mother out so that Annie could talk to Carlene.

Much as Annie wanted to get to know her newly found cousin, she fought the urge to ask her about Milt. "When did you arrive?" she asked.

"Oh, we've been here for an hour or more." Carlene struggled to control Joey, who squirmed in her lap.

"Would you like to come see me?" Annie asked, smiling at the adorable child.

The boy's wary look made her doubt he'd leave his mother, but then his expression softened, and he climbed from his mother's lap to Annie's.

Those blue eyes met hers and stole her heart. Choking back tears, Annie told the boy, "You look just like your father."

Herschel spoke up. "I said the same thing."

"He definitely has Joe's eyes," Carlene added. "I wish…"

"I know," Annie said, patting the boy on the back.

After a moment, Joey climbed down and explored the room.

"Where do you live?" Annie asked.

Carlene smiled. "Near Paris. That's where I'm from."

"It's in West Tennessee," Herschel explained.

"That's where I grew up, before I went to live with my aunt in Brooklyn. I thought it would be a good place to raise Joey."

"I agree," Annie said. "I don't think I'd care to live in New York, at least not for long."

She'd never actually put that thought into words before. A singer would have to live in New York City in order to work and become known. Raising a family there would be a different story. Kids needed to be outside, needed space and friends and a community, not pavement and tall buildings blocking out the sun, not a constant flow of strangers.

"People say you should live around family and my aunt lives there…" She shook her head. "Only my aunt didn't want Joey or me around. We were in the way."

Annie nodded. "I believe you. I met the woman." She shifted her gaze to Uncle Herschel. "You get along with everyone, but you wouldn't have liked her."

He smiled that gentle, all-knowing smile. "Carlene and Joey are here now. With us. And we are delighted to have them, even if it's only for a visit."

Annie glanced at Carlene, whose smiling face glowed with pleasure. Annie's chest swelled with

413

happiness. She had known deep inside that finding Carlene was the right thing to do, that her aunt and uncle needed to have a family and it appeared that Carlene needed them as well.

Until this very moment, Annie hadn't realized how much she longed for a real family, for someone who loved her, for children, for grandparents and aunts and uncles. She didn't want to be alone.

Annie had never had a loving family like the one she saw when she visited Milt's family. She hoped the addition of Carlene and Joey would transform this family into the kind of loving family that Milt had.

"Will you be home long?" Carlene asked just as Joey came running toward Annie.

The boy slammed into her knees and grinned, then he dashed back to his grandfather.

"I managed to get two weeks' leave," Annie replied, chuckling at the boy's antics. "What about you? How long are you staying?"

"Just a few days."

"We've asked her to move here. Live with us," Uncle Herschel said. "Lord knows this house is big enough."

Joey returned to his mother, and she pulled him into her lap.

Annie watched Carlene trying to gauge what she thought of the idea.

"Like I said. I'll think about it," Carlene said, stroking Joey's hair.

"Don't let Uncle Herschel intimidate you."

"Why, I would never do that," her uncle quickly replied. "We'd just love to have her here with us."

Annie smiled at them both. "I'm sure Carlene will

make the right decision."

The girl's answering smile told Annie she appreciated the support.

Annie wanted to thank Milt for his persistence in continuing the search after she left New York. And for encouraging Carlene to get in touch with her family.

She had no idea when, or if, she'd ever see him again.

Maybe she could call his family. Maybe find out his feelings toward her. She'd been the one to send him away. Did he even want to see her again?

She had to know.

****

"Greenlee residence." Milt's father's deep voice rang in her ear.

Annie drew a breath for courage. "Hello. This is Annie McEwen. I'm the nurse who brought Milt home from the hospital a few months back."

"Of course. I remember you. This is his father. I'm afraid he's not here."

"I…uh…didn't expect him to be…Uh… Actually, I wanted to talk to you."

"I see." He paused. "What was it you wanted to talk to me about?"

"To ask how Milt is doing. I haven't seen him in a while, and I just want to make sure he is all right."

"He's doing very well. He had another operation on his face to work on the scarring around his eye."

"That's good." He would feel better about himself if they could improve his looks. "Isn't it amazing what the plastic surgeons can do these days?"

"Yes, it is." Mr. Greenlee paused again. "And how are you doing? We were sorry to hear of your father's passing."

"I'm fine. Thank you. It was very sudden, but we're all doing fine." She sounded so stupid. Why was she so nervous talking to his father?

"Good. And so good of you to call."

He was going to hang up, and she hadn't even said what she meant to say.

"Uh, Mr. Greenlee, would you thank Milt for what he did for my family?"

"You mean finding your cousin's wife and son?"

"Yes. They're here in Chattanooga now, for a visit. If Milt hadn't kept looking and asking questions, I don't think we would have ever found her."

"He wanted to do it, for you and for your family. Milt's the kind of man who finishes what he starts. It may take him a while, but when he puts his mind to it, he does it."

"Yes. I like that about him."

"He likes you, too."

"Does he?" She didn't mean to sound so hopeful.

"Yes. He speaks highly of you."

"What...what did he tell you? About me?"

Mr. Greenlee hesitated as if trying to decide what to tell her. "He says you are a very good singer, so good that you are going to sing professionally. After the war he says you're going to stay in New York, on your own, and start a career."

"I did. I mean, I do want to sing, but I'm not sure I'm cut out to be a professional singer."

"I see."

She could almost hear him pondering what she'd said.

Finally, he spoke again. "Milt will be home this

416

week. On Friday. We're planning a surprise birthday party for him. Why don't you come to the party? You could thank him in person."

"Do you think I should? I don't know if he wants to see me."

"He does. I'm sure of it. Come up on the morning train. We'll all surprise him."

Annie pondered Milt's father's invitation. Did Milt still care for her? The only way she'd know for sure would be to see him in person.

"All right. I'll come."

Chapter 53

Milt hoped to quietly slip in the back door, but Suzanne's mischievous smile met him in the back hallway.

"Welcome home," she said.

"Thanks."

Why the big greeting? She knew he was coming.

"I'll take your bag. You go on in the living room."

Now he was really suspicious. He eased down the hall.

"Surprise!"

Flabbergasted, Milt froze in his tracks. A room full of smiling faces greeted him.

His mother grasped his arm. "Happy Birthday, Son."

He glanced at her smiling face. Then his father was beside him, and Andy. Grandmother Kerr hovered nearby. Familiar faces surrounded him.

"Come on in. See who all's here." His father steered him to the middle of the room.

"I...I wasn't expecting..."

"Exactly. It's a surprise party." Beaming, his father stepped back as the others surrounded him.

"Happy Birthday," someone said.

"Yeah. Many happy returns an' all that."

Milt shook hands with the boys and accepted hugs from the girls, not sure of all the names, even though he knew most of them from childhood.

"Della's made a beautiful cake," his mother said from somewhere behind him.

He turned. "You didn't have to do all that."

"We wanted to."

"Milt." His father's voice drew his attention. When Milt spotted him, there she stood. His chest went tight. The pounding in his ears drowned everyone out. His mouth went dry.

"Aren't you going to say 'Hello'?" Annie asked.

Milt made himself nod in her direction. "Hi," he mumbled.

Annie moved forward until she stood right in front of him. He couldn't breathe.

"I came to wish you a Happy Birthday and to see how you are doing."

He heard himself say something like, "Thanks."

His father touched his shoulder. "I'll let you two catch up." Then he slipped away.

Why? Milt wanted to scream.

He met her gaze. Those beautiful hazel eyes sparkled. "Wh...what are you doing here?" he managed.

"Like I said, to wish you a Happy Birthday."

His head shook. He tried to organize his jumbled thoughts. He finally asked, "As a friend?"

Her face went pink. She looked down. "Yes." then her gaze darted to his. "And maybe more."

At that, he walked away. Made an attempt to mingle and talk to his old friends. Yet he couldn't help glancing back at her every few moments.

I can't do this. Can't talk to her like nothing ever happened between us.

After what seemed like an eternity, his mother called for everyone to come into the dining room. Milt's friends pushed him along and he lost sight of her.

A chocolate cake graced the center of the long table surrounded with trays filled with sandwiches, fruit, and assorted snacks. His father leaned over and lit the twenty-five candles.

"Time to make a wish and blow out the candles," his mother announced.

The guests gathered around. Milt looked at the cake ablaze with light, then he glanced up to take in the faces surrounding him. His gaze locked with Annie's. Time stopped.

"Well, go ahead and blow them out before they burn down." His mother's anxious voice brought him back.

He took a deep breath and blew until all the candles were extinguished. Everyone applauded, called congratulations, and slapped him on the back.

His mother pushed him aside and started cutting the cake.

"What'd you wish for?" an old friend asked.

Milt just shook his head. He couldn't tell them it was Annie.

****

Milt and Andy were talking when his father stepped in and steered Milt over to Annie. He shot the older man a questioning glance.

"I think you two need to talk," was his reply.

"Yes, Milt. I do want to talk to you." Annie sounded as anxious as he felt.

"About what?"

"About us."

His teeth clinched. "There is no 'us,'" he ground out. "Remember? You have other plans."

"Not anymore," she mumbled. "At least I'm considering my options."

"What does that mean? You're not going to marry Brice? Or you're not going to have a singing career?"

She met his gaze. "Both." Her voice resonated with determination.

"And what does that have to do with me?" He wanted to ask what happened with Brice, but he didn't dare. And why would she give up singing?

"In New York I realized I wanted something different. I want a family rather than a career."

"Can't you have a family with Brice? Isn't that what your father wanted?

Mentioning her father clearly hit a nerve. She looked down again, wringing her hands.

"Or maybe Brice doesn't want you?" It was a long shot, but something made him say it.

She looked up then. Tears brightened her eyes. "No, he doesn't. He's engaged to a girl in Washington."

"Oh, I see. So, you thought you'd come crawling back to good ol' crippled Milt. The good-for-nothing bum no one else wants."

By now the people nearby had noticed the argument and stopped their chatter. But Milt didn't care anymore. His chest ached so bad he could hardly breathe, much less care who heard.

"It's not like that," Annie insisted.

"Oh, it isn't?" Sarcasm laced his words. "Maybe it's because my father has a good business, and you knew I had a sure-fire way to make a living. After all, my family's not going to kick me out. They'll find something for this shot up piece of crap to do." He glanced at Andy standing nearby. "Isn't that right, little brother? You'll find some do-nothing job for me, won't you?"

"It's not like that," Andy spoke up. "Even if you can't read, there's lots of other things you can do."

Milt's body burned. Embarrassment made him want to melt into the floor, so he didn't have to see her face.

"What does he mean? Can't read. You never…"

"No!" he shouted. "I never told you. I didn't want you to know." He shot Andy a blistering look. "It's bad enough that my face is a mass of scars, and I have to wear these hideous glasses. Not to mention this useless arm. Why would I tell you I can't read? That without baseball I'll never be able to stand on my own two feet, support myself, much less a family."

Annie's face reflected the shock she must be feeling.

Everyone had gone silent. Acutely aware of his audience…his family, his friends, who all knew his problems to a certain extent, Milt took in their shock. He had never expressed how horrible he felt about himself.

Escape.

Out the door and stumbling down the steps into the yard, hot tears slid down his face.

He wanted to die. Wished he'd never come back. Wished he'd died over there with his friends. They'd all be better off if he'd never come home.

****

"We're a sorry pair, aren't' we?" Annie slipped up behind where he sat under an old tree.

He didn't answer her. She didn't know if that was a good sign or a bad one.

She sat down beside him.

"Now I understand why you didn't want to write to my family," she said.

No response.

"Is that why you got upset with the waiter in that nightclub?"

He glanced at her then, nodded, and looked away down the hillside.

"It doesn't change anything, you know."

"Yeah, sure." He looked at her then. "It makes it worse."

"I don't understand."

"I didn't want you to know. My physical problems are bad enough. You knowing that I can't read…that just…it makes things worse." He turned to face her. "I told you I wasn't good enough for you. That I couldn't give you the life you deserve."

"And what do I deserve? My father hated me. He told me all the time that I wasn't good enough, that my brother's death was my fault, that all I was good for was to marry his friend's son and link our families." She drew a deep breath, trying not to cry. "Joe was his protégé. He was supposed to carry on the family name. Become someone important. After he was gone, my father hated me even more."

"I'm sorry."

"I've never known a loving family like yours."

"So, you want my family."

"No. That's not what I mean. You are part of that loving family. You are kind, you care about others. Everyone likes you. Including me."

423

"That's not enough."

"I know." She pulled her knees up and hugged them. "I've always pushed everyone away...especially men, because I feared I'd get hurt. Because I was afraid they'd end up treating me like my father did." She met his gaze, searching for understanding and for strength. "I realized all this not long ago."

"Because of Brice?"

She nodded. "He was supposed to be the safe choice. No complicated feelings. No chance of getting hurt." She fought back tears, blinking furiously. "I never thought about him not wanting me."

"He's a fool."

"See. You care. You've always cared. I just couldn't see it."

"You're right. I do care about you. That's why I don't want to saddle you with someone like me."

"But you're what I want. You care about me...enough to walk away rather than hurt me. Only you left this big hole in my life. The thought of never seeing you again has been unbearable."

"It's still not going to work." He sounded so sad.

"Milt, I fell in love with you, and it scared me to death. We didn't get to talk about it because Brice showed up...you know."

"You'd already told me it wouldn't work. You wanted your singing career."

"That was just an excuse. The more I pursued it, the more I realized that I didn't want to live in New York. I didn't want to go on the road with a bunch of men of questionable character. It just wasn't for me. I can sing other places, teach music...I don't know...something. I don't have to sing professionally with a big band." The words tumbled out of her. Was he listening? Did he understand?

"You'd rather live in a little town like this?"

"Yes. If you're here."

He stared at her for long moments. Finally, she couldn't stand it. She leaned in and kissed him. At first, she thought he would pull away. Then he kissed her back, a desperate, longing kiss that she hoped would never end.

When they parted, he said "Maybe..."

Unbelievable joy filled her.

"I said 'maybe,'" he repeated. "We can try. See each other, call each other, see if it might work."

"Yes, we can do that. Take it nice and slow. Just to be sure." She held back the giddiness. After all she didn't want to scare him away. Not now, when he'd thrown her a lifeline. Right now, she would hang on for dear life and pray their love would grow.

Chapter 54

Milt and Annie sat at the piano singing an old love song. His family surrounded them and some joined in. Only she and Milt knew the significance of the song, that she had sung it the day they met.

Annie's heart sailed as Milt's voice soared over the others. Such a fine clear baritone full of enthusiasm.

When the song ended everyone laughed and applauded.

She leaned over and kissed Milt on the cheek. The warmth in her heart filled her with more love than she had ever experienced. Those blue, blue eyes smiled back at her, full of love.

Milt had asked her to marry him, finally.

They'd spent months talking on the telephone and traveling back and forth between New York and Tennessee. On Milt's last trip to New York, he'd asked her to marry him, with a little prodding on her part.

They'd agreed she would come to Kerrville to make the announcement to his family. Then they'd tell her family.

Milt hit a key on the piano and repeated it over and over until he had everyone's attention.

"Annie and I have something to tell you all," he said, swinging around to face them.

Annie turned around, too, and grasped his good hand.

With all faces turned toward them, Milt continued. "We've decided to get married."

"Oh my." His mother rushed forward, caressed his face, and kissed his cheek. "I'm so happy for you." She moved to Annie, kissing her cheek, and hugging her close. "Welcome to the family, my dear."

Milt's father shook his hand; fighting emotions and blinking furiously, he only nodded his approval. He clasped Annie's hand in both of his, still nodding. As he turned away, and the others gathered around, Annie saw him swipe his hand over his face.

Grandmother Kerr summed up the occasion. "I thought we were gathering to celebrate the German surrender and Katherine finding her airman. I had no idea a wedding was afoot." She beamed at the two of them. "I'm so pleased my grandson has found such a lovely bride."

Annie's face heated. Milt squeezed her hand.

"You two certainly make beautiful music together. My guess is that you'll make beautiful babies, too."

"Oh, Grandmother." Milt blushed and shot a glance to Annie.

All she could do was nod in agreement. She wanted babies, but, unlike her parents, having children or not having them wouldn't make or break this marriage. She loved Milt so much she knew deep inside that spending her life with him would be enough for her.

****

Milt had never been so happy.

Annie believed in him. Believed he could do anything he set his mind to and, with her at his side, he believed it, too.

She was definitely the best thing that ever happened to him.

And their announcement pleased his family…all of them. Their love and support had given him the courage to ask her. He loved Annie so much, but he'd feared she'd reject him again.

He'd been so stupid.

"Son, have you told Annie our plans?"

Milt flushed. "I told her a little about it."

"We've got the building for the baseball bats half finished. The new equipment will be here any day." His father's enthusiasm pleased Milt.

"I know. I know. I'll take her out tomorrow and show her around."

"What are you going to show me?" Annie asked.

Milt squeezed her hand. "Where we're going to make baseball bats. And then I'll take you to the shoe factory and show you our prototype of Greenlee cleats."

"Sounds lovely." She kissed his scarred cheek.

"And after that…"

"There's more?"

"We're going to the church. See if it suits you for our wedding."

She slipped her arms around him. "Have I told you how much I love you lately?"

He grinned just before she kissed him, a long passionate kiss that expressed her love better than words could.

When she finally released him, he gazed into her twinkling eyes and whispered. "I love you, too………."

A word about the author...

Barbara Whitaker was born in the wrong decade. She loves everything about the 1940's and WWII, so she decided to write about it. Her historical romances embody that fascinating era in history. Visit Barbara's website www.barbarawhitaker.com

Thank you for purchasing
this publication of The Wild Rose Press, Inc.

For questions or more information
contact us at
info@thewildrosepress.com.

The Wild Rose Press, Inc.
www.thewildrosepress.com